A Song *that* Never Ends

HAMILTON PLACE
BOOK I

MARK A. GIBSON

Editing by The Pro Book Editor
Interior and Cover Design by IAPS.rocks

eBook ISBN: 979-8-9880747-0-0
paperback ISBN: 979-8-9880747-1-7
hardcover ISBN: 979-8-9880747-2-4

    1. Main category—Fiction / General
    2. Other category—Fiction / Family Saga

First Edition

This book is dedicated to Henry Hal Gibson.

It was an accident, a terrible tragedy, but it wasn't your fault. You were just a kid.

Rest in peace, Dad. I miss you.

PROLOGUE

NOVEMBER 19, 1967

PERHAPS SOMEDAY HE WOULD BE a farmer of coffee or rice, but that someday was not today. Today, he was Viet Cong. Chu Khahn was not a communist, neither was he a capitalist. In truth, he had no great understanding of, or care regarding, *any* philosophy of government. Mostly, he wanted to be left alone. His parents and his village were aligned against the current South Vietnamese government, and therefore, so was he. His father had once fought against the French Imperialists, but they'd left when the younger Chu was just a boy, only now to be replaced by the Americans. Khahn had no strong feelings, positive or negative, regarding the Americans. Simply, if America supported the South Vietnamese regime, then they were his enemy.

At age sixteen, Khahn was little more than a boy. Days, he worked in the fields around his village in support of his family. Nights, he became Private First Class Chu, a guerrilla fighter with the communist National Liberation Front, the Viet Cong, near the village of Da'k To in South Vietnam.

Within his guerrilla unit, Khahn felt he was special. Most of his comrades were armed with the Type 53 Mosin-Nagant bolt-action carbine or the Type 56, the Chinese version of the Soviet AK-47, assault rifle. There were two RPG-7s and one North Vietnamese K-50 submachine gun in his unit. His unit commander carried the K-50, but only Khahn had the honor of carrying the Type 36 recoilless rifle. The Type 36 was a Chinese copy of the American M18 57mm recoilless rifle used in World War II and Korea. The Type 36 could be fired from the shoulder but was far more accurate used from a bipod or tripod. It was a single-shot, breech loader and had a crew of two—one served as gunner while the other bore ammunition. The Type 36 fired a 1.25-kilogram artillery-type projectile, High-Explosive Anti-Tank (HEAT), or High Explosive (HE), at velocities similar to that of a cannon round but almost entirely without recoil and with better range and accuracy than the RPG-7. Its major selling point from Khahn's perspective was that it fired a projectile rather than a rocket. Because of this, the round did not leave a telltale smoke trail behind to point out the position from which it was fired, making it an excellent ambush weapon.

In truth, Khahn carried the Type 36 less because he was special and more because he was young and in possession of a strong back. His beloved recoilless rifle weighed just over forty-four pounds and was even heavier with the bipod attached. Each round added another five pounds to his prodigious load. To manage the Type 36 required strength, stamina, and a two-man crew. Due to the slow rate of fire and limited rounds carried into combat, he also carried a Type 53 for defensive use. His ammunition bearer, Private Do, carried four rounds for the recoilless and a Type 56 for close support and defense. Khahn loved his weapon and named it *Tie'ng sa'm se't*, which meant "Thunderbolt."

A few months earlier, Privates Chu and Do had snuck to within 350 meters of the American base at Da'k To. After watching the airfield from cover for half a day, Khahn destroyed a fuel truck on the tarmac with an HE round from his recoilless rifle. Afterward, the pair slipped away and returned to their unit without ever having been discovered. With the back slaps and congratulations of his comrades still playing in his mind, Khahn could not wait to bring Thunderbolt back into action again.

Finally, for the past few days, a pitched battle had raged in the hills above Da'k To. Much to his chagrin, Khahn had not been a part of it because his unit was posted on a hill several kilometers north and slightly west of the battle. He pleaded with his commander to allow him to move closer to the action, but his entreaties fell upon deaf ears. The unit had been ordered to this hill, and on this hill they would stay. His commander was unyielding in his resolve, and Khahn dared not defy him.

But his comrades were dying. Khahn could hear the explosions and small arms fire. He could see helicopters circling, landing, and flying away. He could see the jets swooping in to strafe and drop bombs. When the wind was right, he could even discern the unmistakable odor of napalm and of charred flesh, although the latter may have been imagined since Do never seemed to catch the scent.

Still, his commander would not budge.

Hidden atop his hill, Khahn had been a spectator to the battle since dawn. He watched and listened to the battle for yet another wasted day. He'd just settled into his meal of rice and eel when, after a period of relative silence from the battlefield, he heard the unmistakable, deep *pom-pom-pom-pom* of a Chinese .50-caliber machine gun being fired in the distance. He gazed in the direction of the firing and saw an American helicopter rising from a cleared area. The .50 caliber fired again, and the chopper seemed to shudder in the air. Then the craft spun wildly and began flying northward, maneuvering erratically as it attempted to flee the area.

As realization of the copter's path struck him, Khahn couldn't believe his luck. It was coming right at him. He scrambled to find Do and ready Thunderbolt. But the American craft veered away toward the west. The chopper would not overfly his position after all, but it might still be in range when it passed by his hill, just barely. As the helicopter hurtled past in the distance, Khahn squinted into the setting sun, raised the recoilless rifle to a forty-five-degree angle, and fired blindly in the general direction of the Huey. He realized that he had little to no chance of hitting his target, but at least he would have contributed one round to the eventual outcome of the battle. That *had* to be better than sitting on top of this hill and doing nothing.

The helicopter was flying at 110 knots at a distance a little greater than the 450-meter maximum range of the HEAT round Chu launched from his Type 36. With a muzzle velocity of 366 meters per second, the projectile would have to travel almost a second and a half before reaching its target. Over that time, the helicopter would have moved forward almost seventy meters, during which time the projectile itself would have dropped twelve meters. The warhead would then need to fall between spinning rotor blades to find a vulnerable place on the body of the chopper.

A hit on a moving helicopter with an *aimed* shot at that range would have been highly improbable, akin to shooting a duck on wing with a single-shot .22 rifle from a distance of one hundred yards. With his shot being completely unaimed, hitting the chopper was a virtual impossibility. Yet, that is precisely what happened.

The 1.25-kilogram explosive projectile struck the Huey's transmission housing just aft of the main rotor mast, and detonated. The blast shredded the transmission, sending pieces of white-hot metal throughout the cabin and cockpit. A shard of what had once been the transmission's friction damper passed cleanly through the pilot's neck at the base of his skull, killing him instantly. Even if the copilot had not already been killed by groundfire, the chopper would have been doomed. The stricken craft gyrated wildly as it tumbled from the sky. It struck the trees and, an instant later, the ground, where it turned on its side and skidded for several meters before finally coming to rest in a crumpled heap at the bottom of a ravine. Remarkably, there was no fire.

Khahn and Do watched the chopper's demise in shocked silence. Then after a moment, they began jumping up and down and hugging one another, elated by their success. Their Thunderbolt had struck again.

CHAPTER I

1937–1939

W ALTER HAMILTON WAS BORN IN 1919 in an upstairs room of the farmhouse where he still resided with his family. The census would have considered him part of the post–World War I baby boom, although his father hadn't served in the Great War. While he remembered the Roaring Twenties, there hadn't been very much "roaring" going on in the rural South Carolina of his childhood. Truth be told, his life was not so different during the Great Depression years that followed than it had been during the twenties. The family had grown tobacco and feed grains, but the farm had never provided much actual profit. With hard work and favorable markets, it provided enough for a relatively comfortable subsistence but not enough for a luxurious existence.

Walter learned at an early age that hard work and industry got one further in life than empty promises, fancy talk, or pie-in-the-sky dreaming. For any task that needed to be done, you didn't talk about it. You didn't complain about it. You just did it, and you did it well. When the job was done, you didn't brag. Instead, you moved on to the next task and did it well too.

By all accounts, Margaret "Maggie" Butler was a vivacious, funny, and strikingly attractive young woman. Bright, animated, and cheerful, she did well in school and was popular with both boys and girls. Her rebellious streak often got her in trouble with faculty and placed her frequently at odds with her father, a minister for the local Church of Christ.

Perhaps it was her impetuous nature or her love of a challenge that first attracted Maggie to the reserved, phlegmatic Walter Hamilton. Or maybe opposites really do attract. Where she was excitable, high strung, and impulsive, Walter was stolid, unflappable, and calm. In their wildest dreams, no matchmaker ever would have paired the two together, but together they...well, they just worked. Maggie brought a sense of contentment and joie de vivre to Walter's life that he'd never known. In return, Walter provided Maggie a safe, stable foundation from which she could soar to new and unimagined heights with two strong arms to catch her should she somehow fall.

Maggie and Walter were married in 1937, when she was seventeen and he was eighteen. At first, they lived in an old toolshed Walter had spent a month converting into a one-room cabin. Their accommodations, although Spartan, were little different from those of other Depression-era sharecroppers. Walter kept food on the table by working from dawn to dusk on the family farm. Maggie kept a tidy, happy home and always greeted her husband's return with a smile and a kiss. The old toolshed didn't have running water or a source of heat other than the old potbellied woodburning stove Maggie used to cook supper, but the newlyweds kept each other warm enough at night, and eleven months later, they welcomed Mack Lee into their little family. Though they had few worldly possessions, they had each other and little Mack Lee, and they were happy.

One spring day about seven months later, Walter finished work early in the fields. Returning home, he found Maggie slowly rocking Mack Lee's cradle and softly singing "Polly Wolly Doodle."

> Oh, I went down South
> To see my Sal
> Singing Polly Wolly Doodle all the day
> My Sal's a spunky gal
> Singing Polly Wolly Doodle all the day
> Fare thee well, fare thee well
> Fare thee well my fairy fay
> For I'm goin' to Louisiana to see my Susi-anna
> Singing Polly Wolly Doodle all the day.

He stood in the doorway, smiling, listening silently as she rocked his son with a foot while darning a pair of socks. When she finished the song, he said, "I didn't know you could sing!"

Maggie jumped. "Oh, you startled me!"

He stepped inside and went to her, pulling her into a loving embrace.

She swatted him playfully with the sock and cooed, "I have *many* talents that you don't know about."

"Oh really? Name three!"

"One: I can forgo smothering you with a pillow in the middle of the night when you wake me up with your snoring."

"Naw...that's really more of a tolerance than a talent."

She whacked him again with the sock. "I can make your favorite meal, fried chicken, on that old stove."

"Nope...already knew that one!"

"I can give you another little Hamilton. After all, it is the duty of the lady of the manor to provide 'an heir and a spare' for her lord and master," she lilted in an affected British accent.

"Yeah, well, that—Wait, wha...what? Are you sayin'...? Are you...? Are *we*...? Really?!"

Maggie smiled shyly and gave the tiniest of nods.

"*Hot* damn!" he exclaimed loud enough to wake Mack Lee. As the baby groused, Walter gathered his wife into his arms and began jumping and dancing around the old tool-shed like a whirling dervish, just barely missing knocking the skillet off the stove with Maggie's foot.

"So, you're happy, then?"

"Ah," he replied, shaking his head. "I suppose that your third talent is being able to tell when I am happy?" He kissed his wife before she could ponder a reply.

Maggie's pregnancy progressed well with no problems. Her belly grew larger and larger and, although she was uncomfortable because her back *really* ached, she was happy. In fact, she had never been happier in all of her life, and it showed. Her complexion positively glowed. Her face always showed the hint of a smile, even late in her term when her back felt ready to break. During the day, she hummed tunes and sang to her baby. Sometimes, she had conversations with her unborn child about the wonders that he or she would experience upon arrival into the world.

It was clear to Maggie that Walter was happy too. He was in love with her. He had a healthy son and was about to have another. Well, it might not be a son, but even a daughter would be okay, he'd told her. "Especially if she has her mama's pretty olive-green eyes," he'd said. If Walter had concerns about how he was going to support his growing family, it never showed. Days, he worked on the farm, and most nights, he fell asleep with his hand on Maggie's belly, "enduring" kicks and shoves from the upcoming newest addition to the Hamilton family.

When Maggie's time came, she calmly made her way up to her in-law's house and had the midwife summoned while Walter dropped off Mack Lee at Maggie's mother's house. Having already birthed one baby, Maggie knew what to expect and had no fears or worries. There was no reason whatsoever to drive twenty miles just to have a baby at Spartanburg General Hospital.

Walter, on the other hand, was a nervous wreck. He'd been shooed away from his wife's side by the midwife and could only pace the hall like a caged tiger outside the upstairs bedroom where she labored. He walked downstairs to the kitchen for coffee and then returned to his vigil outside of her door. The whole thing seemed to be taking forever. Twice he'd tried to stick his head in the door "just to see if everything was okay," only to be shooed away by the midwife, and the second time, she'd used a broom.

After returning from the door, the midwife bathed Maggie's face with a moist cloth. "Men!"

Maggie and Walter's mother giggled.

"All's well, child. It shan't be much longer now, I think," the midwife said with just the hint of a Scottish burr.

Maggie looked tired but determined. She wasn't worried. She'd been through all this before.

"You just rest a bit. You'll be needin' your strength for pushin' here soon. You'll be holdin' that baby of yours in no time."

Walter was dozing on the floor outside Maggie's door when he was awakened by a strangled scream. He leaped to his feet and bounded to the door, cursing when he found it locked. He was on the verge of breaking the door down when it opened a crack, revealing his mother's face.

"It's just the baby coming, dear. She's starting to push. It won't be long now."

Walter resumed his pacing, drawing on every ounce of strength and willpower he could muster to keep from bursting into the bedroom with each of his wife's screams and gasps. His father, awakened by the commotion, offered him a swig of Gibson's Pennsylvania rye from a bottle he'd hidden behind the dining room corner cupboard. Walter, however, spurned the offer. He preferred to do his fretting sober.

After Maggie's last drawn-out scream, then silence, there was a low, frantic exchange between Walter's mother and the midwife, but on opposite sides of the door, neither Maggie nor Walter could make out the words. As the couple worried with what was happening now, they each realized they couldn't hear...*shouldn't I be hearing...shouldn't there be...crying? I don't hear the baby!* Then, Maggie gave an agonized, "No!" and began sobbing, and unable to wait any longer, Walter burst through the door. There he saw Maggie, crying inconsolably over a little bundle in her arms that was swaddled in the new blanket he'd bought for her last week from Blanton's General Store. In the folds of the blanket, he could just make out a tiny little dusky blue face.

Walter rushed to the bedside and collapsed to his knees, tears streaming down his stubbled cheek.

"Oh, Walter! I'm so sorry! I'm so, so sorry! Oh God! I'm so sorry!" Maggie keened, sobbing uncontrollably. "Our baby..."

"It was the cord...the umbilical," the midwife began.

Walter looked up, uncomprehending.

"The cord was wrapped around her neck three times," she continued, holding up three fingers as though this would make everything clear. "There was nothin' that could be done. Your daughter was born dead. She was strangled to death by the cord. I'm terribly sorry, Mr. Hamilton!"

"Oh, Walter! She was so perfect," Maggie wailed.

The next several days passed as though they were stuck in a bad dream from which they could not awaken. In a daze, Walter picked a tiny little casket from Forrest Lawn Mortuary. *Dear Lord, why do they have to make them so little?* he thought, fighting back tears.

They held the funeral ceremony at the Church of Christ. Reverend Ernest Mahaffy from the First Baptist Church in Chesnee presided since Maggie's father, their church's usual minister, was among the mourners. Walter and Maggie buried their daughter, Myra Louise Hamilton, in the family plot behind the church. They set a small marker bearing her name and the inscription, "Heaven has a new Angel," above her head.

When the ceremony was over, the mourners dispersed. Each went back to their own busy lives, leaving Maggie and Walter alone in their anguish. Cruelly, life went on for the Hamiltons, leaving little time to grieve. Walter, with a spate of new debts incurred from the funeral home, took on odd jobs in addition to his usual work on the farm, just to make ends meet. Too proud to ask his family for help, he left for work before dawn and did not return home until well after dark. He worked seven days a week with no breaks. Gone were lazy Sunday afternoons and sneaking home for lunch or for making love with his young wife. He was always exhausted and had barely the energy to wolf down a late supper before falling asleep in a chair beside the old cook stove. He grieved as he did most things, in complete silence.

Alone with her sorrow, Maggie could not shake the belief that somehow she was to blame for the death of Walter's daughter. With her first pregnancy, he had been almost terrified of becoming responsible for a family. After all, just a few months before, he had been a carefree young man with no responsibilities. In the blink of an eye, he'd had a wife and then a baby who were totally dependent upon him for survival, a daunting prospect for any nineteen-year-old. For nine months, he'd worn a "deer-in-the-headlights" look. But, after Mack Lee was born, he'd more than risen to the challenge. He'd embraced his new role as husband, father, and provider and had excelled at all three. Walter had been so happy when he'd found out she was pregnant again. She'd been nervous about how he might take the news, but clearly, he had been thrilled. Now, little Myra was gone...and most of the time, so was Walter. He said he didn't blame her for the death of their daughter, but Maggie did. She often felt lost in thoughts like, *I could have... I should've insisted upon going to the hospital for the birth even though I really didn't think it necessary. Women have been having babies at home since time began, right? And hospitals are so expensive...and Walter works so hard...and now...* Maggie spent much of her days weeping.

She tried to keep up appearances for Walter, knowing he was suffering. She kept their home neat and clean and took care little Mack Lee, although whenever she tried to play with him, she couldn't help but weep for his lost little sister. When Walter came home nights, she made sure there was always something that he liked to eat waiting on the stove. She even tried to make love with him some nights, but he was always so tired. More often than not, she fell asleep alone in their bed, sobbing quietly into her pillow while Walter snored next to that damned old stove.

Every day, Walter tried to make things as normal as possible for Maggie. He knew she was hurting but had no idea how to make things right again. He worked harder than he ever had before in his life so that she wouldn't have to. It embarrassed him that she'd started taking in laundry from folks around town to help with the bills. He figured it was his responsibility to provide for his family, not Maggie's. He felt like a failure. His father had always provided for *his* family. And so had his father's father. He shook his head in disgust at the thought of the poor example he was setting for his own son to be a responsible husband and father.

His father offered help with the expenses, but Walter's pride prevented him from accepting the assistance. Instead, he worked harder. He took extra jobs and worked until his body could work no more. He was *going* to take care of his family, even if it killed him.

He knew Maggie was trying hard to make everything *appear* normal again in their lives, and that she wanted him to believe she was okay. She was doing all she could to take care of him, their little home, and his son. Sadly, he knew it was all just an act, an attempt to project normalcy. She no longer teased him or laughed. He couldn't remember the last time he'd heard her sing a song or even hum a tune. Walter missed that terribly. The smile that had once brightened rooms and made his heart soar was now forced, and her pretty green eyes were always tinged in red when he finally got home at night.

The "Birthing Tree" was an ancient white oak that once stood in the field behind Walter and Maggie's toolshed home. The massive tree easily had stood for hundreds of years. Popular local history held that the tree had once been a gathering place where displaced Cherokee Indians often paused to allow the pregnant women among them to give birth, before traveling west along the Trail of Tears. As a little boy, Walter had spent countless happy hours playing in the upper branches, or napping in the relative coolness of its shade. He'd always had the expectation that his children and grandchildren would someday enjoy the same.

However, one morning, after a winter thunderstorm, he'd awakened to find the tree on its side. While cutting up the fallen tree for firewood, Walter had been surprised to find it entirely hollow inside. Now, the tree that had cooled him during the hot summer days of his childhood kept his family warm on the cold winter nights of his adulthood.

When Walter looked at Maggie—really *looked* at Maggie—he thought of that old tree. She looked strong and solid enough from the outside, but he suspected that on the inside, she was actually hollow. With one strong wind from the wrong direction, her tree would fall.

Walter wanted to make things better. He wanted Maggie to know she was loved and that everything would be all right. He wanted to assure her that *they* would be okay too, but he didn't know how. He wanted to hold his wife and let her know he was there for her. They'd enjoyed an active sex life before the...well, before. But now, he could not bring himself to make love with his wife. Heaven knew that he wanted to, but he was afraid. What would happen if she became with child again? What if something bad happened...again?

They'd made love once. Exhausted as he was, Walter had dosed off immediately afterward, holding her close as he'd always done before. He awoke a short time later to her silent tears puddling upon his chest. He just couldn't put Maggie through *that* again.

CHAPTER 2

APRIL 1940–DECEMBER 1941

T HE SECOND WORLD WAR WAS a truly horrible event for mankind, but it ultimately brought the Great Depression to an end. Similarly, another terrible event, a death in the family, eventually broke the cycle of misery, guilt, and poverty for Walter and Maggie.

Tobacco is a "thirteen-month" crop. Tobacco farmers must start planning and preparing for the next year's crop before the current one has been cured or taken to auction. Consequently, there is never an "off-season" on a tobacco farm. Late spring, during the planting season, is a particularly demanding time. Fields must be plowed, planted, and fertilized. Chemicals for treating growing plants must be purchased and applied. Additionally, machinery and equipment must be maintained and repaired. Spring is a truly busy time.

The preceding winter had been milder and damper than usual, therefore nematodes and other parasites were expected to be a problem this growing season. Walter estimated about a quarter-ton of nematicide would be required to rid the fields of parasites this year. Additionally, the farm needed another half-ton of high-nitrogen fertilizer to prepare for planting. Thus, on April 2nd, he went to Spartanburg on a procurement run.

The left rear tire on their tractor had developed a slow leak, so Walter's father, Arthur, stayed behind to find and plug the leak. He hoped they wouldn't have to replace the nearly thousand-pound tire, an expensive undertaking and difficult task.

When Walter returned from Spartanburg, he thought it odd that his father didn't meet him at the barn to get the latest news from "the big city." It was already unusual that his dad had sent him to town for supplies rather than going himself. Usually, the old fellow enjoyed hearing all the gossip from his buddies at the hardware and feed stores. With the newspapers and radio talking about Adolph Hitler and how Neville Chamberlain was giving away the store in Europe, the fact that he *hadn't* gone himself was decidedly out of character. Heaven knew the old coot liked to rail about how "Roosevelt is gonna get us sucked into another foreign war!"

Walter actually had some juicy tidbits to pass along this time too, if he could only find the old codger, but figured he'd just finished up early with the tractor and was back up at the house enjoying a glass of iced tea. So he drove down to the barn and off-loaded the fertilizer and nematicide. Finishing, he wandered back up to the house, intending to give his father all the dope from the hardware store checker players and feedstore whittlers, generally agreed to be the two best sources for informed news of the world. But he wasn't there.

Whistling softly to himself, Walter ambled back down to the tractor shed. To his horror, he found Arthur Hamilton lying beneath the rear of the tractor. Apparently, the jack had slipped, causing the tractor to shift so that the rear tire had crushed his father's chest. Walter rushed to his side, hoping against hope to find a pulse or some sign of life. Sadly, the body was already cool to the touch. The accident had likely occurred shortly after Walter's departure that morning.

Having absorbed two major tragedies in less than five months, and with no one there to see, Walter sat on the ground with his head in his hands and wept uncontrollably. After thirty minutes—or maybe two hours, he had no idea—he pulled himself together and walked slowly back to the farmhouse. It was up to him to inform his mother that she was now a widow.

It is a truly ill wind that blows no good. Although this wind brought tidings of heartbreak, it was not a totally malevolent draft. For within the zephyr resided the faintest trace of hope.

After Arthur's funeral, Walter's mother, Mary, insisted that he, Maggie, and Mack Lee come to live in the main farmhouse. With his father dead, the house and property now belonged to Walter, so it would only be right and proper for him to live there with his young family. Mary would move into the upstairs bedroom, and he and Maggie should move into the master bedroom downstairs.

Walter had always been fiercely independent and resisted previous offers to move to the main house. He insisted that his and Maggie's accommodations were little different from most in the area and, in fact, more pleasant than many of the Depression-era sharecroppers living on and near their farm.

Once again, he demurred, insisting that he didn't want to displace his elderly mother in her own home, but Mary was adamant. "I could never sleep in that room or that bed again without Arthur snoring beside me. So I'm going upstairs one way or another. You might as well take advantage of the vacancy. Besides, I'll be closer to my grandson up there. It is decided, Walter. I will *not* take no for an answer!" With this decree, a measure of steel had entered her usually cultured, mellifluous Charlestonian voice.

Having heard that tone many times as a boy, Walter wisely responded with a simple, "Yes, ma'am!" and strode back to the old toolshed to inform Maggie that they were moving.

The old farmhouse would not have been considered particularly large or luxurious by the standards of the day. However, it did possess several significant upgrades compared to the toolshed in which the younger Hamiltons had been residing for the past year and a half. The house had central heat provided by an oil-burning furnace in the basement. It was fully wired and boasted electric lighting throughout with an electric oven/stove and refrigerator in the kitchen. Best of all, it had indoor plumbing with hot water and an indoor bathtub and toilet. For Maggie, it was like moving into the Waldorf Astoria.

The original farmhouse had been a simple two-story structure with two rooms upstairs and two downstairs with a fireplace in each room. A central staircase rose from just inside the front door to access the second floor. During a particularly prosperous time for the Hamilton family in the early 1900s, the detached kitchen behind the house was attached, giving the structure the shape of an offset *T*. Connecting the structure allowed room for a bathroom with tub and toilet, a dining room, and extra space for storage. The formerly detached kitchen comfortably held a break-fast table and featured a large stone fireplace once used for cooking. Beneath the kitchen, the former root cellar had been expanded into an actual basement that now housed the furnace and water heater.

Across the front of the house, along the crossbar of the *T*, a wide, covered porch faced the road. It held several rocking chairs and a hanging porch swing in which the family spent many pleasant evenings talking, sipping lemonade, and watching Mack Lee toddle around in the front yard. With two huge shade trees, one a catalpa and the other a massive sycamore, the porch and yard were always comfortably cool, even on the hottest summer days.

In the backyard grew a huge flowering magnolia, several apple trees, and an ancient scuppernong arbor. The latter, according to family lore, had been old when the Yankees burned the farmstead in 1865. Since the trunk of the old vine was currently two feet thick, the stories may actually have been true.

As they moved in and began settling into their new life in the old farmhouse, Maggie gradually came back to life. The tears became less frequent, and she smiled more often, with more sincerity. Still, on occasion, Walter caught her standing frozen, staring sightlessly into the distance for minutes at a time. Although she was all over the house, cleaning, painting, and washing windows, never once did she step a single foot into the bedroom where she had lost her baby.

While Maggie went about making the old house into *her* home, she was respectful of Mary and always asked for her opinions and recommendations before embarking on any major projects. She planted flowers around the front porch and had Walter build a picnic table beside the scuppernong arbor for alfresco dining during pleasant weather.

Mary was as good as her word. As soon as Walter and Maggie moved in, she happily retired to one of the upstairs bedrooms. She was more than willing to help Maggie with little Mack Lee, and if she objected to any of her daughter-in-law's decorative ideas, she never let on. She even helped with cooking and shared recipes for dishes that she knew to be Walter's particular favorites.

Walter embraced his new role as head of the household and master of the family farm, and he did both well. Now having access to the farm's meager profits, he no longer had to slave away at multiple jobs to provide basic necessities for his family. He embraced new techniques for farming, which improved productivity while reducing costs. With increased profits, he elected to increase the daily wages for his workers. Since many area farms were cutting wages and staff, this move earned Walter his workers' undying loyalty.

Although the farm's profitability had improved, Walter remained unconvinced that tobacco represented the farm's best hope for the future. He was understandably excited when he first heard about soybeans as a potential cash crop. As he researched, his enthusiasm grew.

He didn't believe tobacco would ever be a sustainable crop. Its cost per acre and relative labor intensity made profitability for a small grower an increasingly unlikely proposition. Thus, he'd been contemplating the laborious process of transitioning the farm from tobacco to soybeans, the "crop of the future."

Walter had been introduced to the idea that soybeans might be a viable cash crop during a conversation with another farmer at the feed store in Boiling Springs and had liked what he heard. Apparently, soybeans were extremely drought tolerant and grew well with acidic soils, which were both attractive traits for crops in upstate South Carolina. They were fairly low maintenance and easy to grow. As legumes, soybeans fixed nitrogen in their root systems and thus the plants could be plowed back into the soil as "green manure" to enhance the next year's crop of corn or wheat as part of a crop rotation plan. Alternatively, the plants could be ground into silage for livestock feed or bailed into hay. The beans themselves were very high in protein and oil. The soybean oils could be easily extracted by pressing, and there were numerous commercial applications from cooking to glue to industrial lubricants or even fuel.

By late November of 1941, he'd made the decision to convert the farm totally from tobacco to soybeans beginning in the spring of 1942. All he had left to do was share his plans with Maggie, and tonight was the night. Walter couldn't wait.

In truth, he could wait, and would, because that evening, Maggie had news of her own to share. With their life returning more toward normal, she was, once again, pregnant. Although both were pleased, their joy was tempered by the memory of their recent loss. Consequently, their first step back down this most wonderful of life's roads was tentative.

For the next week, Walter remained on pins and needles, waiting for the perfect opportunity to discuss his plans for the farm with Maggie. This was to be his first major decision since inheriting the farm, and he craved her approval. Although once a flighty girl, she'd become remarkably well grounded since the birth of their son. He knew he could count on her as a voice of reason should his ideas for the future be too impractical or unrealistic. His father had once told him, "Son, the most spirited of stallions will need the steadiest of hands on the reins." For Walter, those hands were Maggie's. If she thought his idea was too risky or impulsive, then he would dial it back or let it go entirely. He just needed the chance to talk with her about it...sometime *after* they had both gotten more used to the idea of her new pregnancy. Maybe, he could talk with her about his plans for their future prosperity this Sunday after church. He figured, with a new baby on the way, what better time could there be to improve the family fortunes. *Right?*

When Sunday finally came, the family dressed and attended as was their custom. Maggie's father was the preacher and droned endlessly, or so it seemed to Walter. With more immediate matters occupying Walter's thoughts than the eventual salvation of his soul, his mind frequently wandered. Maggie had to elbow him in the ribs when it was time to stand and sing a hymn or to pass the offering plate. Eventually, the service ended and Walter complimented a smiling Reverend Butler on his homily, although in truth, he could not remember a word of it...except something about "turning the other cheek," though he couldn't be sure.

Back at home, Maggie started preparing a dinner of fried chicken with green beans and cornbread, one of Walter's favorites, and he uncharacteristically joined his wife in the kitchen rather than retire to the sitting room to read the Sunday newspaper until dinner was ready. Mack Lee had fallen asleep on the way home from church and for the moment, dinner preparation notwithstanding, he had Maggie's undivided attention. As the radio played softly in the background, he laid out his plans for the farm with growing excitement.

Walter was extremely excited by all he'd learned about soybeans. Naturally taciturn, he was uncharacteristically loquacious as he talked with Maggie over a dinner—the noontime meal in South Carolina—of fried chicken, green beans, and cornbread. In the background the radio was set on to warm up so that they could listen to *Fibber McGee and Molly*, the couple's Sunday afternoon treat.

Maggie had never seen Walter being so animated about anything. It was clear to her that he was excited about making the transition from tobacco farmer to soybean grower. She asked a few questions that Walter fielded readily, but she remained unconvinced. Such a radical change seemed sudden to her...and a little scary, especially with a little one on the way. Still, she had no argument that stood up against his logic, and his enthusiasm was soon winning her over.

Maggie was almost at the point of expressing her agreement for Walter's plans when the announcer interrupted the program, and their lives, with an important news bulletin.

We interrupt this program to bring you a news bulletin. The Japanese have attacked Pearl Harbor, Hawaii by air, President Roosevelt has just announced. The attack was also made on all naval and military activities in the principal island of Oahu. We take you now to Washington...

Details are not available. They will be in a few minutes. The White House is now giving out a statement. The attack apparently was made on all naval...all naval and military activities on the principal island of Oahu. The president's brief statement was read to reporters by Steven R. Lee, the president's secretary. "The Japanese attack on Pearl Harbor naturally would mean war. Such an attack would naturally bring a counterattack...and hostilities of this kind would naturally mean that the president would ask Congress for a declaration of war."

"Oh, dear God!" Maggie put her hand to her mouth and fainted.

Just quick enough, Walter caught Maggie before she crumpled to the floor. The bowl of mashed potatoes she was whipping was not as fortunate. It shattered, sending potato and shards of glass flying to all corners of the kitchen. He lay his wife gently on the floor, cradling her head in his lap, then placed a dampened towel on her forehead.

After a moment, her eyelids fluttered open. "Oh, Walter!"

All talk of the farm, soybeans, and the future ended as Walter held his sobbing wife. The next evening, with Mary beside them, the two huddled around the radio and listened in silence to President Roosevelt's address to Congress. First there was static, then a familiar voice came clearly through the speaker.

They waited as the applause died down, unconsciously leaning closer to the radio to better hear.

"Mr. Vice President, and Mr. Speaker, and Members of the Senate and House of Representatives: Yesterday, December seventh, 1941—a date which will live in infamy—the United States of America was suddenly and deliberately attacked by naval and air forces of the Empire of Japan. The United States was at peace..."

The three of them hardly breathed as the president's speech neared its completion.

"I ask that Congress declare that since the unprovoked and dastardly attack by Japan on Sunday, December 7, 1941, a state of war has existed between the United States and the Japanese Empire."

Mary gasped, Maggie sobbed quietly, and Walter stared at the radio in resolute silence. The president's request for a declaration of war didn't come as a surprise to any of them. Each had fully expected it. But expecting something and actually hearing it occur *on live radio* were very different matters. It chilled them to their marrow. Their lives and, indeed, the *world* would never be the same.

News of the Japanese sneak attack on Pearl Harbor and the subsequent declaration of war against the Empire of Japan spread through the little town of Boiling Springs like wildfire. Not surprisingly, nowhere was anyone talking about the upcoming playoff game between the Chicago Bears and Green Bay Packers. Instead, all talk was of war, the draft, the Japanese and the Germans. Pitchforks were being sharpened. Torches were being lighted. Plowshares were being beaten into swords. The townsfolk clamored, ready to "kick them Japs back into the Stone Age!"

Soon, Germany and Italy declared war against the United States, and on December 11, war was declared upon Germany and Italy. A mere twenty-three years after "The War to End All Wars," the world had gone to war again.

As the only male and the sole source of support for his extended family, Walter knew he *could* be exempted from the draft. Even so, he also knew that if war was declared, he *would* do his duty and serve in the military. He'd do his part to avenge the soldiers, sailors, and airmen killed and injured in Hawaii. He hoped that Reverend Butler and Maggie would understand that some atrocities were just too great for turning the other cheek.

Whether the good reverend understood or not was the least of Walter's worries. Maggie definitely did *not*. Consequently, Walter's decision precipitated one of the few heated arguments the couple ever experienced.

"What kind of man would leave his wife and son to go off and fight a war?! You don't even *have* to go," Maggie shrieked.

"The kind of man who wants to do his duty," said Walter, keeping his voice calm and measured like a man trying to tame an angry lion.

"What about your duty to me? And to Mack Lee? And to our baby? How can you say that you love me and then still leave us?"

"That's not fair, Maggie! I'm going *because* I love you! I *have* to."

"But you *don't*," she pleaded. "We need you here!"

"Maggie, sweetheart, I promised to love and protect you. They attacked us."

"Hawaii, Walter! *Not* South Carolina!"

"*This* time it was Hawaii. The Japs invaded Manchuria ten years ago and have since pushed across half of China. Hitler's taken over almost all of Europe and is sitting outside Moscow. How long do you think it will be before they set their sights on us? If we don't stop them over there, they *will* come here. I'll still wind up fighting. The difference is that I'd rather fight 'em over *there* knowing that my family's safe at home, instead of over *here* and having to worry about you every day!"

"But what if you never come back?" Maggie croaked, her throat choked with tears.

"Then know that I died protecting my family, doing what I thought was right, and know that I loved you more than I loved being alive. Know that I died so that you and our children could have a future, even if I won't," Walter replied solemnly, a single tear trickling down his stubbled cheek.

Maggie pounded her fists against Walter's chest. Rage, frustration, abandonment, and fear? She felt them all. But she also knew that Walter would always do what he believed was right—to Hell with the consequences. That was one of the traits she loved most about her husband. The blows to his chest slowed, then stopped. She rested her head against Walter's chest and wept inconsolably. Maggie knew in her heart she was going to lose him.

Walter held his sobbing wife throughout the night, and the next morning, he enlisted into the army. Part of Margaret Butler Hamilton died that day.

CHAPTER 3

WALTER'S WAR 1941–1945

W ALTER HAMILTON HAD BEEN BORN and raised on a farm. All he'd ever wanted was to *be* a farmer. But put him in a tank, and one would've thought he'd been born with a turret hatch over his head. He was a natural tanker. What others learned only after months of rigorous training, trial and error, Walter intuited. For this, there was no explanation except, perhaps, his familiarity with operating tractors and heavy equipment over the family's tobacco farm.

After basic training, he was sent to Fort Knox, Kentucky, to attend the army's Armored Force School. Over a seventeen-week course, he learned tank guns, driving, and maintenance. He initially trained as a driver but, after showing aptitude, was rapidly advanced to the role of tank commander for an M3A1 Stuart light tank crew. The Stuart carried a crew of four: the driver, the assistant driver, the gunner, and the commander.

The driver was Edward "Fast Eddie" LaMotta, a second-generation Italian from the South Bronx, and with his dark hair and olive skin, he certainly looked the part. He was arguably the best light tank driver in the entire class. LaMotta often said that he if had a mind to, he could make the M3 dance the jitterbug, and Walter didn't doubt it. He had seen him do some amazing things. Skilled a driver though he was, his skills paled when compared to his talent as a gambler. It didn't matter whether the game was cards, craps, cribbage, or horseshoes. If there was money to be wagered and won, "Fast Eddie" LaMotta would be the guy with the biggest pile of dough at the end of the night. With his winnings, he singlehandedly put his sister through cosmetology school and helped his cousin purchase a deli in New Jersey. The win for which he was personally the proudest was after he'd drawn to an inside straight, hit and won a 1940 Lagonda V12 convertible off some Brooklyn wise guy a few months before Pearl Harbor. He loved that car.

The assistant driver was a laconic, baby-faced Kansan named Carl Irwin, who at age 19 was the youngest member of the crew. As such, he was subject to the good-natured ribbing of his prank-loving crewmates. Many a day started with him sliding into his seat in the Stuart only to find his viewing port blocked by a baby bottle or a pacifier stuck into his speaking tube. He was a decent enough driver, but where he excelled was as the crew's primary mechanic. There was nothing Irwin couldn't fix. If he'd been available, Humpty Dumpty would have looked like Captain America by the time Irwin got finished with him. Irwin also manned one of the bow-mounted .30-caliber machine guns and helped with loading the 37mm main gun.

Walter's best friend on the crew was Jefferson Folts, who hailed from Flint, Michigan, and was the gunner for the M3's 37mm main cannon. Folts was a terrible shot. He couldn't hit the broad side of a barn at fifty paces. But what he lacked in accuracy, he made up in volume. He seemed to adhere to Joseph Stalin's dictum, "Quantity has a quality all its own." Walter always figured any Japs or Krauts who faced their tank in combat would be certain they were up against at least a platoon of American armor just from the volume of ordnance flying overhead. Although lacking as a gunner, Folts was a gifted scrounger. The crew never lacked for fresh eggs, motor oil, silk stockings, or Scotch whiskey. Any whispered request to Folts, and the desired item or items would soon appear as though by magic. Whether a kleptomaniac or a genie, the crew never knew—or particularly cared. Shortly after the crew had arrived at Fort Knox, Folts procured an entire case of Johnnie Walker, an amazing feat since the base was "dry" at the time.

The tank crew lived, ate, trained, sweat, froze, and slept together. When one laughed, they all laughed together. When one was hurting, the other three were there to provide comfort, solace, or, when necessary, revenge. They fought and bickered among one another, but heaven help the MP or local cop who threatened any one of them. Each man knew intimately the strengths and weaknesses of his comrades. Somehow, each brought out the best in the others. In the process, they formed bonds among them as strong as any family and stronger than most.

After completing training at Fort Knox, Walter's tank crew was assigned to the army's II Corps, then stationed in Manchester, Tennessee. Under the command of Major General George S. Patton, II Corps developed the tactics they'd later employ during Operation Torch, the Allied invasion of North Africa. In Manchester, they terrorized the local populace, speeding their tanks through pastures, over rivers, and around hay fields until II Corps was ready for war.

Just after his arrival to Manchester, Walter received a telegram from Mary, informing him that Maggie had suffered a miscarriage.

Walter was devastated by the news from home. He remembered vividly how Maggie had suffered after the loss of their daughter. He tried his best to get leave from his unit to go home and console his wife, and maybe, draw her back from the abyss. But it was no use. The army was less than understanding.

His commander informed him in no uncertain terms, "There's a war on, soldier. So get your ass back out there and do your duty!"

Walter's duty may have been with the army, but his heart and soul were elsewhere. Had it not been for Folts physically restraining him, Walter would've gone AWOL and hitchhiked the six hours home to South Carolina and Maggie's side. His crewmates prevented him from desertion and supported him as he worked through his anguish. Compounding Walter's distress, his letters home went unanswered, except by his mother. Maggie, the woman he adored, never wrote him back; not even once.

When war came for Walter and his crew, it was in November of 1942 during the Allied invasion of French Algeria as part of Operation Torch. They performed well, but it was rapidly determined that, while the M3A1 Stuart was an excellent scout and infantry support vehicle, it was terribly overmatched by German and Italian armor. Nonetheless, Walter's crew came through the North Africa campaign unscathed.

One morning, Walter clambered up onto his tank to see the name *Dogpatch* painted on the side of the turret. Some wise guy from their unit thought Walter's South Carolina accent sounded like Li'l Abner and had painted the name as a joke. Walter, rather than being angry, liked the name and forbade his crew from removing it. It reminded him of home, he explained. So, the name stuck.

During the invasion of Sicily known as Operation Husky, Walter's crew suffered its first casualty. On August 10, 1943, during the 3rd Division's push toward Messina, Carl Irwin was decapitated by a Panzerfaust round. Folts avenged his death seconds later with an uncharacteristically accurate shot from the *Dogpatch*'s 37mm main gun. But the damage was done, and Irwin was dead just a week before his twentieth birthday.

The death hit LaMotta particularly hard. He felt it should have been him. Suffering from a migraine headache, LaMotta had asked Irwin to switch positions with him earlier that day. Because the younger man wanted more experience driving, he'd leaped at the opportunity and died for his eagerness.

That night, during a lull in battle, the surviving crewmembers got blind drunk with a bottle of gin magically produced by Folts. Walter joined in but not until after he'd finished the hardest job any commander could have, writing a letter to Irwin's parents back in Topeka, informing them that their only son would not be coming home from the war.

After the fall of Messina, Walter's crew was sent back for rest, refitting, and a replacement assistant driver. Their new crewmate was Richard McGregor from St. Louis, Missouri, who was competent, steady under fire, and a pleasant enough chap, but he was never totally accepted by his *Dogpatch* crewmates. The ghost of Carl Irwin was always there, and McGregor, through no fault of his own, was the odd man out. Coincident with his arrival, *Dogpatch* and its crew began to suffer from a run of bad luck. Walter came down with malaria and landed in the hospital for a week. Folts burned his hand clearing the breech of the 37mm cannon. LaMotta's headaches became worse and more frequent. Tank tracks inexplicably broke on smooth ground.

The transmission began slipping, and the engine developed an ominous sounding *ping* during acceleration.

In February 1944, the *Dogpatch*'s crew returned to action as part of the Anzio invasion in central Italy. The first several weeks were without major mishaps, only minor inconveniencies, but after almost two years of fighting, their tank was getting old and worn out. There was scuttlebutt that they'd be refitted with the newer Cadillac-engined M5 Stuart. Many of the other tank platoons had already transitioned into the newer tanks, but no new equipment had yet been delivered for Walter's unit.

Consequently, Walter was still riding the venerable old M3A1 into battle on March 17, 1944. The mission seemed simple enough, to serve as an armored scout for Alpha and Charlie Companies. Intelligence had reported several machine-gun nests along the infantry's line of advance; therefore, light armor support and scouting had been ordered. No German armor was expected to be in the area, so the *Dogpatch* was sent out for solo reconnaissance. Anticipating only small arms resistance and possibly a heavy machine gun, Folts preloaded his cannon with a high-explosive rather than an armor-piercing round.

Dogpatch proceeded along its designated route and soon began taking small arms fire from the tree line off to their left. Walter adjusted his course toward the incoming fire. Folts placed a high-explosive round into the trees, and the firing stopped. It was unclear if the shot had done damage or if the opposing infantry was simply pulling back before superior firepower. Walter advanced cautiously. Coming around a curve in the forested road, he saw a phalanx of three Panzer IVs about a thousand yards distant, each mounted with the long-barreled 75mm cannon. Immediately, he realized that they were outnumbered, outarmored, and outgunned. He shouted for LaMotta to initiate evasive action and reverse back around the curve and ordered Mc-Gregor to pop smoke. Folts took quick aim and splashed a high-explosive round onto the frontal turret armor of the lead tank. It was an excellent shot but did no appreciable damage.

Then the Panzer IVs returned fire. The first round sailed high, exploding into a tree behind the *Dogpatch*. Although a miss, the shot toppled a tree that blocked their line of retreat. LaMotta expertly spun the tank to maneuver around the obstruction. The second round hit short, momentarily hiding their tank behind a gout of mud, rock, and debris. Just as it looked like the *Dogpatch* would get away, the overtaxed engine coughed and hesitated. A scant second later, an armor-piercing round struck the side of the Stuart, easily tearing through their side armor in spite of the oblique angle of the strike. The round tore through the crew compartment and into the engine compartment, where it severed a fuel line and immediately sparked a fire.

Shell fragments from the round killed LaMotta and McGregor instantly as it passed through the crew compartment. Folts was injured but survived only to be trapped behind a piece of equipment. Though he'd received shrapnel wounds to his left knee and hip, Walter scrambled out the hatch, turned, and began clearing the debris that had Folts trapped against the cannon's breech. He'd just pried away a last restraining piece of metal tubing and was pulling Folts through the hatch when the engine fire found a fuel line and erupted, turning the turret into an inferno and immolating his friend. The explosive force blew Walter off the turret and away from the burning tank, saving his life. The last sounds he heard before he lost consciousness were the dying screams of his best friend, his companion, his brother being burned alive before his eyes.

Walter woke three days later in a hospital with a thick plaster cast from his navel to his left ankle and bandages covering almost everything else. He'd suffered a concussion and minor burns to his face, chest, and hands. The orthopedic surgeons did all they could to repair the damage to his leg, but he would suffer pain and a pronounced limp for the rest of his life. Most importantly, he was alive and going home...back to the farm, to Maggie and to his boy.

The next several months were filled with pain, both physical and psychological. Walter underwent extensive physical therapy and two more surgeries on his knee before he was finally released from the military's healthcare system. He didn't mind the pain in his leg. That pain was his ticket back to the home and family that he loved. Physical pain he could deal with. The mental anguish was a different story entirely, though.

As if with a will of its own, Walter's mind constantly played the second-guessing game with him over every decision he'd made on that fateful day in March, in a series of "what ifs."

What if I'd chosen another route for reconnaissance?

But, no...my orders detailed the area to be scouted.

What if I hadn't pursued the Germans firing from the trees? But no...finding and destroying the machine-gun nests along the infantry's line of advance was my primary mission.

What if I'd been more cautious in rounding the bend in the road? No...I was no less cautious at that bend than at any of a dozen others that morning.

What if I'd ordered Folts to load armor-piercing rather than high-explosive ammunition? No...intel had explicitly stated that no German or Italian armor was in that sector and AP shells are less useful in an antipersonnel role. Furthermore, we'd just engaged infantry.

What if I'd seen the Panzers sooner and evaded more quickly? No...the recognition of the threat was pretty quick...just not quick enough.

I got my crew killed...every one of them.

Frequently, he'd mutter, "Why couldn't the Krauts have used an HE instead of an AP round? The 0.75 pounds of TNT in a 75mm shell would've easily overmatched the *Dogpatch*'s pathetic 0.52-inch side armor and blown the tank to smithereens...and me with it."

Walter fought and refought the battle that killed his friends all day, every day. No matter what he did, they still died and, for some reason, he still lived. The doctors called it "survivor's guilt." Walter called it Hell.

Days were bad, but the nights were worse. Every night, the accusing faces of his former friends came to him in his sleep, demanding to know why *he* was alive while they were moldering in graves. During his worst nights, Walter relived the battle in excruciatingly vivid detail. The dream always ended the same way, with him trying to pull Folts through the hatch and away from the burning tank but failing and hearing Folts's agonized screams as his body was consumed by flames. Over and over, Walter awoke screaming in pain and terror at the visions that played like a horror film through his subconscious mind. Over time, he found that his friend's faces could be washed away and the flames extinguished by bourbon—lots and lots of bourbon. And the army seemed more than happy to provide it.

So Walter drank.

Sgt. Walter Hamilton was released from Walter Reed Army Hospital a few weeks before VE Day in 1945. Six months later, he was formally discharged from the army and returned home, exactly four years to the day after Pearl Harbor.

Walter's homecoming was very low key. The mayor of Boiling Springs wanted to declare a "Walter Hamilton Day" and host a parade in his honor, but Walter squashed that plan. All he wanted was to be back home on his farm with his wife and his boy. He wanted normality, not fanfare.

He got neither.

CHAPTER 4

MAGGIE'S WAR 1941–1945

A S WALTER PACKED HIS KIT for basic training, Maggie stood alone at the stove, preparing him his last homecooked meal, breakfast, before he shipped out...and maybe forever.

She slammed the skillet down onto the burner and cracked two eggs into the pan, muttering under her breath through it all. "Why the Hell did Walter have to join the army, anyway? Can't a country as big and powerful as the United States of America manage a war without my husband?" She wasn't buying his sudden overwhelming need to do his "patriotic duty."

The yolk broke. "Oops, guess there won't be any 'sunny-side up,' today. Walter will just have to deal with the disappointment. Patriotic duty, my ass!" She continued to mutter, "He has responsibilities right here at home with me and little Mack Lee...and with our baby. How am I supposed to run a tobacco farm? I'm not a farmer. Who's going to plow the fields, plant the crops, harvest and cure the leaves? What about that new crop Walter wanted to try to raise? What if he gets hurt...or killed? What am I going to do?"

She dropped a pat of butter into the skillet and followed it with a steak she'd picked up from the butcher on Saturday. She felt as though she were preparing the last meal for a condemned man, *her* man.

"I'm going to miss you, Walter Hamilton!" A single tear rolled down her cheek. Maggie was pretty sure it wouldn't be the last.

If Maggie was being perfectly honest with herself, she would have conceded that the farm was running well. Although most of the able-bodied men in the area had gone off to join the military, many of those remaining had chosen to work on the Hamilton farm since Walter always paid the best wages of any farm in the county. But Maggie didn't *want* to concede the point. She was too angry.

She knew that as the sole breadwinner for an entire family, he could have been exempted from service. But she also knew nothing she said would change his mind. She understood his sense of pride and honor. To Walter, *not* fighting for his country, even though not required, would've been tantamount to cowardice. He was going, and once Walter Henry Hamilton set his mind on anything, there was no talking him out of it.

Along with Mary, Mack Lee, and half the town, who were doing the same thing with *their* men, Maggie saw Walter off at the train station. She resigned herself to fighting the Battle of Boiling Springs in his absence. Together with Mary, she dutifully collected copper wire and aluminum cans and made a Victory Garden in the backyard next to the henhouse. She knitted socks and baby booties. She did her best to raise Mack Lee and run the farm. All the while, she kept up a cheerful stream of letters to Walter, telling him all about the farm and sharing news about family and relations, Mack Lee, and how just yesterday she'd felt the baby move for the first time. And every evening, she and Mary dutifully tuned the radio to hear the increasingly distressing news from the war.

All was as well as it could be until one night in early spring when Maggie was awakened from a deep sleep with severe abdominal cramping and blood on the sheets. The cramps abated, but the next morning, Mary drove her to visit a doctor who confirmed her worst fears—she had lost her baby...again. That day, the world stopped turning for Maggie. Time ceased to exist. Her baby was gone. Walter was gone away, perhaps forever. The light in her eyes dimmed. The song in her heart stopped playing. Life ebbed away, and Maggie fell headlong into a pit of despair. She rarely left her bedroom, and when she did, she wore no more than a faded housecoat and slippers. She'd shut herself away entirely from the world and refused to see friends or attend church.

Mary did her best to cheer her up, but Maggie was inconsolable.

Maggie could not bring herself to contact Walter or inform him about the miscarriage. Therefore, Mary took it upon herself to do so via telegram, followed later by a letter describing Maggie's decline into darkness. She tried her best to assure Walter that Maggie would be all right and just needed time to heal.

Had Mary not still lived in the family home, Maggie and Mack Lee likely would have starved. With aplomb, she resumed the role she'd abdicated a few years before as the lady of the house, taking over the cooking, cleaning, and gardening. She made sure Mack Lee was fed, bathed, and schooled, and she watched over Maggie.

Additionally, Mary became the de facto foreman for the farm and kept up the routines of seeding, planting, cultivating, harvesting, curing, and bringing to market their tobacco. For thirty-six years, Mary had watched her husband run the farm, and she'd been an astute observer. Even with rationing and manpower shortages, the farm thrived, helped, no doubt, by an increase in tobacco prices due to government contracts.

Maggie did not thrive. She lost weight and became pale and sickly in appearance. Still, with time, she returned to an attenuated version of her prewar self.

In March 1944, a telegram arrived informing them that Walter had been wounded in action. Frustratingly, there was little additional information, causing the Hamilton women to fear the worst. A few days later, Maggie received a letter from Italy, from Walter. She dropped the rest of the mail in the driveway and tore into the letter. In it, Walter assured her that he was fine. He'd been wounded in the leg, and although it hurt like Hell, he was able to walk and, most importantly, he loved her and hoped to be coming home soon.

Hearing Maggie screaming from the end of the driveway, Mary rushed outside, fearful of the news contained in the letter Maggie held in her shaking hands. She rushed toward Maggie, praying it was good news.

"He's coming home! He's coming home!" Maggie practically sang as she skipped around in circles, waving Walter's letter like a semaphore flag.

The two women walked hand-in-hand back to the house and began making plans for Walter's homecoming.

But Walter didn't come home...at least not as quickly as had been their hope. His recovery at Walter Reed Army Hospital was taking longer than anticipated, and he'd required five additional surgeries. The hoped-for days before he'd come home turned into weeks. The weeks turned to months. Walter remained hospitalized, convalescing.

A full fourteen months after he'd been wounded, Walter still wasn't home. Worse, now, letters to him seldom prompted any reply. By VE Day 1945, Maggie was at her wit's end. The lack of information from and about Walter was driving her mad. It was as though he'd fallen into a vacuum. Thoroughly frustrated and tired of the endless waiting, Maggie—with Mary's wholehearted endorsement—booked a train ticket to Bethesda, Maryland, intent upon visiting her husband. On arrival, she was informed that visitation was not allowed and she must leave. Livid, she marched past the stunned secretary and into the commander's office, determined to get her answers.

What Maggie didn't realize was that *physically*, Walter could've returned home months ago. He'd remained hospitalized not on a physical therapy ward, as she had been led to believe from her correspondence with the hospital administrator, but on a psychiatric ward.

Walter's official diagnosis was "war neurosis" as manifested by nightmares, tremors, and flashbacks. The doctors at Walter Reed believed he was responding to treatment and were adamantly opposed to allowing their patients to visit with family. The commander quoted studies based upon experience gained treating soldiers returning from the First World War and insisted that the best course for Walter was to remain in a perfectly serene but regimented environment with little to no external stimulation until his brain was "fully recovered." He admitted the doctors had no idea how long his recovery might take, but they were convinced that the stress of a visit would trigger a setback and do "permanent psychological harm."

Maggie would hear nothing of it, and when faced by a full-frontal assault from Maggie that would have made

Patton himself proud, the commander relented and gave permission for her to see her husband.

Orderlies brought Walter by wheelchair to a small garden area where Maggie waited on a cast-iron park bench. When she first saw him, it was all she could do to suppress a gasp of anguish. Gone was the strapping, healthy young man she'd seen off at the railroad station four years ago. Instead, a gaunt man with hollow eyes who appeared much older than his twenty-six years had taken his place. Despite her initial shock, Maggie was thrilled to see him. She practically smothered Walter with kisses and held him in a prolonged, loving embrace that he only halfheartedly returned.

Maggie chatted endlessly about the farm, Mack Lee, and Mary. She talked about home and silly air raid marshals, laughing over the absurdity that the Germans might send bombers from Berlin to knock out a grain silo in Boiling Springs. She mentioned nothing about her miscarriage or that the stories she was recounting were secondhand, all repeated from things Mary had told *her* over the three years since the miscarriage.

Walter listened more or less attentively. From time to time he grunted or mumbled a question, but mostly, he remained silent. Before the war, he had been quiet and reserved. Battling his internal demons as he was now, and on enough tranquilizers to bring down a bull rhino, he'd become even more taciturn, if not entirely uncommunicative.

Too soon, the time allotted for the visit came to an end and an orderly arrived to take Walter back to his ward. With a hitch in her throat, Maggie told Walter she loved him and promised to write. Then, after a brief kiss and a half-returned hug, he was gone.

Maggie stared after him as the orderly wheeled Walter away, lost in her thoughts. After a moment, she turned on her heel and strode back to the hospital's administrative offices. Once again, she brushed past the secretary without so much as a second glance, and barged into the commander's office. She stood rigidly before the stunned hospital commander's desk, impatiently tapping her foot as he hurriedly ended his telephone call.

"Mrs. Hamil—" he began.

"Don't you 'Mrs. Hamilton' me!" Maggie snapped. "I have been misled for over a year now, and it's going to stop. Do you hear me?"

"Mrs. Ham—"

Maggie cut the commander off with a glare that would've frozen molten lava. "What I expect"—Maggie quickly read the name plate on the commander's desk—"Colonel Meese, is a weekly update from my husband's physicians or from you—"

Meese rose from his desk and tried, with little success, to talk over Maggie and regain the initiative. "Mrs. Hamilton, this is highly irregular. At Walter Reed, we—"

Maggie continued her assault unabated. "...until my husband is ready to be discharged to home."

"There's not the staff to—"

"And if it is not convenient for you to provide progress reports directly to me, you may forward them to me through the office of our dear family friend." Maggie withdrew a handwritten letter from her purse and placed it upon Colonel Meese's desk. The letter was written on embossed United States Senate letterhead and addressed to "My dearest Mary." She continued, "Senator Burnet R. Maybank. Perhaps you know him as the cochairman for the Senate's Joint Committee on Defense Production or, perhaps, the

Appropriations Committee? He has promised to help us in any way possible."

Maggie swiped the letter from Meese's desk an instant later, not allowing him an opportunity to peruse its contents. This was totally a bluff, but Maggie played her cards expertly, and the commander folded.

In truth, the letter was little more than a thank you to Mary for a five-dollar donation she'd made to Maybank's 1942 senatorial campaign. Mary had given it to Maggie before she'd left for Bethesda, thinking it might help lubricate bureaucratically rusty hinged doors, and it—along with Maggie's poker face—had worked marvelously. Consequently, when Maggie left Walter Reed, it was with Colonel Meese's promise for frequent and detailed communications regarding Walter's progress.

Although the reunion was less joyful than Maggie might have hoped, the doctors could not have been more wrong. Rather than precipitating a setback, Walter began to improve. Once again, Maggie became his guiding star—his link to the normality that he so desperately craved but heretofore had believed unobtainable. Coincident to her visit, he began "cheeking" his pills—a combination of sedatives and antipsychotics—and spitting them into the toilet when the orderlies weren't watching. Consequently, as the drugs washed out of his system, Walter was able to think clearly once again. Gone was the drug-induced miasma through which he'd muddled for the past several months. In its place, he had clarity. He became more interactive with staff and other patients and even began writing letters home to Maggie and Mary. He started taking walks in the garden and exploring the grounds, slowly recovering his strength. By Thanksgiving, totally ignorant of his noncompliance, and thoroughly convinced that their treatment regimen had miraculously worked, Walter's doctors began making plans for his discharge from Walter Reed. Per an edict from the hospital commander, they informed Maggie by mail and telegram of their plans.

Maggie was elated, and immediately began planning for Walter's return. She, Mary, and little Mack Lee would meet him at the rail depot. Then, he'd be home!

Walter was scheduled for discharge on December 8, 1945, but when one of the orderlies wrangled him a ticket home a day earlier, he jumped at the chance to leave.

On the day of his hospital discharge, the doctors gave Walter a large bag of pills with instructions that they should be taken four times per day. Additionally, they scheduled him to return to Walter Reed in a month for a follow-up evaluation. The hospital orderly dropped Walter at the train depot, handed him a ticket to Spartanburg, and wished him well before driving back to the hospital. As soon as the orderly was out of sight, Walter dropped the bag of pills into the garbage bin next to the ticket booth. Then he sat on a bench and smoked cigarettes while patiently waiting for his train home.

All Walter wanted was to be back home. He wanted to work his own land and sleep in his own bed. As for the doctors? Well, as far as he was concerned, they could all go straight to Hell. He never took another pill and never again did his shadow darken the threshold of Walter Reed Army Hospital.

CHAPTER 5

DECEMBER 1945–AUGUST 1955

W ITH NO HOME TELEPHONE, WALTER was unable to get in touch with Maggie to inform her of his accelerated discharge date. Consequently, when he arrived at the depot in Spartanburg, no one was there to meet him. Unfazed, he picked up his suitcase and started walking. He figured it was *only* nineteen miles, not a big deal for a soldier used to marching twenty or more miles while carrying a rifle and sixty pounds of equipment on his back. However, he neglected to account for the facts that basic training had been four long years ago and that he'd suffered major damage to his leg and hip at Anzio. After a mile, he sat down on his suitcase by the roadside and waited. Soon, he was able to thumb a ride the rest of the way home in the back of a passing farm truck. The farmer was a veteran of World War I and was all too happy to assist a fellow vet's homecoming. Rather than taking him into town as Walter had suggested, the old man insisted upon going miles out of his way and dropped Walter off at the end of his driveway. Walter thanked the man and limped painfully up to his house, thankful to finally be home.

As he neared the house, he heard faint sounds of singing coming from the kitchen.

> In Dublin's fair city,
> Where the girls are so pretty,
> I first set my eyes on sweet Molly Malone.
> As she wheeled her wheelbarrow,
> Through streets broad and narrow,
> Crying, "Cockles and mussels, alive, alive, oh!"
> "Alive, alive, oh,
> Alive, alive, oh,"
> Crying, "Cockles and mussels, alive, alive, oh."

Walter smiled. He'd not heard his wife sing in too many years. Although her song was more melancholy than once her songs had been, the sound still made his heart leap for joy. The singing continued as he entered the kitchen. Maggie's back was turned, and she was kneading dough for biscuits. He smiled, watching his wife. She had flour in her hair and on her apron and her hips swayed as she sang.

> She died of a fever,
> And no one could save her,
> And that was the end of sweet Molly Malone.
> But her ghost wheels her barrow,
> Through streets broad and narrow,
> Crying, "Cockles and mus—"

Walter cleared his throat.

The lump of dough skittered across the countertop as Maggie spun toward the sound and shrieked, "*Walter!*" as she ran to embrace her husband. Mary rushed in at the commotion and gasped at the sight, as thrilled as Maggie that he'd finally returned home. Mack Lee, with no recollection of his father, hid behind Mary's skirt and ran away screaming when Walter moved in his direction.

Mack Lee had no memory of his father from before the war and had grown into an unholy terror during the years Walter had been away. He was headstrong and selfish with a tendency toward laziness, traits that were anathema for Walter after four years in the army. As Walter, Maggie, and Mary settled into new routines, everyone adjusting in their own ways to Walter's return, his patience was pushed to the limits by a son who seemed only to do his chores under duress and constant supervision. Consequently, the relationship between Walter and his son was, at best, strained.

Maggie tried to bridge the gap between father and son, but she was dealing with issues of her own. Although she put on a brave face for her husband, she was prone to bouts of deep depression and often found it difficult to get out of bed each morning.

If the damp, dreary winter weather bothered Mary's rheumatism, she gave little indication. With Walter's return, she was more than happy to relinquish her roles on the farm. Instead, she spent her days bustling about the house, helping Maggie cook, clean, and care for her grandson. Evenings, however, she was content to sit in her rocking chair by the kitchen fireplace, reading a book while waiting for a cake or pie to come out of the oven. The human dynamo, it seemed, was beginning to wind down.

Walter Hamilton didn't talk much about the war. In truth, he didn't talk much about anything. But when he did deign to communicate verbally with the outside world, never, ever was the exchange about his experiences during the Second World War. That did not, however, suggest those experiences were ever far from his mind. On the contrary, they never left. Though happy to be home safe from the war and ready for his life to once again move forward, Walter was still troubled by nightmares for which he frequently self-medicated with alcohol.

His drive for working the farm had faded during his years away. His enthusiasm for transitioning from tobacco to soybeans was dampened somewhat by the high prices still being paid for tobacco in the post-war markets. Realizing that the post-war boom wouldn't last forever, he made a few desultory moves toward the transition, but Walter's heart was no longer in the endeavor.

Nor was Walter's heart into any other endeavors. The joy from his homecoming was short-lived. That is not to say that Walter wasn't happy to be home, for certainly, he was. It's just that he'd left the part of his soul that believed in a future, somewhere along the road from Anzio to Rome. How was it fair that he was here at home, alive and enjoying the love of his family, when better men than he, Irwin, Folts, LaMotta, and McGregor—his brothers—were moldering in their graves. If only the Krauts had fired a high-explosive shell instead of an armor-piercing one...he'd be with them.

Of course, they were here with him now too, at least at night.

His nightmares persisted, although their subject matter had changed. Whereas before, he relived the final battle with the three Panzers repeatedly, now he just saw the faces of his fallen comrades. They stared back at him in silent accusation as though to say, "Why aren't you here with us?" Honestly, Walter was unsure which set of bad dreams was the worst.

He'd once tried to talk with Maggie about his nightmares—a huge step for one not prone to talking—but it had been a disaster. She couldn't understand why he should feel sad. She told him that he should just be happy being at home, and thank the fates for allowing him to be there. That, she said, would keep the dreams at bay.

As for his son, Walter just had to shake his head. The boy was lazy, insolent, and a liar of biblical proportions. He was the snake in the Garden of Eden. If Mack Lee told anyone that the sky was blue and the grass was green, they'd better check it out for themselves lest they be fooled.

For her part, Maggie was thrilled to have Walter home again. However, it was clear to her that he wasn't really *here* with her, even now. He'd always been quiet, so his silence wasn't a great change. Before, Walter had always been quiet, but he'd also been present, caring, and kind. Now, however, he generally seemed a million miles away and, more often than not, angry.

It was the war—the same goddamn war Walter had not *had* to go off and fight—that was the wedge holding the two of them apart. Maggie knew it! Apparently, he'd not gotten enough of it while he was away. He even *dreamed* about the damned war at nighttime. To top it all off, his time in the military had left him with bad habits. He constantly drank. Walter tried to hide it, but a wife always knows.

What galled Maggie the most, however, were her husband's interactions with Mack Lee. Walter seemed to have no time or patience for that dear, sweet child. He always seemed angry with Mack Lee and had no appreciation for him or his active imagination—that boy could really tell some tales.

As for Mary, she could see that Walter and Maggie's relationship was strained. To a degree, it was to be expected. The couple had been apart for four long years, and over that time, both had changed. Knowing how much they'd loved one another, she was certain that they'd eventually get the family back on the rails. They just needed time; time to get to know one another again, and time to heal.

Mary was right, as she usually was, and in 1947, Maggie announced that she was pregnant.

When Maggie found out she was pregnant, the news was more terrifying for her than joyous. Maggie was careful to hide this dichotomy of feelings. Outwardly, she was appropriately happy, as convention dictated she should be. She was only twenty-seven, but after one still-birth and a miscarriage, she was perfectly content to never put herself through all that again. Besides, she already had one perfectly delightful child, did she really *need* another? Additionally, although her relationship with Walter was improving, he continued to drink more than she'd like and was prone to angry outbursts. Was another baby *really* going to help with that? Maggie thought not.

Thankfully, Maggie's pregnancy was uneventful, and on August 27, she and Walter welcomed a little boy, they christened James Wiley Hamilton, into their family. When specialists in Spartanburg informed Maggie she would not likely be able to become pregnant again, she was secretly relieved, a fact for which she felt terribly ashamed.

It was therefore quite a surprise two years later when Maggie gave birth to a little girl they named Anna Marie. Maggie called Anna her "miracle baby," and she was perfect! She had bright blue eyes and curly, corn-silk blonde hair. She was a good baby and grew into a delightful, loving child, the apple of both her mother and father's eyes.

The early 1950s were happy times for the Hamilton family. Even though the farm prospered, Walter continued his plan for transitioning from tobacco to soybeans, albeit slowly. His nightmares become much less frequent, and he'd largely given up drinking.

Following Anna's birth, Maggie seemed to have been cured from her depression. Puppies, kittens, and giggling little girls can bring a smile to the most stolid of faces. She worked tirelessly around the house, making sure that Walter and the children were well fed, well clothed, and well loved.

After running the farm and holding the family together during the war years, Mary decided that she'd like to visit her sister in Key West for a while. Her arthritis had begun to limit her ability to be helpful around the house anyway. A little time in the warmer latitudes might do her aching joints some good. After arriving in the Keys, she found she loved it there and decided to stay.

Mack Lee evolved from petulant child into rebellious teenager, constantly getting into mischief around town and returning home in the back of a patrol car many an evening. He was a standout in sports and a star on the high school football team, thus his hijinks around town were largely tolerated. He was significantly less tolerant of his younger siblings and teased and mocked them both mercilessly.

Walter was constantly frustrated by Mack Lee's antics and total lack of discipline. His efforts, however, to correct these deficiencies were hobbled by his wife. For Maggie, Mack Lee represented a link to an earlier, happier time in her life. Consequently, he could commit no sin that his mother was unable to absolve entirely or explain away, and Mack Lee was all too happy to play this "Get Out of Jail Free" card with impunity.

James became the classic middle child, lost in the shuffle between his star athlete older brother and his adorable younger sister. Remarkably, living in the shadows of his elder and younger siblings did not seem to faze him at all. He had nothing in common with his brother. Where Mack Lee was brawny and athletic, James was quiet, even tempered and bookish. He excelled in school and maintained interests well beyond the grasp of his age-matched peers. He was a peacemaker around the house and seemed to embrace his role as Anna's companion and protector.

All was well in the Hamilton household until black shank hit. Then, everything fell apart. Walter had planned on having the farm fully transitioned away from tobacco to soybeans within the next three years. When black shank hit, less than a third of the farm had been converted. Their entire tobacco crop had to be plowed under and the fields burned, leaving the family with no viable cash crop and virtually no income. They rapidly burned through the meager savings they'd banked during the war years. Luckily, they owned their house and land outright and so for the moment were safe from creditors. But the respite was only temporary, since Walter had to take a mortgage out on the land in order to purchase seed beans for the next year's planting and to cover the lost revenue from this year's tobacco crop. Even if there was no income, the workers had to be paid, equipment had to be purchased and serviced, and the family must be fed. So, for the first time since 1665, the bank held paper on the Hamilton family farm.

With the combined stresses of an expanded family, new debt, and lack of income, Walter's nightmares returned with a vengeance. Consequently, he resumed self-medicating with alcohol. He refused to drink around Maggie and the children, instead drinking away from the house, hiding his bottles in the hay loft. Alternatively, he had a bottle tucked behind a keg of nails in the toolshed and still another safely ensconced in the tractor shed under a pile of rags. Each morning, he went off to "work" on the farm. On good days, he got some work accomplished. On bad days, which became increasingly frequent, he drowned his failures in a sea of bourbon, rye, or Scotch and returned home hopelessly drunk at night.

Maggie hadn't signed up for this. She'd given herself to a man she loved, a man with a strong work ethic who she knew would always take care of her and her children. And, right up until Walter decided he wanted to run off and play soldier, he'd been just that. The indomitable force that had gone off to war had never returned from Italy. Now, it seemed, with every little bump in the road, Walter fell apart. War had been Hell on the home front too, and nobody saw *her* turning into a sniveling, spineless dud of a man.

Maggie had conveniently forgotten that she'd spent most of the war in bed, with Walter's mother caring for her and her son. So, rather than easing her husband's burdens as Mary had done for her, Maggie berated the man constantly, which did little to support Walter's flagging self-worth or his mental health.

CHAPTER 6

1947–1953

THE HAMILTON FARM OF THE 1950s represented the remaining postage-stamp-sized sliver of a much larger parcel granted to the family by a proprietary charter from the king of England back when South Carolina was still part of the British colony, Carolana. The original charter had granted to their great-great-great—and perhaps a few more greats—grandfather "all the lands between the Pacolet and Broad Rivers in the Carolana Colony by hand of King Charles II in 1665." The charter documents had been lost, ostensibly, during a house fire some two hundred years later. Family lore held that the fire was arson, set by a foraging party from none other than General William Tecumseh Sherman's army.

The family's acreage had been steadily whittled away—down to a scant forty-six acres—through three hundred years of marriages, wills, and sales so that only this small farm remained in the family's name. About a third of the farm was wooded and fenced for cattle. On the rest, the Hamiltons grew tobacco, or at least, they *used* to grow tobacco. The unfortunate brush with black shank had permanently destroyed the farm's ability to produce marketable leaves.

The Hamilton's were not a wealthy family—far from it, in fact—but because they'd always owned their farm outright, rather than the bank, their situation had been slightly better than most of their neighbors. Selling livestock and hay, they were able to barely keep their heads above water. However, with a farm that no longer produced a significant cash crop but for which taxes routinely came due, the land was more of a liability than an asset.

The Hamilton children, at least the two youngest, were totally and blissfully unaware of their penury. Although there was not always much to eat, the dinner table was never empty. The garden provided a steady supply of fresh vegetables in the summer, and their mother religiously canned and pickled the surplus for their winter fare. The cows supplied fresh milk, and once a year, one would be sent to the slaughterhouse to be magically transformed into beef. Similarly, the smokehouse was full of hams and sides of bacon from pigs who'd suffered similar fates.

The eldest of the Hamilton children, Mack Lee, had a very different perception of the family's general state of affairs. He hated the farm and everything about it. Had it been left up to him, their tobacco plants would've been planted in raised beds. *Everybody* knew raised beds made their tobacco less susceptible to infection with black shank. If there wasn't any black shank, then they'd still have a viable cash crop. If they had a cash crop, then the farm would be profitable. If the farm was profitable, then he wouldn't have to work like a pack mule from dawn to dusk on the farm and Dad could buy him a car. If he had a car, then he could get Sherri Lynde to go steady with him. And if what the guys said about her was even *half* true...Well, he dared not even to dream!

Mack Lee was at once omnipotent, egocentric, and drowning in hormones. In short, Mack Lee Hamilton was a teenager.

Mack Lee had no time for the younger Hamilton children. He was far more interested in cars, friends, girls, and hunting than he was his younger siblings. Besides, he had more important things to occupy his time than two "babies." The children were barely tolerated and, wherever possible, ignored outright.

He also hated the farm and all things related to farming. As the star running back on the Boiling Springs High School football team, he was often allowed to skip out on his chores for football practice, which was fine by him. He determined very early in his life that, although he didn't know exactly what he wanted to do for a living, it sure as *Hell* would not entail working a tobacco farm.

His best friend Robert Morrison, Bob, was already six feet four and weighed 240 pounds. He was the starting center on the football team and had caught the attention of several universities, although he was only a sophomore. Already, recruiters stalked the stands and hung around after games just to shake his hand. On the field, Bob opened the holes and Mack Lee ran through them. Bob had a head for numbers and was near the top of their class in school. He was, by all accounts, a good kid and looked forward to a bright future. Mack Lee, although a decent running back, did not share Bob's work ethic on or off the field. Consequently, he would never rise beyond the level of average. Nonetheless, the two made an unstoppable pair on the football field and were nearly inseparable off field as well. They shared similar interests—mostly girls, cars, and beer, although not necessarily in that order. Neither boy had any interest in life as a farmer after finishing high school. Both athletically and academically gifted, Bob's future ability to avoid that fate was all but guaranteed. Mack Lee's prospects for the future seemed much less assured.

Near the end of their sophomore year in high school, the pair came across the find of a lifetime while working for Old Lady McDaniel. She'd hired the two boys to clean out her barn and haul away all the old junk therein, much of which had been there since the turn of the century. She was willing to pay ten dollars, and if the boys wanted to do it, the job was theirs. Mack Lee and Bob leaped at the opportunity. For them to actually get paid to do something that did not entail sweating in a tobacco field was one step short of heaven.

The barn was a large structure with corrugated metal walls and a tin roof. In the front was a pair of massive rolling doors secured by a padlock and clasp. The place looked like an aircraft hangar large enough to comfortably house a B-29 bomber. The rollers for the barn doors were frozen with rust, and their tracks were in a similar state of disrepair. After two hours on ladders sanding, oiling, and pounding the rusted tracks with a ballpeen hammer, the boys finally freed the frozen rollers well enough to force the door open a crack.

The sight they beheld while peering through that crack left them speechless. Apparently, Old Man McDaniel had been quite the pack rat, a hoarder par excellence, back in his day. The barn was piled from floor to rafters with a half-century's worth of detritus.

Bob quipped, "Jeez! If we open that door all the way, it'll take them a month just to dig our bodies out from under all that stuff."

Always quick to feel slighted, Mack Lee replied, "How are we supposed to get rid of all this crap? That old bat's out of her mind. All this...for a lousy ten bucks?! We've been robbed."

After a moment of reflection, both agreed. This barn was *still* better than a tobacco field though, so they forged ahead.

Bob's concern, although well-founded, ultimately was proven unnecessary. The mountain of debris was so tangled and interwoven that when the pair finally forced the doors fully open, the mass did not budge. In fact, the army could have used the pile as a rather effective tank trap. Maybe they should sell this junk to them, an idea not totally devoid of merit.

Having spent an inordinate amount of time simply gaining access to the barn and its mound of hoarded content, the boys then tackled the problem of removal. Trying to clean this place out was going to be like Hercules cleaning the Augean stables. Unfortunately, there was no convenient river to redirect to do the job for them. Cleaning this place out was going to be nothing but backbreakingly hard work.

So, on a warm August morning, the two began their task. The boys borrowed a horse and wagon from the Morrison farm and drove it into the shade of an oak tree near the barn. Then they began dragging free the hoarded mess. By noon, when it was almost a hundred degrees outside and significantly hotter inside the barn, still they worked.

The boys recovered a variety of farm implements, some serviceable but most not. The tools appearing in best repair, they placed aside. The rest, they tossed onto the wagon destined to be hauled away to a deep gulley behind the pond on the McDaniel place. They found old saddles, yokes and halters, old horse-drawn plows, and hay rakes. They saved the best while the rest made its way to the gulley. There were kegs of rusty nails and jugs of what they took to be moonshine, although neither trusted the vile-smelling contents enough to give it a taste. The liquid was highly flammable and made a wonderful accelerant for burning some of the lesser junk items that didn't merit the work of being hauled away.

The gulley that was to serve as their landfill was located behind the dam on the effluent side of an old mill pond. After every couple loads, the boys dove into the pond to cool off, much to the displeasure of a mama duck and ducklings who called the pond their home.

After a full day of working, they'd made it no farther than ten feet into the barn's interior, not even a quarter of its depth. The boys hauled closed the barn door and trudged wearily to the McDaniel house. They wanted to update Old Lady McDaniel on their progress and needed to verify her wishes regarding disposition of the still serviceable contents they'd recovered.

"Burn it! Sell it! Haul it away! I really don't care. I thought you'd be finished by now. What's taking so long anyway?" Mrs. McDaniel replied, clearly annoyed.

"But some of the stuff is still good," started Bob.

"I want it gone, all of it. Just get rid of it. That's what I'm paying you good money to do and that's what I expect!"

"Yes, ma'am," the boys replied together.

At seven o'clock the following morning, the boys resumed their labors. After another day of sweating, hauling, and cursing, the idea of diverting a stream was becoming far more appealing. Hercules had had it easy!

On day two, they dragged free an old cider press, several stove-in barrels, and what appeared to be an ancient still. The cider press was in decent shape, but sadly, the still had been smashed beyond repair.

By the afternoon of day three, the boys glimpsed the back wall for the first time, but only for an instant. While pulling a broken chair from the pile, Mack Lee initiated a chain reaction. The chair hung on something, so he gave it a yank. This dislodged an old truck tire, which fell on the end of a rickety wooden ladder, which cartwheeled toward the ceiling and cleaved a previously unseen, basketball-sized hornet's nest from one of the rafters. Angry hornets boiled from their damaged home, intent upon revenge, and brought the day's work to an abrupt and painful close.

Before sunrise on the morning of day four, as the eastern sky was beginning to show a faint light, the boys returned to the darkened barn. Entering the inky interior, they found the hornet's nest, doused it with moonshine, and set it ablaze. The ensuing conflagration settled the score once and for all, ending all possibility of future vespoid-borne reprisals.

As the burning nest crackled, hissed, and popped, the light provided the boys their first decent look at the barn's dark, previously unlit interior.

"Hey, Mack Lee." Bob pointed to a ratty canvas tarpaulin buried under a mountain of broken furniture and spattered liberally with bird droppings. "What do you think that is? Back there in the corner?"

The light rapidly waned as the nest burned away, and the tarp faded again into the gloom.

Rubbing multiple inflamed welts on his forehead from the previous day's brush with the hornets, Mack Lee sneered, "Probably Old Man McDaniel's rattlesnake pit!"

Having been unpleasantly alerted to the possibility that there might be additional inhabitants of the barn who may not *totally* appreciate their industry, Bob and Mack Lee decided to wait for full daylight before proceeding with what they hoped would be the final day of their clean-up project. Kicked back in the shade of a towering black walnut and smoking pilfered cigarettes, the boys surveyed the products of their past three days' labor and deliberated what to do next.

They'd amassed a nice pile of serviceable furniture and tools they thought could be taken to the trade lot and sold. With no overhead, everything they sold would be pure profit. God knew this job should have paid them more than the measly ten bucks they had been promised. Besides, if Old Lady McDaniel didn't want any of it, why shouldn't they sell the stuff that was still good enough to be useful to somebody? Anything else would be...well, wasteful.

As the morning sun rose above the trees, the boys forced the barn door open wide and resumed their work. They found more old tires, broken furniture, and rusted tools. Nothing, unfortunately, appeared to be in any condition even close to salable. It was all junk, more junk, and nothing but junk.

Until Bob raised a corner of the tarp. He stepped back and let out a whistle, then called over his shoulder, "Mack Lee, you have *got* to see this!"

"Let me guess...another broken couch? A washing machine? Maybe it's a—" Turning toward Bob, Mack Lee's jaw dropped as he gaped in awe. "Holy shit!"

Under the tarp sat a 1929 Ford Model A Roadster.

The boys stared in open-mouthed amazement. The car body was in decent condition and had been painted black. The spoke wheels were, or rather, had been, cream colored. The white wall tires were all flat and cracked from dry rot. The brown leather door panels and seats were similarly cracked, and it appeared that a family of rats had made their home in the rumble seat. There was a stick shift and a huge four-spoke steering wheel. In the center of the dash was a rounded, diamond-shaped chrome instrument cluster upon which the odometer read 4390 miles. And the key was in the ignition.

Bob popped the latches and raised the wings of the hood. Partially hidden under a pile of clothing scraps and hay—apparently placed there by cousins of the rumble seat rats—was a rusty, two-hundred-cubic-inch, inline four-cylinder engine. He pointed out various components to his friend. "This is *awesome*! Look at this, Mack Lee."

"Hot damn, we got us a car! I can see us now, cruising down Main Street. We'll absolutely *rule* this town. The chicks are gonna *love* this," crowed Mack Lee, already imagining the lovely Miss Lynde sliding toward him across the bench seat while watching a flick together at the Bijou Drive-In Theater. Excitement welled up inside him. This was going to be great!

"We can fix it up and make it run again. We can work in my old man's garage. He won't care. Maybe we put a real engine in it, something better than this 40HP sewing-machine motor. Get it a new paint job, maybe something with flames or somethin'. And we can—" Bob stopped suddenly. "No, we can't."

"Whaddaya mean, we can't?"

"We gotta tell Old Lady Mac about this. It's *her* car, not ours."

"Screw the old biddy! If she wanted it, she shouldn't have told us to haul away or burn everything in the barn. You heard her when we asked about the other stuff!"

"Mack Lee, man...this is different. That other stuff was junk. We might get a couple bucks out of it, but this is different. This is a *car*! And it belongs to her."

"It's not like the old bag has it registered to her. Nobody will ever know. It's ours, man!" Mack Lee argued.

"I gotta tell her about it. It's the right thing to do!"

"Says who?"

"Says me!"

"Don't do it, Bob! I'm tellin' ya! Don't!"

"Or what?"

"I'll stop you!"

"Yeah...right, you and who's army?" Bob said, turning toward the McDaniel house.

"Nooooooooooo!" Mack Lee screamed, launching himself at his friend's legs.

Bob collapsed in a heap but managed to take Mack Lee down with him. The two grappled and rolled around on the ground and even traded a few punches, although no real damage was done by either combatant. With one boy outweighing the other by at least seventy pounds, the outcome of the scuffle was never really in doubt. Soon, Bob was sitting atop the smaller boy's back. With one hand, he twisted Mack Lee's arm, and with the other, he drove his friend's face into the dirt.

"Do ya give up? Say uncle!"

"Hell no!" Mack Lee hissed, trying to shake Bob from his back.

Bob simply applied more pressure on the arm and face.

"All right, all right...uncle."

"What was that? I don't think I heard you."

"Uncle!"

"What?"

"Uncle, uncle, uncle...goddamn it! Uncle!"

"That's what I thought you said." Releasing his hold, Bob jumped to his feet and began brushing the dirt and grass from his clothes.

He offered a hand to help his friend up from the ground, but Mack Lee peevishly slapped the hand away and rose unassisted, swiping at a thin trickle of blood running from his nose.

"It's the right thing to do, Mack Lee...even if we don't like it." Bob called over his shoulder as he trudged toward Old Lady McDaniel's house.

He returned several minutes later, a dejected look on his face. "I told her about the Roadster. She said that it was her husband's car. He used to drive it running shine. Apparently, there's a compartment under the rumble seat where he'd stash the bottles. He got caught and was sent up the river. He died in the pen before his sentence was up. She said he loved that car," Bob said, affecting an air of feigned despondency. "It killed him. Because of that, she *never* wants to see it again. She said that *we* have to *keep* it!" Bob brandished what appeared to be a handwritten bill of sale over his head.

"We have to...We w-what?" Mack Lee stammered.

"It's ours, man! It's ours!"

"You mean, we get to keep it...really? You're not pullin' my leg?"

"It's ours! It's ours!" Bob screamed, clinching Mack Lee in a bear hug and swinging him around like a sack of flour— a very happy sack of flour.

For the next two years, Bob and Mack Lee worked nights and weekends restoring the Roadster and transforming it into a hotrod. Bob often worked in his father's garage, and tractors and other farm implements were constantly breaking down and needing repair on the Hamilton farm. Thus, both boys knew their way around a wrench. To pay for the restoration, the boys worked odd jobs in addition to their usual chores around their respective farms. They picked cotton, mucked stalls, painted sheds, repaired fences, and patched roofs. They even worked in the tobacco fields and barns without grousing. No job was too menial if it paid, and all funds were pooled for parts and tools. They were on a mission.

Progress, while excruciatingly slow, was steady, and the boys worked tirelessly. They stripped the car down to its chassis and painstakingly scraped and sanded away a quarter of a century of rust and grime. They rebuilt everything from the ground up. They removed the fenders, leaving the wheels naked, and replaced the original twenty-one-inch rims with seventeen-inch wire wheels from a '34 Ford, lowering the ride. They eliminated the running board, giving the car a more streamlined appearance. The original four-cylinder "sewing-machine motor" was gone, replaced by a 350HP Chevy small-block V-8 they'd found in a junk yard. This, they coupled to other junk yard finds: a four-speed manual transmission and an updated rear end, differential, and brakes. They left the bonnet off to showcase the small-block with its new aluminum radiator and decorative chrome air cleaner, headers, and pipes.

A local upholstery shop reworked the Roadster's door panels and recovered the front bench and rumble seats with a soft, tan leather. The boys retained the instrument console and choke but had them rechromed and set into a burlwood dash plate. They also rechromed the horn, steering-wheel spokes, and gear shifter. The ball atop the latter, Mack Lee replaced with an eight ball he pilfered from the local pool hall.

The only major disagreement during the restoration process occurred while the two were selecting the exterior paint scheme. Mack Lee wanted to paint it black with blue and white "ghost flames" on the sides and hood. Bob favored a more classy, refined appearance and favored British Racing Green without a lot of frills. Their discussions became heated and at times, the boys nearly came to blows. Ultimately, the decision was made easy by Jerry's Body Shop in nearby Chesnee. Jerry had recently been commissioned to recondition the town's only fire truck. His assistant, unfortunately, overordered the pigment and Jerry was left with several gallons of red paint he couldn't use. However, he was quite willing to sell it to the boys at cost just to clear out his storeroom. He'd even allow them to use his painting bay and compressor for the paint job. Hence, their hotrod came to be colored a bright fire-engine red. Bob even compromised and agreed to have yellow and orange flames stenciled onto the sides and doors.

One Saturday afternoon in February, while the boys were working on the rear brakes, Bob, imagination whetted by half a dozen beers, opened a conversation regarding their plans for the hotrod once the work would be completed. Beyond the immediate and obvious plans to cruise Main Street on Friday nights, pick up chicks, and go to the drive-in, neither had given it much thought.

"As long as I get Sherri Lynde in that rumble seat, I don't really care," chirped Mack Lee airily. "She only dates guys who have cars."

"Aw, be serious, man."

"I *am* being serious! I mean, what could be more serious than those ta-tas? Those hooters are the *promised land*. Wooohoo!"

"Jeez, Mack. Are you drunk or still thirteen years old?"

"I didn't hear you complaining when I got you set up with Lori Horton...behind the bleachers...eh?"

"Christ, Mack Lee, use your head gasket and stop thinking with your stick shift. I'm being serious here."

"Okay, okay, you win. What do *you* think we should do?"

"I dunno. I was thinking, maybe we drive out to California..."

"Yeah! We can bring the girls!"

Bob sighed and shook his head. "Dude, you're hopeless."

"No, actually I am *very* hope*ful*, but why California?"

"Street racing. I was reading about it at the barber shop last week. It's really big in California. I think we should be street racers. Think about it! We just put 350 horses onto a very light chassis. With that power-to-weight ratio, this thing's gonna run faster than Sherri Lynde when she sees you coming her way!"

"Ha ha ha," said Mack Lee, throwing a greasy rag at Bob's head.

Bob caught it easily. "Just kiddin', man. Seriously, this car's gonna be faster than greased lightnin' once we've got it finished. I figure, we get it dialed in, win a few races, and make us a stake. You drive and I pit..."

"Wait, you want *me* to drive?" Mack Lee was immediately interested and excited.

"Yeah, I'm too big for racecar driving. Besides, I'm a better mechanic than you."

"Asshole!" Another rag fluttered past Bob's head.

"And you throw like a girl," Bob teased. "Like I was sayin', we win a couple races and use the winnings to stake us into one of those NASCAR races."

"NASCAR?"

"Yeah, NASCAR...it's a stock car racing series. The idea for NASCAR began with old bootleggers back during Prohibition. The bootleggers needed to be able to distribute their product and evade detection and incarceration, so the drivers modified their cars for speed and handling but retained the exterior appearance of the original car. Sometimes, like Old Man McDaniel, they'd have hidden compartments for their product just in case the cops got too nosey and started pokin' around."

"Why bother? Couldn't they just outrun the cops?"

"Camouflage my friend, camouflage. By not altering the outside looks, they could hide in plain sight. A bootlegger could drive right past a cop and the cops would be none the wiser. If the cops *did* catch on? Well, that's when they kicked in what they had underneath the hood and left the boys in blue eatin' dust instead of doughnuts."

"But that's still not a race. I don't get it."

Bob continued, "Bootleggers, like everybody else, like to brag. What's the point of having the biggest, the fastest, the best if nobody *knows* you've got it. So, drivers got together and started racing each other. People liked to watch these races and even started betting on the outcomes. After a while, bragging rights and side bets gave way to cash purses provided by promoters. Legend has it that some of the promoters were unscrupulous and skipped out on the drivers without paying them anything. So, in the late 1940s, a guy named France founded the National Association for Stock Car Auto Racing, NASCAR, to regulate the sport and make sure everybody got paid. NASCAR held its first big race at Daytona Beach in 1948. Since then, stock car racing has really taken off. I tell you, man, it's gonna be *huge*...and just think, *we* could be a part of it."

CHAPTER 7

1953–1955

WALTER AND MAGGIE HAD NAMED their second son, James Wiley Hamilton, after Walter's great-grandfather. Maggie was the only one who ever called him James. His father just called him "JW" or "Boy." To his friends, he was Jimmy. But to Anna, his adoring little sister, he was forever "Jibby." When she was younger, Anna had suffered from frequent colds, which made it nearly impossible to pronounce the *m*s in his name. Whenever she tried, her stuffy nose caused his name to come out "Jibby" and a nickname was born.

Jimmy and Anna were inseparable. Jimmy liked how her riot of blonde curls bounced when she ran and the way she giggled whenever he said something funny. Making Anna laugh was one of his favorite pastimes, and he loved how her big blue eyes stared adoringly up at him whenever he read stories to her at night. Big brothers were supposed to be annoyed by bratty, tagalong kid sisters, but that was never the case with Jimmy and Anna. Jimmy actually *liked* having a little sister, or at least he did now that she wasn't crying all the time or wearing stinky diapers. He called her "Brat" or "Rugrat" or "Anna-panda."

Since Anna loved *anything* that had to do with animals, "Anna-panda" was her particular favorite. Anna adored Jibby. He was her guide, protector and bestest friend. He was in the third grade, and to first grader Anna, that meant he was almost all grown-up. He was her hero.

Jimmy awoke every day before dawn and milked cows, mucked stalls, and fed the family's pigs for about two hours. Morning chores completed, he returned to the house, washed up, and had a quick breakfast before setting out for school. Regardless of the weather, he walked the three miles into town each day with Anna in tow. After school, he waited for her and together they trekked back home, sometimes stopping to check in on a nest of baby bunnies he'd found.

In the afternoons when his homework and chores were completed, Jimmy was free to do whatever an active, inquisitive boy wanted to do. If a tree needed climbing, he climbed it. If a rock needed throwing, he threw it. If the weather was hot, he swam in the pond. He caught fish, frogs, crawdads, and the occasional June-bug, and every step of the way, Anna-panda was right behind him doing it too. Together, they rode broomstick horses and took the three o'clock stagecoach into Dodge City, where they fought Billy the Kid and, sometimes, Sitting Bull. Rural South Carolina was a great place to be a kid.

Rainy days found Jimmy and Anna playing in the hay loft or sometimes in the attic of their home. Sometimes, Jimmy would read books aloud for Anna. He liked to read and spent an inordinate amount of time in his school's library. Although he was only seven, he was reading at near high school levels. While his peers were still struggling through *Fun with Dick and Jane*, Jimmy was devouring works by Dickens, Kipling, and Robert Louis Stevenson. Anna's favorites were *Heidi* and *The Wizard of Oz*, but

Jimmy could've read her the New York City telephone directory and she still would've sat spellbound, hanging on every word.

There was always something to occupy their time and minds. Consequently, boredom was a concept foreign to both children. If the will is present and the imagination strong, there is always something to do. The world was Jimmy's oyster and Anna, his pearl.

With all his heart, Jimmy believed the family stories about the charter documents. Often nights he dreamed about the charter, and wondered might it be lost rather than destroyed? If only lost, might he not find it?

Once, while searching the crawlspace underneath the house, Jimmy had found fragments of charred timbers from the original structure. Afterward, he spent hours digging near the house's foundation, hoping he might find the charter, where—in his imagination—it might have been secretly buried for safekeeping before the arrival of the Yankee arsonists.

But alas, it wasn't there.

While playing hide-and-seek in the attic one cold, drizzly November afternoon, Jimmy and Anna discovered an antique steamer trunk buried beneath a pile of boxes and old clothes. It was large, probably four feet by two-and-a-half feet by three feet, and made of some kind of dark wood with lighter-colored wooden slats held in place by tarnished brass clamps. On the domed lid was some kind of metal, perhaps tin, stamped with a pattern like he'd seen on fancy saddles. On the front were two rusted brass draw-bolts and an old-fashioned, hinged lock-plate slotted for a small round key. Around the whole chest, held in place by studded brass tabs, were two cracked leather straps, each fastened by an ancient iron buckle.

Jimmy couldn't believe his luck. Around the farm, he'd often found old marbles, nails, and broken tools. Once, he'd even found part of an old cast-iron hinge while plowing the garden, but *never, ever* had he found anything so grand.

What treasures lay inside? Maybe it was a pirate's booty full of gold and jewels, enough that Mama and Pa wouldn't have to look so worried all the time. Maybe there would be a magic lamp with a genie who would grant him three wishes. Or perhaps, he did not dare to hope, maybe this trunk was the hiding place of the family's long-lost charter. Oh, how impressed would his friends at school be when he brought in a genuine charter signed by the king of England himself, to show-and-tell?!

Jimmy simply couldn't wait to open the chest. With trembling fingers, he tried to work the stiff leather straps through the rusted buckles. He successfully unbuckled the first, but the second strap was too brittle and crumbled in his hands.

"Oh no, Jibby! You broke it. You're gonna get in trouble!"

"You worry too much, Anna-panda. Nobody even knows this old chest is up here. Mama and Pa sure won't care, 'specially if it's full of treasure!" Jimmy released the two draw-bolts easily enough, but try as he might, he couldn't open the trunk's lock.

In a lilting voice, Anna asked, "How you gonna open it without a key, Jibby?"

Jimmy sat for a moment, thinking. "I've got an idea." He rummaged through the attic and found the item he desired—Pa's claw hammer.

"No, Jibby! Don't!"

"I ain't gonna hurt nothin'," he said, working the claw beneath the lock's clasp.

Prying gently, he was rewarded with a metallic *pop*, and the clasp sprang open. Then, with heart pounding a tattoo, Jimmy slowly raised the lid. The rusty hinges creaked and groaned as the domed lid swung open. It was heavier than he'd expected, and he lost his grip as the lid passed vertical, causing it to crash open with a bang and a cloud of dust.

Anna screamed, and Jimmy leaped backward. Creeping forward again to peer inside, the children were met with the musty aroma of mothballs and rat urine. To Jimmy's disappointment, no light reflected off gold or jewels heaped to the trunk's edges. The inside was lined with peeling paper of some kind of hunting scene with horses jumping over a fence. There was a wooden tray filled with old letters and a big pile of what at first looked like oversize dollar bills. The bills were an odd color and featured a funny-looking old man on the front, wearing a frilly bowtie and big, fancy 50s on the front and backs. The bills sure didn't look like any money Jimmy had ever seen, although admittedly, he hadn't seen much in his seven years.

"Confederate money...worthless," he muttered. To his profound disappointment, nothing in the tray looked remotely like a charter. "Garbage...nothing but garbage. But maybe it's under the tray." Jimmy lifted out the tray and set it aside, his disappointment unaffected by what he saw there.

He rummaged through contents but saw only old clothes. There was a light gray wool jacket of some sort with a half-inch moth hole in the front. Beneath that was a threadbare pair of patched trousers and a long, folded, cream-colored linen shirt with another moth hole and a big rust stain all over the front and left side. Then he tossed the clothes aside in a pile and, to his wonderment, there it was. Pay dirt! He'd found the charter.

Nestled in one corner at the bottom of the trunk was what appeared to be a dark blue folding leather folio with fancy gold filigree framing the front cover. Jimmy had never seen a proprietary charter before, but what he was seeing would be *perfect* for holding one, he was certain. It was about twenty-two by fifteen inches and had a fancy binding on its spine. He held his breath and reached for the folio with trembling hands. In this chest was the discovery of a lifetime. He'd be famous and might get invited to the White House to meet President Truman. His family would be rich beyond all belief and never have to worry about tobacco bugs or black shank or anything else...*ever again!*

Slowly, Jimmy lifted the folio from the trunk and reverently placed it atop a box of old clothes.

Anna clapped and bounced excitedly. "What is it, Jibby? What is it?"

"It's our family's charter," was his awed reply. "We've done it, Anna!"

"Yay, we've done it! We've done it!" Then quizzically, "What did we do, Jibby? What's a charter? Lemme see."

Jimmy gently opened the cover of the folio. He'd seen a picture of a charter once in the *Encyclopedia Britannica* in the school library, and the image was burned into his memory. He knew precisely what it would say, "Charles the Second, by the grace of God, king of England, Scotland, France, and Ireland, Defender of the Faith, etc....blah, blah, blah, blah, blah...witness Ourself, at Westminster, the thirtieth day of June, in the seventeenth year of our reign. *Per Ipsum Regum.*"

In an instant, Jimmy's excitement turned to despair. In reality, the title page read:

THE

BIRDS OF ASIA

BY

JOHN GOULD, F.R.S.,

LOTS OF SOCIETY NAMES

DEDICATED TO THE HONOURABLE EAST INDIA COMPANY.

IN SEVEN VOLUMES.

VOLUME I.

LONDON:

PRINTED BY TAYLOR AND FRANCIS, RED LION COURT, FLEET STREET.

PUBLISHED BY THE AUTHOR, 26 CHARLOTTE STREET, BEDFORD SQUARE.

1850–1883

"It's just a dumb old book!" Jimmy grumbled, throwing it down in disgust.

The book fell open to a picture of a bird, thrilling Anna. "Birdies! I love birdies! Look, Jibby, look! Oh, what's this one? It's so pretty!" she chattered excitedly, thumbing through the pages. "I like this one too! What's it called, Jibby? What does this say? I think I like charters."

"This isn't a—" Clearly, she was *significantly* more impressed by their find than her older brother.

"Ooooh, I *really love* this one! What is it?" she asked, indicating a bird with a bright green chest and body, darker green wings and back, a yellow throat, and bright blue tail. "Look, he's wearing a black football helmet! Hee hee hee..."

Although still feeling dejected from his failure to save the family farm and the realization that President Truman would not soon be sending him any invitations asking for Jimmy to show him a dumb old book, he nonetheless recognized his little sister's unabashed glee. "That's a long-tailed broadbill," and then read the overleaf description aloud to her.

"What's this one?"

"That's a saker falcon."

"How about this one?"

"Mantled kingfisher...mountain trogon...Great-billed Eurylaime...Edwards's pheasant..."

On and on they went, with Anna pointing and Jimmy dutifully reading. Lost in his little sister's obvious delight, Jimmy soon forgot the day's disappointments, and when it became too dark to read any longer, the children descended the attic stairs with *The Birds of Asia* tucked safely beneath Jimmy's arm.

Thus, the children began what was to become a nightly ritual of Anna pointing and Jimmy reading aloud to her about her beloved birds.

CHAPTER 8

AUGUST 27, 1955

I T WAS A SATURDAY, AND it was going to be the best day ever! It had taken the two of them almost two years, but the hotrod was finally finished. Hitchcock's *To Catch a Thief* with Cary Grant and Grace Kelly was playing at the drive-in, and Mack Lee and Bob had a double date planned for that night with the busty Sherri Lynde and the pliant Jessica Wharton. It was going to be a night to remember. They'd cruise Main Street in downtown Boiling Springs and take the girls to the Beacon Drive-In restaurant for burgers and shakes, then it was off to the movies with Bob and Jessica up front and Mack Lee and Sherri in the rumble seat. And all this was possible because they had a car and could actually *drive*! This night was going to be one for the record books, indeed.

But that was tonight. This morning, Mack Lee finished his chores early and decided to spend the afternoon hunting. He'd flushed a covey of quail from a nearby corn field last week and wanted to try his luck again. Even if there were no quail, there were always mourning doves, squirrels, and rabbits, which he could easily add to the stewpot. Failing that, he just liked shooting things. To make his hunting expedition even more enjoyable, he'd secreted a six-pack of Falstaff beer into the creek to cool that morning. Those beers should be just about perfect by the time he fished them out of the water in the afternoon, for the perfect start to the perfect night.

Mack Lee grabbed his shotgun, a Mossberg Model 183 bolt-action .410, along with a handful of number 7 ½ shot for quail and number 4 shot for rabbits. Then he set off for the creek, where he found his beers perfectly chilled and promptly downed the first two. Seeing no rabbits or squirrels, he headed toward the field where he'd flushed the quail. While walking, he polished off another two beers. After each, he tossed the bottle into the air and took a shot at it...and missed. Arriving at the field and hating to let his two remaining beers get warm, he sat in the shade of a tulip poplar at the edge of the field and popped the tops. Soon his wild shots were missing *those* bottles as well.

"Damn, if this isn't a great day," he said to himself.

After chugging the entire six-pack over a half-hour span and finding himself rather comfortable in the poplar's shade, he leaned back against the trunk and promptly dozed off.

Sometime later, Mack Lee woke with a start at hearing the sound of a horn blaring back at the house. He looked at the sky and realized the sun was already low over the horizon. "Fuck! That must be Bob! How long have I been asleep?" he said, grabbing his shotgun and sprinting to the house.

By the time he arrived, Mack Lee was panting like a hound on a hot summer day. But there was Bob, waiting in the driveway with their car, and it was chrome-plated. *Cool!*

"Hurry up, man! The girls are waiting. Get a move on," Bob shouted.

Mack Lee gave him a thumbs-up and then raced upstairs to the room he shared with James. Eschewing the gun cabinet because his father would pitch a fit if any unclean weapon was found there, he threw the shotgun on one of the twin beds and quickly changed into a clean shirt. Five minutes later, he and Bob were off to begin their best night *ever*!

CHAPTER 9

AUGUST 27, 1955

I T WAS A SATURDAY, AND it was going to be the best day ever! Although all Saturdays were pretty great, this one was going to be the best because today was Jimmy's birthday. He was officially eight years old and super excited about it. Ma had promised him a chocolate cake for his birthday and said there might even be ice cream!

Jimmy rose early and fed the chickens and pigs and brought eggs up from the henhouse. With no other chores to do and no homework since school had only been back in session for a week, he and Anna went down to the duck pond where he taught her to skip stones. Well, he *tried* to teach her. She just couldn't seem to spin the rocks fast enough to make them skip. Nonetheless, it was a fun morning for both children. They came back up to the house for lunch and then went back outside to play.

Today, they played hide-and-seek. Anna wasn't very good at hiding, but Jimmy always pretended he couldn't find her. She giggled hysterically as he searched under flowerpots and behind trees no bigger around than his wrist. Finally, she'd shout, "Here I am!" but Jimmy still pretended not to see her. Then she'd start running to base, and he'd chase her around in circles until both collapsed on the ground, laughing.

They could play like that for hours, and usually did. The day was hot and humid as was common for August in South Carolina, and Anna was prone to becoming overheated, so they stopped early and went back to the house. There, they each had a glass of ice-cold lemonade and Anna asked Jimmy to read to her from their bird book, and he was only too happy to comply.

Jimmy drew the book from under his bed and dutifully paged through the entire volume, reading about each of the birds for his little sister and listening to her comments. As usual, her favorite was the long-tailed broadbill. Something about that bird always made her laugh, which in turn made Jimmy feel all warm inside. Jimmy knew Mack Lee was Mama's favorite. That didn't bother him one bit. Jimmy knew *he* was Anna's favorite, and that was good enough for him!

After Jimmy read *The Birds of Asia* twice from cover to cover, Anna gave a yawn and announced that she was tired. With that, she padded across the hall to her room to "take a little nappy."

Jimmy went back to his own room and carefully slid the book back underneath his bed. He shared the room with Mack Lee and knew that if his brother ever got ahold of the book, he'd likely tear it apart and use the pictures for target practice. Then he went quietly downstairs to check on the progress of his birthday cake.

He was still in the kitchen thirty minutes later when his brother's friend, Bob Morrison, showed up in their driveway. After a short wait, Bob began honking on the horn of that shiny red car he and Mack Lee had been working on for the past couple years.

A few minutes later, Mack Lee burst through the door, slapped Jimmy on the back of the head—because he could—and practically flew up the stairs. A moment later, he rushed back down the stairs, out the door, and into the front seat of the car. Just like that he was gone.

With the commotion, Anna woke from her nap and stumbled sleepily down the stairs.

"No, sweetie, it's not time for dinner yet. You and Jimmy go play," said Mama with a smile. "Remember, after dinner we're having birthday cake and ice cream, so be good!"

"Yay!" Anna cried and turned back toward the stairs with Jimmy following behind.

Arriving in Jimmy's room, Anna called and pointed excitedly, "Look, Jibby! Your birthday present...it's up here. Come see!"

Jimmy rushed into his room and, following Anna's outstretched finger, he saw it. On his bed was a toy gun, and it was the best toy gun *ever*! It looked totally real. But there it was, and there could be no doubt. It was right on his pillow. He picked the gun up, finding it was much heavier than his other toy guns. But it was really nifty, the best birthday present ever.

Then Anna raised her hands out and over her head and began to waddle, rocking from one leg to the other toward him. "Grrrrrrrrr," she growled. "I'm a big ol' baarrr. Grrrrr!"

Jimmy laughed and cried out, "Oh no! It's a bear!" and swung the barrel of the toy gun playfully toward Anna.

Anna growled again and made a swipe with her big bear claw. Her hand struck the barrel of the gun, jarring it in Jimmy's hand and causing his finger to brush the trigger.

The gun bucked and roared in his hands.

The discharge tore the gun from his hands and sent half an ounce of number 4 lead shot into Anna's chest at point-blank range. She was immediately thrown back against the doorframe where she crumpled to the floor. Wide-eyed, she gaped down at the enlarging red circle on her blouse and cried, "Jibby! Jib...bey..."

Maggie was upstairs in an instant, kneeling beside Anna's trembling little body. "Anna!" she screamed. "James, what have you done?!"

Jimmy stared in horror, his mouth opening and closing but unable to utter a sound.

"What did you do?! Go and get you father! *Now!* Don't just stand there...*go!* Go, goddamn you! Go!"

His mother cursing brought Jimmy out of his shock well enough that he was able to squeeze past Anna and his weeping, hysterical mother. As he slipped past, he noticed that the wound seemed to bubble and wheeze with every labored breath.

"Please don't die! Please don't die," Jimmy mumbled through his tears. Then he ran down the stairs and to the barn where Walter was working on a tractor.

One look at the terror on Jimmy's tear-streaked face and the color drained from Walter's. He'd seen that look too many times back during the war, and it was never because of anything good. He dropped the wrench from his hand and began running toward the house as fast as his injured leg would allow.

The next several hours passed in a blur for Jimmy. His father had bundled Anna's limp little body into the cab of their pickup truck, and the four of them had raced the twenty miles to the hospital in Spartanburg. Anna was rushed into surgery, leaving him and his folks to wait...to hope...to pray. Eight hours later, Jimmy remembered the surgeon coming to the waiting room and shaking his head. Ma had given out an anguished scream and collapsed into the floor in a sobbing pile. Then Jimmy noticed a single tear running down his Pa's cheek. Somehow, his father's reaction seemed even worse to Jimmy than his mother's. Jimmy had never seen the man cry before.

And nobody seemed to notice Jimmy was even there.

CHAPTER 10

AUGUST 28, 1955

WELL, MAYBE THIS WASN'T THE best day ever after all for Mack Lee. Sherri Lynde had resisted all of Mack Lee's advances, and Bob had made out no better with his date. The two dropped their dates off after the movie and went down by the railroad tracks to drink beer. Even if the girls had turned out to be a little more prudish than they might've hoped, nobody could argue that having a car wasn't totally awesome. He loved the way all heads turned toward them as they cruised Main Street. He knew he'd wear Sherri down eventually. And if he didn't, well, there were always other fish in the sea, and Mack Lee was planning on landing a trophy catch.

Arriving home around midnight, Mack Lee was surprised to find no lights on inside or outside the house. He assumed everyone was asleep, which was fine with him—nobody to bitch him out for coming home late...or drunk. When he got to his room, he didn't turn on any lights. Better not to wake anybody. As he entered his bedroom, he stepped in something sticky by the door and automatically assumed his stupid little brother had probably spilled something. Well, the little shit could clean up his own mess in the morning.

He threw his clothes in a pile and promptly passed out on his bed.

The next morning, Mack Lee woke to the sun shining through his bedroom window. His head was pounding, and his mouth felt like it was full of chalk dust. He rolled over and glanced painfully at his brother's bed. Finding it empty, he muttered, "Wonder where the little turd's off to so early?" In the dim light, he made out what he took to be a puddle of spilled paint on the floor. He knew his mother was *not* going to be happy about *that*! He smiled at the thought of his goody two-shoes brother getting in trouble instead of him for a change. That would be a nice change of pace! Then, smiling, Mack Lee promptly fell back to sleep.

He awoke hours later to voices downstairs, lots of them, and to the sound of his mother wailing uncontrollably. In between her sobs, her heard her wail, "I want my baby...my poor, sweet little girl!" over and over again.

Mack Lee rapidly dressed and went downstairs to see about the commotion. The house was packed with friends and neighbors. The pastor from the church was there, which was odd since this was a Sunday morning. As he pushed his way into the room, Maggie gasped, pointing toward his feet and the splotches of reddish-brown that he had tracked in on the rug, and fainted. Apparently, he'd stepped in the puddle of paint in his socked feet as he'd rushed from his room.

But it wasn't paint.

CHAPTER 11

AUGUST 28, 1955

IT WAS A TERRIBLE ACCIDENT—A senseless tragedy—and it had been entirely preventable. After terrible accidents and senseless tragedies that are entirely preventable, there is no shortage of blame, recriminations, vitriol, or anger. This occasion was no different, and the lion's share of the blame, recriminations, vitriol, and anger—rightly or wrongly—landed firmly upon the trembling shoulders of a heartbroken eight-year-old little boy.

When the Hamiltons returned from the hospital, the house was already full of neighbors and extended family. Everyone spoke in hushed tones, and from time to time, Jimmy noticed them making furtive glances in his direction before shaking their heads. He couldn't hear what they were saying but knew without a doubt what they were thinking. He supposed they were just waiting for the sheriff to come and take him away. After all, he *was* a murderer.

Almost on cue, a black-and-white police car pulled into the driveway. Sheriff Clower got out, hitched his gun belt up over his belly, and ambled to the Hamiltons' front door.

Jimmy was sitting on a stool in the kitchen, staring at his forgotten, partially iced birthday cake when he heard the knock at the door. He glanced out the kitchen window and saw the sheriff's car in the driveway, then swallowed hard and stumbled to the front door, ready to accept his fate. He wondered what it would feel like to be in handcuffs and leg irons and if he'd have to wear a ball and chain.

Jimmy opened the door and craned his neck to look up at Sheriff Clower, a big man, tall with an enormous gut.

The sheriff spoke with a slow, pronounced southern drawl, "Mis-tuh Hamilton, I pre-sume?"

"Y-yes, s-sir. I-I'm J-Jimmy H-Hamilton."

"I need to speak with yo' mama and daddy. Are they he-yah, son?"

"Y-yes, S-Sheriff C-C-Clower. They're in there with the pr-pr-preacher," Jimmy stammered, pointing the lawman toward the living room as he continued contemplating his future as a convicted felon.

It was called the living room, but the room showed no evidence whatsoever of life. It practically oozed death. The air was stale and still. The curtains were drawn, leaving the interior dark and somber in stark contrast to the bright, beautiful, late summer's day outside. No lamps were lit, so there was no light to burn through the miasma of gloom. Neighbors and close family friends milled around the room, speaking in the most muted of tones, if they bothered to speak at all. The preacher was there, kneeling in front of Maggie's chair and murmuring what seemed to be a muted prayer. Pa sat by her side, stoically holding her hand.

Maggie stared blankly toward the door when Jimmy arrived with Sheriff Clower in tow. Upon seeing Jimmy, she pointed at him with a trembling finger and began shrieking and wailing anew.

Jimmy retreated back across the threshold until he was, again, out of her view. There, he paused and listened. After several minutes of her sobbing, Pa and the preacher seemed to get Mama calmed down again.

"Mis-tuh and Missus Hamilton, I'm sorry to intrude, but they are some questions I need to axe you," the sheriff began.

"Sheriff, can't this wait?" asked the preacher in his nasally voice.

"I'm sorry, but protocol dictates that any time they is a death..."

Jimmy listened from outside the doorway as the sheriff asked for details about Anna's death. Walter explained in a monotone voice that the children had been playing upstairs and Jimmy had unknowingly picked up a loaded gun and the gun had gone off. The little girl had been struck in the chest and died at the hospital. No, he didn't wish for a coroner's inquest, and no, they did not anticipate filing any charges. It was an accident...a terrible, terrible accident.

Jimmy was wondering what a "coroner's request" was when the sheriff nearly knocked him down, leaving the living room.

The sheriff stopped and knelt by Jimmy, his fetid, salami-and-chewing-tobacco breath practically curling the boy's nose hairs. "Now, son, that was a turr'ble thang to have happened...a turr'ble thang! Ya gotta learn to be more careful with guns, boy, ya hear?"

Tears welled in Jimmy's eyes. "I didn't know it was real! I thought it was my birthday present."

The sheriff nodded his head. "I reckon maybe you did. Mighty sorry 'bout your sis-tuh, though."

With that, Sheriff Clower stood, spit a gobbet of tobacco juice into a convenient pot of geraniums, and ambled back to his patrol car.

CHAPTER 12

AUGUST 1955–DECEMBER 1956

FUNERALS ARE *SUPPOSED* TO HAPPEN on stormy days. That's how it is in all the movies. The family and mourners huddle together beneath a tent as the preacher prays and the dark clouds shed commiserative tears—but not today.

Jimmy glanced furtively up from his shoes. The day was perfect; not too hot—not too cool, and not a cloud in the sky, dark or otherwise. It was a day Anna would've loved. In a nearby oak, a pair of cardinals flitted from branch to branch, calling happily. Anna loved birdies. At the thought, another tear rolled down his cheek, joining the hundreds of earlier arrivals now dampening the collar of his best Sunday shirt.

Immediately, Jimmy returned his blurry gaze to his feet. He could feel the stares of the mourners around him boring into the back of his neck. He knew what they were all thinking. *There's the murderer...the one who got off on a technicality.* Of course, nobody actually *said* that to him directly; nobody except Mack Lee. But Jimmy knew they were thinking it. How could they not be? Jimmy thought it, himself.

The family had received friends at the funeral home last night, and for Jimmy, it had been a disaster.

Jimmy hadn't seen Anna since she'd been whisked away and into the operating room four—or was it five?—days ago. But there she was at the mortuary, wearing her best powder-blue dress, the one with the frilly collar and cuffs, lying in a casket. Her hands were crossed over her heart as though hiding the place Jimmy had shot her. Her hair had been neatly curled and was arrayed over the pillow, perfectly framing her cherubic little face.

Jimmy wondered why she was wearing makeup. Without thinking, he reached out and touched Anna's face. Jimmy hadn't known what to expect, but whatever he *had* expected, it certainly wasn't this cold, firm mask that now was his sister's face. He snatched back his hand and backpedaled away from the coffin in abject terror, tripping over Mack Lee's foot—no doubt, an accident—and in the process, knocking over a flower arrangement.

Maggie screamed at Jimmy and slapped him hard across the face. She was about to deliver another blow when Walter and Mary pulled her away. From the look in her eyes, had they not done so, she likely would've beaten the child to a pulp right there on the mortuary floor.

Afterward, Mary spirited Jimmy away to the relative safety of the funeral home's kitchen. There, the two spent the rest of the family visitation time playing Go Fish and snacking on cakes and pies brought in by family friends.

In the weeks and months after Anna's funeral, life at the Hamilton farm improved very little. Jimmy did his best to avoid his mother. When she was around, he made himself scarce, often hiding in the attic or in the crawlspace beneath the house. Now, however, he no longer searched for the family's charter. Instead, he just hid, and remembered Anna.

The image of her clutching her chest and sliding down the doorframe in his room was indelibly imprinted on his brain, as were her final words, "Jibby! Jib...bey..."

Mack Lee remained entirely unrepentant and failed even to acknowledge his role in Anna's death. Initially, he'd claimed total innocence, stating he'd not left the gun out at all, and that Jimmy must've gotten it from the gun cabinet himself. When Walter pointed out the oil smudge on Jimmy's pillow—Mack Lee was always bad about over-oiling his weapons—he finally admitted he'd left his shotgun there, but claimed it had been unloaded. When Walter began refuting this falsehood as well, Maggie swept Mack Lee away protectively and forbade Walter from pursuing the matter any further.

Mack Lee had always had a cruel streak, but after Anna's death, it had gotten even wider. He reveled in making Jimmy's life a living Hell. He took great pleasure in sneaking up behind his little brother and yelling, "BANG." If after the initial tears, Jimmy objected, Mack Lee, safely under Maggie's protection, would challenge him to do something about it. "What ya gonna' do about it? Shoot me?"

The one positive to come from Anna's death was Walter. Her death seemed to galvanize him and give him the impetus to change. He recognized Jimmy's pain—it was so similar to what he'd experienced himself—and tried to help. It was, however, a case of the blind leading the blind. Walter, even before the war, was unable to easily express his emotions. With his own struggles, he was hardly the ideal person to aid Jimmy with his, but alone among the denizens of Hamilton Place, he, at least, made the effort. He did his best to protect Jimmy from Maggie and Mack Lee's persecution, albeit with only limited success.

The first Christmas after Anna's death, Walter purchased a cast-iron fire truck for Jimmy and the child had loved it. The toy truck had a spring-loaded motor so that if one rolled the wheels backward, it wound the spring. Releasing the truck engaged the spring and propelled it forward. Maggie was angry with him for spending so much money on a gift for Jimmy, but Walter didn't care. It was the right thing to do. Besides, he loved his son and wanted him to be happy. He smiled nights listening to the sound of the little firetruck racing back and forth across the attic floor, often for hours at a time.

Walter was changing. Ever so slowly, he was again becoming the man he'd been before the war. He'd lost his friends. He'd lost his daughter. He was losing his wife, if he hadn't lost her already. He was at risk of losing his farm. He had one son who was a lazy, lying hellion, and the other was...well, broken.

On that kind of a losing streak, something had to give. In his case, it was the alcohol. Some holes are too deep to climb out, but if Walter was ever to have a chance, Walter knew first he'd have to stop digging. Walter's new demons battled his old ones to a draw, and he finally stopped drinking. This time it was for good, but it was too little, too late.

With the loss of their daughter, the light went out of Maggie's eyes forever this time. The depression against which she'd struggled so valiantly for the past decade took hold and, this time, wouldn't let go. The happy-go-lucky girl whose smile had brightened every room died just as surely and just as permanently as had their daughter. Both were gone for good and were never to be seen again. In her place was left a brooding, spiteful, vindictive wraith whose venom was directed solely toward the person who, in her eyes, had taken her daughter away from her. Jimmy.

Even with his own demons placated, Walter was totally incapable of drawing Maggie back to the light. He tried his best, but with no effect. He tried to explain that Anna's death had been a terrible accident and that young Jimmy was not solely to blame. He pointed out that he, personally, had never taken the time to teach Jimmy about firearm safety and that Mack Lee had been careless to leave a loaded gun in an unsecured area. But she'd hear nothing of it. He tried to point out that Jimmy had adored his little sister and was hurting just as much as they were and that Jimmy, as a child, did not have the mechanisms to cope with the loss that they, as adults, had. He explained to her that now more than ever, their son needed the love and support of his family. But all his entreaties fell upon deaf ears.

If Jimmy was unlucky enough to happen into the same room as Maggie, she would immediately fly into a murderous rage. Over the next year, Walter began to fear for his son's very life, but had no idea what to do about it.

Once again, it was Mary, Walter's mother, who came to the rescue. Her younger brother, Howard Hines, was a physician who had a general medical practice in a small town near Raleigh, North Carolina. Howard's wife had died recently, and his health was beginning to fail. He had no living children, and it would be helpful for him to have someone living with him to help with heavy tasks around the house. Mary gave him a call, and, yes, Howard would "love to have young James come for an extended visit." Howard could come and pick him up after Jimmy's school's fall term ended that year. That way, Jimmy could start school with the spring term in North Carolina and suffer no time lost. Problem solved.

And just like that, Jimmy was shipped off to North Carolina to live with Uncle Howard.

CHAPTER 13

DECEMBER 1956

THE LIFE HE'D KNOWN AND everything and everyone Jimmy loved receded into the distance between the tail fins of his grand-uncle's brand new '57 Cadillac Eldorado Brougham. He watched out the back window as the old farmhouse grew smaller and was eventually lost from view entirely when they traversed a curve. Still, Jimmy stared out the rear window.

What did he hope to see? Mama or Pa running after him, calling out that it had all been a mistake and he should come back home? Or maybe Anna skipping along behind the car, begging him to come back and read their bird book to her?

No, no one was there, nor would there be. He'd been banished, sent away from the only home he had ever known.

Still, he stared.

Jimmy had brought almost nothing with him into exile. The tiny cardboard-sided suitcase that contained every stitch of clothing he owned was lost in the depths of the Caddy's massive trunk. On the white leather seat beside him were the only two possessions he cared anything about. One was a bright red cast-iron firetruck that had been a gift from his father the Christmas after Anna died. It was the only present he'd received that year. The other was his ancient copy of Gould's *The Birds of Asia*.

He didn't really know his grand-uncle, or at least not well. The man had always been nice to Jimmy at family reunions and Fourth of July picnics. He used to sit and engage Jimmy in conversations, just like he would one of the grown-ups. Jimmy liked that. He also liked the peppermint candy the old man used to slip him when his parents weren't looking. Now Jimmy was to go live with him "for a while," until things became more settled at home.

Howard was an old country doctor who lived near Raleigh, North Carolina. His son had been killed outside Nijmegen during Operation Market Garden in 1944, and his wife, Doris, had died a year or two ago. The old codger didn't like living alone. He had a bad heart, and his greatest fear was that he might die alone at home with no one around to help—or to know.

Jimmy missed his mother and father. Even if they didn't want him around anymore, Jimmy still loved them both. He didn't blame them for wanting him gone. He'd killed Anna, after all. How could they possibly forgive him? How could they even still love him? He released a long, broken-hearted sigh and stared unseeing out the car window.

Jimmy missed Anna most of all. He could still hear her giggling as she played with one of the new piglets. He could hear her saying, "Read me the birdies, Jibby! Read me the birdies!" "It's read *to* me *about* the birdies, Anna-panda," he'd tell her. "And you should always say please."

For a moment, the memory made him smile. Then he remembered she was gone and it was all because of him, and the moment slipped away from him.

Jimmy liked Howard's car. He had never been in a car that nice and certainly not a brand new one. It was long, black, and shiny with a silver roof and white leather seats. The front had four headlights, a huge chrome grill and, rather than a standard bumper, it had two chrome, bomb-shaped nose cones that protruded forward. The rear doors had deep air scoop vents on the sides and there were shark fins over the fenders in the back. He felt like he was riding in the Batmobile!

Maybe Uncle Howard is really Bruce Wayne in disguise? Nah, he thought. *Too old for Bruce Wayne, but maybe he could be Alfred?*

The journey to Howard's house in North Carolina took a little over six hours. Along the way, Jimmy watched the countryside scroll past his window. To pass the time, he invented a game he called "Counting Cows." The object of the game was to see whether there would be more cows on the left or right side of the road by the end of the trip. To make the game more interesting, he added rules. If the car drove past a body of water, but it was only on one side of the road, then half the cows on that side of the road would drown and be lost. If the car crossed a river, then both sides would lose half of their herds. On passing a graveyard or cemetery, all cows on that side of the car would be lost. Passing a hospital caused a 10 percent increase in the herd lucky enough to be on that side of the car.

By the time the trip ended, there were 184 cows in the left sided herd, but the right had suffered catastrophic losses at a cemetery outside of Buckhorn, North Carolina, and only had seventeen head of cattle left standing. Jimmy couldn't be entirely certain his count was correct since he'd fallen asleep at one point during the trip. Howard assured him that he'd kept the count going during his nap, but Jimmy wasn't entirely convinced.

Technically, Howard lived in Holly Springs, about twenty miles outside of Raleigh. Jimmy found the symmetry interesting in his move from Boiling Springs to Holly Springs. At the names, all similarities ended. As the crow flies, the distance between Jimmy's old home and his new one was exactly 203 miles, but in all other aspects, they were worlds apart.

Gone was the ramshackle old farmhouse with its rusting tin roof. In its place was a bright yellow two-story Queen Anne Victorian with lime-green shutters, a wraparound veranda and a round turret, a steeply pitched roof, and lots of fancy trim work. The house sat on a hundred acres of wooded hills, and Howard referred to it as a farm. There was one large barn, but Jimmy saw neither field nor fences. The only domesticated animal in sight was a huge mackerel tabby sunning herself on the front porch railing.

Seeing the boy staring at the cat, Howard volunteered, "That's Kitty Lamarr. This is really her house. She just lets me live in it."

"Kitty Lamarr? That's a funny name," Jimmy said, laughing.

"Well, she's a funny cat...and very smart, just like her namesake."

"Her namesake?"

"Yessirree! She's named after Hedy Lamarr, the actress and inventor."

Wide-eyed, Jimmy stared at his uncle in disbelief. "An inventor?"

"Oh yes, absolutely! She invented lots of things."

"Really? Like what?" Jimmy challenged, strongly suspecting that Uncle Howard was pulling his leg.

"Her most famous invention was a frequency-hopping technology for torpedo guidance systems, but she also made glow-in-the-dark dog collars and figured out a way to make airplanes more aerodynamic."

"A *film actress* did all that? That's really neat!"

The old man had already engaged in more conversation with him in the past five minutes than his father had over the past month. And even *that* had been more conversation than he'd had with his mother.

Howard led Jimmy into the house and showed him around. They walked through downstairs first, through the kitchen and dining room, a living room, and a huge library. The rooms were large and well appointed, and the floors were wide heart pine planks, stained and worn smooth by a century of feet. The ceilings were high, and big windows made each room bright and cheerful. The library was a sight to behold, with books shelved from floor to ceiling in beautiful wooden cases. Jimmy thought there had to be at least a thousand volumes—more than in the entire library at his old school in Boiling Springs. On one wall was a huge fireplace featuring an ornate black wrought-iron mantel. Over the mantel was a framed needlepoint piece that read, "Do Right and Fear Not." Before the fireplace sat two leather armchairs with accompanying companion tables. In the corner ticked a burlwood grandfather clock. A thick oriental rug covered the floor, and thick-framed hunting scenes adorned the dark-paneled walls. Incongruously for the room's formal decor, a framed drawing of Mickey Mouse signed by Walt Disney himself hung over the fireplace in the room's place of honor. From the coffered ceiling hung a chandelier, which, along with several strategically positioned lamps, supplemented the light from the windows, giving the room a light and inviting feel.

Jimmy's room was upstairs. It had been Howard's son's room before he left home for college, and no attempt at redecoration had been attempted thereafter. It looked like a 1930s time capsule. There was a single pipe-frame twin bed with a blue-and-white quilted bedspread on one wall. On the opposite wall hung a huge map of the world studded with pushpins. The third wall featured a built-in bookcase and writing desk. Jimmy briefly perused the spines on the shelves. Classics like *Moby Dick, Treasure Island, The Old Man and the Sea,* and *The Last of the Mohicans* immediately caught his eye.

The bed looked comfortable. The world map was interesting, and Jimmy was certain he would thoroughly enjoy the shelves of books. However, by far the best part of the room was the exterior wall with a large alcove created by the turret. Upon seeing it for the first time, his imagination went into overdrive.

This could be a castle tower, the redoubt on a fort, or a rocket ship! Wait until Anna sees—

Jimmy's shoulders sagged. In a subdued voice he said, "Thank you for showing me my room, Uncle Howard. I'm kinda tired from the trip." He lovingly placed *The Birds of Asia* on the desk and plopped onto the bed with his head down, staring at his shoes.

The old man tousled his hair and said, "That's all right, son. You just rest and get used to the place. We'll have supper in about an hour. I'll call you down when it's time to wash up." Howard moved toward the door.

Jimmy ran to the old man, wrapping his arms tightly around his ample midsection, and bawled, "I miss her so much, Uncle Howard...so much! Why'd she have to die?"

Howard held the boy until his shuddering sobs downgraded to sniffles. He thought how unfair it was. The accident had taken Jimmy's sister only the year before, and now his family had banished him—just sent the child off into exile like some kind of criminal—and just a week before Christmas! It made Howard angry enough to spit nails. It just wasn't right. *Poor kid!*

When Jimmy had calmed, Howard gave him his handkerchief and said, "I'll be downstairs if you need me. Mrs. Tucker is making barbecue chicken and mashed potatoes for supper tonight." Then with a smile and a wink, he continued, "And she even mentioned something about apple pie. I'll see you in about an hour, son."

"Yes, sir," Jimmy said. Eschewing the handkerchief, he blew his nose on his sleeve.

As Howard left the boy's room, he paused at the open door of his bedroom across the hall. From his bedside table, a framed photograph of Doris lovingly smiled back at him, just like she had forty-nine years ago on their wedding day. On Doris's bedside table, under a pair of half-moon reading glasses, lay her unfinished copy of Françoise Sagan's *Bonjour Tristesse*.

"I know exactly how you feel, son!" He whispered, "Love ya, Doris." With his accent, her name came out sounding more like *Darse*. "And I miss you every day," he continued, dabbing a tear from his eye, allowing his mind to wander back in time as he stood staring at her photo.

Howard maintained a medical office in downtown Holly Springs, where he saw patients each day. As a general practice physician, he saw all comers, taking care of patients from cradle to grave. He occasionally delivered babies and, when there was a need, did house calls. A few summers earlier, Howard, a.k.a. Dr. Hines, had received a call late in the day from Lucille Barker. She and her husband, Edward, had a farm outside of town where they raised corn, pigs, cows, chickens, and kids. The pigs, or rather one of them, was the problem.

Bocephus was the Barkers' six-hundred-pound prize boar that they had raised from a piglet. He was almost sixteen years old and had not mellowed well with age. In his youth, the pig had had a sweet disposition and tolerantly allowed small children to ride on his back. As he'd gotten older, his upper canines had grown into a pair of feral-appearing curved tusks, and his attitude had evolved to match. He became territorial and overtly aggressive. He serviced the sows, wallowed in the mud, and ate anything dropped into or near his food trough. Beyond that, the old boar preferred to be left alone.

While feeding the pigs earlier that day, Edward had slipped in the mud near the pig trough. Bocephus, perceiving Edward as a potential rival for a particularly scrumptious-appearing slice of rotten cantaloupe, promptly moved to protect his territory. He delivered a nasty gash to Edward's lower leg before slurping down the cantaloupe and waddling back to his mudhole. By the time Edward made it back to the house, his pant leg was soaked in blood and he appeared deathly pale. Lucille had taken one look at her husband and called Dr. Hines.

The good doctor had arrived soon thereafter and cleansed the wound with warm, soapy water and packed it with gauze. He gave Edward a tetanus shot and a shot of penicillin. Additionally, he wrote prescriptions for oral antibiotics and something for pain.

"Ain't ya gonna sew me up, Doc?" asked Edward.

"Nope, wound's too dirty. If I sew it closed, that guarantees it'll get infected, and you might lose the leg."

"Well, don't do that, then," said Edward, his eyes huge.

"I wasn't planning to. You'll need to take out the gauze and repack the wound twice a day. That'll let it heal from the inside out and give all that pus somewhere to go besides into your bloodstream. If you start running a high fever, say over 101.5 degrees, or if you start seeing red streaks running up your leg, come and see me *immediately*. Otherwise, I'll see you in the office next week. Oh, and no working on the farm until I see you next week."

"But I—"

Dr. Hines cut him off. "No buts! Not if you want to keep that leg. What's the point of having seven kids if they can't help out on the farm?"

"Number eight's on the way-ay," said Lucille rubbing her belly.

"You two *really* need to get a hobby!" Dr. Hines said with a good-natured laugh. "I mean, another hobby. Failing that, could you at least have this one during daylight hours? The last three of your kids came between midnight and four in the morning. I'm an old man and I need my sleep! But, seriously, congratulations to you both."

The Barkers laughed. Edward replied, "Thanks, Doc, and thanks for coming out! So, what do we owe you?"

"We'll worry about that when you come into the office next week."

"Well, at least stay for some pie! I have an apple pie in the oven that should be out in a few minutes," said Lucille.

Apple pie was Dr. Hines's favorite, and the aromas of freshly sliced apples, cinnamon, sugar, and a buttery cheddar crust wafting from the kitchen were more than any mere mortal could possibly resist. "Well, maybe I could stay for just one little slice," he replied.

One slice soon turned into two, and by the time Dr. Hines turned into his driveway, he was already an hour late for dinner.

"Darse, I'm home," he called as he walked through the front door. "I got called over to the Barker's place. Ed got hooked by that damned boar of his, and can you believe it, Lucille is pregnant aga—"

As he reached the dining room, his eyes fell upon Doris lying crumpled on the kitchen floor.

"Darse!" He ran to her and knelt by her side.

Her lips were blue, and he could find no pulse.

The pot of green beans on the stove boiled dry and began belching thick, acrid smoke.

Howard shook his head to clear the memory. Doris had died over three years ago, but in Howard's mind, the day was etched in granite. When he'd left for work that morning, Doris had been dropping Alka-Seltzer into a glass of water. Instead of suspecting she was experiencing the early symptoms of a heart attack, he'd teased her about her putting too much seasoning on the porkchops they'd had the night before for supper.

"Some brilliant diagnostician, I am," Howard whispered to himself.

Then, he'd delayed coming home from the Barker's that night. When he'd finally arrived, Doris was dead but clearly hadn't been so for very long.

"I should've been here. Maybe I could've..." his voice trailed off.

Everybody, and especially an experienced physician like Howard, knew there was no treatment for a heart attack. That there was nothing he could have done to save Doris did nothing to absolve him of his guilt. He knew had he been there, at least she wouldn't have had to die alone.

Now Jimmy, a little boy who clearly was dealing with a load of his own guilt, had come to live with Howard.

"Helluva pair we make," Howard said to himself before turning to wash up for supper.

CHAPTER 14

MAY 1957

MACK LEE COULDN'T BELIEVE HIS senior year in high school was almost over. Graduation was tomorrow, and it couldn't get here fast enough. He'd long ago come to the realization that he hated this one-horse, Podunk little town and hated life on a farm. He'd made a promise to himself that five minutes after graduation he was going to blow this popsicle stand and hit the road. He was headed to Nashville, Tennessee, for diesel mechanic school. After that, he'd never set foot on this stinking farm again, and *that* was something to celebrate. Boiling Springs could kiss his lily-white ass!

And celebrate was precisely what he was planning to do. Bob was coming to pick him up before dark, and then the two would be off for one last wild night on the town. They'd pick up some chicks, have some fun, and paint the town red.

Bob Morrison had been heavily recruited to play college football. When he and Mack Lee had started working on the Roadster, he stood six feet four inches and weighed 240 pounds. Over the past two years, he'd gained another two inches in height and close to forty pounds in weight, and it was just about all muscle. He received scholarship offers from Oklahoma, Tennessee, and Georgia Tech. Ultimately, he'd accepted Tech's offer for two reasons. The first was that the coach at Georgia Tech had assured him he'd be a starter his freshman year on a team with a legitimate shot at a National Championship. The second, the Russians had just launched Sputnik, and he was very interested in space and rocketry. As the valedictorian of Boiling Springs High School, Tech had offered him a full academic scholarship majoring in Aeronautical Engineering even if he elected *not* to play football. His future by anyone's estimate was bright, and not even the sky would be his limit.

That was the future. Tonight was all about the past and saying goodbye to his old hometown and friends. The most important of them was Mack Lee. The boys had been best friends since grade school. Bob strongly suspected that, although they'd been close through the years, tonight would be their last hurrah. It had been fun restoring the old Roadster, but the two seemed to be growing apart. Bob was growing up and moving on in his life. Mack Lee, at least emotionally, seemed destined never to truly *leave* high school. Bob was sure that he'd still see his friend whenever he was home for school breaks but doubted they'd have much in common and even less to talk about. There is only so much mileage one can get out of reliving the championship game against Woodruff, bragging about playing "back-seat bingo" during their double dates, or drinking beer. It had become painfully clear to Bob that Mack Lee was *never* going to grow up.

Bob swung by Mack Lee's house just before sunset, and they headed to their favorite hangout, the Beacon Drive-In, for sliced barbecue sandwiches and a milkshake or three. The place would be rockin' with good music playing on the speakers, and the chicks would be out in force. There was no telling where the night might lead, but it should be a good time.

"Dude, you got me outta there just in time!" said Mack Lee as he hopped into the car. "Let's burn rubber."

"How so, compadre? What gives?"

"The place is Deadsville, man. There'd be more excitement in a mortuary. I mean, it's always dark, Ma cryin' all the time and Pa doesn't do anything about it. Ever since the little ankle biter got blown away, everybody's still acting all sad-sack and all."

"Jeepers, Mack Lee! Show some respect! That 'little ankle biter' was your kid sister, for Christ's sake! She died what...eight, nine months ago?"

"My point exactly! After that long, why aren't they back to normal yet? I am. Like, Ma doesn't even cook anymore. I thought it was gonna be better after they shipped the dweeb off to live in North Carolina, but nothin's changing, man!"

"Dude, give it a rest already!" said Bob, turning the dial on the radio that he'd mounted to the dash.

Elvis Presley's "Hound Dog" sprang from the speakers and successfully squelched Mack Lee's childish rant.

Bob shook his head in disgust and wondered what he'd ever seen in his old friend. He'd always been selfish and quick to take offense, but this behavior was over the top even for Mack Lee. Somehow, his friend had gotten a free pass for his role in Anna's death—hardly even a harsh word—and it had made him even worse than he already was. Mack Lee lied at the drop of a hat, blamed everyone else for his problems, and had a mean streak a mile wide. Bob realized he didn't even like being around him anymore. Without football, they had nothing in common. Sad though it made him, Bob was certain tonight would likely be their last as friends.

The evening began well enough. There was a good crowd at the Beacon Drive-In, and as usual, the girls, music, and food were all top-notch. Bob was having a great time talking with a cute blonde named Tana who was also planning to attend Tech that fall, remarkably as a math major. They might even wind up in a few classes together since his engineering degree would have many math requirements. She had a particular interest in computing machines, and the more she talked, the more interest Bob developed in them as well—anything to keep the conversation flowing.

As usual, things started going downhill the moment one of the guys produced a bottle of gin, and before long, Mack Lee was falling-down drunk. He usually did pretty well if he stuck to beer, but any time liquor was involved, there was going to be trouble. Mack Lee wasn't mellow or happy when intoxicated. He was a mean drunk, plain and simple. Consequently, he was prone to getting into, and usually starting, fights.

Bob was unfortunately drawn away from the charming Tana by a ruckus in the parking lot and the sound of Mack Lee's raised voice. After quickly exchanging phone numbers, he rushed outside to see what kind of trouble his friend had gotten into *this* time. He found Mack Lee on the ground by the Roadster's front fender, surrounded by four greasers in matching leather jackets. They were taunting him, calling him "farm boy" and "hayseed." Mack Lee was on the ground with a rapidly blackening eye and bloody nose. The four took one look at the angry-looking giant bearing down upon them and raced off, each in a different direction to complicate possible pursuit.

"Come on, Mack Lee, let's get you outta here," Bob said with the implacable air of someone who'd clearly had to do this before.

"No, man! I can take them. Let me go!"

"Just shut up and get in the car, Mack Lee, or I've half a mind to let you go and try. Those four would tear you to shreds."

"Not if you—" Mack Lee began.

"Not a chance, my friend. No way I'm gonna put my scholarship at risk for the likes of those four."

"But—"

"No buts, Mack Lee. Case closed. Give it up! Just get in the car and try not to bleed or puke on the seat. We're outta here."

Mack Lee stomped his feet and then climbed into the driver's seat, slammed the door of the Roadster, and fired up the engine as he stared straight ahead with both hands on the wheel.

"I'm not sure that you ought to be driving," Bob said, reaching for the driver's door handle.

Mack Lee truculently cut him off. "It's not *your* car, Bob! It's *ours*. We agreed. You drive half the time. I drive the other half. You drove here, so I'm driving back. Are you getting in or what?"

"All right, all right, you drive home, but let's give it a while...you know, maybe we let some of the gin wear off. Besides, I met a really cool girl tonight and I'd like to hang around for a while longer...you know."

Bob slipped into the passenger seat and leaned to take the keys from the ignition. Before his hand could reach the ignition, Mack Lee popped the clutch, threw the Roadster into gear, and floored the gas pedal. The Roadster fishtailed out of the parking lot in a storm of flying gravel and squealing tires as they turned onto the black top.

"Jesus, Mack Lee, pull over!"

"Quit your bitchin' and pass me a beer!"

Bob started to object further. But, reflecting that this was going to be his last night ever with his old friend, muttered, "Ah, t' Hell with it," and popped open a beer.

Twenty minutes later, the Roadster was tearing down State Road 221 with the speedometer needle bouncing around eighty miles per hour. The top was down, and the boys were drinking beers and singing "Suzie Q" along with the radio. As they emptied bottles, they flung them toward the blur of mailboxes racing past along the sides of the highway.

As they passed the Tumbleston farm, Mack Lee killed the last swallow of his beer and drew back to chuck his bottle at their mailbox. As he did, the right front tire slid off the asphalt and onto the graveled shoulder. He overcompensated and jerked the wheel to the left, causing the Roadster to career sideways across the road and into the opposite ditch. The car went airborne and flipped twice, ejecting both boys before coming to rest in a smoking heap upside down against a roadside juniper.

Mack Lee woke in agony. His right leg felt like it was on fire. Looking down, he found there was no fire, but his entire lower leg was twisted and bent ninety degrees to the left at the knee like a puppet with its strings cut. He called out to Bob but received no answer. Calling again, he was rewarded with a muffled groan coming from out in the darkness to his left.

"Bob, you okay?" Mack Lee yelled back.

"Yeah, I think so. But something's on my legs and I can't move them," came Bob's immediate reply. "Come get it off me!"

"My leg's broke. I can't."

"Just help me move whatever it is. I can't reach it. Get it off me, then I'll go for help."

After several agonizing minutes of arguing back and forth, Mack Lee finally dragged himself painfully toward Bob's voice. Arriving at his friend's side, he saw nothing pinning the legs. "Asshole! You made me drag myself all the way over here with a broke leg, and there's nothing even on you, you som' bitch! Now, get your ass up and go get help!"

"Nothing on my legs? What do you mean?! Mack Lee! I can't move my legs. *Oh, God!* Oh, God...oh, God. I can't *feel* my legs," Bob moaned in panic as awareness washed over him. "Oh, God, please, no!"

CHAPTER 15

DECEMBER 1956–DECEMBER 1957

WITHOUT MUCH FANFARE, CHRISTMAS CAME and went a week after Jimmy arrived in North Carolina. Jimmy assumed his uncle had been too busy to decorate the house for the holidays. He *was* a doctor after all. Jimmy didn't mind the non-festive air; he wasn't feeling much like celebrating, anyway.

To Jimmy's surprise, Howard gave Jimmy a Christmas present. He certainly wasn't expecting anything, so the gift took Jimmy totally by surprise. It was a pair of Buster Brown shoes. The dog on the box looked really creepy, but the shoes inside were just his size...and Jimmy *needed* shoes. He'd held the soles of his old shoes on with bailing twine for the past month.

"Oh, Uncle...thank you! How did you know I needed shoes?" Jimmy asked.

"Not me, James. Your mom and dad wanted you to have those shoes," had been his uncle's reply.

Jimmy knew there had been no packages taken from the house in Boiling Springs when he left last week. The trunk of his uncle's car had been empty save his one tiny suitcase and the spare tire. But Jimmy let it go without further comment.

Later, when he found a receipt from a department store in downtown Holly Springs inside the shoebox, he maintained his silence. He needed the shoes wherever they came from.

Christmas afternoon, Howard told Jimmy he had to leave for a while but should be back in a few hours—well before supper. Jimmy, assuming his uncle was heading off on a house call, assured him that he'd be okay. Jimmy didn't mind. He wanted to write a letter to his mom and dad to thank them for his new shoes...just in case.

It took Jimmy several weeks to adjust to his new way of life. Although Howard referred to the acreage around his house as "the farm," there no were animals to be tended and no crops in any of the fields. Consequently, there were no chores for Jimmy to do on a daily basis. Wilma-Jean Tucker, his uncle's housekeeper, took care of all the household chores and meal preparation. Jimmy's sole duties were to mow the lawn and trim the hedges once each week after school. Otherwise, there was little that he *had* to do. Having never been afraid of hard work and with an enterprising nature, he began mowing lawns for neighbors, and soon, a cottage industry was born.

When not mowing lawns or doing schoolwork, Jimmy spent his afternoons exploring the property and familiarizing himself with all of his surroundings that were within walking distance. In an outbuilding behind the house, he found an old bicycle, which, with Uncle's permission, he refurbished. Thereafter, the radius of his empire was expanded still further.

Although he was happy enough staying with his uncle, Jimmy longed for home. He missed his mother and father... and even Mack Lee, at least a little. He wrote countless letters home but never received a response, unless, of course, one considered the return of his letters with *"Return to sender—Addressee unknown"* scrawled across the front in his mother's handwriting to be a reply. Initially, Jimmy kept the returned letters from his family in the desk drawer in his room. As their numbers grew, he transferred them to his shoebox from Christmas, certain that they'd be safe under the watchful eyes of Buster Brown and his dog, Tige.

With the nearest telephone to his parent's house being in the Rexall Pharmacy in Boiling Springs, Jimmy was effectively cut off from his family.

Most evenings found Jimmy and his uncle in the library, which Howard referred to as his study. For the first few weeks, Jimmy only paged through *The Birds of Asia*, but then Howard smiled to himself when one night Jimmy brought Zane Grey's *The Last Trail* down to the study. The next night, he had a copy of Mark Twain's *The Adventures of Huckleberry Finn*, and the next night, Jack London's *The Call of the Wild*. The following night brought a collection of works by Rudyard Kipling. Howard watched as the boy flipped through *The Jungle Book*, *Rikki-Tikki-Tavi*, *Gunga Din*, and *Captains Courageous* in rapid succession.

"You realize that it's acceptable to read entire books, don't you? I think you'd enjoy them more if you'd take the time to finish the stories," Howard admonished after watching the progression of books over several nights in a row.

"Oh, I finish them. I just read fast," Jimmy replied, absently turning a page.

The following evening, Jimmy had Herman Melville's *Moby Dick*, and to his uncle's satisfaction, he brought it with him again the next night.

Finally, Howard thought, smiling inwardly. *He's reading the whole book.* Then to Jimmy, he teased, "So Moby

Dick has held your attention for a second night? I'm impressed!"

"Well, yes...I finished it last night, but the language was a little confusing. I wanted to reread it tonight and try to figure out the symbolism Melville was employing with the colors black and white in the novel. At first, I thought it was just good and evil...you know, the usual stuff. But then I started thinking about them and Queequeg's tattoos in terms of race and religion and thought I had better read through it again before I could be sure what Melville was trying to relay to the reader."

Howard stared open-mouthed at his grand-nephew. "You're only nine. How do you even *know* about that stuff?"

"I found an *Advanced English Composition and Literature* textbook under the bed in my room."

"Christ, son! Charles took that class when he was a senior at Duke."

———————

Howard's arms flailed and slashed as though wielding an invisible saber, hacking away at the Russian cannoneers. His doughy face was flushed from exertion as he acted out the scene with a Shakespearean earnestness. The rich baritone of his voice boomed in an escalating cadence:

> *Half a league, half a league,*
> *Half a league onward,*
> *All in the Valley of Death*
> *Rode the six hundred.*
> *"Forward the Light Brigade!*
> *Charge for the guns!" he said:*
> *Into the Valley of Death*
> *Rode the six hundred.*

After the second verse, Jimmy, "riding" beside his uncle toward the guns, chimed in with the refrain:

Cannon to right of them,
Cannon to left of them,
Cannon in front of them
Volley'd and thunder'd;
Storm'd at with shot and shell,
Boldly they rode and well,
Into the jaws of Death,
Into the mouth of Hell
Rode the six hundred.

Minutes later, after Tennyson's final verse had been completed, the two collapsed in a fit of laughter. Howard pulled Jimmy in for a long hug and kissed the boy on the top of his head. When his breathing had returned sufficiently to allow for something resembling normal speech, Howard bade Jimmy goodnight and sent him upstairs to bed.

Howard was reasonably certain, before that night, Jimmy had never even heard of the Crimean War, Alfred Lord Tennyson, and certainly not *The Charge of the Light Brigade*. Yet tonight, after a five-minute read through, Jimmy had recited—Hell, he'd *performed*—it flawlessly. Clearly, the child was gifted.

Howard had always been proud of Charles, and rightly so. His son had been at the top of his class at every level of schooling, all the way through college. Had he not been killed during the war, he would've had the world at his feet. He could've done anything he wanted to do, and would've done it very well. Yet Jimmy, at only age nine, would've run circles around Charles. If the boy played chess, he'd be Bobby Fischer.

Of course, Howard supposed there might be problems associated with having a gallon-sized intellect in a pint-sized body. Jimmy might have the brain of an adult genius, but he only had the life experiences and coping skills of a child.

Alone in his study, Howard contemplated Jimmy and the death of little Anna. Even for an adult, dealing with an accidental death like that would've been difficult. He reflected upon his own struggles after Doris's death. For a child, it must be Hell.

Howard turned out the lamp and climbed the stairs to his bedroom. He sighed, "Poor kid."

On good nights, Jimmy heard his sweet sister calling to him, "Read me the birdies, Jibby! Read me the birdies!" On bad nights, though, it was, "Jibby! Jib...bey..." as crimson blossoms appeared on her blouse and she slumped to the floor. With the latter, Jimmy would wake in a cold sweat or screaming, or both.

During one such night, Howard rushed into Jimmy's room only to find him tightly balled up with his knees under his chin, rocking and breathing in shuddering gasps. Howard sat on the bed and pulled the child to him, wrapping him tightly in a supportive embrace as he reassured, "There, there, son. It was just a dream."

"No!" Jimmy sobbed. "The blood...the blood! Make it go away!"

"It was only a dream. Everything is all right," he said in his most soothing "we're going to get that thorn out of your paw, Mr. Lion" tone.

"No, Uncle! It was real. I shot her...and the blood...the blood was everywhere! Anna is dead and it's because of me." Another wave of sobs racked the boy's body.

A bolt of lightning daggered through Howard's soul. *Doris*, he thought. He shook his head as though to clear it, then continued aloud. "Yes, son, Anna is dead. But *you* didn't kill her. A series of events leading up to a horrible accident caused her death. Not you."

"But I killed her, Uncle. It *was* me!" His tears soaked the old man's night shirt.

Howard nodded his head slowly. "True, it was you holding a gun you *thought* was a toy and it went off. You didn't know it was real. That makes it an accident. You weren't trying to hurt anybody."

"I should have known! I was too dumb."

Howard held the boy away from him and looked directly into Jimmy's eyes, saying in a stern but even tone, "Son, there has *never* been a dumb Hines and *you* are not going to be the first!"

"But I'm not a Hines, Uncle. I'm a Hamilton," Jimmy squeaked.

"Dammit, son, you're one-quarter Hines and that's more than enough. There has *never* been a dumb Hines!"

"But what about Mack Lee?" Jimmy sniffled.

"Even Mack Lee," Howard replied, stifling a chuckle. "He's not stupid, just lazy."

Jimmy gave a choked half-giggle.

"Son, all of us make mistakes. The important thing is not the mistakes that we make, but rather what we do to correct them. The key to life is learning from our mistakes so we don't repeat them."

"But Anna is dead! I can never correct that."

"You're right. You can't correct that mistake, but you *can* learn from it."

Jimmy laid down again, and Howard pulled the covers up and tucked the boy into bed.

"Uncle," Jimmy began, still sniffling. "I don't think I want to be Jimmy anymore." With his nose stuffy from crying, Jimmy pronounced his name "Jibby."

Howard nodded, understanding the boy's feelings all too well. "Well, son, what would you like to be called?"

"Can I be Jabes, instead?" he asked with another sniffle.

"I think we can do that," Howard replied reassuringly.

"Thank you, Uncle. Good night."

"Good night, James. Sleep well!" he said and turned out the light. "I'm just across the hall if you need me."

In his room, Doris smiled back at Howard from her picture frame. She looked happy, he thought before he turned out his lamp. "Love you, Darse!" he whispered.

"I love you too, old man!" he imagined Doris saying as he drifted off to sleep.

Much to James's relief, Howard mentioned nothing about the spectacle of the night before over breakfast. Nor was anything mentioned over supper that evening.

Later, in the library, Howard, using care to call the correct name, said to the boy, "James, I have a book I think you'd like reading. I know it's here somewhere." He stared up at the bookcases. "Ah, here it is." He reached and selected a volume from the top shelf.

James clearly appreciated his uncle remembering their earlier conversation. His eyes were as big as saucers when he accepted the proffered book. It was bound in leather and had to be three inches thick. Opening to the title page and very unsure, he said, "Les Miser...ables?"

Uncle smiled. "*Les Misérables* by Victor Hugo. It's a story about a man named Jean Valjean...a man who made a mistake and then spent the rest of his life trying to atone for it. *Les Mis* deals with love and sincerity, sacrifice for others, justice and injustice. It has it all. I think you'll like this book.

It's one of my favorites. And it will probably take longer than a day to read. I hope you enjoy it!"

Three evenings later, James turned the final page of *Les Misérables*. Closing the book, he said, "Uncle, I think the world needs more Jean Valjeans. I mean, he could have stayed bitter about the way he had been treated, but after Bishop Myriel saved him, he really changed his life. He wasn't really responsible for Fontine's problems or for her losing her job but vowed to take care of her daughter anyway. He gave up his own happiness so Cosette could live a life untainted by his past sins. He sacrificed everything, even his own life, so she and Marius could be happy...although neither of them appreciated what he did for them, until they finally 'got it' on the day he died. I hope someday I'll be like Jean Valjean."

Howard tousled the boy's hair. "If anybody can, son, my money's on you."

Howard and James slipped into the comfortable habit of reading and discussing books or life together each evening. Over time, Howard's loneliness and guilt, constant companions since Doris's death, began to slough away. Evenings, he rushed home from the office to spend time with the boy. James seemed so much like Charles...only smarter.

As for James, the guilt over Anna's death was never far from his mind, but through his uncle, he learned to deal with it more effectively. Finding himself in a loving and caring home, he slowly began to come out of his shell. He laughed often and soon began looking forward to the nightly dialogue with his uncle.

After noticing James seemed to particularly enjoy James Fenimore Cooper's *Leatherstocking Tales*, Howard planned a surprise for him. Only a few days earlier, he had left his office and found a flyer tucked underneath the windshield wiper of his Cadillac. He was about to throw the advertisement in the curbside trash basket—waste of good paper and ink—when the red-and-black bull's-eye on the brochure caught his eye. The flyer stated that famed marksman and trick shooter, Herb Parsons, would be performing a "fancy and trick shooting" exposition at the State Fairgrounds in Raleigh the following weekend. The exposition was sponsored by Winchester & Western. Tickets for the event cost $0.25 and could be purchased at the Western Auto in Holly Springs. Howard had slipped the flyer into his jacket pocket. That evening, he showed the flyer to James, and as he'd expected, the boy was beside himself with excitement.

"Do you think this Herb Parsons person is as good a shot as Natty Bumppo was with Killdeer, Uncle?" James asked, clearly excited. "How about Lew Wetzel?"

"I don't know. They were both crack shots. I suppose we'll just have to see for ourselves. That is, if you want to go," Howard said, trying to hide his smile.

"Oh, can we go, Uncle! That would be just swell!"

The next weekend, while riding home from the fairgrounds after watching Parsons's exhibition, James couldn't stop talking. "Uncle, can you believe it?! That aspirin tablet just went *POOF*, right off the top of the balloon. One minute it's an aspirin tablet. The next it was aspirin powder blowing away downwind, and the balloon didn't even pop! Then, when he cut that Ace of Spades card in half by shooting it... wow! At first, I thought it was a trick, but he let me put another card into the holder...did you see...and he did it again! It was a *real* playing card, not a trick card. I could tell! And then, he blew out ten candles by shooting rapid-fire from the hip, one after another. Crack-crack-crack, one after another out-out-out went the candles...one, two, three, out they went. Ten in a row in, like, five seconds. He was like a real-life Natty Bumppo, just like in *The Last of the Mohicans*. Uncle, did you see? Did you see?!"

From time to time, Howard was able to wedge an "uh-huh" into James's nonstop after-action play-by-play, but mostly he just listened, smiled, and nodded as the two of them drove back from Raleigh. James was still babbling about Herb Parsons and Natty Bumppo as he tucked the boy into bed that night.

In his bedroom, Doris smiled at him from the bedside table. Howard smiled back and turned out the light.

CHAPTER 16

1957

W ALTER SHOOK HIS HEAD IN disgust. He knew the boy was milking his injury for all it was worth, and then some. The car wreck had been bad; there was no debating that point. When he'd been thrown from his little hotrod, Mack Lee had suffered major ligament damage to his knee, and he'd likely always walk with a limp because of it. But, as Walter knew only too well, a limp wouldn't keep a man from doing an honest day's work. Or at least, it shouldn't.

Mack Lee had been the lucky one in that accident. That other boy, the Morrison kid, had suffered a broken back and, because of it, would spend the rest of his life in a wheelchair. Even with paralyzed legs, Morrison had still gone off to college and was gonna make something of his life. Walter supposed with enough drive, you could always make somethin' of yourself, even with a broke back.

And without that drive, you had Mack Lee, who, in Walter's estimate, would never amount to much of anything.

Mack Lee's leg was no worse than Walter's—in truth, it was significantly better—but that mattered not. Maggie, distraught over the near loss of her "perfect" son, had totally bought into her son's invalid act hook, line, and sinker.

When Walter had suggested that Mack Lee should pitch in and help out around the farm, Maggie would hear nothing of it. She insisted, "After such a grievous injury, certainly Mack Lee cannot possibly be expected to perform physical labor."

At this, Walter wondered incredulously if Maggie'd ever taken more than a cursory glance at *his* own injured leg. She certainly didn't seem to have any problem with *him* toiling away from dawn 'til dusk on the farm.

"What's good for the goose oughta be good for the gander," he'd grumbled quietly, albeit wisely in a tone too soft for Maggie to hear. Otherwise, there would've been Hell to pay.

Maggie coddled Mack Lee, and the more *she* did, the less *he* did. Throughout his childhood, Walter had known Mack Lee to shirk work. If his son had put even *a third* as much effort into working as he put into avoiding it, the farm would've been running along like a well-tuned engine. He didn't, and it wasn't.

The boy was just lazy.

On the rare occasions when Mack Lee deigned to do any chores at all, Walter almost wished he hadn't bothered. Invariably, whatever Mack Lee had done, Walter'd have to go back and redo. The lesson Walter had stressed so often to Mack Lee as a child—"If you've got time enough to do a job twice, then you've got time enough to do it right the first time"—had been totally forgotten by his own son by adulthood.

The thought of nearly losing Mack Lee, especially after all she'd been through, was too terrible for Maggie to bear. She'd stayed at his bedside the entire time he'd been in the hospital after his accident and was determined to protect him from even the *possibility* of future injuries.

It angered her that Walter was trying to force Mack Lee to get out and work. He was in such frightful pain, and she and Walter paid farm hands good money to labor on the farm anyway. Why should her boy have to slave away like that? Had he not suffered enough already?

The person who angered her even more than Walter was that Bob Morrison boy. In the hospital, Mack Lee had told her *all* about the accident and how Bob had been drunk, but insisted on driving anyway. Her dear sweet son had tried to stop him, but Bob would hear nothing of it. Then, Bob had flipped their little car and nearly killed both of them. Poor Mack Lee would never walk again without pain, and that Morrison boy had broken his back. As far as Maggie was concerned, Bob Morrison had gotten just what he deserved!

CHAPTER 17

1957

J AMES'S FIRST YEAR LIVING IN North Carolina passed quickly. He found school there to be no more challenging than it had been back home in South Carolina. His classes were easy to the point of boredom. He passed each one effortlessly and with perfect grades.

The relative ease with which he completed his coursework made him less-than-popular with his classmates. James was always the guy in class who blew the grading curve, scoring a perfect 100 percent when the next closest score was a "C." Consequently, he was an outsider, just like he'd been at his school in Boiling Springs.

James enjoyed the time with his uncle. Howard was always kind to him, and James learned significantly more from the old fellow just talking over books in his study than James ever learned from any of his classes at school.

It was nice living at Howard's house, but for James, it still wasn't home. When he went to bed each night, he said a little prayer, asking to hear from his parents the next day, telling him to come back home. It had taken James almost six months just to move his clothes from his suitcase and into the chest of drawers and closet in his room. Before that, he always repacked his suitcase each night, just in case to-morrow was the day. After a year of tomorrows *not* being the day, he finally settled in for the long haul.

———————————

Regardless of the book that accompanied him to the library each evening, James finished his day with *The Birds of Asia*. He'd found a can of saddle soap in the barn behind the house and every night lovingly worked it into the cracked leather binding of the old book. Soon, the leather was as soft and supple as it had been when it first rolled out of the book binder's shop in 1883. Each night before turning out his light, he studied one of the lithographs and read aloud to the angels about one of the birds just in case Anna was listening. Only then would he go to sleep.

Like a parent who's read the same bedtime story to their toddler every night for months, James was soon able to reel off the descriptions by heart for all seventy-six of the illus-trations in Volume I, although his Latin pronunciations may have left a bit to be desired. Soon, James made this nightly ritual into a game. He'd turn to a random illustration and then recite the overleaf. When this was no longer a chal-lenge, he began copying the illustrations themselves into one of his notebooks from school. His initial drawings were rudimentary, but he rapidly improved. As he perfected his technique, he found he actually enjoyed drawing and began to draw items around the house, first a vase, then Kitty Lamarr, and, later, the house itself.

James didn't realize that his uncle had noticed his bud-ding interest in art. The old man certainly had made no com-ment if he had, but one evening after their book discussion in the library, James found a sketch pad and artist's pencil set waiting for him on the desk in his room. Beside the desk, an easel sat propped against the wall. He stared wide-eyed at the artist's set, then practically flew down the steps to the kitchen where he gave the old man a Kodiak-sized bear hug. Howard put down his pie fork and returned the embrace with a polar-bear-sized grin of his own.

With his new artist's supplies, James redoubled his efforts at learning to draw and sketch. He worked some with watercolor, acrylic paints, and pen & ink, but found that his favorite media were pencil or charcoal. He liked the way different shades of gray gave his pictures depth and mood.

James practiced his artwork every day. Typically, his drawings were still-life sketches where he could practice shading, perspective, and scaling. His fire truck, which he lovingly kept on the shelf above the desk in his room, was his most common subject. The ladder, grill, and hoses provided lots of interesting details. The pencil cup on his desk, his bed, and a sleeping Kitty Lamarr also garnered a fair number of pages in his sketchbook.

A pile of filled sketchbooks began to accumulate in the floor of James's closet. Sometimes, he pulled them out and flipped through the pages, doing a self-critique of his earlier works to assess his "artistic growth." He was a harsh and unforgiving critic too. Sometimes he looked at one of his early drawings and shook his head in disgust. Often, he wanted to tear out the offending page but somehow was able to check the impulse. On the occasions when he found his talents to have been particularly lacking, he'd recreate the subject with similar lighting and perspective and redraw the picture, often repeatedly, in his current sketchbook. When he was finally satisfied with the image, only then would he turn to a new page. In this manner, he taught himself to draw. This was an effective method for learning to draw, but as a perfectionist, James went through a *lot* of sketchbooks and pads, which his uncle was only too happy to supply.

The old Victorian was beautiful and full of nooks, crannies, and niches. but it lacked closet space. By Christmas, the tiny closet in James's room was so packed full of art supplies and used sketchbooks that there was hardly room for his clothes. Not wishing to dispose of any artwork, James sought and received permission from Howard to transfer some of his older works into the attic. He filled a cardboard box with assorted sketchbooks, loose art, and pads. The process should have been the work of a few minutes, but James felt compelled to flip through each one before he consigned it to the box. Several he could not bear to hide away—these he set aside and returned to his closet. The rest he lugged up the rickety fold-down stairs into his new ancillary archive.

In the attic, James found dozens of boxes similar to his own. Most were in orderly stacks and carefully labeled with a black marker in a neat, rounded script. He knew in an instant that the writing was not his uncle's. *His* handwriting was atrocious! It must have been his grand-aunt Doris's hand that had lovingly placed those labels. There were boxes labeled for each holiday, Valentine's Day, Easter, Independence Day, Halloween, Thanksgiving, and Christmas, and there was even a box for Saint Patrick's Day. Apparently, Doris had liked to decorate, which James thought was odd.

Remembering back over the year and a half he'd lived with his uncle, not once had there been any attempt to decorate the house. In fact, the more he thought about it, from day to day, month to month, year to year, *nothing* in the house ever changed. The furniture stayed in the same places. When Mrs. Tucker cleaned the house, she replaced shelved items in precisely the same position as they had been before she began dusting. No fresh flowers ever graced the niches inside the house. James cared for the lawn and hedges, but the flower beds remained untended. Except for his room, the entire house seemed to have been frozen in time. He'd not paid much attention to this before that very day, but now it struck him as odd. Even his *mom* had kept flowers around the house and put up a Christmas tree—or, at least, she used to.

Having spent the year at his uncle's home, living more like a temporary boarder rather than a resident, James had hardly noticed the static day-to-day appearance of the house. If he'd thought it odd that the house wasn't decorated for the holidays, James made no mention of it. Why should he? He was only a guest in the house, after all.

As James's second Christmas with Howard loomed near, he found himself far more comfortable in his environment. With no visits from his family and each of his letters having been returned unopened, it became clear to him that *this* house was now his home and he longed to make it *feel* more festive for the holidays.

In James's mind, much like last year, his uncle was too busy with his medical practice to decorate the house. So, this year, James resolved to decorate it for him. He found the box labeled "Christmas" and brought it from the attic to his room. The next morning after his uncle left for the office, James began the task of decorating the house for the holidays. He found an axe in the shed and set off into the woods behind the house, where he felled a cedar tree and dragged it into the library. After standing the tree up in a corner, he found the lights and a box of glass ornaments and placed them on the tree. Mrs. Tucker even made popcorn and gave him a carton of cranberries with which to make a garland.

When he finished trimming the tree, James went back out to the woods and cut a wheelbarrow load of spruce boughs. Taking this back to the house, he fashioned a wreath for the front door and garland for the porch railing. Then, exhausted from his day's labors, he returned inside to await his uncle's return and promptly fell asleep on the sofa.

James was still asleep when Howard arrived home and thus did not hear the car pull into the drive. Mrs. Tucker, however, *did* hear and slipped outside to intercept the doctor before his storm had a chance to break over the boy. She met him as soon as he opened his car door.

"What in the tarnation is this?!" he said, gesturing to the porch and already red in the face. "You know dang well that I—"

"You stop right there!"

"Well, I—"

"Not another word, Howard Hines!" Mrs. Tucker had never called him by any other name than Doctor, and certainly had never spoken harshly to him, so he was momentarily taken aback.

"You..." he began again, only to be arrested by the look on Mrs. Tucker's face.

She poked him in the chest with her forefinger, punctuating every word. "That little boy has been working his behind off all day, trying to decorate this house and make it look nice and festive for Christmas."

"But I don't—"

"Well, you *do* now! That child has been through *enough* already. He's buried under a mountain of guilt about his sister. He's been kicked out of the only home he's ever known, and his own mama can't stand the sight of him. He shouldn't have to live in a mausoleum, Howard Hines...and neither should you!"

"But—"

"No! What you are going to do if you *ever* want to see another bite of pie in this house, is to sit your rump back down in that big, fancy car of yours, back out of the driveway, and then drive back in. When you get back *this* time, you are going to be happy about what that sweet little boy has done for you. He's mighty proud of the work he's done here today, and dammit, Howard Hines, you're gonna be too!"

At this, she turned on her heels and marched back into the house.

Thoroughly cowed, Howard started his car and backed quietly from the driveway. A moment later, the Caddy roared back into the driveway. The slamming of the car door woke James from his slumber, and he rushed to the library to await his uncle.

Howard came through the front door and said, "Mrs. Tucker, did you do all this decorating? And is that apple pie I smell?"

"Why, Doctor Hines," she replied, her voice dripping with honey, "how was your day? Of course, there's apple pie! I know it's your favorite, and they had the best-looking apples at the market this morning...not too sweet and not too tart. Oh, and no, James has done all of this decorating. Isn't it just grand?! I think he's waiting for you in the library."

Looking contrite, Howard dipped his head and obediently went off to find the boy in the library. He entered, finding James fidgeting and bouncing on the balls of his feet next to the saddest, most bedraggled, moth-eaten excuse for a Christmas tree he'd ever laid eyes on. It was horribly misshapen with large brown sections and multiple missing limbs. A homemade star drooped from the topmost branch, but the branches were adorned with colored lights, ornaments, tinsel, and garland. Most importantly, the excitement of the boy standing next to it could not be denied.

"D-do you like it, Uncle?"

Howard took in a deep breath and, slowly nodding his head, said, "Son, that's got to be the most incredible Christmas tree I have ever seen! You did all this? And did you do the garland on the front porch too or did Mrs. Tucker help?"

"Nope, just me," James beamed with pride. "So...you really like it?"

Whether he was thinking about the tree or apple pie, Uncle answered with a smile, "Yeah, I think I do."

And James rushed him with a hug the old man was only too happy to return.

"Now you two get washed up for dinner, and remember to save some room. There's pie-ee," an approving Mrs. Tucker called from the kitchen.

CHAPTER 18

CHRISTMAS 1957

Christmas morning, James woke to a dusting of snow on the ground and Kitty Lamarr curled up on the pillow by his head. The cat, wholly unimpressed by the concept of Christmas, watched him dress in jeans and a sweater through half-closed eyes and then promptly went back to sleep when he rushed out the door to head downstairs.

To his amazement, James found his uncle in the kitchen. During the entire time he'd lived there, never once had he seen him in the kitchen except to pass through en route to the breakfast nook. To the best of James's knowledge, the old man didn't even know how to turn on the stove, much less cook. Yet there he was, standing by the stove with a half-pound of bacon sizzling in the skillet, a steaming mound of scrambled eggs large enough to serve a battalion, and a plate of toast on the counter next to him. Everything smelled wonderful.

Rubbing his growling stomach, James said, "Good morning, Uncle Howard, and Merry Christmas! I didn't know you could cook."

"Merry Christmas, James! I learned in the army a hundred years ago," came his rumbling baritone reply. "But don't tell Mrs. Tucker! If she ever finds out, she'll want me to peel potatoes or chop salad or something like that every night for dinner."

James gave him a solemn nod. "It will be our secret, sir."

Howard filled two plates for them, and James bounced to the breakfast table beside him. They ate heartily, both eager to finish up and share their gifts with the other.

After breakfast, Howard excused himself to his study. He wanted to make certain the gift he'd secreted there for James was placed perfectly beneath the tree. He hummed "Oh, Holy Night" and thought about this Christmas day. This was the first time since Doris had died that he had looked forward to the day, and it was all because of James. He was a good boy and deserved to be happy and to feel loved. "And dammit, he is," Howard said to himself, adjusting the position of James's gift for a third time.

In the kitchen, James hurriedly cleared the table and washed all the dishes, leaving them to dry on the rack. Then he joined his uncle in the library.

Under the Christmas tree were two brightly colored packages. One was a flat rectangle about two feet across and wrapped in a haphazard fashion. James had wrapped it himself using silver foil and a big green bow. He'd worked diligently on this gift for over a month and could hardly wait for his uncle to open it.

The other gift, he had never seen. It was a little over four feet long and about six inches across. Beautifully wrapped in striped red and gold paper, it was tied up with a red ribbon and bow.

James's eyes practically glowed as bounced with excitement. He could not for the life of him stay still. "Can we open the presents now, Uncle? Can we?"

"Well, it is Christmas morning, so of course we can."

Needing no further encouragement, James raced to the tree and to his uncle's amazement, selected the smaller package from underneath. He then practically danced to Howard's side and handed the present to him.

"Open it, Uncle! Open it!"

"Don't you want to open your gift first?"

"Huh-uh! You open yours. Open it! Open it!" His words came out like quarters from a slot machine jackpot.

Howard removed the ribbon and bow from the package, but not fast enough for James.

"Rip it open, Uncle!" said James, his cheeks flushed with excitement.

Obediently, Howard tore open the foil and stared wordlessly at his gift, a tear glistening in the corner of his eye. Inside a homemade barn-wood frame was a charcoal drawing of the farmhouse as it had appeared on the day James first came to live there. It was complete with rocking chairs on the porch and Kitty Lamarr perched on the railing beside the front door. He had added a single addition to the scene, which caused a lump to come into the old man's throat. In one of the rocking chairs on the porch sat Doris, wearing a gingham dress and smiling just like she had on the day they were married.

"Do you like it, Uncle? Do you like it? I *hope* you like it! I used the photograph in your room so that I could draw Aunt Doris. I didn't really know her that well. I hope that was okay! Do you like it?!"

Howard continued staring wordlessly at the picture. With a tear now running down his cheek, he stood and walked toward the fireplace holding the drawing in both hands. The uncured, green wood in the fireplace crackled and popped as it burned.

"No, son, I *don't* like it."

James watched in horror as his uncle paused before the fire. Then Howard reached up and took down his Mickey Mouse drawing, propping it on the floor next to his chair, and hung James's picture in the place of honor above the mantel.

"No, I don't like it. I *love* it! James, I think this is the most wonderful gift I have ever been given. It's perfect! Come here, son!" he said, his arms wide.

The hug that followed lasted a full minute, punctuated by laughter, a few more tears, and not a few kisses to the top of the boy's head. And James beamed.

When they finally broke from the hug, Howard pointed to the tree and said, "Looks like there's still another present under there, son. Why don't you see what it is?"

"For me?" James began in a meek voice.

"Well, it sure as heck isn't for me."

"Uncle, you didn't have to get me anything. You already got the art supplies for me!"

"Oh, hush and open your present!" his uncle said with a smile.

James complied, ripping into the paper with abandon. Inside, he found a wooden box branded with a galloping horse and rider under the word *WINCHESTER,* which had been stenciled in red. With trembling fingers, he worked the two brass clasps and opened the hinged top, then immediately slammed it shut, recoiling in terror from the rattlesnake inside the case. Of course, there wasn't one, but there may as well have been.

The box contained a Winchester Model 52 bolt-action .22 rifle with a five-round box magazine.

"Get it away!" James cried, dropping the box. He had enjoyed reading about Buffalo Bill, Calamity Jane, and Natty Bumppo and been thrilled to see Herb Parsons performing tricks that were even beyond the abilities of his literary heroes. But to see an actual rifle before him after what had happened to Anna? That terrified the boy.

Howard recognized his mistake an instant too late. Having seen how much James enjoyed the shooting expo, he'd been certain the boy would love to have a rifle of his own. After all, who was Hawkeye without Killdeer, his long rifle? He hung his head. *All true,* Howard thought. *But this is a little boy who accidentally shot his sister. I am such a damned old fool.*

Well, old fool, Doris's voice told him in his head, *go to that boy and you make it right! And you can make it right.*

Howard thought for a moment, nodded his head, and motioned for James to sit in the chair next to him. "James, I made a mistake and hope that you will forgive me."

"It's all right, Uncle," James said in a shaky voice.

"No, I did something that upset you, and that was definitely not my intention."

"It's okay, you didn't mean to."

"You're right, I didn't mean to hurt you...and *you* didn't mean to hurt Anna either. What happened to you and Anna was a terrible accident. You didn't realize the gun you were holding was real or that it was loaded. If you had, it never would have happened."

"But..."

"Just last week, Elmer Brannon brought his son Albert into the office with a gash on the side of his head that needed to be sewn up. Albert's horse had shied and threw him off. His head hit a fencepost as he fell. He needed twenty-seven stitches to close up his scalp. Was that the horse's fault?"

"No, but—"

"Hear me out!" Howard interrupted gently. "When I was a little boy, my pa was splitting wood behind the house. My job was to stack the split pieces next to the house for Ma to use in the cookstove. Well, one time I moved in to grab a piece of wood a little too soon. It shouldn't have been a big deal, but the axe head wasn't tight on the handle and it picked that very instant to fly off. It nearly took my ear plumb off. Was that my pa's fault?" Howard brushed back his hair, displaying an ugly scar behind his left ear.

"No."

"Right. It was because of the tool. Maybe if the head had been on tighter, it wouldn't have happened. Maybe if I hadn't been so eager, I wouldn't have been in the way of the axe head and my ear wouldn't look so funny now. The point is, it was an accident caused by a tool."

"Okay."

"A gun, whether it is a rifle, a pistol, or a shotgun is a tool. Understood and used properly, they are as safe as any other tool. Understand?"

"Yes, but—"

"With all tools, there are rules that must be followed while using them to make them safe."

"Yes, sir."

Howard reopened the box and removed a single typed page. "These are my rules for firearm safety."

He handed it to James who read aloud, "Number one. Every gun is real until *you* prove that it is not. Number two. Every gun is loaded until *you* prove that it is not. Three. Never point a gun at anything you do not intend to shoot. There are only two exceptions to this rule: the sky and the ground. Four. Always clearly identify your target and know what is downrange. If you're not 100 percent sure, don't take the shot. Five. Keep your finger on the trigger guard, well away from the trigger until the moment you are ready to fire. Six. Always transport and store guns unloaded. Seven.

Always clean your gun immediately after use and check that the barrel is clear of obstruction before using it each and every time, but with the appropriate tool, never by looking down the barrel (see rule number three). Eight. Never run or climb a tree or fence with a loaded weapon. Nine. Make certain the ammunition you are using is right for the gun you're using."

Then Howard added, "One more that is my personal philosophy, but I think it's a good one. If hunting, shoot to kill cleanly and *never* to wound. It is cruel to leave a wounded animal in the field. Don't ever be cruel."

James nodded his head in earnest agreement. "Yes, Uncle."

"If you understand and follow these rules, then your rifle is just as safe as the axe you used to cut down our Christmas tree or the needle you used to thread the garland. You had great respect for Hawkeye in *The Last of the Mohicans* and for Lew Wetzel in *The Last Trail.* You can be like them if you like, and I will be proud to teach you. But if you would rather, I can return the rifle and let you pick out another present for Christmas. It's your choice, son."

James glanced pensively at the box, then said, "I think... I'd like to keep my rifle and learn to shoot like Herb Parsons, Uncle."

Howard plopped heavily onto the ottoman next to James. "Then let's get a better look at that new rifle of yours!"

With that, James reopened the box and gazed inside. The stock and grips were a highly polished walnut and exquisitely checkered. The galloping horse and rider from the case lid was also engraved onto the butt plate. The butt plate and barrel were both blued but had an oil can finish, which gave them a rainbow sheen in bright light. There was an aperture rear sight and a tunnel sight at the muzzle. The rifle was beautiful, and it was obvious even to James that it had not been cheap.

James carefully lifted the rifle free of its case, careful to keep it pointed well away from his uncle and Kitty Lamarr, who'd finally come downstairs.

Howard smiled at the boy's obvious care, then asked, "Is your rifle loaded?"

"No, sir!"

"Really? How do you know?"

"It just came out of the box."

"Remember, rule number two says that every gun is loaded until *you personally* prove that it is not."

James's gaze jerked from his uncle back to the rifle. He suddenly felt very unsure and a little scared again. "How do I do that, Uncle? How do I check?"

"That's okay. Come here and I'll show you."

James handed the rifle to his uncle.

"First, you push this lever to release the magazine. Then, you work the bolt twice like this"—he demonstrated working the bolt—"to make certain that the breech is clear."

"Twice?"

"Yep, twice. If there's a round chambered, that guarantees it will be ejected and you have a safe weapon. The only way you could hurt someone with it now is if you clubbed 'em over the head with it."

"That's neat, Uncle! Can we go outside so you can teach me to shoot?" James asked, his excitement clearly having returned.

"It will be my pleasure, but not today. We'll give it a try tomorrow."

"Awwww...tomorrow?" James said, allowing just a little bit of a whiny tone to creep into his voice.

"Yes, tomorrow. We have something else important to do today. So go get your coat, and I'll meet you in the car."

James felt a flicker of hope. *Maybe Uncle's taking me to see Mom and Dad?* He thought before racing upstairs to his room.

A few minutes later, James met his uncle at the car. He started to open the rear door as was his custom, when his uncle told him, "Nope, you're up front with me today." As James obediently slid into the front seat, he glanced into his usual spot in the back and saw that it was crammed full of grocery bags.

"Uncle, would you like me to take the groceries in before we go?"

"No, they're fine right where they are."

"Okay. But won't they go bad if we just leave them?"

"They'll be fine."

"If we aren't taking them in and we aren't leaving them, then what are we doing?"

"Just wait, son. You'll see."

With this, Howard started the car and pulled out of the driveway, onto the blacktop. After several miles and many twists and turns, the blacktop became rougher and narrower with every turn. Finally, he turned onto a rutted dirt lane and then from that into a muddy driveway in front of a run-down clapboard-sided house. He nodded for James, implying this was their destination. James exited the car and walked around to his uncle's side.

Howard opened the driver's side rear door and leaned down to James's ear. In a conspiratorial voice, barely above a whisper, he explained, "Lenny Wilkie worked for the Clinchfield Railroad for almost twenty years. About the time you came to live with me, Lenny had an accident at the rail yard and lost both of his legs. He has a pension from the railroad, but without any other income, it's not enough to keep three kids fed and clothed. Martha takes in washing for folks and cleans houses, but they're still only scraping by. James, grab that bag back there...no, not that one, the one next to it...yeah, that one."

James selected the correct bag and walked with his uncle up to the house and onto the porch. There, Howard knocked on the front door and waited. A minute later, a tired and frazzled-looking woman in her forties opened the door.

"Merry Christmas, Martha!" bellowed his uncle. "How are Lenny and the kids?"

"Why, Doctor Hines! What on earth are you doing here? And Merry Christmas to you as well."

"I was talking to the guys at Wilson's Barbershop last week and they wanted me to bring a few things by for you and the kids," he said, handing over James's grocery bag.

"Well, that was very nice of them. Oh, Lenny, *look*! It's a whole ham and new shoes for each of the children! Oh, Doctor Hines, thank you! Please pass my thanks along to everyone at Wilson's. Oh, this is just too wonderful. I think I'm going to cook up some of this ham right now. Would you like to come in?"

"That's very kind of you, Martha, but we have other stops to make. Take care, and Merry Christmas!"

Mrs. Wilkie gave him a kiss on the cheek and turned back into her house. Closing the door behind her, she excitedly called the children to come get their new shoes; Buster Browns, James noticed.

Howard and James rode back to the blacktop and, several turns later, stopped in front of a wood-framed house with peeling white paint and sheets of plastic stapled over the outside of each window.

"Who lives here, Uncle?" James asked upon meeting his uncle on opposite sides of the back seat again.

Howard replied, "Johnnie and Emily Turnbull. Johnnie is an excellent carpenter. He used to work at one of the furniture mills west of here but was in the wrong place at the wrong time and sucked cleaning solvent into his lungs. It messed them up really bad, and the mill laid him off. They figured that if he couldn't do the job, they shouldn't have to pay him. He got exposed while helping one of his buddies at work. Since it wasn't part of his job, the company said the Workman's Compensation Laws didn't apply. He's getting better, but it will still be a while before he's strong enough to work again."

Again, Howard knocked at the door and was greeted by the lady of the house. "Merry Christmas, Emmy! It's wonderful to see you again. How's little Laura Leigh? I was talking to the guys at Wilson's Barbershop last week and they wanted me to bring a few things by for you to help brighten the season."

James presented Mrs. Turnbull with a bag containing another ham and a winter coat about the size a six-year-old girl might wear. Again, Howard begged off the offer to come inside for refreshments and they returned to the car.

This process was repeated at the Martinsens', the Pettigrews', and the Braxtons' homes. Each time, the same story was offered and tear-filled hugs or kisses were received.

Walking back to the car after leaving the Braxtons' front porch, James asked, "I don't understand, Uncle. You don't even go to Wilson's Barber shop. Mrs. Tucker cuts your hair. But you tell everybody that it was 'the guys at Wilson's' who took up a collection or something like that. Why?"

His uncle smiled. "But *they* don't know that it wasn't from Wilson's."

"Why don't you just tell them it was from you? It is, isn't it?"

"It is."

"Then why not tell them the truth?"

"But it *is* the truth...from a certain point of view."

"Huh?"

"Charlie Wilson has arthritis. Hank Sutton has diabetes. Cecil Darcy has gout. I treat every one of them and probably two-thirds of their customers. They pay me to treat them, so technically, the money I'm using to help these people came from the good folks at Wilson's."

"Don't you want them to know everything was from you? Shouldn't they know that?"

"Son, the important thing is that the good gets done—not who gets the credit for doing it. Besides, don't you think it would be a nice thing for all the folks we've seen today to know that their neighbors and friends around the town are thinking about them and their families at Christmastime? Shouldn't Christmas be about love, caring, and good will? I think it should!"

James remembered the shoes he'd received last Christmas and his uncle's coy response when he'd inquired about their origin. As the realization dawned over him he said, "I hope that someday I will be as good a man as you, Uncle!"

The old man reached across the seat and patted the boy's shoulder. "I'm betting you'll be even better. One more stop, then we go home."

"But we're out of bags?"

"That's okay. For this stop, we won't need one."

About fifteen minutes later, they stopped in front of a dilapidated white one-room country church with a stubby steeple and four windows on each side. It was elevated about eighteen inches off the ground by a rickety-looking stone foundation. The white paint was peeling and, in many places, the silvery-gray patches of its wooden side planks were visible. The door, which might once have been black, now was a sad, dark gray and bore no latch or fixtures.

The rusty hinges screeched in protest as Howard pushed through the door and entered, just in time to see an opossum disappear through a hole in one of the floorboards. The interior of the church was bare except for an ancient potbellied stove in the back corner. On the walls, there was more lath visible than plaster. The latter being found mostly in piles along the baseboards, intermixed with rat droppings. The rafters were bare, and shafts of sunlight beamed like searchlights through holes in the roof. Dust motes floated like barrage balloons swirling slowly in unseen drafts.

"Fifty-one years ago," Howard began in a faraway voice, "this place was a sight to behold, especially from where I was standing. The floors were polished, and six rows of wooden pews lined the center aisle. There were lanterns hanging from the rafters, and each of the windows had an evergreen garland underneath and a poinsettia with holly boughs on the sill. Of course, I was standing up front next to the altar with Preacher Bailey. The most beautiful thing I had ever seen in all my seventeen years was walking toward me, holding a spray of pink sweet peas. And that smile...God, I loved her smile. There was this little gap between her front teeth that she hated, but I thought it was cute. Her smile that morning was so wide the corners of her lips could have just about met in the back of her head...and best of all, she was smiling at me! I could never forget that! The rest of the day is a blur, but I remember that smile."

James listened in silence beside his uncle.

"She was sixteen years old, and her folks were none too happy about her getting married. They wanted us to wait until I was 'better established,' but Darse would hear nothing of it. She told them that she was getting married and they could either come and be a part of it or stay home and she'd tell 'em about it later. They came. Darse was always good about putting her foot down and getting what she wanted." As though in a fog, the old man drifted past the site that once held the altar and through a side door.

James followed and found himself in the church's graveyard, which was in no better repair than the church. Weeds grew almost knee high, and the picket fence that had once guarded the yard was mostly gone. Some of the headstones had fallen over and others sat at crazy angles, not yet totally having succumbed to gravity. But over one gravesite in the shadow of an ancient sycamore, the grass was carefully mown and entirely free of weeds. Its headstone stood straight and proud and had a spray of flowers, possibly sweet peas, at its base. To James, it looked like a tropical island rising from a sea of crabgrass and broom sage. Here, Howard stopped and bowed his head. The freshening breeze ruffled the tuft of white hair atop his head, making his combover flutter like the tail of a nervous albino squirrel.

"Darse loved this place. She always did. So, when she died, I knew she'd want to be here...even if the church wasn't. I come by at least once a week to keep things cleaned up and bring by new flowers."

James watched as his uncle knelt before the grave, removed the faded flowers, and replaced them with a sprig of holly that he magically produced from an inner pocket of his coat. He murmured a few words James couldn't quite catch and then stood again.

James read the words engraved upon the headstone:

DORIS YVONNE HINES

April 12, 1892 – October 2, 1955

BELOVED WIFE AND MOTHER

An untimely frost upon the sweetest flower.

"Uncle, what does the quote about an untimely frost mean?" James asked.

"It's Shakespeare, from *Romeo and Juliet,* Act IV, Scene V. 'Death lies on her like an untimely frost upon the sweetest flower of all the field.' Darse loved Shakespeare. She loved Christmas too. That's why we got married on Christmas Day. She loved decorating for all the holidays, but Christmas was her favorite. She would've loved what you did with the house, by the way. It would've made her proud. I think maybe I'd forgotten that. Thank you, son, for reminding me." He dabbed a tear from the corner of his eye. "Now, let's head on back home. I think Mrs. Tucker should have dinner just about ready by the time we get back, and there might even be pie."

The day after Christmas of 1957 was a Thursday. Even so, Dr. Hines had closed his office through New Year's. Of course, had anyone needed him, he would've happily made a house call. Such was the nature of medical practice in a small town. The doctor went wherever and whenever there was need.

The morning dawned chilly but not cold. The dusting of snow from the morning before had disappeared from the ground except in a few shady spots where the sun could not reach. The sky was blue except for a smattering of cottony white clouds. It had all the makings of a beautiful winter day.

James woke at first light. His uncle had promised to teach him how to shoot his new rifle, and he was more than ready. Howard was still asleep, but James was pretty sure he knew how to wake him. He figured what better alarm clock could there possibly be than the aroma of frying bacon wafting up the stairs. That he'd never attempted to cook anything before that day did not faze him at all. He was eleven years old now, after all, so how hard could it be?

Dashing down the stairs to the kitchen, James found the cast-iron skillet from the morning before and placed it on the stove with a loud *CLANG*. Since the smell of breakfast cooking was supposed to rouse the sleeping bear from his hibernation, he thought a little "pan music" to accompany his preparations wouldn't harm a thing. They'd had scrambled eggs the morning before, so he decided to make pancakes. He'd watched Mrs. Tucker make them before, and it had looked easy enough.

First, he heated the skillet and tossed in several slices of bacon. In no time it was sizzling and popping. But no matter what he did, he could not make the bacon get crisp. Soon, the skillet began belching a thick, acrid smoke. At this he removed the pan from the burner and scraped the smoldering bacon onto a waiting plate where it crumbled into a thousand scorched pieces. Undaunted, he repeated the process again and, unsurprisingly, achieved the same result. This cooking stuff was a snap, he decided.

The bacon having been so plated, he turned his attention to his pancake batter. Mrs. Tucker used flour, water, baking powder, eggs, and sugar to make her batter. James wasn't sure how much of each ingredient he was to use but thought he had a pretty good idea. He found the largest mixing bowl in the cabinet and poured in half a bag of flour, then added a cup of sugar and a few eggs. He couldn't find the baking powder, so he substituted baking soda instead, thinking himself quite clever to be able to make such substitutions "on the fly." It was like he was a real chef. He guessed that a half-cup should be about right and then dumped in a little extra just to be safe. He mixed it all together with a long wooden spoon, stirring until his arms got tired. Then, figuring that he'd done as much as he could for his gourmet pancake batter, he placed the skillet, still awash in scorched bacon drippings, back onto the burner. As he waited for the skillet to heat up again, James picked the largest of the eggshells from the batter. When it was good and hot, he dumped half the contents of the mixing bowl onto the scalding grease, filling the bottom of the skillet. Soon, his blob of batter was bubbling and smoking like the La Brea Tar Pits.

Whenever Mrs. Tucker made pancakes, she was able to flip her pancakes with a simple flick of the wrist. Her perfectly browned, light, fluffy cake would rise a foot out of the pan, perform a flip that would make an Olympic gymnast jealous, and settle lightly back into the pan to brown the other side.

James's pancake flip did not turn out quite as well. No woolly mammoth ever found themselves trapped so securely by the bubbling goo at La Brea as that pancake was. Flick, flip, shake, and pry though he might, James simply could not break the bond of batter to pan. Finally, using both hands, he gave the skillet a mighty heave and, remarkably, the batter chose that precise moment to release its hold upon the pan. The goo sailed high into the air, hovering for an instant just below the fourteen-foot kitchen ceiling, before performing a perfect hammerhead turn and diving back toward earth like a fighter plane strafing a locomotive.

Off balance from the toss, James missed the strafing pancake on its plummet toward the center of the earth. Consequently, it splatted loudly upon the kitchen floor, forming a perfect brown, black, white, and yellow Rorschach test blot.

At this moment, Howard strode into the room and stopped suddenly just before the stove, taking in the carnage that had once been his kitchen. It looked like Pearl Harbor on December 8. A blizzard of flour, sugar, and baking soda formed drifts over the cabinets, a window, and one eleven-year-old boy while still falling in a light flurry from the rafters. A perfectly cured, cast-iron skillet foundered in the kitchen sink under a miasma of greasy brown water and steam. A crumbled pile of smoldering bacon dust sat in heaps on two dinner plates. Seeing the little boy standing proudly in the midst of this most unnatural of disasters, it was all Howard could do to keep from sweeping the boy up into a monstrous hug. Instead, wordlessly, he skirted around the blob of scorched batter in the floor, thinking, *Hmmf, looks like two bats playing tug of war over a witch's cauldron.* Then, he reached out and turned-off the stove, and tousled the boy's hair, displacing a cloud of white powder.

With a big smile, Howard said, "I vote Wilma-Jean's Café for breakfast this morning."

James sneezed violently, then solemnly raised his mixing spoon. "I second the motion, sir."

During the drive to Wilma-Jean's, breakfast, and the eventual return home, Howard did not say a single word about the morning's kitchen disaster. Instead, they talked about books and James's rifle. Upon their return home, James set himself to the restoration and repair of his uncle's kitchen.

CHAPTER 19

A FEW HOURS LATER, JAMES AND Howard reconvened in the study, ready for James's first shooting lesson. Much to his chagrin, the lesson had little to do with actual shooting. Instead, it focused upon familiarization with the rifle, its inner mechanisms and how/why each one worked. He learned how to break his rifle down for cleaning and how to reassemble the parts after everything was cleaned and oiled. Howard had him repeat the process dozens of times until James was certain he could've performed these acts blindfolded.

Howard went over his nine firearm safety rules again and made certain James understood each. Only then did he begin to discuss how to use the rifle. He explained the safety, stressing that the safety was to remain in the safe position until only an instant before firing. He demonstrated to James how to load and unload the magazine and how to work the bolt. Next, he demonstrated how to hold the rifle so it would be the most stable. Finally, he discussed the rifle's sights and, with an empty chamber, demonstrated how to use them to aim.

"Your rifle has an aperture sight. Basically, the rear sight is a peephole. Because of this, some people call it a peep sight. Peep sights are more accurate than standard iron post and groove sights. They are the sights used by the US Rifle Team in the Olympics. A telescopic sight may be more accurate over, say two hundred yards, but there's nothing better than a peep for hitting a moving target, and a peep sight won't fog up on you on a cold day."

"It looks kinda weird. How do you aim with a peep sight?" James asked.

"Simple. Look through the rear aperture and focus on the front sight. Place the dot of the front sight on or just below what you want to hit. Pull the trigger and hit your target."

Howard demonstrated proper aiming technique and handed the rifle to James. He was pleased to see that as soon as the boy had control of the rifle, he ejected the magazine and worked the bolt twice to verify it was not loaded. Only then did he bring the rifle up to his shoulder and aim toward a distant tree beyond the window.

"That looks about right, but keep both eyes open. I know that isn't what they do in the movies, but it'll make you a better shot, especially if your target's moving."

"Uncle, is it my imagination or do things look sharper and more focused through the sight?"

"Great observation! Peep sights can actually boost your vision. That's because your focus sharpens when you look through a small gap. It's like a camera lens. The field of view gets longer and sharper if it is stopped down to a tiny aperture."

"Huh?"

"Never mind. Just know that looking through a pinhole improves your optics. Ready to give this thing a try?"

"Yes, sir!" James almost ran to the door.

"Aren't you forgetting something?" Howard asked, gesturing to the rifle.

Looking sheepish, James walked back and picked up his rifle. Then together, the two walked into the woods, toward the millpond.

Arriving at the back of the dam, Howard set several dirt clods and small sheets of loose bark on the trunk of a pine tree that had been downed during an ice storm last winter. He then stepped off twenty-five paces and turned back to the fallen tree. Satisfied that the range was clear and the berm of the dam would provide an appropriate backstop, he handed James a box of .22 long rifle ammunition. He carefully watched as James slipped five rounds into the magazine and slid it home with a click.

Stepping behind his grand-nephew and pointing, Howard said, "You see that biggest piece of bark? The one on the far left?"

James nodded.

"Without chambering a round, I want you to grip your rifle like you are ready to shoot and aim at that big piece of bark."

James complied, and Howard adjusted his hand position on the fore stock and had him rest his cheek lightly against the stock. "Good, just like that. Now bring the rifle down and take it back up into the firing position again." James did as he was told, and Howard said, "Good. Now do it again... and again."

James followed his uncle's instructions, and each time his movements became more fluid and natural.

After he was happy with the motion, Howard said, "Okay, now chamber a round. Do *not* release the safety. Leave your trigger finger on the trigger guard and try it again."

James stiffened and struggled through the maneuver that he'd just done flawlessly more than twenty times.

"Relax! Nothing's changed. Just bring your rifle up, and aim...good...just like that...perfect. Excellent! Now bring your rifle back down and release the magazine...good. Now clear the bolt."

James did so, then looked up expectantly at Howard.

"Good. Now let's take the bullets out of the magazine and slide it back in."

"Yes sir."

"Good. Now, that you've assured yourself it's unloaded, take it back up to the firing position."

James did so smoothly.

"Aim at the same piece of bark. Look through the rear sight and place the dot on the front sight in the middle of your target. Good. Now, use your thumb to disengage the safety."

James lowered the rifle's barrel and fumbled the safety into the *FIRE* position. Only then did he bring the rifle back level.

"Okay, now thumb the safety off again...good...but this time when you bring the rifle back up, I want you to leave it up and level and deactivate the safety with your thumb without bringing your rifle down and without looking. Do it by feel."

James struggled initially but soon was able to perform the feat without losing sight of his target downrange or lowering the rifle.

"Great! Now engage your safety and bring your rifle back down."

James complied instantly, beginning to appreciate his uncle's somewhat pedantic, albeit effective, teaching technique.

"This next time, after you bring your rifle up, I want you to aim, disengage the safety—by feel—and then slip your finger from the trigger guard to the trigger and pull the trigger. When you pull the trigger, slowly and gently apply pressure straight back until the sear releases and you hear a snap. It's not a good habit to dry fire a weapon, but until you get used to shooting, it should be okay."

"Why's that, Uncle? What happens if you dry fire?"

"For a center fire rifle, very little. Your rifle is a rimfire, however, and if it gets dry fired excessively, it will cause peening, which is a dent that forms where the firing pin strikes the chamber mouth. A frequently dry fired rimfire rifle is prone to malfunction and misfiring."

"Okay, that makes sense. But a few dry fires are all right?"

"Shouldn't pose much of a problem," Howard reassured him.

After several tries, James quickly learned how to ease the trigger rearward and not to flinch at the snap of the firing pin.

"Now, let's try it for real. Go ahead and reload your magazine and go through each step just like you practiced."

Even with all of his practice and preparation, James flinched at the crack of the rifle, causing a puff of dirt to fly up a full two feet to the right of his target.

"That's all right, son. You'll always get a flier on the first shot out of a cold gun barrel. Go ahead and eject your round and try again," Howard said, patting the boy on the shoulder.

CRACK

"Eject, and again."

CRACK

"Eject. Again,"

CRACK

"One more time."

CRACK

By the fifth shot, James was no longer flinching as the rifle fired but was disappointed that none of his rounds had even nicked his target. All struck off to the right.

"Good job," Howard said. "Now for your next lesson, you'll need to learn how to adjust your sights. You see this screw? That's your windage, and this one's your elevation."

"Windage?"

"Windage is for right and left. If you are missing to the right of your target"—Howard produced a tiny screwdriver from his back pocket—"you turn the screw so that your rear sight moves left and vice versa. The same concept works for elevation, for high or low."

Howard flexed and released his hand several times. The cold was wreaking havoc with his arthritis.

"So I need to move my sight to the left?"

"Maybe."

"Maybe? But you said—"

"And what I said is correct, however, you were shooting offhand standing. When trying to sight a rifle, it is better to use a stable rest, like this tree stump. Here, take my jacket and roll it up. Put the jacket on top of the stump. Now, kneel down and rest the fore stock of your rifle on the jacket. That reduces movement as you aim. Good! Now try it again with another five rounds, using the stump to stabilize the fore stock and barrel."

James did as he was told. He still missed his target, but the cluster of puffs on the berm were much closer, although still low and to the right, of his bark target. Only then, did Howard allow him to adjust the rear sight. His joints protesting, he allowed James to make the adjustments. It was good practice for him, anyway.

After several more five-shot cycles, James was hitting the target but struggled to hit close to the center. Howard, however, had made several shots and easily grouped them all in a tight pattern near the target's center.

Becoming frustrated, James sighed and hung his head. "I guess I'm just not a very good shot."

"Don't worry, son! You'll get better with practice."

James suddenly brightened. "Maybe I just need glasses?" he said hopefully.

"No, that's not it. We checked your vision in my office when we did your school physical last summer. You were better than normal—20/15 in your right eye and 20/10 in your left."

"Okay," James replied, shuffling his feet in the leaves as he began trudging back toward the house. "I guess not." He shuffled along, barely holding back tears.

"Wait a minute!" Howard called after him. "I've got an idea. I want you to try something."

Totally deflated, James ambled back to Howard's side, his enthusiasm of the morning now a distant memory.

"Are you right-handed or left?" his uncle asked.

James held up his right hand, too dejected to speak.

"That's what I thought. Now, see that oak tree over there?"

James nodded.

"Good. I want you to hold your thumb up right in front of you so that it's lined up with the trunk of that oak. Do it with both eyes open."

James did.

"Focus on that tree and don't move your thumb. Now I want you to close your right eye. Now open it and close your left eye. Now right. Now left."

James felt foolish but did as he was asked.

"Now, when you open just one eye, through which one does it look like the thumb is still aligned with the tree?"

"This one," James replied, pointing to his left eye.

"Hot damn!" Howard shouted, dancing around like he had just won the Moose Lodge raffle. "I knew it! You're not a bad shot, son. You're left-eye dominant! Come on, let's walk back up to the house and I'll explain."

On the way back, Howard explained to James that everyone has a dominant eye. Typically, right-handed people are right-eye dominant and left-handers are left-eye dominant. However, about 25 percent of right-handers will be left-eye dominant. In daily life, this has little bearing, but for a shooter it can be challenging. One can learn to shoot passably well with their nondominant eye but will usually be more accurate if they conform to their dominance.

All James needed to do was learn to shoot left-handed.

"I don't know if it's true, but I think I remember reading somewhere that Annie Oakley was left-eye dominant," Howard confided in a conspiratorial tone.

"Annie Oakley? Really!"

"It might've been Calamity Jane, but I'm pretty sure it was one of them."

Of course, Howard had made it up on the spot, but his little white lie had had its desired effect. James was once again *very* excited about his prospects for becoming a marksman.

After breaking down his rifle and cleaning it thoroughly, James began the process of teaching himself to shoot left-handed. He set himself to the problem with all the industry he had displayed while teaching himself to draw. Over the next month, he spent countless hours in his room going through each of the drills his uncle had taught him initially, albeit now, left-handed. After a great deal of effort, he mastered the movements. He found his biggest challenge to be operating the bolt action of his rifle with the "wrong" hand.

After James had mastered the processes of aiming, firing, and working the bolt left-handed, he and Howard returned to the dam for more target practice, and the contrast in his accuracy shooting left- versus right-handed were striking. Left-handed, James rarely missed. He was routinely able to hit quarter-sized dirt clods from a range of fifty paces. At that range, Howard could barely see the clods, at least not until they exploded in a puff of powder. Left-handed, James was a natural marksman par excellence.

When Howard was convinced that James had mastered all the rules of firearm safety, he allowed James to practice his marksmanship alone. The only caveat was that someone, either he or Mrs. Tucker, had to be home and within earshot while he was practicing. James found this restriction to be limiting. Except for weekends, his uncle was rarely home during daylight hours, especially during the shortened daylight hours of winter. Similarly, Mrs. Tucker, with all the house windows and doors closed, would not be able to hear him call out from the dam.

James's solution was to build a rifle range in the backyard. There, Mrs. Tucker would be able to hear him easily should he need help, and she could watch him through the back kitchen window. He found a book in the Holly Springs Public Library detailing how to build a rifle range and found most of the materials he would need to create his range in the barn. Howard was impressed by James's firing range plans and readily gave his approval for the project.

In the years before her death, James's Grand-Aunt Doris had loved gardening and ordered a truckload of railroad crossties to be used for building flower beds around the house. After completing the project, she'd stored the left-over ties in the barn for future projects but never had opportunity to use them. James cut them to length using an old crosscut saw and created a six-foot square he positioned along the back wall of the barn. He filled the space within the ties with several wheelbarrow loads of sand from the creek behind the mill pond.

To create a rear baffle for his range, he used a six-by-six-foot section of quarter-inch boiler plate he'd found in the barn. The plate had once been used as a temporary patch for the footbridge down by the town's grist mill. Howard had salvaged the four-hundred-pound slab of steel for use in some long-forgotten project, stored it in the barn, and promptly forgot about it. With a block and tackle and considerable straining, James successfully positioned the boiler plate flat over the freshly created sand pit. He drilled a hole near the leading edge of the plate through which he mounted an eye bolt. With the base plate wedged against the base of the barn wall as a fulcrum and a series of pulleys he mounted to an overhanging eave, he could raise and lower the plate like a hatch cover without much effort. He drove nails into the barn's wall so that the pulley chain could be secured with the baffle positioned at a forty-five-degree angle, guaranteeing that spent projectiles would ricochet safely downward into the sand pit rather than in a less-safe direction. He figured that when not in use, his boiler-plate baffle could double as a cover to prevent the sand pit from filling with water during rainstorms. Finally, he wound baling wire around the baffle to provide an attachment point for paper targets.

With his sand pit and baffle finally completed, James used string to set out firing positions at 25, 50, 75, 100, and 125 yards. He fashioned cubes of wood from another crosstie and drove two 40-penny nails side by side into the bases of each, leaving three inches of the nails sticking out to anchor the cubes to the ground. This alleviated the need to remeasure distances each time he used the range and allowed him to pull them from the ground whenever he needed to mow the grass.

Having promised his uncle that he wouldn't try out his firing range until it had been officially "inspected and approved," James impatiently waited...and waited. Never having been comfortable with idle hands, he carefully planed and sanded each of the blocks and then painted range numbers onto each. Unfortunately, his wait lasted well past dark, and by then it was far too late for Howard to inspect his handiwork. But that didn't prevent James from chattering about his range all through dinner and well into the night.

Howard had been dubious when James initially described his plans for the rifle range project. Although he'd thought the design well-conceived, he'd doubted that James would be able to execute them. There was no harm in letting the boy try. Now, faced with a completed, totally functional, totally safe rifle range, he couldn't help but be impressed. Howard shook his head in amazement. That boy was a wonder.

After receiving his uncle's blessing on the range design, James began marksmanship training in earnest. Every sunny day after school, he spent at least two hours practice shooting. Each night, after the evening spent reading and discussing books with Howard, he drew new targets in his sketchbook for the next day's practice.

As he practiced, James often thought of Anna. And through practice and in his burgeoning skill, he found peace. Howard had been right—a gun really *was* just a tool, and he was going to make *darned* sure nobody was going to be hurt by one of his tools *ever* again. So motivated, his interest never waned. With a box of fifty .22 LR cartridges costing only twenty-five cents, he was able to fire off thousands of rounds each month for the cost of mowing two lawns. He practiced shooting offhand, kneeling, seated, and prone. By spring, he routinely was able to put fifty rounds into a grouping the size of a quarter from his fifty-yard firing position.

When his marksmanship abilities were no longer challenged at fifty yards, James extended his range to seventy-five and later one hundred yards. Beyond that, he noticed more influence of wind upon his accuracy. He struggled until he placed a small flag atop the barn with which to better estimate wind speed and direction. Thereafter, he could shoot respectably tight groupings from 125 yards. His abilities beyond 125 yards remained unchallenged due to lack of space. There simply was no additional room for him to extend his firing range.

Hemmed in by lack of real estate, James turned to the types of trick shots that had so impressed him back during last summer's exhibition. If Herb Parsons could do it, then why couldn't he?

James found that the easiest to replicate of Parsons's tricks was snuffing out a candle. That trick he was soon able to accomplish with regularity from as far out as a hundred yards. More challenging was shooting the aspirin tablet from atop a balloon. This he performed easily at fifty yards and eight out of ten times at seventy-five yards but seldom at ranges beyond that. Initially, he struggled at cutting a playing card in half, but after another month of practice was routinely successful at a range of twenty-five yards and occasionally even at fifty.

There were two tricks James did not attempt to replicate or master. The first was the rapid-fire demonstration that had so thrilled him at the expo. Parsons had employed a lever action rifle for this feat. With James shooting left-handed while using a right-handed bolt-action rifle, reproduction of the trick was an impossibility.

The second trick, James declined to attempt due to safety concerns. This was shooting at charcoal briquettes that had been tossed into the air. Citing Howard's fourth firearm safety rule, he declined to try. Although he was reasonably confident that he could easily hit the target briquettes, there was no way of knowing where his bullet would fall thereafter.

Rather than risk it, James created a couple tricks of his own. For the first, he mounted an axe head atop a gallon paint can. Behind and to each side of the axe, he placed a soda can. The object was to shoot the axe head, split the bullet, and have a piece of the bullet strike each of the soda cans. He was able to perform this shot routinely from fifty yards and at least half of the time from seventy-five. Having already mastered the ability to cut a playing card in half, James did not find this trick to be at all challenging, but it *looked* impressive to spectators.

Another trick James mastered but later discarded from his trick-shot repertoire was that of shooting the bottom from a soda bottle from his fifty-yard firing position. For this shot, he set the bottle into the fork of a branch driven into the sand. The object of this shot was to shoot the bottom out of the bottle by firing through its mouth, while leaving the bottle's neck and mouth undamaged. Although an impressive feat of marksmanship, he abandoned it after cutting his trigger finger on glass shards while setting up a subsequent shot. It took twelve stitches and almost month before his finger healed well enough for him to resume his target practice.

In addition to the stitches in his hand, James had required another six on the back of his head due to his reaction to the first injury. There had been very little pain associated with the gash on his hand, but when James saw the blood spurting from his forefinger and base of his thumb, he became nauseous. His face had lost all color and, a moment later, he felt as though the ground was sucking him into it. He collapsed, striking his head on a stone paver, and woke a few moments later in Howard's arms, being carried to the house.

At the house, Howard cleaned and then sutured James's two lacerations.

"Uncle, what happened?" James asked as his head cleared a bit.

"You passed out and hit your head. You'll be fine," the old man replied with a kindly smile.

"Okay, but why? Is there something wrong with me? Does this mean I have a brain tumor or something?"

Sensing the boy's anxiety, Howard explained, "You had a vagal event. It happens to lots of people, say with pain, shock, or at the sight of blood."

James's natural curiosity immediately kicked in. "Vagal event? What's that?"

"The vagus nerve—"

"Like Las Vegas?"

"No," Howard replied. "*V-A-G-U-S.*"

For most of his patients, Howard—Doctor Hines— would've left the explanation at that. But with James being so bright and inquisitive, he decided to go into full-on professor mode and lay out the details.

"As you know, the brain controls all movement and bodily functions. The vast majority of the impulses from the brain travel down the spinal cord to the body. There are twelve pairs of nerves, called cranial nerves, that get to their destinations in the body *without* using the spinal cord to take them there. The vagus nerve is the tenth cranial nerve. It leaves the brain and goes through a tiny hole in the base of the skull. Then it runs down the carotid arteries in the neck, down to the gut and back up to the heart."

"How would that make me pass out?" James asked.

"Well, the job of the vagus nerve is to control digestion, heart rate, and blood pressure. So, if you overstimulate the vagus nerve, it causes the heart rate to slow and that makes the blood pressure drop. If your pressure falls far enough, you pass out, and quite often you'll feel very nauseated before you go down. It can happen to anybody."

"That makes sense. But why does it happen to *me*?" James asked, once again feeling concerned.

Howard smiled. "It's because you're so dang healthy!"

"Huh?"

"Yep! Your blood pressure usually runs a little on the low side, which is healthy. People usually start becoming light-headed with a systolic—that's the top number—blood pressure of around 90 millimeters mercury. A normal systolic blood pressure is about 120. Yours usually runs no higher than 100. So, you don't have as large of a safety margin if your blood pressure drops like the rest of us. Stimulate your vagus nerve and down you go. It will be more likely to occur if you aren't drinking enough fluids and are a little dehydrated."

"Thanks, Uncle! Still, I think I'll leave the Coke bottle trick out of my shooting exhibition," James said, nodding his head in understanding.

"I think that's maybe a good idea," his uncle agreed.

When James was finally able to resume shooting, the trick shot he found to be the most difficult to master was that of using a rifle bullet to light a standard wooden kitchen match. The key to successful execution was to barely graze the striker patch on the matchhead's tip without damaging the match. He practiced this trick first from fifty yards. He was able to knock the head off the match or cut the matchstick, but try as he might, he couldn't cause a strike. Finally, he gave up and moved up to twenty-five yards. There, on his second shot, the match sparked into flame. With another week of practice, he rarely failed to achieve a light and was commonly successful at fifty yards.

Sometimes, when he wanted to show off for Howard or Mrs. Tucker, James would drag them out to his range where he placed a candle slightly above an unlit match. Then he'd fire two shots in rapid succession. With the first, he lit the match, which in turn, lit the candle. With his second shot, he snuffed the flames of each without damaging either the matchstick or the candle. This, he found, was always a crowd pleaser.

CHAPTER 20

MAY 1958

AS WINTER TURNED INTO SPRING and spring to summer, James found he had less free time for target practice because of the demands of his busy lawn-mowing business, ongoing art projects, and school. Many weeks, he was only able to practice on weekends, and not even then if the weather didn't cooperate.

School was the part of his life that demanded the least of his time. There, everything came easily. James's only issue with school was that he had little in common with his fellow students. He was far more interested in discussing rocketry and Sputnik with his teachers or politics with the school janitor than he was talking with his classmates about Stan Musial's latest home run, the adventures of Matt Dillon, or Red Skelton's latest TV skit. Lack of interest with peers notwithstanding, James got along quite well at school. He had no conduct issues, and his academic performance was superlative. Therefore, he was justifiably surprised when Mrs. Ledford, his English Literature teacher and school counselor, sent him home with a note for his uncle requesting a "parent-teacher" conference at the end of the 1958 spring term.

The note was cryptic, only stating that she wished to speak with Dr. Hines about school issues and James's future on the following Thursday at close of school. Frowning, Howard read the note and, after James assured him that he was as much in the dark as he regarding the reason for the meeting, penned his response, which James delivered the next day.

When Thursday arrived, Holly Springs was in the throes of a mini-epidemic of stomach flu. Consequently, at the appointed time, Dr. Hines still had a dozen patients in the office who'd been suffering from vomiting and explosive diarrhea. Unable to leave, he called the school and extended his regrets to Mrs. Ledford, offering to reschedule their meeting to another date. Rather than rescheduling, she responded that she'd be quite happy to have the meeting later that day, after school and office hours. She suggested she could wait at the coffee shop down the street from his office, and he should swing by whenever his clinic was finally empty. No, it would be no inconvenience at all. She had plenty to keep her occupied while waiting. Over his objections, she assured him that she would be just fine until he arrived and he shouldn't worry or try to rush.

More than a little frazzled, Dr. Hines rushed into the coffee shop three hours later. "Mrs. Ledford, please accept my apologies for being so late," he blurted as he puffed up to her table. "I swear, half the town must be sick, and I—"

"Never you mind, Dr. Hines," she said, smiling warmly and putting down a copy of *Anna Karenina*. "You are a doctor, and these things are to be expected. Besides, Mr. Tolstoy has been outstanding company during the wait, and Florence has kept my coffee cup full the whole time. Would you like a cup?"

Mrs. Ledford's voice was pure Vivien Leigh from *Gone with the Wind*. It would not have surprised Howard one bit had she responded to his tardiness with, "Well, fiddle-dee-dee."

"Well, don't just stand there, Doctor. Do sit down!" she said with a flourish, clearing her stylish leather portfolio from the table.

Howard settled into the booth opposite Mrs. Ledford. It had been a long day in the office and his back was killing him. It felt good just to be off his feet.

"Thank you. And, yes, coffee would be wonderful," he responded. Then he motioned to her copy of *Anna Karenina* and quoted the book's first line, "Happy families are all alike; every unhappy family is unhappy in its own way."

Behind Mrs. Ledford's tortoiseshell, cats-eye glasses, her brown eyes immediately brightened. "Oh, you are familiar with *Anna Karenina*, Doctor Hines." With her honied southern accent, it came out "Doc-tuh," and somehow "Hines" had at least two syllables. "That's just grand! Most of the people I have met here in Holly Springs have been more familiar with Louis L'Amour than Tolstoy, not that there's anything *wrong* with liking Mr. L'Amour's books, of course."

"Certainly not!" He laughed. "I take it that you're not originally from around here?"

"You are correct. I was born and bred in New Orleans. I moved here after the war...after my husband died. Let's just say there were too many ghosts back in the Crescent City for me to stay. A teaching position came open in Holly Springs, and I have been here ever since. I've been happy enough. After all, 'If you look for perfection, you'll never be content,' at least according to Mr. Tolstoy."

The two chatted companionably about books, backgrounds, and family. All the time, Florence kept their coffee mugs filled. Howard appreciated Mrs. Ledford's easy laugh, and their conversation flowed effortlessly. After what seemed only to have been a moment, Howard glanced at his watch. Then he looked again. They had been talking for over *two hours.*

"Oh my, look at the time! It's just so nice to talk with someone so well read. Usually, the only person who seems to enjoy these conversations is James."

"Goodness, yes...James." Mrs. Ledford appeared momentarily flustered. "Yes, I asked to see you today so that I could talk with you about James. As you may be aware, I am James's English teacher, but I also serve as school counselor."

"I hope that he's not been any trouble."

"Oh, gracious, no! He is an absolute delight."

"Is he having problems in your class?"

"Absolutely not. He could probably *teach* it."

"So..."

"That's just it. I've talked with his other teachers and he's not having problems in any of his classes."

"And this is a problem?"

"Heavens, no! It's just that he's not being challenged at all by anything in *any* of his classes. I have talked with his other teachers, and I, well...we all believe that instead of James going into the eighth grade next semester, we should move him up to the tenth grade instead."

"I know that he's bright, but do you really think that—"

"Doctor Hines, James is more than just bright. I performed an abbreviated IQ test on him, and his score returned at 166. With a full test, he would likely score even higher. In all honesty, he could easily perform college level work."

"But you only recommend moving him up two grades?"

"Yes, as I was saying, he could easily do college work, but from a developmental stage, that would be quite a leap for a twelve-year-old boy. He is something of a savant. He has a genius-level IQ but only the coping skills and understanding of a little boy. He's already rather quiet and reserved, something of a loner, and I understand that he was involved in some kind of family trauma?" She raised her eyebrows, then continued, "Eventually, his body will catch up with his mind, but I'm afraid if we force him too far, too quickly, it might do him harm."

"I've seen that, and I agree. And, yes, James definitely suffered a family trauma, as you say." He proceeded to give Mrs. Ledford an abridged version of James's story and then asked, "Have you discussed any of this with him yet?"

"No. We wanted to talk with you first."

"A hundred and sixty-six?" Howard mused. "That doesn't surprise me at all, not one bit. Yes...yes, I will talk with James about this this evening...well, too late for evening. I'll talk with him tonight. He, of all people, will understand what this means and should be involved in any decision. Mrs. Ledford—"

"Please, call me Charlotte!"

"Yes, of course...Charlotte. Thank you for bringing this to my attention." After a moment's hesitation, he continued, "And thank you for a lovely evening. However, if I'm to call you Charlotte, then you must refer to me as Howard."

"All right, Howard it is!" she said, flashing a smile.

He grinned. "Nothing is so necessary for a young man as the company of intelligent women."

"Isn't that from *War and Peace*? You really do know your Tolstoy! You are simply delightful, Howard. We should...do this again...sometime?"

Howard surprised himself. "Why yes. Yes, we should! May I...walk you to your car?"

"I'm right out front, but yes."

Charlotte collected her things and walked to the door, which Howard, like the true southern gentlemen he was, opened for her. At the car, she turned and offered him her hand. At the last instant, she pulled back her hand, and instead planted a quick kiss on his surprised cheek. A moment later, she sped away, leaving Howard shocked, standing in a swirling cloud of dust...and feelings.

And an old man too, he thought, remembering the quote from *War and Peace.*

Howard sat in the coffee shop's parking lot with his car engine idling for quite some time. He'd had a wonderful evening with Charlotte. The time had seemed to fly by. Now, he needed to think. He had to make sense of his scrambled thoughts before going home to talk with James. Absent-mindedly, he caressed the spot on his cheek where Charlotte had kissed him. It was the first time since Doris...

"Ahhh, I'm just an old fool, imagining things that aren't really there," he muttered to himself. "What am I thinking? Charlotte can't be a day over fifty...". Then he shifted the Cadillac into gear and drove home, lost in thought.

———

James was in the library reading *Flowers for Algernon* by Daniel Keyes when he heard his uncle's car pull into the drive. Nervous that the meeting with Mrs. Ledford had lasted so long and fearing the worst, he met Howard at the door.

"Hi, Uncle. How was the meeting with Mrs. Ledford?"

"It was…fine," came Howard's distracted response. He was still flustered by the time spent with Mrs. Ledford—Charlotte—and the kiss that punctuated their evening, and needed a few minutes to process his feelings.

"Mrs. Tucker left your supper plate in the oven for you. It's liver and onions," James said, scrunching his nose up in distaste. "So…how'd it go?"

"Fine. We can talk later. Go on back to your book. Do you know if Mrs. Tucker made any pie?"

"Does peach cobbler count as pie?"

"Close enough."

"Would you like to talk while you're eating? I don't mind sitting at the table with you," James asked hopefully, his insides doing flips.

"That's okay. I won't be long. Just go back to your book. What are you reading tonight?"

"*Flowers for Algernon.*"

"I'm not familiar with that one. What's it about?"

"A man named Charlie Gordon. He isn't very smart, but he agrees to undergo an experimental surgical procedure to increase his intelligence. The procedure worked for a mouse named Algernon, and the scientists want to try it on a human. I just started it, but I think it has a lot of ways that it can go and it's written like a series of diary entries. It should be interesting."

"Sounds like it…I'll be there in a few minutes. We'll talk then," Howard said before disappearing into the kitchen, his mind still on the kiss. What had it meant? Nothing? Something…?

James stared up at his uncle. "Yes, sir."

James felt a wave of dread, thinking the meeting with Mrs. Ledford must have gone really badly if his uncle didn't even want to talk with him about it. Dutifully, he returned to the library where he fidgeted nervously until Howard ambled in several minutes later. James watched as he browsed the shelves, finally selecting a leather-bound copy of *Anna Karenina* and settling into his usual chair by the fireplace.

Rather than reading, Howard simply held the book in his lap and stared unseeing toward the mantel.

Howard usually didn't act this way and his face *did* seem a bit flushed. Maybe he was ill? "Uncle, are you okay?" James asked, a worried expression on his face.

James's apparent concern for his well-being snapped Howard from his reverie.

"Oh, yes, dear boy...I am quite well. Thank you for asking. I'm just an old man lost in old man thoughts. Think nothing of it," Howard said with a reassuring smile, once again acting like himself.

"How was the meeting with Mrs. Ledford?" James asked in a tremulous voice.

"Yes, yes...Charlotte and I had the most wonderful meeting..."

Charlotte? James thought.

Howard went on to reassure that James that he'd not been implicated in any mischief in school, and there were no issues with any of his classes. On the contrary, the reason for the meeting was his superlative academic achievements and how his teachers believed he needed to be more challenged than was possible at his grade level. Because of this, they believed he should jump to the tenth grade next term.

Although relieved to hear he wasn't in trouble, James was totally nonplussed by the idea of advancing so rapidly. True, he found little challenge in the basic algebra, simple grammar, and social studies that his teachers had gone over this past school year. He had been far more intrigued by the physical chemistry, analytic geometry, and multivariable calculus textbooks his cousin Charles had left underneath his bed when he'd graduated from college and left for the army. It was also true that even after two years in Holly Springs, he still felt like an outsider with his classmates. Most of them had been together since first grade or even longer. Holly Springs, though larger than Boiling Springs, was still a small town, after all. Most of the kids in his classes had parents who'd also grown up together. They formed an insular group, one that was difficult to crack, especially for an introverted loner with a mysterious background. That James refused to discuss life before Holly Springs only served to widen the chasm between him and his fellow students. He had a few friends, but there was no one with whom he felt particularly close...and there was no one even remotely like Anna.

Howard explained that he and Mrs. Ledford had discussed the pros and cons for skipping grades and believed it would be in his best interest. He also assured him that, ultimately, the final decision would be James's and he would support whatever decision he made.

For the first time since he had come to live with his uncle Howard, James was unable to concentrate on the book open before him. He just couldn't bring himself to focus on the page. So, after an hour of desultory page turning, he bade his uncle good night and went upstairs to bed.

Howard laid *Anna Karenina* on the armrest of his chair and gave James a hug and kiss good night. Watching him climb the stairs and, for the umpteenth time over the past two years, thought how much James reminded him of his son, Charles.

Safely ensconced in his room, James was a caged tiger, pacing back and forth between his desk and the turreted window. As he paced, he gave his inner thoughts voice.

"Uncle says I'm a genius. He's the smartest person I know, so he must be right. I don't feel like a genius. But how's a genius supposed to feel, anyway? If I move up two grades, I won't have any friends. But really, I don't have any now. I'm already an outsider. What's there to lose? I think tomorrow, I'm gonna tell Uncle and Mrs. Ledford that I want to move up."

His decision made, James stopped pacing, and took down Gould's *The Birds of Asia*. He sat on the side of his bed and read to Anna the section about the long-tailed broadbill—her favorite. Finishing, he placed the book on his nightstand, turned out the light, and immediately fell asleep.

Alone in his study, Howard's thoughts wandered to his afternoon and evening with Charlotte. He absently rubbed his cheek. "Nah...I'm old enough to be her father," he mumbled to himself.

Howard shook his head, stood, and returned *Anna Karenina* to its place on the bookshelf. Then he hobbled slowly up the stairs to his bedroom, his arthritic knees protesting every step.

There, from his bedside table, a framed photograph of Doris lovingly smiled back at him, just like she had fifty-one years ago on their wedding day. On Doris's bedside table, under a pair of half-moon reading glasses, still lay her unfinished copy of Françoise Sagan's *Bonjour Tristesse*.

Howard did a double-take and stared back at Doris's picture. This time, she *wasn't* smiling back at him just like she had on their wedding day. Tonight, she was smiling... *approvingly*?

CHAPTER 21

1958–1964

W ITH NOTHING TO HOLD HIM back, James elected to make the jump to the tenth grade. The challenge would be fun. In spite of lacking the prerequisites for many of his classes, he graduated two years later at age fifteen from Holly Springs High as valedictorian for the class of 1964. That fall, after accepting the offer of a full, $175-per-year academic scholarship, he made history by becoming the youngest student ever to matriculate into the University of North Carolina at Chapel Hill.

There, James majored in biology and took a minor in chemistry. Individually, he found the classes to be little more challenging than those he'd taken in high school. Time management was more of a struggle because the sheer volume of material being covered contemporaneously was daunting. Nonetheless, James excelled. He even had time to tutor his roommate, Cliff, in precalculus math and general chemistry.

Cliff Waters had been a standout strong safety for his high school team in New Jersey and recruited to play football for the Tar Heels. Cliff was eighteen, and upon meeting his bookish new fifteen-year-old roommate, was immediately disdainful. He teased him mercilessly about being too young to shave, date, or drive, and James often found himself the butt of practical jokes and pranks. As the academic year progressed and Cliff found himself on academic probation and at risk of losing his football scholarship, he began seeing his roommate in a new light.

After a month of James's tutoring, Cliff's F- in chemistry and F in precalc had risen to a C+ and B- respectively. Tar Heels's head coach, Jim Hickey, was pleased by his strong safety's sudden academic turnaround and inquired of Cliff what had changed. Cliff gave all the credit to James, and soon Coach Hickey was paying James ten dollars per week to serve as team tutor, with four other team starters soon coming under his tutelage. Always willing to help the athletes with their classes, he soon became the team's de facto *little brother*. He was invited to all team events and even traveled with the team for away games. For the first time in his life, James *belonged*.

James enjoyed the attention received from his extended football family and, by extension, from ever-present coeds who hung around the team like groupies. However, much to his chagrin, the latter *also* treated him like *their* little brother. That he was shy and prone to blushing probably didn't help him appear more grown-up either. The girls told him that he was "so cute" and pinched his cheek, but they *never once* offered to kiss it.

Although he still loved and missed his estranged parents, James now considered Holly Springs his home. He continued to write letters to his family, but he'd long ago given up hope of receiving any reply. Similarly, he'd long ago stopped pestering Howard about wanting to visit his parents. Sometimes, they'd receive bits of family news through his grandmother, Mary, but it had become increasingly clear that, in the hearts and minds of the Hamiltons of Boiling Springs, James Wiley Hamilton no longer existed.

Still, James was happy and his life was full. With classes and his responsibilities with the football team, his days were quite busy and he rarely had the opportunity to return even to Holly Springs for visits. His one extended visit occurred during the summer between his freshman and sophomore years at UNC. He had a full slate of summer classes and tutoring work but returned home for the entire week of July 4th for his uncle's wedding.

During their meeting in the coffee shop, Howard and Mrs. Ledford had discovered that they had a great deal in common and a relationship had blossomed. They each loved books and could easily spend hours discussing them. Often, they did precisely that. They both enjoyed fine dining, travel, and shared an appreciation for fine wines. Consequently, their honeymoon was to be held at the Tenuta Tignanello Estate and Vineyard in Tuscany. Afterward, Howard planned to close his practice and retire from medicine, sell the farm, and move to Scottsdale. The hot, dry weather there should be good for his arthritis. From there, together, the world would be their oyster.

James was thrilled to see Howard so happy. He was also proud and greatly honored that his uncle had chosen him to serve as his best man.

CHAPTER 22

AUGUST 27, 1964

T O CELEBRATE JAMES'S SEVENTEENTH BIRTH-DAY, Cliff and several friends from the football team decided to take him out on the town. The plan was to get him drunk and, if possible, get him laid. The guys were reasonably certain they'd be able to accomplish the first. The second would pose more of a challenge, especially if James was to be left to his own devices. But they had worked out a play that just might work.

Around his friends from the football team, James was quick-witted and incisive. He possessed a dry sense of humor that flew outside the scope of the average person's radar. He had the ability to verbally chop, dice, and puree any opponent. Not until hours later would that person even realize they'd been insulted. James could wax poetic for hours about Plato's *The Republic*, Euclidean geometry, or particle physics and never break a sweat. But put him around someone with a pair of X chromosomes and he'd become as timid as a rabbit living under a hawk's nest. His formerly golden tongue turned to lead. It was alchemy in reverse.

The plan was to take James to Minsky's Tavern near campus. After a few brewskis, he might just lighten up enough to give himself a chance—or at least enough to get out of his own way. They even knew a girl who liked guiding boys along the road to becoming men, and she was an experienced guide, sort of a...coed Sherpa. Since a guy never forgets his first time, by her math, she would be fondly remembered by about half the football team, two members of the basketball team, and at least one member of the faculty.

After football practice, Cliff would pick James up at the dorm and conduct him to Minsky's. There, they'd meet the rest of the guys, who would start buying rounds and getting him drunk. Ginger would just happen to drop by with some of her girlfriends and be introduced to the birthday boy. The two would talk for a while and then slip out back to Cliff's Studebaker...bada-bing, bada-boom, instant manhood. What could possibly go wrong?

And the plan worked flawlessly—right up until the point where it didn't.

For his part, James had no desire or intention to celebrate his birthday. True, the day was the seventeenth anniversary of his birth, but this was also the ninth anniversary of the worst day in his life. He planned to pass this birthday as he had the past eight—lost in remembrances of Anna. Alone in his dorm room, he filled several pages of his sketchbook with her likeness. In one, her cherubic face with its impish grin was framed by perfect ringlets that danced upon her slender shoulders before church on Sunday morning. In another, James's favorite if he was being totally honest with himself, her hair had bits of straw sticking out of it and was wild like Medusa's. Her face shone with unabashed joy as she gazed down at the baby bunny she cradled in her tiny little hands. That was the way he most liked to remember her. In yet another, the image caught her with her little feet a few inches off the ground in midjump. Her hands were clasped together, and he could almost hear her begging him to, "Read me the birdies, Jibby. Read me the birdies!"

There was one image that he never committed to paper but was never far from his mind. It was of Anna clutching her chest as her life blood bubbled out and stained her tiny little fingers, a look of shock and terror on her face as she slumped to the floor. "Jibby! Jib...bey!"

With a tear in the corner of his eye, James shook his head to clear the image from his mind. *I'm so sorry, Anna! Please forgive me!*

Just then, Cliff burst into the room. "Jim-boe, whatcha' doin', buddy? Wipe that hang-dog expression off your face! Get dressed! We're goin' out on the town," he said, his usual New Jersey machine-gun delivery set to fully automatic. "Get a move on! Chop-chop!"

"Ummm...I don't think—"

"Nope! We're goin' out, you and me. No buts about it. Got big plans for you tonight, my man. Biiiiiig plans! Why you still sittin' there?"

"No, I—"

"Not gonna hear it. Get your ass dressed. We're goin' out tonight." Then, closing James's sketchbook, he said, "Nice lookin' kid! You draw this? Ya gotcha some talent there."

"But—"

"No buts, amigo! It's your birthday. There's a beer out there with your name on it, and I'm buyin'!" He tossed James a clean shirt from his wardrobe. "Get a move on, buddy-boy!"

James sighed. "All right, maybe just one."

"That's the spirit, Chief!" Cliff said and started singing, "Everybody Loves Somebody."

Cliff actually does a pretty decent Dean Martin, James thought as he changed his shirt. *Let's get this over with...it might even be fun.*

The owner of Minsky's Tavern was Oleg Kominsky. He'd lost three fingers in an industrial accident in a Pittsburgh steel mill in 1947. After the accident, the union had filed suit on his behalf, claiming that an unsafe workplace and improper management had caused his injury. They'd won the case and with the settlement money, Kominsky had moved south and opened a tavern in Chapel Hill.

He named his bar Minsky's Tavern figuring that Kominsky's would sound too foreign for an insular southern town. There used to be another bar in Minsky's location, but its owner never came back from the war. Consequently, Kominsky was able to buy the place, lock, stock, and whiskey barrel for a song. The bank wanted it off their books, and he wanted a bar—win-win. Over the next year, he'd gutted and totally remodeled the entire building. By the time he'd finished, all that remained from the original establishment was a beautifully restored mahogany bar and a giant mounted moose head.

The moose head hung behind the bar and quickly became the centerpiece of the establishment. It was an immediate hit with his patrons and became known as "Minsky's Moose." It was so popular, Kominsky commissioned a drawing of a moose to be incorporated into the Minsky's Tavern sign and had it printed on his bar napkins. At Christmas, the moose wore a Santa hat. Around Easter, it sprouted bunny ears. For Halloween, it was adorned with spider webs. And in his storeroom, Kominsky maintained a cardboard box nearly filled with sundry items he'd found decorating his moose.

Cliff and James arrived just after dark. There was already a decent crowd, especially for a weeknight. Manfred Mann's "Do Wah Diddy Diddy" was playing on the jukebox when they walked in. From a corner table, Tim Gabrish, a defensive end James tutored in English composition, saw them and waved them back. Already there and a few pitchers into their evening were the team's middle linebacker, Joey Cooley, also known as Joe Cool, and William Orzechewski, their starting defensive right tackle.

"Yo, yo, yo! Happy birthday, Ace!" said Orzechewski, sliding a glass of beer to James.

"Thanks, Ski!" James replied. "Cliff didn't tell me you guys would be here."

"What? And miss your birthday? Not a chance!" said Cooley.

"Happy boithday, Hamilton!" said Gabrish with his sharp New Jersey accent, slapping him on the back and causing James to spill beer in his lap. Then, sotto voce to Cliff, "The girls will be here soon. Ginger's down with it. She gets off on this kinda thing. We're all set. The kid's gonna have his most memorable boithday ever!"

"Thanks, guys!" James smiled dutifully, sponged the beer out of his lap, and took a sip from what was left in the glass. He liked the guys from the team, and they seemed genuinely to like him. The least he could do was *act* like he was enjoying himself.

An hour and two pitchers of beer later, James was feeling rather mellow. As the jukebox played "I Get Around" by the Beach Boys, four girls materialized at their table as though by magic. One was Cliff's on-again, off-again girlfriend, Patricia, but James didn't recognize the other three. Introductions were made all around, and promptly, as though choreographed, the girls paired off with the guys.

Patty stayed with Cliff, and Debbie immediately began chatting with Ski, suggesting that they were already acquainted.

Joe Cool gave off something of a "bad-boy" vibe, so the girls seemed to just love running their fingers through his wavy, swept-back blond hair. James couldn't understand it. He liked Joey well enough, but he treated women like dirt. No matter what he did, the girls kept coming back for more, couldn't seem to get enough of him. Do girls actually like that sort of thing? They must, for less than five minutes after arriving to their table, Myra was sitting across Joey's lap and feeding him Beer Nuts as he groped her ass.

James sighed and shook his head.

"Hi, I'm Ginger...Ginger LaVire," said girl number four in a squeaky, breathy Brooklyn accent that incongruously sounded equal parts Marilyn Monroe and Betty Boop. Whatever the combination, it didn't work well together, at least not to James's ear. "What's your name?"

"Um, James...James Hamilton, but everybody calls me James," he answered, extending a hand. "Nice to meet you, Ginger."

"Now, aren't we being formal?" she said, taking his hand.

To James, her voice was like nails on a chalkboard. In the middle of almost every one of her short sentences—he was reasonably certain if she ever strung more than ten words together, she'd strain something—she affected an annoying squeak.

"James, just like James Dean? I just loved James Dean. It's terrible that he had to die like that. And Buddy Holly too...he died too, ya know. If Frankie Avalon ever died, I just don't know what I'd do with myself," she said, releasing his hand and placing hers casually on James's knee.

A few moments later, the hand slid to midthigh, causing a prickly sensation inside the crotch of James's still-damp jeans. He shifted uncomfortably in his chair.

"So, LaVire," he squeaked. "Is your family French? There is a river in France named the La Vire, you know."

"I dunno. A river? Maybe that river was named after my family? Or maybe my family was named after the river. Who's to say?" she cooed, staring weirdly into his eyes.

James had spent almost no time in the dating pool in his seventeen years, but was pretty sure Miss LaVire was from the shallow end.

Wanting to be polite, he changed the subject.

He asked, "Did you hear? Gracie Allen died today."

"Gracie who?"

"Gracie Allen. You know, George Burns and Gracie Allen?"

"Oh, yeah, I think I saw them once on *American Bandstand.*"

"Ayeee, yeah, I...don't think so. They had an act on vaudeville and a TV show back in the fifties." He almost had to yell over the din of the patrons singing along with the Drifters' "Under the Boardwalk."

"Oh, *that* Gracie Allen. Of course! Why didn't you just say so?" she said, waving her hand in dismissal.

James could think of nothing else to say, and their conversation died for several minutes. All the while, Ginger's hand remained in place on his inner thigh, her fingers stroking and lightly scratching the denim of his jeans like he was her pet cat. Then, the hand slid farther up his thigh. Taken by surprise, he yelped like a scalded puppy, leaped backward off his barstool, and collided with a burly biker-dude.

The biker had been carrying a pitcher of beer back to his table but now wore half of it down his front. Immediately enraged, he wheeled upon James. "Hey, buddy, watch what you're doin'!"

"Sorry, sorry, sorry...I didn't mean to—"

"I oughta' belt you one and teach you some manners," the biker said, drawing back a fist.

Before the fist could be brought forward, it was caught by one of Gabrish's ham-sized hands. He held the fist with all the effort it took to turn a doorknob. At six-foot-six and 260 pounds, he towered over the now-terrified biker. Gabrish slowly shook his head and growled, "I don't think so."

"I didn't mean nothin' by it! We was just foolin' around... you know, having some fun. Right, kid?" the biker wheedled, turning to James with a pleading look in his eyes.

"It's all right, Tim. I accidentally spilled his beer."

Gabrish gave the fist a firm squeeze, then released his grip. The relieved biker scampered back to his table, cradling his hand to his chest. James could have sworn he'd heard a knuckle pop when Gabrish squeezed, although that might just have been the *POP* from "Lollipop" playing on the jukebox.

"Oh, you were so brave, standing up to that motorcycle person like that!" Ginger exclaimed, placing her hand on James's chest.

"No, I...it was..."

With her index finger drawing figure eights on James's chest, she purred into his ear, "It's so hot and crowded in here. Would you step outside with me for a few minutes?"

"Well, it is rather warm. Oh...yes, of course," James stammered.

"Truly it *is* so hot in here!" Then, quick as a flash, she reached behind her back and an instant later was holding her silky, white brassiere over her index finger. "There, that's bet-tuh!" Then, without looking, she tossed the bra back over her shoulder.

James watched in amazement as the garment fluttered through the air like a pair of chickens with their feet tied together. As Ginger drew him toward Minsky's rear door, the two lacy leghorns came to roost across the uppermost tine of the moose's left antler. Cliff fist-pumped and pressed something into James's hand as he walked past. Mission accomplished!

Ginger led James to the secluded corner of the parking lot where Cliff had parked his car. As she walked, she released another button on her blouse. In the bar, her ample bosom had been barely contained. Now free of the constraining brassiere and down to just one tiny little button to hold them back, her breasts danced and shuddered like two spirited thoroughbreds waiting at the starting gate at Pamlico, ready to burst free. Arriving at Cliff's Studebaker, Ginger stopped and turned to James. She suddenly leaned forward, expecting a kiss and offering him a better view of her impressive cleavage. At the same time, James glanced down at his hand and was stunned to find that he was holding a condom. He was so shocked, he dropped it. Out of reflex, he lunged forward trying to catch the condom as it fell. With Ginger bending forward, James's forehead caught her square in the nose, eliciting a sickening *crack*.

Blood gushed from Ginger's broken nose, instantly covering the front of her white blouse. She held a hand to her ruined nose, blood dripping between her fingers.

James beheld the tableau before him and promptly fainted.

CHAPTER 23

SEPTEMBER 1965

J AMES WAS EXCITED TO BEGIN his junior year of college. The first two years had largely been filled by general education classes and low-level introductory material—simple prerequisites for his major. This year, he'd finally get a crack at the really interesting stuff. P-chem was definitely going to be interesting. The professor had a reputation for being totally brilliant and for being something of an asshole. James didn't care—he wasn't planning to marry the guy, just learn from him.

"I am Professor Medbury. Welcome to Chemistry 311, Physical Chemistry." Medbury scrawled his name and the course title on the center of the five blackboards on the lecture stage, then continued. "Those of you who are political science or business majors might want to save yourself a lot of time and frustration and go ahead and submit your DROP-ADD cards now. Enroll instead, in Chemistry 100, also known as 'Betty Crocker Chemistry.' It's held down the hall next to the cafeteria and not in *my* classroom. This is a *real* chemistry class."

Medbury stalked back and forth in front of five green-colored blackboards as he delivered his introductory monologue. James's mind wandered briefly. *Are they still called blackboards if they're green?"*

To James, Medbury's oration sounded overly rehearsed; like he was playing to his *reputation* as a snarky professor, rather than actually being one. James smiled inwardly and thought of the line from *MacBeth* as he watched Medbury "strut and fret his hour upon the stage..." Time would tell.

Focus, dammit, James silently chastised himself.

Medbury continued without pause. "What is physical chemistry? P-chem is a broad branch of chemistry concerned with the application of the techniques and theories of physics to study chemical systems. It covers quantum chemistry, thermochemistry, kinetics and statistical mechanics."

"Quantum chemistry is generally about trying to understand scenarios on an atomic level, modeling systems in convenient mathematical representations, and..."

At this point, Medbury's lecture was interrupted by a graduate assistant furtively approaching the lectern. She handed the professor a note, and like a puppy caught in the act of peeing on the master's shoes, immediately scurried back toward the relative safety of the exit door.

"This had better be important," Medbury groused. "Interrupting my class like this." He read the note, lips moving as he read. Finishing, he raised his eyes to the bank of student desks. "Is there a James Hamilton in this class?"

From a desk two-thirds up the lecture amphitheater, James timidly raised his hand.

"Mr. Hamilton, you are wanted in the chancellor's office at once. Perhaps it's regarding your DROP-ADD card," he offered derisively. "Take your books when you go."

Perplexed, James obediently collected his notes and textbook, and made his way to the lecture hall exit.

Medbury picked up his lecture immediately. "Where was I? Yes, convenient mathematical representations and making the appropriate..."

The door slammed shut, and James heard no more. Arriving at the chancellor's office, he paused briefly at the secretary's desk.

Before he could say a word, she asked, "Are you James?"

James nodded.

"You can go right on in, hun. The chancellor is expecting you."

Bewildered, he knocked on the chancellor's door.

"Enter!"

Entering the well-appointed office, James stood with a sense of foreboding before a huge, burnished oak desk. "Doctor Sharp, I'm James...James Hamilton. They said you wanted to see me?"

Chancellor Sharp rose and walked around his desk. He shook James's hand and motioned him to a couch beside the door. "Please sit down, James. I am afraid that I have some bad news to share with you."

James sat in terrified silence, his thoughts racing. Had he done something wrong? Was there an issue with his scholarship? Was Howard okay?

"Son, we received a telegram this afternoon from your mother." The chancellor handed it to James.

SEPTEMBER 8, 1965

JAMES WILEY HAMILTON

UNIV. OF NC

CHAPEL HILL, N.C.

FATHER DIED LAST NIGHT STOP HEART ATTACK STOP COME HOME

MOTHER

11:46AM

James stared speechless at the page for what felt like several minutes. He was vaguely aware the chancellor was saying something, but had no idea what it might be. Probably some words of sympathy or condolence. James didn't know and didn't really care. Pa was dead! His eyes watered, and his thoughts swirled. Pa was dead, but Mama wanted him to come home. He hadn't been home or even seen his parents in eight long years. A tear trickled down his cheek. James buried his face in hands. His thoughts cycled between grief, elation, guilt, and then back again.

Chancellor Sharp patted James's shoulder. "Yes, I know, son. Let it all out."

James's thoughts swirled. For the longest time, all he'd ever wanted to do was to go home, and now he was going to have the opportunity, but at what cost? He grieved for his father and felt an immense sadness because of his loss. However, now his mama wanted him to come home. She needed him. She still *loved* him?

All the while as James battled complex and contradictory emotions, the chancellor did little more than spout pithy platitudes. "These things happen, and everything happens for a reason..." the chancellor droned. "Your father is in a better place now, son. This too shall pass, son. Let me know if there's anything I can do to help..."

It took all James's willpower not to shout, "I've just lost my father and all you can do is spout vapid bromides. How the *Hell* did you rise all the way to the chancellorship of a major university?!" But instead, he just said, "Thank you, sir. I will."

After departing the chancellor's office, James sleep-walked back to his dorm room. His thoughts and emotions continued to kaleidoscope. He hoped that Howard could help him find clarity, but when he called his uncle in Scottsdale, the housekeeper informed him that Doctor and Mrs. Hines were out of the country on a tour of Egypt and the Great Pyramids and were not expected to return for another month. James smiled at the thought of his uncle bumping along the Giza plateau on the back of a camel. Then, with no one to help him focus his thoughts or provide counsel, he walked to the admission's office and withdrew from school for the rest of the semester. He figured he'd be back for the spring term.

Then, he packed his clothes, said his goodbyes to the team, purchased a train ticket, and returned home to Boiling Springs.

No one was at the train station to meet James when he arrived the next morning. He wasn't surprised. No doubt, the family was busy with funeral arrangements. It wasn't a big deal. He could easily hitch a ride from the train station to the hardware store in Boiling Springs. From there, it would be an easy walk to the family farm.

As James walked, he spent the time reminiscing. Over there was the old Hansen place. He'd spent many a weekend there playing ball and fishing with Seth Hansen. He wondered where he was now. Seth had been a year ahead of him in school, so maybe he was working somewhere. He supposed he would have graduated last June and might even have gone on to college. Seth had had a little tagalong sister. What had her name been? James tried to remember. *Betty? No...Rhonda? No, that isn't it either. Rebecca? Yes, Rebecca, Becky...and she'd been in Anna's first grade class at school.*

James sighed. The thought of Anna sent a pang of regret through to his marrow. No matter where he was, the pain of her death never seemed very far away. He began to wonder if coming home was even the right thing to do. Of course, in his soul he knew it was, but it was going to hurt.

But Ma needs me.

James rounded the bend onto Oconee Street, bringing the old farmhouse into view. The last time he'd seen his boyhood home, it had been fading into the distance between the tail fins of his uncle's old El Dorado. Now, rather than fading, it was growing in his vision. Instead of leaving, James Wiley Hamilton was coming home.

They say you can't really come home again. Things viewed through a filter of childhood innocence rarely appear the same through adult eyes. Although James would not have considered himself an adult, nothing seemed the same. Nothing felt the same. Nothing *was* the same.

The grand old farmhouse of his memory was far more ramshackle than he remembered. The tin roof was stained by rust. The front porch sagged in the middle, and the white paint was peeling from the sides of the house. The giant sycamore tree in the front yard of his youth didn't seem so imposing as it once had. The flower beds were more weeds than flowers, and the front yard grew more clover than grass. The tobacco fields around the house had gone fallow. It looked like it had been years since they'd seen a plow. There was nothing time hadn't touched. Everything seemed so different from what he remembered.

The front steps were badly cracked, and James nearly lost his balance when a brick shifted beneath his feet as he climbed to the porch. He considered knocking at the front door but thought better of it. He grasped the latch and furtively pushed it open. Seeing no one in the entryway, he called, "Maaaaa...I'm home."

No answer.

James stepped back onto the porch and grabbed his suitcase—the same one he'd taken when leaving home nine years ago. He gave a rueful smile. "I guess not everything changes," he thought aloud. He left the suitcase in the entry hall and set out in search of his mom, calling out periodically to avoid startling her.

When James finally found his mother, she was in the kitchen sitting at the breakfast table with Mack Lee. Cigarette smoke curled from an empty coffee cup she'd repurposed into an ersatz ashtray. Her lips were tightly pursed and displayed the ray-like linear wrinkles of a chronic, heavy smoker, which he found odd since he'd never known her to smoke during his childhood.

The expressive emerald-green eyes that had watched over him as a child were now muddy, glazed and lifeless. An array of pill bottles was scattered over the table next to a plate of half-eaten scrambled eggs and toast. James knew his mother had tiptoed around the diagnosis of depression for years, but now it appeared that she'd stepped into it outright, and with both feet. Her hair was a listless mop, which had turned completely gray. In his memory, his mother had always been slim, petite, and lively. Today, she looked to have gained at least a hundred pounds that was tentatively held up by legs like fence posts. Her legs, or at least what he could see of them between the hem of her house coat and her pink, fuzzy bedroom slippers, were a deep reddish-purple hue with skin as thick and rough as tree bark.

Maggie made no attempt to rise as James entered the room.

"Ma, I'm home!" James said with excitement, practically skipping across the room to offer his mother a hug.

Maggie glanced briefly at him through hooded eyes, then returned her gaze to Mack Lee. "I can see that." Her monotone reply was entirely devoid of inflection and practically sucked the oxygen from the room. She made no attempt to return, or even nominally participate in, James's embrace. "Took you long enough to get here."

"I came as soon as I got your telegram about Pa."

"Don't you back-talk me! You should have been here yesterday," she snapped.

"I'm sorry, Mama. I went straight from the chancellor's office to admissions and submitted my course withdrawal form. Then I took the first train from Chapel Hill. I don't know how I could have gotten here any sooner."

"You could have hitched a ride."

"But I did! From the train station in Spartanburg to the hardware sto—"

James was interrupted by a slap to the face. "I *told* you not to back-talk me!" Margaret was suddenly stirred from her torpor. "Your Pa's funeral is tomorrow, and there's work to do."

"Yes, ma'am. I'll get right to it. Where do you want me to put my things?"

"I don't!"

"Pardon?"

"*I* don't *want* you to put them anywhere. If it were up to *me*, you'd still be the *Hell* away from my house at your hoity-toity university!"

"But your telegram said—"

"*I* didn't send any telegram! The *preacher* at the hospital sent it and signed my name."

"But—"

"It was your Pa who wanted you here, *not me*. The preacher said it was his 'dying wish,' " she snarled, making air quotes.

James stood thunderstruck. "Yes, ma'am. I'll just put my things in my old room."

"That's *my* room!" Mack Lee said in a flat tone. Like his mother, Mack Lee hadn't risen to greet James when he'd entered the room, instead electing to remain slouched in a chair by the table. The pile of cigarette butts in the saucer before him suggested he'd been there awhile, and the sneer he wore suggested he planned on being there awhile longer.

Like everything else in the old homeplace, Mack Lee had changed, and had not changed. When they'd been young, he had always worn his hair in a flattop. He still did, but now the look had evolved into what James's friends at college called a "Chicago Boxcar," a flattop with the sides swept back into a Brylcreemed ducktail. A grease-stained wife-beater T-shirt flaunted still-muscular arms but also did little to restrain the well-developed beer-gut that lopped over the waistband of grimy mechanic's trousers. The one constant of Mack Lee's appearance, James noticed, was the sardonic Elvis Presley smirk he'd learned to hate as a kid.

"Hey, Mack Lee. It's good to see you, brother, although I wish it was under other circumstances. Your room? You mean, you still...live...here?"

"Yeah, college boy. I live here. What of it? I work at the gas station in town and stay here to help out Ma."

"I don't know what I'd do without Mack Lee. He's been such a blessing," Maggie interjected.

"With you off in *college*, somebody had to pitch in," Mack Lee said with a sneer.

"It's good that you've been able to help," James agreed. "Where do you want me to put my things?"

"Across the hall, in Anna's old room."

James's face lost all color, and he felt his knees go weak. "Anna's...room?" His mouth went dry, and the room began to spin. He reached a hand toward the door frame to steady himself.

James woke a moment later on the floor. His mother was at the sink, casually washing dishes and Mack Lee, still seated at the table, was gazing down at him in disgust.

"Too much to drink last night, *college boy*?" Mack Lee jeered. "You better get upstairs and get changed. Them stalls ain't gonna muck themselves. I'd help, ya know, but I got this bum leg."

CHAPTER 24

SEPTEMBER–OCTOBER 1965

THERE HAD BEEN A GOOD turnout for Walter's service. All around James were faces he recognized, but there were none he *knew*. He felt like an outsider at his own father's funeral. To James, everyone was from a time and place long distant. When well-wishers offered him condolences, he thanked each one effusively, but deep down, he knew he was just going through the motions. He, of course, had loved his father, but the outpouring of grief he'd expected just wasn't there. Perhaps this was not surprising. For everyone else, Walter's loss was new and acute. James had had over nine years over which he'd gotten used to his father's absence.

The only time James had felt any strong emotion at all was when he noticed the headstone standing just to the right of the open hole in the family plot. It was Anna's. Were it not for the strong hands of Russell—James couldn't remember his last name but knew he'd been the produce manager at the Community Cash Grocery store—supporting him, James might've passed out. Apparently, James's vagus nerve was still alive and well and up to its old mischief. Some things never change.

Having dreamed of little more than "coming home" for the past nine years, James found the reality to be much less than he'd hoped. The relationship with his mother had not improved. She seemed barely to tolerate his presence, and certainly took no joy from it. Mack Lee, sensing exploitable weakness, took every opportunity to goad him about Anna's death and, perhaps out of jealousy, constantly belittled James about his college education.

James remained in close communication with his Uncle Howard—or at least, as close communication as was possible with the old fellow's world travels. Most of their communication was by mail. James had been surprised to see a wall-mounted telephone in his mom's kitchen when he'd first arrived home. He was not surprised, only disappointed, that she'd declined to allow him to use it to place long-distance calls, even if he promised to call collect. Therefore, for any verbal conversation he'd like to have with his uncle, he had to walk into town and use the payphone outside the post office in downtown Boiling Springs.

He didn't mind the walk and made it about once each week. It got him out in the fresh air and pleasantly away from the house and farm. James would've liked talking with his uncle more often, but felt guilty sticking his uncle with the bill. His last call had cost $3.85!

After his father's funeral, James's life devolved into a mind-numbing routine. Each morning, he did whatever chores were required on the farm, but none required any great expenditure of time and certainly no thought. The fields, having lain fallow for years and with no plans for this to change, required no tending. The farm's outbuildings were largely in disrepair but no longer in use, so no repairs were deemed cost efficient. A few pigs and cows remained but required only a nominal degree of husbandry.

After the constant stimulation he'd known at his uncle's house and in college, James slid slowly into ennui and despair. He rapidly came to the realization that rather than dropping out of school, perhaps he should've just come for the funeral and then returned to university. Such thoughts tormented him, keeping him awake nights. But the die had been cast, and there was no use perseverating. Instead, he decided to make the most of his time in Boiling Springs and then return to school for the spring semester. He resolved to ask Howard his opinion when he returned from his latest travel adventure, a marlin fishing expedition off Cairns near the Great Barrier Reef, but was pretty certain he would agree with James's plans.

James looked up many of the friends he had known before his banishment to North Carolina. Sadly, he found that their life experiences and interests had diverged significantly from his during his time away. Consequently, they no longer had much in common.

With a toxic environment at home and little to do while awaiting spring term, James took a part-time job at the Rexall Pharmacy in Boiling Springs. In addition to being a typical drug store, the Rexall featured an active lunch counter and soda fountain. He became its newest "soda jerk." For the lunch crowd, he manned the griddle, turning out hamburgers, hotdogs, and french fries. Afternoons and evenings were spent dipping ice cream, making malted milkshakes, and servicing the old Rock-Ola jukebox for the high school kids. James thought it odd that he considered the students to be "kids" even though many, if not most, were his age.

He enjoyed his job at Rexall. The work wasn't challenging, but he devoted his full attention to doing it well and rapidly mastered the counter. Remembering his uncle, James smiled. The old man had always told him, "Whatever you do in life, do it well. If you are digging a ditch, then be the best damned ditch digger there ever was!" Uncle Howard would be proud.

The pharmacy's owner, Mr. Boyter, was slight of build and stood a full head shorter than James. He had wispy, faded red hair over his ears, but the top of his head was as hairless as a newborn opossum. Out of doors, he was seldom seen without a crisp white fedora protecting his bald pate from the sun. His gray eyes were narrow-set over a long, protruding nose, which gave him something of a ferret-like appearance. He sported a nicotine-stained lampshade mustache over a ready smile of similarly tinted teeth. A dapper little man, he always wore a seersucker suit with a starched white shirt and red bowtie. One could tell the day of the week by Mr. Boyter's suit color. Mondays, he wore classic light blue, with red, green, gray, and dark blue set to the rest of the workweek. The suit color might change, but the bowtie always remained fire-engine red.

After a week, James knew each of the regulars by sight and could predict their orders. Most were creatures of habit, and after two weeks, he felt confident enough to begin preparing orders for certain patrons as soon as they walked through the door. He was almost never wrong and was deft enough behind the counter that if someone did deviate from their usual order, there was seldom any waste. Noting more rapid turnover of well-satisfied customers, Mr. Boyter, gave James a twenty-five-cent per hour raise and offered him a full-time position.

Rain or shine, Monday through Saturday, James walked the three miles into town for work. He arrived an hour before the lunch rush and changed into the uniform he kept in a storeroom at Rexall. After the lunch rush died down and the café area had been cleaned, he had free time until the kids arrived for the after-school rush.

"Hey there, Soda Pop," teased a pretty girl as she slid onto a stool at James's counter. "I'll have a—"

James smiled and slid a root beer float in front of the girl.

Having been into the soda counter every day for the past two weeks, she'd caught James's eye. He estimated that she was sixteen or maybe seventeen. The skin of her face was as pale and smooth as a porcelain doll except for a tiny dimple on her left cheek. She had coal-black hair that today she wore pulled back into a ponytail. Her widow's peak, high cheekbones, and delicate, narrow chin made her face appear slightly heart shaped. Her most striking feature, however, was her eyes. They were a brilliant sapphire blue, and when she smiled, as she was doing at that very moment, they practically danced.

"How did you know..." she began to ask.

"That you wanted a root beer float?" James finished the question with a raised eyebrow and a wink.

The girl blushed and nodded her head.

"It's simple. She's a banana split," he said, nodding to a red-haired girl in the corner. He then pointed around the room, pausing at each patron. "Coke, chocolate malted, Orange Crush, chocolate sundae, vanilla ice cream, Cherry Coke, regular Coke." He leaned forward and whispered in a conspiratorial tone, "But when he comes in alone, it's always Nehi Grape." He nodded his head with great solemnity as though about to confer upon her a sacred confidence. "And you, Miss Ponytail, are a root beer float."

She slapped at him playfully. "How do you do that?"

"Simple. I just pay attention."

"I could never pay *that* much attention!" she said wistfully. "But, hey, what happens if I change my mind and order something different? What then?"

"Then I suppose I'd make you whatever you came up with for your new order, then *I* would get to enjoy a delicious root beer float!" Caught up in their banter, James reached up and playfully deposited a tiny dollop of whipped cream on the end of her nose.

He recoiled in horror when he realized what he'd just done and scrambled to give the girl a clean cloth. He quickly glanced around to see if Mr. Boyter, or anybody else in the pharmacy, had seen his impetuous act. Then he realized she was laughing, and he was able to breathe again.

"You're blushing!" She giggled, wiping the whipped cream from her nose. "That's so cute!"

Just then, the bell over the pharmacy's door tinkled and in walked a strawberry malted and a Coke with two squirts of vanilla. James turned away from the girl to prepare their orders. Customers continued to trickle in, and he never quite made it back to the pretty girl to continue their conversation.

When the after-school rush had ended, James was pleasantly surprised to find the ponytailed girl still in one of the rear booths. Her friends had already left, and she had books and graph paper scattered over the table. It appeared she was working on her algebra homework. He smiled and opened two bottles of Coca-Cola, then walked over to her table.

"Here, take this. Algebra goes better with Coke." He sat one of the colas before her and slid into the seat opposite. *No-no-no! Could anything sound cornier than that?!* he chastised himself silently as his face flushed again. *No, probably not.*

"I didn't order this." Then she gestured to the bottle in James's hand and teased, "Did you finally get an order wrong? Oh, and do sit down."

"Things go better with Coke...get it? It's the Coca-Cola ad campaign...Never mind," he said with a weak, apologetic smile and a shrug, so flustered he almost spilled his own drink. He spluttered, "Well, I...um...no...I mean...it's on the house." Abruptly, he stood from the booth, bumping the table and causing his Coke bottle to teeter dangerously. His hand shot forward and barely caught the bottle before it tipped completely, but not before it splashed a few drops onto her algebra textbook.

"Nice catch, Soda Pop. Didn't know you could juggle. What *other* talents have you been hiding away? Oh, sit down. I'm just ribbing ya," she said as she nudged his hand playfully.

"Thanks, I just..."

"Oooo, you're blushing again. That's so *cute!*" she teased, her voice rising to a squeak.

James buried his face in his hands. Even his ears were a flaming red. Eventually, his flush returned to a light pink, and he was finally able to speak. "Other talents?" he asked. "Hmmm, well, I know that you are graphing quadratic equations...or at least, you're trying to."

"How do you know that?"

He gestured to her algebra textbook and the many sheets of graph paper strewn over the booth's table, many smudged from multiple erasures.

She nodded, "Yeah, I can't seem to get it. It makes no sense to me."

James glanced at the problem she was attempting and said, "Here, let me show you! If...you...don't...mind, of course?"

"Mind? Why would I possibly mind? If you can make this stuff actually make sense, I'll probably kiss you!"

James shook his head slightly to clear his mind. "It's actually easier than in looks. You remember the formula $y = mx + b$?"

She hesitated for a moment and then nodded.

"That's the formula for grafting a straight line. In the formula, x and y are just points on their respective axes, m is the slope of the line and may be positive or negative. b is the point where the line crosses the y axis. So, if you know the slope and the y intercept, all you have to do is plug in numbers and draw your graft. Piece of cake! Similarly, if you don't know the slope of the line but have the other information, you can solve for it by rewriting the equation as $m = (y-b)/x$."

"You're so smart! And you make it sound so easy."

"It is...try it!"

She worked a problem...and then another. "This is great! You should be teaching this stuff instead of old Mr. Swofford."

James smiled without the slightest hint of a blush, happy to be back in familiar and comfortable territory. "Proud to have been of some assistance, Miss Ponytail!"

"Why do you keep calling me that?"

"Same reason you've been calling me Soda Pop. You have a ponytail, and we've not been formally introduced. I'm James, by the way, but my friends call me Jimmy."

Maybe it was being back in his home town, or maybe he just wanted this girl to be a friend. Either way, and for whatever reason, he wanted to be Jimmy for her.

"Bytheway, what a funny name," she said, feigning puzzlement.

"I..." Jimmy felt himself beginning to flush again.

"Just teasing ya. I'm Rebecca, but everyone calls me Becky, Becky Hansen," she said smiling and holding out her hand to shake.

"*You're* Rebecca Hansen? Little Becky Hansen? It's me, Jimmy Hamilton. We used to walk to school together." The words bubbled out from his mouth like water from a spring.

"I know. You were Anna's big brother."

The smile faded from Jimmy's face, and his eyes bored holes in the floor.

Rebecca watched as Jimmy deflated like a beachball stuck with a pin. "It was very sad about Anna." She reached across the table and placed her hand gently underneath his chin, raising it so that his eyes met hers. "Mom and Dad told me it was a horrible accident. It must have been so terribly hard for you."

"Yeah, but it was my fault! She'd be alive today but for me. And I miss her still."

"It was an accident...and you were just a little kid." Rebecca placed her hand gently over Jimmy's. "And then you went away. That was sad too. But now you're back, and I'm glad!" she said with a shy smile and chewing on her bottom lip.

Jimmy smiled weakly.

The bell over the lunch counter door tinkled.

Jimmy took a deep breath and clamped his eyes tightly closed for several seconds. When they opened again, he screwed on a smile, turned back to the counter, and resumed his Oscar-worthy performance as Happy Soda Jerk for a half-dozen new customers.

After his customers departed, Jimmy was pleased to see Rebecca still ensconced in her back booth. "How goes the homework?" he asked as he approached her again, this time on less wobbly legs.

"I think I'm done, but I'll be back again tomorrow. Maybe you can help me?" Rebecca slid from the booth and collected her homework.

"It will be my pleasure," Jimmy replied. He carried Rebecca's algebra book as he accompanied her to the door.

Jimmy watched her go. Then, he practically floated back to the lunch counter. Maybe it hadn't been such bad idea taking a semester off from school after all?

Rebecca did return the next day, and the day after that. And Jimmy was *always* happy to help.

The Boiling Springs Post Office was around the corner from Rexall. During his break after the lunch rush, Jimmy liked to walk over and check the mail. Like most families in the area, the Hamiltons had a mailbox on the street for routine mail. Even so, his pa had always maintained a post office box in town for "important" mail. He'd said that it was "more secure." Having seen many a roadside mailbox flattened by speeding motorists, Jimmy couldn't argue against the practice. Besides, it gave him opportunity to chat with Marvin, the postal clerk, behind the counter.

The Hamiltons did not receive much mail. The sympathy letters had dried up within a week of Walter's death. Now, there was rarely anything in the postbox other than utility bills or the occasional Sears & Roebuck Catalog. The latter was particularly useful for passing the slow times at work. Last week, Jimmy had received a postcard from Howard and Charlotte as they continued their round-the-world tour. The postcard had made Jimmy smile. It was obvious that in his former teacher, his uncle had found a worthy companion *and* happiness. Jimmy hoped someday he'd be as lucky.

Jimmy had only been at home for a month and, other than the postcard from Howard and Charlotte and a couple sympathy notes from Cliff and the guys, he'd not received any other mail. He was disappointed but not entirely surprised that his college friends hadn't written more often. He knew that they were busy with classes and football season was in full swing. Still, he'd hoped to hear more from them.

It was, at least transiently, a pleasant surprise when Jimmy found a letter addressed to James Wiley Hamilton nestled between a property tax notice and the electric bill from Duke Power. Curious, he immediately ripped into the envelope and began to read.

SELECTIVE SERVICE SYSTEM
ORDER TO REPORT FOR INDUCTION

LOCAL BOARD NO. 186
SPARTANBURG COUNTY
88 CHURCH STREET
SPARTANBURG, SC   29302

The President of the United States

(LOCAL BOARD STAMP)

To

James Wiley Hamilton

Oct 4, 1965
(DATE OF MAILING)

GREETING:

You are hereby ordered for induction into the Armed Forces of the United States, and to report...

One by one, the other envelopes fell from his grasp. The letter in his hand began to shake. Actually, the letter was quite calm—it was Jimmy's hands that shook like an oak leaf in a tornado. He staggered against the wall and slid slowly to the floor. There he sat, head in his hands and elbows on his knees. "Oh no, no, no! I'm being drafted!"

He'd had a draft deferment for college and every intention of returning to school for the spring term, but the moment he'd withdrawn from college, Jimmy had lost his draft deferment. He'd always assumed he'd be back in school again with a new deferment before the draft board even got wind of his change in status. Consequently, he was shocked to find that he'd been drafted less than a month after walking out of the chancellor's office.

"I'm such an idiot!" he muttered to himself.

When Jimmy had sufficiently recovered his wits, he gathered up the rest of the mail from the floor and absentmindedly crammed the other letters back into the postbox. Slamming the box closed, he thought, *Taxes and Duke Power can wait. I'm being drafted.*

He continued reading as he walked back to Rexall. "Geez...how cold is that. 'Greeting.' They could've at least made it a little more personal with, 'Greetings.' "

As Jimmy read on, he realized there were no loopholes through which he might wriggle to escape induction into the army. He'd gone from 2-S Draft Classification to 1-A as soon as he'd left the UNC Admissions Office. He had no one dependent upon him or his income and no disqualifying medical conditions. He was screwed!

When he read the section about life insurance, he had to fight down a wave of nausea.

He read on. The board would provide transportation, lodging, and meals. "How thoughtful," he muttered acidly. "Bet they'll be happy to provide transportation to Vietnam too."

Willful failure to report at the place and hour of the day named in this Order subjects the violator to fine and imprisonment. Bring this Order with you when you report.

If you are so far from your own board that reporting in compliance with this Order will be a serious hardship, go immediately to any local board and make written request for transfer of your delivery for induction, taking this Order with you.

Jimmy swallowed hard. The bastards had thought of everything. He flopped onto a barstool at the lunch counter and buried his face in his hands.

Mr. Boyter suddenly materialized behind the counter. "What seems to be eatin' ya there, Jimmy-boy?"

Jimmy startled at his boss's sudden appearance. It was probably the first time in his life the kindly old gentleman had ever scared anyone, a more milquetoast soul the world had never known.

"Didn't mean to startle ya, sonny! Ya look like ya were a million miles away," said Mr. Boyter in his cheerful drawl.

"No, sir, just a little over nine thousand," Jimmy replied with a sigh.

"Huh?"

"Sorry, sir. I'm just a little preoccupied."

"I'd know that look anywhere...girrrrl troubles," the old man said, nodding his head in understanding. He sucked air between his teeth and continued, "Ya jest got a letter from some gal back at that university and she's done gone and broke ya heart. Well, I remember back when I was your age, there was this li'l gal...and she was a looker too...well, she just tore out my heart and stomped that sucker flat. Ya just go right on and tell ol' Uncle Robbie all about it, son!"

"I did get a letter, sir, but it wasn't from a girl. I wish it *had* been," Jimmy said, sliding the letter to his boss.

"Ooooh, I see. It's one of *those* letters." He folded the letter and handed it back to Jimmy. "I understand completely! I got me one of them once, back in '19 and '17. They were plannin' on sendin' me over there to teach the Kaiser some manners. Guess our dear Uncle Sam is gonna be wantin' ya to do the same for some commies."

"That pretty well sums it up, sir."

"Ya don't look so thrilled about it, though."

"Again, sir, you hit the nail on the head."

"Well, I wasn't none too thrilled about it either. Ya' remember that girl I was tellin' ya about?"

Jimmy managed a smile in spite of himself.

"Ya know, ya don't necessarily *have* t' go t' the army."

"Yeah, I could just accept the fine and go to prison," Jimmy snapped.

"Naw, naw, naw...not *that*! Ya misunderstood me. Ya can do like I did. When I got my letter, I went and joined the navy. Best decision I ever did make. I did that an' spent the war as a pharmacist's mate on the ol' D-73, USS *Stockton*. I think I just 'bout threw up my toenails a coupla times, but otherwise, I made it back here without so much as a scratch, and it worked out pretty good for me, iffin I say so myself," he said, making a sweeping gesture with his hands toward the pharmacy...*his* pharmacy.

As if on command, as Mr. Boyter's arm passed the front of the pharmacy, the door banged open with the first of the after-school crowd.

Jimmy took a deep breath and slipped the draft letter into his pocket. "Thanks, Mr. Boyter!" Then he stepped behind the counter, put on his game face again, and immediately began mixing a chocolate malted and a vanilla ice cream with chocolate drizzle for his first two customers. In short order, he created a banana split, a chocolate sundae, two cherry cokes (one with a squirt of vanilla), and a half-dozen Coca-Colas.

A few minutes later, Rebecca came in and went directly to her—their—booth, and Jimmy met her there with a root beer float.

"Look, look," she said, waving a piece of paper excitedly. "This is my Algebra II test. One hundred percent, and it's all because of you. I'm so glad you're home again!"

Jimmy beamed, but then his smile faded again. "Unfortunately, it looks like I'm about to be leaving again soon."

"No! You can't leave! Who's going to teach me to graph quadratic equations if you leave? And we're doing parabolas next!"

"Just remember $y = ax^2 + bx + c$, or if it's easier, $y = a(x - h)^2 + k$ where h and k are the vertex coordinates."

"See, you've *got* to stay! How else will I ever learn that stuff? Why do you want to leave so soon already? You just got here," she wheedled.

"I don't...want to leave, that is." Jimmy gave a despondent sigh. "I got my draft notice this morning, and I'm to report for induction into the army in less than two weeks."

"No!" Rebecca exclaimed. "Seth got one of those letters too at the end of the summer..." Her voice trailed off.

"How is he doing? Where did he get sent for basic training? I'm betting Fort Jackson. That's the closest army base to us."

"He...ummm...didn't go."

"Didn't go? Did they wash him out? Medical?"

"No, nothing like that. He went to live with our cousin in Winnipeg. He took a job in a lumber mill there."

"In *Canada*?"

"Is there another Winnipeg?" Her voice dripped with sarcasm.

"I...uh...I just..." Jimmy fumbled for words.

"Don't worry about it! I shouldn't have snapped at you. I'm sorry." Then, by way of explanation, she continued, "It's just...well, it was sort of a scandal around town. The local flag-wavers don't take kindly to draft dodgers."

"That's okay. I was just surprised."

The long silence that followed was finally broken by the tinkling of the bell over the front entrance.

"I'll be right back," Jimmy said before turning to the counter and scooping out a vanilla ice cream cone.

When he returned to Rebecca's table, the tension had abated.

"I'm sorry you're going to be leaving, Jimmy. I'm just getting used to having you back. Besides, who's gonna tutor me in algebra?" She pouted.

Jimmy gave a rueful smile. "Guess I'll just have to stay. You can bring your algebra book by the penitentiary on visitation days, and we'll do homework. They probably don't put guys in solitary for skipping out on draft. Alternatively, you can write to me in Vietnam, and I'll walk you through quadratic equations in between dodging bullets."

Rebecca threw an eraser at him.

Jimmy caught it. "I really don't have a choice, Becca. I've lost my college deferment. I have no disqualifying medical conditions, and I can't go to Canada. I've gotta go."

"Becca? I like that! Beats the heck out of *Ponytail* or *Root beer*," she said, tilting her head to the side and smiling. "But it sucks that you have to leave!"

I could get used to a smile like that, Jimmy thought. Then aloud he said, "Seriously, you actually could write to me. I might not be able to help with homework, but it would be great to hear from you. And other than my uncle, I really don't have anybody to send a letter to."

"What about your mom and brother?"

Jimmy shook his head dolefully. "No, I'm not exactly on the best of terms with Ma, and Mack Lee isn't exactly the writing kind."

"Deal," she said, holding her hand out to shake.

Jimmy took her proffered hand, thinking how small and soft it was. "Deal," he said, smiling.

CHAPTER 25

NOVEMBER 1965–FEBRUARY 1966

J IMMY STEPPED OFF THE BUS at Fort Jackson along with fifty-nine other new inductees, immediately receiving a warm welcome—if that's how an onslaught of curses, spittle, and demands to "drop for push-ups" is best described—from Sergeant First Class Dowhauer, their senior drill instructor.

Welcome to basic training, thought Jimmy with a wry smile, which promptly earned him twenty push-ups.

The first days of basic training passed in a blur of shaved heads, ill-fitting uniforms, physical training, and classes on army tradition and the Code of Conduct. Jimmy had been cautioned about "bad" army food before his arrival, but he actually though it was pretty decent. There was just never enough time to enjoy it.

His bunkmate and best friend was Slater "Slat-head" Watts. Slat-head was from Chesnee, a town less than twenty miles from Jimmy's childhood home of Boiling Springs, and he had also grown up on a tobacco farm. They immediately bonded and helped one another through the rigors of basic.

Early in basic training, Jimmy discovered that he couldn't march worth a damn. At drill, he was constantly harangued by Staff Sergeant Bucholz, one of his platoon's assistant drill instructors, for marching like he was "plodding along behind a mule." Jimmy couldn't help it; that was just the way he walked. Try as he might, he couldn't seem to "step out smartly and swing his arms nine inches to the front and six to the rear" as he marched. It just wasn't natural. Compounding his awkward gait, Jimmy was a book person and totally unaccustomed to listening to music. To him, the heavy beat of the drum sounded just like the light one. Although this was of no concern in the civilian world, in a military where one was expected to march in step to a drumbeat, this was a calamity of epic proportions—one step short of not knowing which end of a rifle the bullet came out. Had it not been for Slat-head, who marched behind him in formation, softly whispering the cadence, "left, left, left, right, left," Jimmy may have never survived to graduate from basic training.

Jimmy was happy enough to return the favor by helping his friend learn to break down and clean his rifle and shine boots and brass, skills that came easily to Jimmy but seemed to elude Watts.

One evening after Jimmy's platoon had been at basic for several weeks, Sergeant Dowhauer rolled the men out and had them line up in formation before their barracks. Such impromptu formations were not unusual. They gave the DI a chance to exercise capacious lungs and display his impressive vocabulary of expletives, and this evening's formation was little different.

"Reee-cruits, aaah-*ten-shun*," Dowhauer bellowed.

Jimmy's platoon snapped to attention.

"Paaa-*rade* rest!"

The platoon briskly complied.

After a short pause, Dowhauer gave the next command. "Stand at *ease*! Eyes to me."

The drill instructor paced back and forth before the men. Their heads swiveled as he paced, to keep the DI in the center of their vision just like they'd been trained. Dowhauer was a short fireplug of a man who wore his "brown round" Smokey-Bear hat low over his forehead, so much so that only the lower third of his nose was visible beneath the brim unless a recruit was unfortunate enough to be looking up after having "assumed the position" for push-ups. The men didn't need to see his face. They knew he was there, and he held their full and undivided attention.

"Reee-cruits, I have just had the distinct pleasure of sharing a chat with Captain Parsons. Whereas I generally enjoy conversations with our training company commander, this one was less than pleasant. The good captain had a bee in his bonnet over some kinda shit. And what does shit do?"

The men snapped to attention and shouted, "It rolls downhill, Sergeant!"

"And who's at the bottom of the hill?"

"We are, Sergeant!"

"You're goddamn right you are," Dowhauer continued. "It seems the captain got a call from the major. The major had gotten a call from the colonel. And the colonel, in turn, had gotten a call from the member of Congress representing East Bumblefuck. That member of Congress, it seems, had received a call from *somebody's* mama sayin' she hadn't heard from her dear, sweet baby boy since he went away to join the army lo' these many weeks ago, and she's worried.

"So, the member of Congress called the colonel to check on Mama's little boy, to let him know that Mama would love to hear from her little angel. The colonel called the major and suggested that he have the man write home to soothe his mother's anxieties. The major called the captain and told him to have the goddamn recruit write home because Mama's worried. And the captain chewed my *ass* for the past half hour because one of you panty-waste losers hasn't written his mama! Show of hands," Dowhauer demanded. "Who here has written their mama since you been here?"

Over the years Jimmy had amassed an impressive collection of letters he'd written to his mother. Each had returned to him unopened. He'd kept them all, carefully collated and curated in the old shoebox at his uncle's house, on the off chance that someday his mother would forgive him and might like to read about her son's life and experiences. After his induction into the army, Jimmy gave up this childish fantasy. Sometimes he wondered where that box had wound up—likely in an incinerator—after his uncle's move to Scottsdale. Nowadays, when his letters home were returned to him at mail call, he just threw them away. Still, dutifully he wrote.

Of the fifty-three remaining recruits in Jimmy's platoon—attrition had claimed six—only about half raised their hands, and Jimmy was one of them. It had been his habit to write his mother at least once a week since he'd gone to live with Howard, and he'd resumed the practice once more after leaving for basic training. Of course, now as before, he never received a reply, but then, he'd stopped expecting responses from her years ago. Were it not for routine letters from Becca and Howard, Jimmy would've been totally cut off from the outside world.

After an extended stream of expletives, the recruits were released for the night and given strict and unambiguous orders to write their "goddamn mamas!" And if they didn't have a goddamn mama, they should write to their rabbi, their sweetheart, or their goddamn dawg if need be!

Regardless, each and every man was to produce a two-page letter for Dowhauer to post before reveille the next morning or they'd "be skinned."

Jimmy returned to his bunk, thought for a moment, and took out pen and paper to write to Uncle Howard.

November 28, 1965

Ft. Jackson, SC

Uncle Howard,

I didn't realize that you and Charlotte had returned to the States already. Does this represent a stopover or do you two world travelers intend to stay for a while? If you're in this part of the world and have the opportunity, I would love to invite you to my graduation ceremony at the end of basic training.

After basic, I will travel to Fort Sam Houston in San Antonio for combat medical training. Then it's off to Jump School at Fort Benning. I'm beginning to feel a little nervous about possibly jumping out of an airplane. Perhaps this thought should have struck me sooner. Hmmm... makes one wonder about my sanity.

I have a great story from basic that I think you'll enjoy. It's about my first day on the firing range at Fort Jackson. We were issued our rifles and spent quite some time learning the M14 rifle, how to break it down and clean it, etc. By the way, the M14 uses the same sights as my old Winchester Model 52. After the time you spent teaching me, learning the M14 was a piece of cake, but lots of the guys in my platoon struggled with it. Thanks for that, Uncle—I *owe you! When we finally got to the range, my drill instructor was none too happy when I informed him that I am left-eye dominant and shoot left-handed. But I think I made my point...*

"On my command, you will each fire five rounds from each firing position: offhand standing, kneeling, seated, prone, and then twenty rounds fully automatic," the Range Master's voice boomed across the firing range like a howitzer. "To qualify with the M14 rifle, you must successfully place rounds on target from one hundred, two hundred, and three hundred yards. Today, you will begin in the offhand position and fire at the two-hundred-yard target. Is that clear?"

"Hoo-rah! Yes, Range Master!" Jimmy's squad shouted in unison.

Jimmy raised his hand.

"Reee-cruit Hamilton! Do you have a problem?" the RM, a former drill instructor, bellowed.

Jimmy thought absently, *Do DIs even have a normal voice, or are they born shouting? I wonder if he calls cadence to his wife when they're in bed or screams, "Pass the salt!" at the dinner table at his mom's house on Sundays. Do they even have wives...or mothers?*

"Does something amuse you, Reee-cruit?"

"No, Range Master!"

"Then wipe that smirk off your face!"

"Hoo-rah! Wiping away the smirk, Range Master!"

"Now, what is the recruit's problem?"

"No, Range Master...I mean...yes, Range Master. I mean, the recruit has no problem, only a question, Range Master!"

By now the Range Master was in Jimmy's face with the brim of his Smokey-Bear hat pressed firmly against Jimmy's nose. After an extended tirade of shouted expletives and responses, it was determined that the recruit was left-eye dominant and would complete the range drills firing left-handed.

"Will there be anything else, recruit?"

"No, Range Master!"

The RM stalked to a central position behind the squad and barked, "Reee-cruits, *read-y!*"

The squad assumed the "ready" position.

"Take aim!"

Rifles came to shoulders up and down the line.

"Fire!"

Rifles cracked.

After two rounds, Jimmy stopped firing and began to fiddle with his M14's rear sight.

"Cease fire! Cease fire!" The RM practically flew to Jimmy's firing bay. "Reee-cruit Hamilton, is there a problem with your weapon?" he roared.

"No, Range Master. My rifle is firing high and to the right. I'm just adjusting the sights."

The RM practically erupted, spittle flying as he screamed, "Reee-cruit, do you think you're better at sighting this weapon than the battalion armorer? The same one who's been sighting rifles on this range since you were suckin' on your mama's tit?"

"No, Range Mast—"

"You're goddamn right you're not! If you think your rifle is firing high and to the right, then aim *low and to the left!*"

"Yes, Range Master!"

The RM returned to his central position. "Now, if Reee-cruit Hamilton is ready to proceed," he yelled, glaring at Jimmy, "re-sume firing!"

Once again, rifles cracked up and down the line. The squad completed each firing position and automatic firing burst at the end. The RM noticed that bay #17, Jimmy's bay, had completed the shot sequence several minutes before the rest of the squad.

The RM shook his head and muttered to himself, "Little bastard's not taking this seriously enough. Guess Mr. Left-Eye Dominant is gonna be the object lesson for this class of recruits. There's one in every group."

When firing had ceased, the RM stalked to firing bay #17. Through the intercom, he asked, "How many strikes are on number seventeen?"

The intercom crackled a barely intelligible, "Three—" before a burst of static drowned the remainder of the response.

"Bring me number seventeen on the double!" the RM ordered. Feeling more than a little smug, he called the squad. "Gather around and take a knee. Let's see how our Davy Crockett did with his shiny new M14."

While the range assistant was retrieving Jimmy's target, the RM began, "Gentlemen, this is the US Army. The mission of the US Army is to project force if necessary to secure and protect this great nation of ours. My job is to teach you recruits to shoot in support of the army's mission. Now, some of you"— he glared at Jimmy—"might *think* you know how to fire a weapon..."

The range assistant returned with Jimmy's target, which contained only three holes. One was ragged, about the size of a silver dollar, and had obliterated the center X of the bullseye. The other two formed a perfect figure-eight three inches high and to the right of where the X *used* to be but still well within the bullseye circle.

The RM stared at the target, then at Jimmy, and then back at the target. "Squad dis-missed! I want those rifles broken down, cleaned, oiled, and ready for inspection in ten!" Without another word, he turned on his heel and strode into the range office, where he met the RSO, Range Safety Officer, Captain Brightman.

"Cap, take a look at this!" The RM slid the target across the desk.

"Great-looking target, RM! Nice job zeroing your scope...at what, a hundred yards?"

The RM shook his head. "Not my target. No scope. *Two* hundred yards, and before you ask me, offhand, no sandbag!"

"You're shitting me! Who, then?"

The RM nodded toward Jimmy, who was busily reassembling his rifle.

"Day-um, who the Hell is he? Sergeant Alvin fuckin' York?"

Afterward, I was called to see the RSO, a Captain Brightman, who tried (without success) to convince me to change my MOS from medic to sniper. I thought you might enjoy hearing about the fruits of your tutelage. :-)

I miss you, Uncle!

James

P.S.: Please pass along my thanks to Charlotte for the snickerdoodles. They were a big hit with my squadmates!

In retrospect, changing Jimmy's military occupational specialty from combat medic to sniper might have been a good idea. Certainly, the change in career fields would've saved him a great deal of pain and embarrassment. No doubt, had he been a typical draftee rather than someone who "volunteered" after receiving his draft notice, the army wouldn't have hesitated to send him to sniper school. However, as a volunteer, Jimmy had received a contractual guarantee allowing for self-selection of his MOS. If the contract specified he become an army medic, then an army medic he would be, provided that he successfully completed the training course.

Upon finishing basic training, Jimmy received orders to Fort Sam Houston to begin the army's ten-week Combat Medic Course. There, Jimmy and his classmates learned about hygiene and the basic tenets of triage. They were taught how to treat broken bones, gunshot wounds, burns, amputations, and basic healthcare—to include, but not limited to, the recognition and treatment of venereal diseases.

Jimmy and his cohorts watched dozens of training films. They learned to give shots, start intravenous lines and draw blood; perfecting their techniques upon one another.

The course featured lectures on pharmacology, physiology, anatomy, and countless other topics they'd need to perform well as medics in the field.

In addition to the classroom portions of their training, Jimmy's class also received practical training. They learned how to transport patients using a fireman's carry or stretcher. They practiced on each other and upon patients with moulage (simulated) wounds under the watchful eyes of their instructors. Jimmy loved every moment of his instruction and excelled in each phase of the combat medic course, or at least he did, right up until the final exam.

The course's final examination was practical, rather than classroom, which didn't worry Jimmy. He'd done well treating simulated wounds over the preceding nine weeks and had no reason to expect that he'd have any additional difficulty during the final. He was unaware, however, that the wounds he and his three teammates would be treating that day would not be moulage. They'd be real.

The day of the final dawned unseasonably warm, even for San Antonio. Jimmy and his team donned full combat gear and packs before being marched twenty miles to a field on the fringes of Fort Sam Houston. By the time they arrived at the field, they were all hot and sweating profusely, but there was no shade. There, they were told to wait for further instructions.

After two hours' waiting, Jimmy's team was startled by a loud explosion and the sound of automatic weapons fire. This was followed by animalistic screams and frantic calls of "MEDIC!"

Jimmy's team grabbed their gear and sprinted toward the sound. As they crested a rise, the team observed six wounded and dying pigs and a coterie of instructors standing mute holding clipboards.

The team hesitated, unsure what to do.

One of the instructors again shouted, "MEDIC!" and the team moved forward, intent upon putting to practice the knowledge they'd gained during the course.

Jimmy cautiously approached a grievously wounded boar. It was thrashing wildly and had a coil of intestine hanging from a massive, open wound in its abdomen. It looked to Jimmy like the poor animal had been close to a grenade when it exploded. As he neared the animal, he was hit simultaneously by the smell of ruptured bowel and a gout of hot arterial blood—right in his face.

Immediately, he felt a wave of nausea. This was followed by everything in the field around him losing color—just dimming to gray—and the ground coming up to smack him, although he never felt himself hit.

Jimmy awoke a few moments later to find a bag of IV fluid running into his arm and one of his teammates tending to a laceration on his forehead. Nearby, two of his instructors stared at him, shaking their heads in disgust.

Nearby, the pigs still screamed.

Jimmy struggled to his knees. He shrugged off assistance and crawled back to his own wounded pig. As saline ran into his own arm, he tended to the animal's wounds. When he finished, he moved on to another. Twice, he felt lightheaded and was forced to stop and take several deep breaths before getting back to work, but he managed not to completely pass out again.

Two of the four instructors wanted to fail Jimmy on the spot for having passed out at the sight of real blood. The other two, however, pointed out that, although he had been "wounded" during the exercise, Jimmy had returned to render aid to the other animals until the exercise was over. They argued Jimmy's actions were *precisely* those expected of a medic in an actual combat situation and were therefore laudable.

With two instructors voting to fail, and two voting to pass, Jimmy's fate rested solely with the school's commander.

The commander, noting Jimmy's superlative performance on the didactic portion of the course, and with knowledge of the urgent need for medics, elected to sign off on Jimmy's combat medic certificate.

With that stroke of his commander's pen, Jimmy was shipped off to Vietnam.

CHAPTER 26

MARCH 1966

A FTER COMPLETING THE COMBAT MEDIC training course at Fort Sam Houston, Jimmy traveled from the US to South Vietnam by boat. He'd never been on a ship before and, God willing, he never would be again. As a country boy, he'd never been in a boat larger than a rowboat or a body of water larger than a mill pond, and he was immediately beset by sea sickness. He spent the entire voyage alternating between moaning in his bunk, retching over the aft rail of the troop transport, and praying to be allowed to die. By the time his voyage ended at Cam Ranh Bay, he'd lost almost twenty pounds.

Jimmy hitched a ride in the back of a deuce-and-a-half to his regiment's base camp near Da'k To in the Central Highlands of Vietnam. The transfer was hot and bumpy, but after the torture of the past month at sea, he felt close to euphoria. His orders dictated that Jimmy report immediately to Headquarters Company of the 503rd Regiment on arrival. There, he'd been informed, the first sergeant would get him "squared away."

Although he'd done well in the "land navigation" portion of basic training, Jimmy wouldn't have believed it that day.

He got lost three times between the motor pool and the first sergeant's tent, and had to ask for directions. His problem? Without signage, the landmarks described as waypoints by the helpful strangers all looked the same to Jimmy.

Finally, he found his destination and rapped smartly on the bunker's doorframe. Inside, the first sergeant had been shaving, and when Jimmy knocked, he'd given himself a nasty nick on his Adams apple.

From inside the bunker, Jimmy heard a string of expletives. An instant later, the door was flung open. Jimmy cringed reflexively. Before him, wearing nothing but his skivvies, stood a bear of a man. Half the man's face was covered with shaving cream and a thin rivulet of blood trickled down his neck toward the matted jungle of black hair on his chest.

"Who the Hell are you and what the fuck do you want?" the man demanded.

Master Sergeant Holloway had been in "this man's army" since the late days of World War II. While just a green recruit, he'd distinguished himself outside of Bastogne during the Battle of the Bulge in December, 1944. Later, in Korea, he'd been wounded near Wonju in February of 1951 as part of the 173rd Airborne Regimental Combat Team. Now, he was the HQ Company "first shirt" for Second Battalion, 503rd Regiment of the 173rd Airborne Brigade. After three wars and twenty-two years of soldiering, he wasn't a patient man and didn't suffer idiots.

Before him stood an idiot. *Jesus H. Christ, I ask for a medic and the replacement depot, in their infinite wisdom, sends me this wet-behind-the-ears piece of shit*, he thought as he stood appraising young Jimmy.

"Who the *Hell* are you?" Holloway growled.

"Um, Private Hamilton, First Sergeant! I was told to find you." Jimmy riffled through his pockets searching for his orders.

"I don't need your goddamn orders. I know who you are!" Holloway dabbed at his bleeding neck with a towel.

"I have a styptic pencil if—" Jimmy began helpfully but was cut off by a glare from the first sergeant. "Never...mind."

"I know who you are, Hamilton. I've heard *all* about you. You're that piece of shit medic who can't stand the sight of blood. What's this fucking army coming to?!"

Jimmy went pale.

"And what the fuck do you think you're wearin'?!"

Jimmy looked down. "My uniform, First Sergeant?"

"Of course you're wearing your goddamn uniform. What are you? Some kind of fuckin' comedian? The red crosses, dumbass!"

"Um, I'm a medic, First Sergeant?"

"Of course you're a goddamn medic!" The vein bulging from his forehead looked ready to burst.

Jimmy wondered if the first sergeant was about to have a stroke.

Then in a controlled tone like someone talking to a simpleton, Holloway continued, "Those red crosses out there in Indian country...Mister Charlie Sniper sees 'em"—he yanked his thumb toward the jungle—"and thinks, *Now ain't that a convenient goddamn target,* then, *BANG!* I need another dumbass medic. This is a fuckin' war, not a dress parade! Don't they teach you guys anything back at Fort Sam?!"

Holloway sighed and shook his head. "Just lose the fuckin' crosses. You're assigned to HQ Company. As such, you may be pulled into the field by any of the line companies as need arises. Check in at the dispensary, and they'll show you to your billet. Sick call runs 0700 to 0900 every day when you're not actively deployed. That's your baby to rock. You can draw your weapon from the armory. It's that bunker—"

Startled, Jimmy interrupted, "Weapon?"

"This is the fuckin' army, Hamilton. Of course you'll draw a weapon! As a medic, you have the option of the M16, a piece of shit in my opinion, or a .45-caliber—"

Foolishly, Jimmy interrupted again. "But I'm supposed to be a noncombatant, First Sergeant."

Holloway stared daggers at Jimmy and resumed speaking, enunciating every word like the former drill instructor he was. "*Or* a .45-caliber pistol. Yes, Private Hamilton, in the eyes of the US Army, you are a noncombatant. When Charlie's shoving a bayonet through your goddamn liver, you just go right ahead and tell *him* you're a noncombatant. I'm sure he'll stop and apologize! Charlie don't give a hoot in Hell about you bein' a *fuck-ing* noncombatant! So, you go and draw your goddamn weapon, and when Charlie comes with his bayonet, you send him to commie Hell!"

"Yes, First Sergeant!" Jimmy said meekly.

Having made his point, Holloway softened his tone. "Look, Hamilton, your job out there is to take care of your platoonmates. You take care of them, they take care of you. That's the way it works. In the best of worlds, you'll never fire your weapon. You won't be walking point. You won't be playing tunnel rat. Still, it's better to have a weapon and not need it than need it and not have one."

Duly chastened, Jimmy took Master Sergeant Holloway's "advice" and reported to the armory bunker. There he drew his weapon, a Colt M1911-A1 .45-caliber pistol, and a cleaning kit and three magazines. After checking in at the dispensary and dropping his gear off at his assigned tent, he made his way to the camp's makeshift firing range and began to familiarize himself with his new sidearm. Over the subsequent weeks, he became rather proficient. Not as much as he had with his .22 rifle back home, but he always hit where he aimed and was able to routinely create a two-inch grouping at fifty yards. Beyond that range, he felt the pistol was little more accurate than a blunderbuss. Still, that was more than acceptable, especially since he wasn't planning on using the thing anyway.

Jimmy's camp accommodations were by no means luxurious, but at least he was off the ground and, sweat notwithstanding, dry when he slept each night. The tent flaps could be raised to allow air to circulate whenever there was a breeze, which wasn't often. Given the number of insect wings beating just outside his mosquito netting, Jimmy figured there should be at least gale-force winds. But alas, this was seldom true. The wall of sandbags that surrounded his tent did little to improve ventilation but was a most welcome feature during mortar or rocket attacks.

Sharing the tent were Adam Riggs and Colton "Goose" Lampley. A few months later, they were joined by Isaiah "Ike" Wigfall. All were draftees who had been lumped together in the melting pot that was the army.

Adam Riggs was short and powerfully built, and he needed to be. He was a radio operator. The radio itself only weighed thirteen-and-a-half pounds, but with extra batteries and the obligatory encryption device, the pack he carried weighed almost fifty-five pounds. This was in addition to his personal weapon, ammunition, canteen, and other standard pack items. His father owned Smokey's BBQ in Kansas City, and he loved to regale his messmates about dry-rubs, ribs, and pulled pork as they chowed down on C-rations. After the war, he planned to go back to KC and open a second

Smokey's location with his dad and maybe someday start a franchise.

Colton Lampley came to the army from Leighton, Alabama. He was a rifleman and had a long, thin neck. With his large, hooked nose and standard issue BCGs (birth control glasses) with their thick black frames and Coke-bottle lenses, he bore a striking resemblance to a goose, and a sobriquet was born. He'd been raised on a peanut farm, but his passion was music and he boasted of having once met Percy Sledge at a function back in Leighton. When not serving as rifleman, he spent most of his time picking his Gibson B-25 acoustic guitar.

Ike Wigfall haled from Detroit, where he'd been a standout basketball star in high school. At six-foot-six even without his pre-army afro, he'd been recruited heavily to play college ball for both Michigan and Indiana, but his grades didn't reach either school's minimum admission requirements. He had applied to a finishing academy to rehab his GPA, but that hadn't been enough to protect him from the draft. Therefore, now instead of shooting at baskets, he shot at hidden Viet Cong, and usually on full-auto. In his helmet, he always carried a photograph of his kid sister, who resembled a young Diana Ross, and if Ike was to be believed, she could sing even better than the original.

Frequently, Ike and Goose had good-natured arguments regarding the relative merits of their hometown musical styles. Ike strongly declared the superiority of Smokey Robinson and Marvin Gaye, whereas Goose was equally steadfast in his support of Wilson Pickett and Percy Sledge. Each, firmly convinced that their preferred style of soul and R&B music was the best, often co-opted Jimmy to serve as judge, having him listen to record after record. However, since he was tone-deaf, Jimmy's judicial renderings did little to bring the matter to a close.

Jimmy got along well with his bunkmates, and though they seemed to like him well enough, it also seemed that whenever he was selected to join patrols, each unit was ill at ease about having him with them in the field. He suspected that his reputation for passing out at the sight of blood had preceded him. It worried him too. What would happen if the men needed him, but he was too incapacitated to help?

Once, Jimmy had overheard a group of guys from A-Company complaining about being uncomfortable with a particular medic. Although his name was never mentioned, he was pretty certain they were talking about him. Distraught, he wrote Uncle Howard, who wrote back and assured him he was not the only GI to be nervous before going into battle for the first time. Although Howard had been certain that when the time came, Jimmy would "do okay," he recommended that maybe he should talk through his concerns with the camp chaplain.

Captain Charles Campbell was the chaplain assigned to Jimmy's unit. He had been in-country for ten months and was scheduled to rotate back to the States in another two months. He had a reputation for kindness and for being uncannily steady under fire and, unlike most officers, was actually approachable. Campbell was sitting on his footlocker when Jimmy knocked on his tent frame.

"Chaplain Campbell, do you have a moment?"

"Enter! Ah, Private Hamilton, what can I do for you, son?"

"Sir, I—" Jimmy began.

"Don't stand there, son. Sit-sit-sit," Campbell said with a disarming smile, motioning to his cot. "And in this tent, as in the eyes of God, there is no rank. Speak freely, son. How may I help?"

"Well, sir..."

Campbell gave him an amused look over top of his wire-rimmed glasses. "Sir?"

"It's a southern thing, sir. If I didn't call you 'sir,' my granddaddy would come up out of the grave and get me!"

Campbell chuckled. "Well, we wouldn't want *that* to happen, now, would we, son? You were saying?"

Jimmy gave a brief history of his childhood trauma with Anna and his violent reactions to the sight of blood thereafter. "Sir, I'm afraid I won't be able to do my job when...well, you know...when I need to. The guys trust me to take care of them. What happens if they need me out there and I freeze? Or worse? Everybody says you're always calm and steady. How do you do it?"

Chaplain Campbell nodded thoughtfully. "I can see where you might be concerned. A medic who can't stand the sight of blood...that's a difficult burden to bear."

Jimmy stared at his feet, too ashamed to meet the chaplain's eye.

Campbell continued, "Look at me, son."

"Yes, sir."

Campbell smiled. "Let me tell you a story. Right after I arrived in-country, I joined in on a routine patrol...a search-and-destroy mission. Intel assured us that there were no Cong in the area, so I decided to tag along. It seemed like a good way for me to get to know the men, and I thought it would be good for them to see me out in the field...the whole 'shared bond of combat' thing.

"On our third night out of base camp, we were splashing this rice paddy when our point-man tripped a mine and lost a leg. A moment later, a flare went up and we started getting hit by automatic weapon fire from the dike to our front and small arms and mortar fire from somewhere to our right. We lost half of the lead platoon within the first two minutes. I was with the company commander near second platoon when he went down with a piece of shrapnel in his neck. By the time I got to him, it was clear he wasn't going to make it. So, I gave him last rites and moved on to another gravely wounded man and another after that. I helped the ones I could and prayed for the ones I couldn't.

"After what felt like forever, we called in arty, and that drove the Vietnamese away. Intel had been right," he said with a sardonic grin. "There were *no* VC in the area, but there *was* a battalion of NVA Regulars.

"It's funny the things you remember when you're under fire. What I remember most was the smell of shit. The smell was everywhere. After the battle was over, I still smelled it. I noticed that my legs were wet and thought, *Oh no, I've been wounded*. It was only then that I realized I'd shit myself when we got ambushed. When nobody was looking, I dropped into the paddy and rinsed out my drawers. Nobody ever knew, or if they did, they didn't care 'cause they were too busy cleaning their own drawers.

"Bottom line, son," Campbell said, placing a reassuring hand on Jimmy's shoulder, "when the time comes, you're not going to be any more scared than the guy next to you. When it's all over, you might have to clean your drawers, but you'll be no less a man for having done so. You *will* do your job...and you'll do it well. When those boys need you, you'll be there and they'll be damned glad you were with them. You'll take good care of them when they're wounded, and you'll be there for them when they're dying. That's all any soldier can ask."

"Thank you, sir!" Jimmy rose from the bed and began to salute. Remembering the chaplain's earlier admonition, his hand froze midway to his brow, where it was grasped by the chaplain's own, in a handshake.

"You're welcome, son."

Jimmy felt better after his conversation with Chaplain Campbell. He supposed no one *really* knows how they'll react to combat until the bullets began to fly. A weak smile broke over his previously worried face.

Maybe Uncle and Chaplain Campbell were right. Maybe he'd do okay.

CHAPTER 27

APRIL–MAY 1966

O VER HIS FIRST SEVERAL WEEKS in-country, Jimmy felt like an outsider, even on post. He was uncertain if his exclusion was the typical old-hand's predisposition toward eschewing newcomers—don't get too attached to the newbies lest they get killed too soon—or if his reputation for fainting at the sight of blood had preceded him, as it had with Holloway. Either way, nobody stood too close to him while out on patrol.

During basic training and the combat medic course, Jimmy had learned how to be a soldier and how to keep himself and the soldiers entrusted to his care alive. He felt like he'd learned a lot—and he had—but once he got to Vietnam, he found out precisely how much he *didn't* know. And it scared him.

Perhaps it was because he was the medic whose job it was to keep *them* alive, or perhaps it was out of pity. Regardless the reason, a few of the old hands eschewed superstition and took Jimmy under wing, teaching him how to *not* get killed while operating in hostile territory.

The patrols Jimmy was tasked to accompany over the first month were generally "milk runs" contained well within the boundaries of base camp's green zone, areas previously cleared of enemy combatants in which direct hostile action was not expected. The operative word was *direct*. On these patrols, Jimmy learned the myriads of diabolical indirect ways a determined foe could inflict injury or death upon their enemies.

One of the first lessons he learned was never to walk on a path or game trail. Such trails were inviting when traversing dense Vietnamese vegetation but were prime spots for placement of booby traps or ambuscade.

Booby traps were low tech, improvised setups designed by the Viet Cong and were intended to injure or maim, more so than to kill. They knew well, injuring a single man would slow or stop an entire platoon much more effectively than killing that same man. And the traps they devised were both ingenious and effective.

There were punji sticks, snake pits, flag bombs, bamboo whips, maces, and tiger traps. Another particularly insidious trap involved a rifle cartridge placed on a hole against a striker, usually a nail. An unsuspecting person stepping in the hold would drive the cartridge against the striker and cause it to fire up through the foot. This trap, commonly known as a toe-popper, was particularly dreaded because it was almost impossible to detect.

Thankfully, each of Jimmy's early patrols ended without incident, giving him opportunity to test his recently learned skills, or his vagus nerve.

Back at the base camp, Jimmy slipped into the routines and responsibilities of his post. He was still worried, albeit less so after his conversation with Chaplain Campbell, about what would happen when he was faced with the sight of blood again.

When not in the field, most of his time was spent in garrison where he ran a daily sick call for the troops and manned clinics for the Vietnamese people who surrounded the camp. With little or no hostile action in his sector of Vietnam, he gave vaccinations and treated all manner of afflictions, minor and major, that did not require hospital-ization. He generally enjoyed this aspect of garrison duty, but often he ended his day shaking his head in dismay and, sometimes, in disgust.

"Damnation, Ballentine! What the Hell have you been doing? Actually, don't answer that. I already know," Jimmy said shaking his head. It had been a fairly busy morning in sick call with the usual assortment of aches, pains, and rashes. Rick Ballentine, a machine gunner from Alpha Company, took today's prize.

Ballentine grinned. "Nothin', Doc...I swear!"

"Dude, you've got four *different* kinds of VD! Man, that takes talent. If you keep this shit up, that thing's gonna fall off."

"Maybe so, but until it does, I'm gonna get as much as I can!"

Ballentine's tongue seemed a little thick as he spoke and, as Jimmy suspected, the whites of his eyes looked like bright red road maps.

"You're not on duty today are you, Ballentine?"

"Naw, man. Why?

"Nothin', just making sure. You look like you might still be a little high."

"Yeah, Doc. Roberson had some really good shit last night. He's got more. You oughta come by later. He'll fix you up too, and he's got a girl over there that will blow your choir-boy mind."

Jimmy cut him off. "I'll pass, thanks. And if she's the one that got you here," he said, motioning to Ballentine's crotch, "then you should too!"

"Naw, Nanay, she's good, Doc!"

"Uh-huh." Jimmy was unconvinced. "Still, I'll pass. Take these pills for a week and keep your 'bayonet' sheathed for a while. And, Ballentine, lay off smoking that shit when you're headed to the field. You might get yourself or somebody else killed out there if you don't."

"I hear ya, Doc. I hear ya."

Shaking his head, Jimmy watched him leave. *He'll be back*, he thought. Then he called to the queue outside the sick call tent, "O'Brien, you're the next contestant. What can I do for you today?"

And so it went as Jimmy did his best to keep the men in fighting form, as often from their own stupidity as from injuries due to the war. After that particularly grueling day in the clinic, he returned to his tent and wrote Becca.

May 2, 1966

Dear Becca,

In yesterday's letter, I mentioned the Vietnamese children and had planned to expand on the topic in that letter. However, I had to get to sick call and never got back to writing before mail call, which is the only time we can post letters. It also gave me an excuse to write you again today—as though I need one.

I mentioned before the things that one notices immediately upon arrival to Vietnam. Heat, humidity, smell, and bugs took the top spots. Coming up strong behind those are the children. The children are at once warm... and break my heart.

As you know, my family, like just about everybody else's in Boiling Springs, was not wealthy. However, compared to the people here, we lived and ate like kings! Almost all of the children here are rail thin and malnourished. There are huge rats around the garbage dump that the children whack on the head and take home to eat. Dogs and cats, the few that are here, don't survive very long before suffering similar fates.

The kids are always begging us for scraps from our C-rations. A piece of candy or bite of chocolate earns their undying affection. After I gave one little girl a whole C-rat box, she offered to marry me. She couldn't have been more than twelve years old, and she was *serious*. She even brought her father by my tent to prove that she was sincere. I declined the offer, by the way. Instead, I gave her father a whole case of C-rations that I had bartered away from the guys in the mess tent. Every day since then, when I come back to my tent after sick call, I find the tent swept out, my spare boots shined and cleaned, and a pressed uniform on the foot of my cot. I can't get her to stop. It breaks my heart!

Some of the more desperate kids offer to sell themselves, or their sisters, to us for just scraps of food. And it disgusts me that some of my fellow soldiers actually take them up on it! And command turns a blind eye!

Just outside base, drugs and brothels abound. Just about anything a boy, not only away from home for the first time but thousands of miles away from that home, could desire can be had for less than a buck!

Some of these guys have no clue whatsoever! I guess they figure if they can be killed tomorrow, what do they have to lose today?

Sorry about the depressing letter! Thanks for listening... rather, for reading. I miss your smile. I could use it today!

Sincerely,

Jimmy

CHAPTER 28

MAY 1966

NOW THAT JIMMY HAD TWO people to write to who actually wrote him back, his letter writing became even more prolific than the once-a-week letters he'd written his mother all those years. Most days, he posted at least one letter to his uncle or Becca, or to both. And once each week, he still dutifully posted a letter to his mother. As before, Margaret Hamilton deigned not to reply. Letters home that had always come back "Return to Sender" now seemed just to disappear into the void, or more likely the kitchen garbage can. Still, he wrote.

In the months before Jimmy's arrival to Vietnam, his unit had been involved in heavy fighting. Afterward, they'd been moved back to their base camp, located in a relatively pacified part of the country, for a period of rest and refitting. Thus, for a full two months, Jimmy only had opportunity to treat minor injuries, giving him no opportunity to test his skills...or his overly sensitive vagus nerve.

One day in May, an event occurred that cured him once and for all of his doubts regarding his ability to care for his fellow soldiers. Afterward, back in his bunk, he proudly related the event to Howard.

May 10, 1966

Dear Uncle,

Thank you for your letter! As always, your words of encouragement and advice were most welcome. I can only hope someday that I will be as wise as you.

Much has changed since my last letter, and I am feeling more confident about my role here. I won't say I feel completely comfortable, but I do think that I will be able to do my job when called.

A few weeks ago, a group of VC snuck to within a few hundred yards of the base and blew up a fuel truck. Our commander went totally apeshit, convinced the base was under imminent threat of attack. He had guys stringing new concertina wire along the perimeter and digging even more machine-gun emplacements all week. I swear, this whole camp is little more than sandbags, razor wire, and mosquitos! Even the improved fortifications were deemed inadequate. So he ordered a new mine field be put in near the perimeter fence. Unfortunately, it was also close to one of the off-base bars run by the locals... a favorite watering hole for off-duty GIs.

Rick Ballentine, one of the guys from A Company, was off base at the bar and got totally wasted on a combination of booze and God knows what else. After staggering back to the main gate, he realized he'd left his favorite tiger-striped boonie hat at the bar. Rather than go back the way he had come, he decided to take a shortcut along the wire. A week before, there would have been no problem with his improvised route. This time, it took him right through the middle of the new minefield...

Before anyone could stop the drunken soldier, a mine exploded with a muffled *CRUMP*, followed immediately by screams of pain. Overhead, something twirled lazily in the air before landing with a sickening *splat* beside the main gate. It was the soldier's lower leg, still laced into his combat boot. Immediately, panicked cries of "Medic!" went up from the gate guard and several onlookers. Although each was within thirty yards of the wounded man, none dared venture into the minefield to render assistance.

Jimmy was in his tent writing a letter when he heard the call. Immediately, he grabbed his M5 medic bag and rushed toward the main gate. Without thinking, he ran straight to the wounded man, placed a tourniquet on the leg, and gave him a shot of morphine.

After the morphine kicked in, Ballentine became lucid enough to notice blood all over his crotch. He grabbed Jimmy's arm and, in a trembling voice, spluttered, "Did I...did I...oh God, do I still have my..."

Recognizing the source of Ballentine's panic, Jimmy cut away the blood-soaked trousers and took a quick look. Affecting a grave expression, he said, "Ballentine, I've got some good news and some bad news."

"Oh God!"

"The good news is, you're going home!" Jimmy shook his head somberly. "The bad news is, I think you've got VD again."

Relief swept immediately over the wounded man's face.

Only then did it dawn upon Jimmy that he was squatting in the middle of a minefield. Beads of sweat immediately broke out on his forehead. He gave Ballentine a cigarette and another shot of morphine.

"Ballentine, I'm going have to carry you out of here. I'm not going to lie to you, it's gonna hurt like a bitch, but I need you to stay perfectly still. Otherwise, we're both fucked!"

Ballentine nodded understanding and flicked his cigarette deeper into the minefield.

Jimmy threw his M5 bag to one of the onlookers and took Ballentine into a fireman's carry. He retraced his steps, careful to step only on the footprints from his earlier headlong dash to Ballentine's side. Arriving safely to the minefield's boundary, someone relieved Jimmy of his burden and rushed Ballentine to the hospital tent. Immediately, Jimmy collapsed to the ground and became violently ill, projectile vomiting his lunch. A moment later, breakfast followed and then what looked like last night's dinner.

Afterward, I couldn't stop shaking. Funny thing is, the guys didn't seem to notice. They kept slapping me on the back, shaking my hand, and offering to buy me beers. Later, I talked with Chaplain Campbell. He said the commander was going to put me in for a medal, a Silver Star, I think he said. I don't understand. All I did was what I was trained to do... that and **NOT** get blown up. On another positive note, there was blood everywhere, but I didn't pass out! That was a nice change!

I've got to run. Time, tides, and sick call wait for no man.

Yours truly,

James

CHAPTER 29

JUNE 1966

THE EPISODE WITH BALLENTINE IN the minefield had a markedly transformative effect upon Jimmy. His confidence soared, and he no longer feared being unable to care for his wounded comrades. The effect spilled over into the way he was viewed by his fellow soldiers too. Before Ballentine, when he was assigned to a patrol, his presence was met with eye rolling and not-so-subtle jibes. As word circulated around camp about Jimmy's dash into the minefield, he became the medic the soldiers *wanted* to join them for patrols. When he was with them, they felt safe—or as safe as any soldier can feel on patrol in a hostile environment. In an instant, Jimmy had been transformed from pariah to messiah.

A few weeks later, Jimmy got to test his newfound confidence and verified that, indeed, he'd lost his aversion to blood, although not in the manner one might have expected.

He was sitting on his cot practicing his most common off-duty pastime, writing a letter to Becca, when from outside his tent he heard a loud, high-pitched screech sounding like a child in severe pain. Soon, there were multiple voices, but the cries continued. Immediately concerned, he dropped his pen and paper, grabbed his medical bag, and sprinted into the compound. Behind his tent, by the perimeter fence, he saw a cluster of GIs milling about, and the cries seemed to be coming from within their midst.

Jimmy pushed through the throng of GIs and found, hopelessly ensnarled in the concertina wire, a huge orange tabby. Apparently, the cat had been seeking a safe place to hide, likely from pursuing camp kids intent upon having cat for supper, and had run into the coils of wire where it had become trapped. It thrashed, twisted, and struggled. With each move, the razor wire produced deep painful gashes through the cat's coat, which only further enraged and terrified the animal.

All attempts to rescue the poor cat had ended with GIs being clawed or bitten or cut to ribbons by the wire. One of the military police, a gate guard, was just drawing his sidearm to put the animal out of its misery when Jimmy arrived on the scene. Jimmy stayed his hand, hoping to have better luck than his brothers in arms at rescuing the feline.

He dropped to the ground and rifled through his M5 bag, soon withdrawing a vial of ether. It wasn't standard issue for a medical bag, but he'd snagged the vial from the dispensary, believing it might someday prove useful. He doused a piece of gauze with the ether and gingerly reached through the coiled wire toward the cat. He received a painful slash on the back of his hand but was able to clamp the ether-soaked rag over the cat's nose for several seconds. Soon, the animal stopped struggling and went limp. No longer fighting against his rescuers, they were able to extract him from the tangled wire.

The poor cat was a bloody mess from his nose to the tip of his tail. Part of one ear was missing, and the tail had been skinned down to the bone. The cat's entire body was a road map of lacerations, all bleeding freely.

Jimmy took the cat back to his tent where he transformed his cot into a makeshift operating table. There, he shaved, cleaned, and sutured the animal's many wounds. Seeing no way to save the cat's avulsed tail, Jimmy re-dosed him with ether and amputated the distal third. By the time he finished tending to its many wounds, the poor animal looked more like Frankenstein's monster or a mummy than he did a cat. Conservatively, he gave the cat a fifty-fifty chance of recovery. Hopefully, the feline had another life or two left of his nine. He was gonna need 'em!

When he finished caring for the animal, Jimmy looked around his tent. Blood, gauze, and matted cat fur covered his cot. Only then did he notice the four parallel slashes oozing blood from the back of his hand—wounds received while rescuing his patient from the wire. A moment later, he felt a wave of relief wash over him. In spite of all the blood and gore, he hadn't fainted!

I guess I really can *do this, after all,* he thought.

Over the next few weeks, Jimmy's patient made a full recovery, although a more tattered, patched-up cat he'd never seen. He figured since the cat had lived, he probably should have a name. Fondly remembering Kitty Lamarr, Jimmy wanted to choose a name that fit the cat. With all his wounds, the poor cat looked like a pirate, but for his coloration, Calico Jack would have been an obvious choice of name. Failing that, Captain Kidd-y was an early favorite. Later, after the cat had recovered further, Jimmy noticed it demonstrated definite communist, collectivistic tendencies—everything Jimmy owned now also belonged to the cat. Thus, for several weeks he referred to the cat as Chairman

Meow. Ultimately, it was an event in late June that served as catalyst for the feline's official nom de guerre.

Army intelligence, G-2, reported several large weapons caches being used by the Viet Cong in the area. Delta Company was tasked with a search-and-destroy mission, and Jimmy was deployed with them. The company was successful in their mission and never saw any enemy combatants. Nonetheless, they suffered several casualties from mines, booby traps, and snipers along the way. Consequently, when Jimmy returned to his compound, it was well after dark and he was exhausted.

On Jimmy's return, he found the tent empty except for Chairman Meow, curled up asleep on the foot of his cot. His bunkmates, apparently, were still out on patrol. Jimmy tossed his gear on the unoccupied portion of the cot, disturbing the poor cat's slumber, and padded out of the tent in search of a much-needed shower. When he returned from his shower twenty minutes later, the cat was no longer on the bed. Instead, he was underneath the cot, next to Jimmy's hastily discarded combat boots, batting about a piece of black rubber tubing.

Jimmy lit a lantern and reached down to take the tubing away from the cat, wondering where the animal had found it. Immediately, he yelped and jerked his hand back. What had appeared in the half-light to be rubber tubing was in actuality a two-foot-long king cobra. Thankfully, on closer inspection, he found the snake to be dead, recently killed by his cat.

Thereafter, Jimmy called his cat Rikki-Tikki-Tabby, after the mongoose that saved the children from a poisonous snake in Rudyard Kipling's *Rikki-Tikki-Tavi,* one of the books he'd read after first going to live with Howard.

CHAPTER 30

JUNE–NOVEMBER 1966

T HROUGH HIS LETTERS WITH BECCA, Jimmy kept
up with current events in Boiling Springs. Initially,
he wrote chatty letters about his daily life and the
lives of his friends. Over time, a change became evident in
the tone of his letters. He started talking about his hopes,
dreams, and plans for the future and how Becca might fit
into those plans. From half a world away, Jimmy was falling
in love.

He enjoyed the country of Vietnam and genuinely liked
the people, finding them to be hardworking and industrious
with strong family ties. He enjoyed treating the locals in his
medical clinic and had a blast playing with the camp kids
during his downtime between missions. Their poverty sad-
dened him greatly, and he did everything within his power
to alleviate their suffering and improve their daily lives.

Interestingly, Jimmy held no malice toward the North
Vietnamese soldiers or local Viet Cong fighters. He believed
them to be brave and respected their tenacity and ability to
effectively oppose a better trained and supplied force.

Jimmy also thought them ingenious, and although he
respected the North Vietnamese fighters, he found their

booby traps and tactics often to be diabolical. Few situations can make a man feel more helpless than watching a tripwire pulling taught against a buddy's leg. For Jimmy, it was like watching someone fall off a building. You see it happening, but there's nothing that can be done to stop it. And invariably, it was his job to deal with the aftermath.

He rarely spoke about the battles he fought or the terrible things he saw in his letters to Becca. These topics he generally reserved for Uncle Howard.

One exception occurred in August of 1966, after a particularly difficult battle in which Jimmy lost several friends and was himself lightly wounded. He wrote:

August 21, 1966

Dearest Becca,

My unit was involved in major fighting last week. On a routine patrol, we were ambushed by a vastly larger force of VC and NVA Regulars. Casualties were heavy. Wigfall was killed. He took a piece of shrapnel to the neck, and there was nothing I could do to save him. I held him as he died. We also lost Seigel, Roberson, and Strickland.

About half the platoon was wounded, including yours truly. It is nothing serious. I got grazed by a shell fragment just above my left ear. Luckily, my head was too hard for it to do any real damage. Still, I bled like a stuck hog and have had blinding headaches for the past week. I really cannot complain. I was lucky. I still have all my appendages attached and no holes or scrapes that won't heal. That's plenty better than most.

Wigfall said he wanted me to have his records and player before he died. He's lying there dying and thinking about music. I hope it gave him some peace...

I'm going to cut this short. I'm having a hard time focusing on the page. Maybe it's the headache... maybe it's the tears. Either way, everything is all blurry.

Listen to some good music for me... and think of Wigfall.

Always,

Jimmy

Jimmy's wound healed rapidly, but afterward, he didn't seem like himself. His usually positive affect darkened, and he became short-tempered with his fellow soldiers. He even started snapping at the camp kids he so adored. Something was wrong.

In addition to the shift in personality, he intermittently suffered severe headaches. Initially, his symptoms were limited just to the headaches, but over time, he began to experience severe drowsiness, nausea, balance problems, and episodes of confusion. When he developed double vision and difficulty speaking, he finally sought out the camp surgeon.

The surgeon took one look at Jimmy and had him medevac'ed to Japan to be seen by a specialist at Camp Zama near Tokyo. There, Jimmy found himself sharing an open ward with nineteen other wounded GIs evacuated from Vietnam. Camp Zama served as a way station of sorts. Many of the wounded would be rehabbed and returned to the fighting. Others with more serious injuries would be shipped back to the States.

Jimmy met Aaron Lipinski, an army neurologist from NYU who was brusque, almost to the point of being rude, during his intake evaluation. Perhaps it was because Lipinski initially suspected Jimmy of malingering, or perhaps, he was simply overworked. When the man's attitude didn't change even after testing proved *definitively* that Jimmy was not a malingerer, he suspected the latter, or possibly it was just the doctor's nature. Some people were just jerks.

Dr. Lipinski stood at the end of Jimmy's bunk and cleared his throat repeatedly. Eventually, Jimmy woke and struggled to a sitting position. Through blurry eyes, the wall clock *looked* like it said three forty-five. Since it was dark outside the ward's only window, Jimmy assumed it was early morning.

Without preamble, Lipinski began speaking, "Soldier, you are being sent back to the States via this afternoon's air evac flight. You'll travel from here to Tripler Army Hospital in Honolulu. From there, you'll go to Madigan Army Hospital near Seattle, and from there, on to Walter Reed in Bethesda."

Still foggy from sleep, Jimmy stammered, "Excuse me, sir. What? Why? Huh?"

"Have your kit packed and be ready for transport to the flight line no later than thirteen hundred hours."

"But, sir...why? Did you find something on my scans?"

Doctor Lipinski stared at Jimmy like he was stupid, then answered, "No, soldier! The army thinks you need a little vacation. *Of course* we found something, soldier! You need brain surgery."

Dumbfounded, Jimmy pressed, "Sir, but...but why?"

"Nobody's told you?" Lipinski sounded incredulous.

Jimmy shook his head. "No, sir!"

Lipinski's attitude softened but only a little. He pulled up a metal chair to Jimmy's bedside and sat down hard, expelling a long, slow sigh. "Son, your chart says you received a head wound back in August...a shell fragment?"

"Yes, sir, but my helmet took the brunt of it. I still got a nice gash behind my ear. But it's all healed now. See?" He turned his head so the doctor could see his healed scar.

"True, it's healed on the *outside*. Inside's another story. Apparently, that shell fragment knocked free a splinter of bone from the inside of your skull. The splinter appears to have punctured one of the veins in your subdural space, causing a slow leak. This leak caused a pocket of blood, called a subdural hematoma, to form in the space between your cranial vault and your brain. This subdural hematoma has likely been slowly expanding since your initial injury. As it expands, it puts increasingly more pressure on the brain, displacing brain tissue. Untreated, it can lead to hallucinations, seizures, paralysis, herniation, and death.

"Subdural hematomas are treated by trephining a burr hole to relieve intracranial pressure. Your symptoms should abate almost immediately if the procedure is effective. If not, or if surgery to repair the rent in the vein is required, a craniotomy—that's removal of a section of the skull—may be required. Neither of these procedures are we set up to do here. Therefore, you get an all-expense paid trip to Bethesda in about nine hours."

At that, Dr. Lipinski stood from the chair and, before a stunned Jimmy was able to formulate any follow-up questions, strode from the ward without another word.

Jimmy sat on his bunk in the half-light of the ward, staring blankly at the opposite wall. His thoughts swirled as he contemplated his need for brain surgery. He sat motionless, but try as he might, he was unable to focus on any thought for more than an instant. Then, after what felt like hours but more likely was just several minutes, he was finally able to focus and hold his mind on one clear image.

Becca.

Jimmy reached into the drawer of his bedside table, removed a pen and paper, and began to write.

November 12, 1966

Dearest Becca,

You may notice this letter is being posted from Japan. Why, you ask? It appears that my head wound may have been more significant than was initially believed.

I continued suffering severe headaches from my wound long after the graze had turned to scar. They were bad, but I was still able to do my job. After a few weeks, I started having double vision. It came and went with little warning, but still, I was able to function, at least most of the time. Then, my balance started going all screwy and I started stumbling around like I was a on a seven-day drunk. The battalion surgeon saw me and sent me to see a specialist here in Japan. Now, the specialist says I have to go back to Walter Reed for brain surgery! He says that if I don't, then over time I will be unable to walk... or maybe worse.

I freely admit that I was scared of my own shadow when I arrived in Vietnam. After plunging into the minefield after Ballentine, that all seemed to go away. Firefights and artillery barrages don't seem to faze me anymore. I just took care of the guys around me. I didn't want to get hit, but the possibility that I might be injured wasn't paralyzing. It wasn't something that I feared.

This is different! I am embarrassed to admit it, Becca, but the possibility of brain surgery terrifies me. What if this changes the person I am? I have always been able to learn and remember things easily. I have always loved to read and to sketch. I have always loved music and art. Some people think I have a goofy sense of humor and a kind, warm heart. What if this changes me? What if I'm not ME after my surgery?

I don't know if I can do it... certainly not alone.

I know am only a guy you knew when we were kids and who later, briefly, helped you with math homework. Then I was just a lonely GI with whom you exchanged letters from overseas. I fully realize this. Still, it would mean the world to me if you were able to visit me while I'm at Walter Reed after my surgery. You should be on Thanksgiving Break from school around that time, so the timing might work?

I have no right to ask this of you, and you have every right to refuse.

If it would make your mom and dad more comfortable, one or both may come along to chaperone. I have saved tons of money (there's nothing to spend it on in Vietnam) over the past year and will be happy to pay for lodging and transportation if you say yes.

If you're able to come, it would mean the world to me! Uncle Howard and Charlotte are in Rio until sometime after New Years, or I would ask them. Otherwise, I have no one else to ask.

Think about it and let me know. Please forgive me for asking!

Your ever humble,

Jimmy

CHAPTER 31

NOVEMBER 1966

B ECCA WALKED DOWN THE HIGH school's main hall-
way to her locker, lost in conversation with her best
friend, Shelby Sutton. Becca had received Jimmy's
letter the previous afternoon telling her about his upcoming
brain surgery, and she was in a tizzy about what to do. Mrs.
Melton's home economics class could wait. This was more
important.

Should she go to him, the man she loved? Or should she
stay home and forget him? Becca knew her parents would
choose the latter option, which was *precisely* why she was
seeking Shelby's advice and *not* theirs.

Becca knew Emmitt Hansen had had it in for the Hamiltons ever since Walter purchased a plow and seed spreader
from a store in Spartanburg, rather than from *his* hardware
store back in 1960. Her father was generally a good man,
but was prone to holding grudges, sometimes for decades.
His distaste for the Hamilton clan persisted even after Walter's death and was little assuaged by Mack Lee's reputation
about town for being a shiftless rounder and reprobate.

Shelby, upon whom Jimmy had once placed the moni-
ker *Banana Split with Extra Chocolate Syrup*, was saying,

"Becca, you simply have to go! You love him. He's so cute! Even if he has the dorkiest smile ever, those dreamy green eyes are to die for. You *have* to go!"

Becca sighed. "I want to, I really do. But Mom and Dad will have a Class-A meltdown if I just wander off to Maryland."

"Then do like Jimmy suggested in his letter. Take one of them with you as a chaperone. He even promised to pay for transportation and board."

Becca shook her head, looking dejected. "They'd never agree to go. They don't even like that he's corresponding with me."

"You know, there *is* another way," Shelby started.

Suddenly hopeful, Becca turned to her friend, placed a hand on each shoulder, and shook her gently. "Don't just stand there. Tell me!" she demanded.

"Well, you don't *have* to tell them."

Becca's shoulders slumped. "I can't just run off to Maryland without telling them."

"No. Hear me out," Shelby insisted. "I can take you to the bus station in Spartanburg. You buy your ticket and, just before you board the bus, you call and tell them where you are and where you're going. That way, you get to go *and* you let them know so they'll not have to worry that you've just disappeared or something. By then, it'll be too late for them to stop you."

"Do you really think it will work? I mean..."

"Of course it'll work. It's not like they're gonna send the state police out after you," Shelby said with a solemn nod. "It's one of life's greatest truisms. 'It's easier to beg forgiveness than to ask permission.' You'll go. You'll get to see Jimmy, and you'll come back. It's as easy as that. And you *might* even get to kiss him!"

"Oh, you're bad!" Becca giggled and gave her friend a playful shove. "You know, you *could* come with me," she suggested hopefully.

"I would, but I can't." Shelby shook her head. "The family, along with yours truly, is traveling to see Grandma in Nashville for Thanksgiving. She had a stroke last summer, so there's no way I can get out of the trip. Sorry."

Becca sighed. "Okay, I've made my decision."

"And...?"

"I'll do it! I'll go to Maryland and see Jimmy." Becca gave Shelby a fierce hug. "Thank you!"

With that, the two practically skipped down the hall to Mrs. Melton's classroom, laughing and chattering away about Becca's upcoming adventure.

On Thanksgiving day, 1966, scarcely a week after receiving Jimmy's letter, Becca snuck out of her house and made her way to the Greyhound bus terminal in Spartanburg. A thoroughly frazzled and wearied Becca finally stepped off the bus in Bethesda late in the afternoon of the twenty-fifth. With scheduled stops along the way and a delay caused by a flat tire, the trip that was expected to last less than fourteen hours had ballooned into almost twenty-three. But Jimmy needed her, and she was there now, right where she wanted to be.

Undaunted, she gamely picked up her overnight bag and walked the three blocks to her motel, the Travelodge on Old Georgetown Road, feeling the way the chain's Sleepy-Bear logo looked—totally exhausted. There, she checked into her room and enjoyed a much-needed shower and change of clothes. Afterward, she dabbed on a bit of makeup to hide the dark circles under her eyes and added a light touch of lipstick. Jimmy needed her to look pretty, after all.

Preparations for seeing Jimmy completed, Becca closed her eyes, took a deep breath, and reached for the phone. This was not going to be the least little bit pleasant, but she knew she *had* to let her parents know she'd arrived safely. She *was* a good girl, after all, and didn't want them to worry about her unnecessarily.

With trembling fingers, Becca dialed the phone. Her call was answered on the first ring. As expected, Mama and Daddy were livid. Daddy had just launched into a tirade, demanding her immediate return when, inexplicably, their connection was lost.

After three seconds, Becca removed her finger from the switch hook on the phone's cradle and hung up the receiver. Giggling, she said to herself, "Long-distance calls are just *so* unreliable these days. They just drop with no warning at all, right out of the blue."

Then she gathered up her purse, went to the lobby, and took the next shuttle to Walter Reed Hospital.

CHAPTER 32

NOVEMBER 1966

J IMMY UNDERWENT SURGERY ON THE day after Thanksgiving. At 0500, he was wheeled into the surgical theater, where his head was shaved and prepped for surgery. Then a rubbery mask was placed over his nose and mouth and he was told to count backward from one hundred. Jimmy vaguely remembered hitting ninety-four but had no memories thereafter.

Once he was asleep, the surgeon peeled back Jimmy's scalp and applied the trephine. As soon as the burr punctured the skull, a gout of black blood spewed from the burr hole. Given the large quantity of blood released, the surgeon elected to perform a craniotomy to search for the offending bone fragment and seal the rent in the vein.

The latter was easily accomplished, but the bone shard could not be located. It was not visible by X-ray and did not turn up when they strained the blood suctioned from the subdural space. The surgeon *hoped* the fragment had ejected with the initial effluence from the burr hole, but he feared—and in truth, suspected—that it was tucked away in one of the brain's gyri and could cause more problems down the road.

Jimmy's surgeon understood both the risk of leaving the fragment in situ and also of rooting around the brain, attempting to find it. Without imaging capable of localizing the bone fragment, finding it would be like searching for a needle in a haystack. And when the haystack in question was someone's brain, the search could do as much, or more, harm than the needle itself...and the fragment *might* not still be in there anyway.

The most important part of Jimmy's procedure, the evacuation of the subdural hematoma and relief of the pressure on his brainstem, had been accomplished. Although the surgeon would have liked to locate and remove the offending splinter, prudence dictated that he replace the section of cut-away skull, sew up his patient, and call the surgery a success.

Jimmy woke back in his room several hours after his procedure. His vision was fuzzy, but he was pretty sure there was an angel sitting next to his bed. Somewhere in the back of his mind, he figured he was dead, so he might as well go back to sleep.

When he woke the next time, the angel was still there and she was holding his hand. The hand felt soft and warm in his. Then, his vision cleared.

"Becca? You came!" he croaked. His tongue felt thick, and his lips were cracked and dry. Yet, he managed a smile and then promptly fell back asleep.

Becca watched Jimmy sleep until visiting hours ended at 2000 hours. She wondered why the military couldn't just say "eight o'clock" like the rest of the civilized world, and hoped Jimmy would be proud of her for learning to speak in military time.

Visiting hours began at 0800 hours on Saturday morning, and by 0805, Becca was back at Jimmy's bedside, feeding him a bowl of unsalted chicken broth, the hospital's postoperative day, number one breakfast of choice.

"I can't believe you really came," Jimmy said, smiling his lopsided smile in between slurps of the tasteless clear liquid.

"You couldn't have kept me away if you tried." Becca happily ladled another spoonful of broth into Jimmy's mouth. She thought to herself, *I could get used to taking care of this man.*

"I wasn't sure if it was a dream—you know, you being here and all."

"Nope, I'm real."

"Then it is a dream...a dream come true."

Becca beamed. Then, Jimmy decided to have a little fun with her.

"And you brought your sister too. Becca, I didn't know you had a twin sister."

"What?"

"Your sister? What's her name?" Jimmy asked, pointing to an empty spot beside Becca.

Becca's puzzlement turned to alarm. "Jimmy, I don't have a sister. Do I need to get the doctor?" She began to rise from her chair. "Somebody, HELP! He's starting to see..."

Jimmy began laughing, but abruptly stopped. Laughing made his head hurt. He reached out and grasped Becca's hand in his. Still grinning, he said, "I was just joshin' with ya..."

Becca's face flushed and, without thinking, she snapped him on the nose with the plastic spoon, sending a bolt of pain through Jimmy's craniotomy incision.

Becca recoiled reflexively at Jimmy's expression of pain. Then he started to laugh.

"Serves you right, mister! Just for that, I'm keeping the lime Jell-O for myself," Becca scolded, but there was no anger in it. It took every bit or her willpower just to keep from kissing that smirk right off his adorable face.

Jimmy's surgeon dropped by to talk with him before his discharge from Walter Reed. He discussed the procedure and the missing bone splinter, explaining that it might be gone or it might still be lodged somewhere, hidden between the gyri of his brain. If simply inside the skull, trapped in the subdural space, it might just scar in place and cause no problems. There was also a chance, he explained, that the shard could move and cause recurrent problems in the future. Knowing what would happen was anybody's guess. Hopefully, the fragment was gone, but if Jimmy began experiencing recurrent headaches, seizures, visual changes, balance issues, or hallucinations, those would be indications that the fragment was still inside his head and possibly migrating. For that, Jimmy should immediately return to Walter Reed for additional surgery, an idea that filled Jimmy with a terrible sense of dread.

Becca popped by the hospital again Sunday morning. She just missed seeing Jimmy's surgeon when he came by on rounds. Jimmy, knowing Becca had very little time before she'd have to leave to catch her bus back to South Carolina, elected not to relate to her the ambiguities of his prognosis. Why should she worry unnecessarily? After all, he was going to be fine.

By noon, Becca was back on a Greyhound bus, two hours into her return trip to Boiling Springs. She was on cloud ninety, which was ten times higher than cloud nine. If she was unsure before about whether she was really in love with Jimmy, this trip had removed all doubts. He'd needed her, and she'd been there for him. When he woke up and saw her, she could see the relief on his face. And later when he smiled his lopsided little grin, Becca's heart had just melted.

Becca's parents met her at the bus station and were, understandably, incensed. How could she possibly shame them in such a way? They couldn't believe her nerve, an eighteen-year-old girl traipsing across the country to see a boy, and a soldier at that! Even worse, the soldier-boy was the kid brother of that good-for-nothing Mack Lee Hamilton. They also informed her that she was grounded until she turned *sixty*.

If Becca heard, she didn't care. She'd just spent the weekend with the man she loved. They hadn't so much as kissed—unless you counted that one time she'd kissed him while he was still asleep—but she now knew beyond all doubt, James Wiley Hamilton was the man she was going to spend the rest of her life with.

CHAPTER 33

DECEMBER 1966

JIMMY'S POSTOPERATIVE RECOVERY WAS RAPID and complete in only a few days. His headaches abated, and his vision and coordination, to the relief and amazement of his neurosurgeon, quickly returned to normal. By November 30, he showed no residual neurologic symptoms from either his injury or the surgery and was ready for discharge from Walter Reed.

After his discharge, he had thirty days of convalescent leave before his required return to Vietnam for the completion of his first tour of duty, and he knew precisely where and how he wanted to spend them.

Becca had come all the way from South Carolina to Maryland just to see him. Now, Jimmy fully intended to return the favor. *If she can come here, then I can, and will, go there.* There was nothing he wanted more than see Becca again. Jimmy could say very little positive about the war in Vietnam. It had, however, taught him that life is short, and opportunities for happiness should *never* be wasted.

Jimmy spent his final days at Walter Reed making plans. He'd return to South Carolina for his convalescent leave. While there, he'd spend as much time as possible with the woman he loved. With a smile, the thought struck him, *I really do love her.* Yes, he'd pass his leave time in Boiling Springs, but *not* at the family farm, mucking stalls. Instead, he resolved to book himself into a hotel and earmark every waking moment for Becca.

Uncle Howard had sent a telegram informing him that he was returning early from his trip to South America to be there for him, but with Jimmy's rapid recovery, he was released from the hospital before his uncle's arrival. That did not stop the old man, however, from transforming Jimmy's room into a veritable florist shop full of flowers, gifts, and cards.

Howard's reaction to Jimmy's surgery was in direct contrast to that of his mother and brother. From them, Jimmy heard nothing.

But Becca had come to see him in the hospital, and Jimmy resolved that if it was the last thing he did on this earth, he was going to make that girl his wife, and that certainty made him feel warm all over.

On the day of his hospital discharge, Jimmy paid an orderly five dollars to collect all the flowers from his room and distribute them around the floor to other rooms. He hated the idea that such beautiful flowers should be discarded, and if they might brighten the day for his fellow soldiers, then so much the better.

Then, Jimmy called his uncle's home in Scottsdale and asked the housekeeper to inform Howard that he'd been released from the hospital and asked her to pass along his thanks for the flowers. He also wanted her to let him know that he was heading back to Boiling Springs but that he hoped to see both him and Charlotte before his eventual return to Vietnam at the end of December.

With that, Jimmy boarded a bus bound to see his future wife.

Jimmy's orders listed the Hamilton farm as his leave address. While he thought no one likely to check up on his location, he felt obligated to, at least, stop by his mother's house while he was back in town.

There, he was not surprised to find his mother's enmity toward him unabated. Her and Mack Lee's contempt no longer fazed him. Unsurprisingly, neither asked where he was staying or how long he'd be in town, nor did they offer for him to stay at home. Jimmy didn't care. He was going to see Becca, and that was all that mattered.

Seeing Becca, however, proved to be something of a challenge. After she'd returned from her visit to Walter Reed, her parents had placed her practically under house arrest. She went to school every day, but nothing else was allowed. She could not use the telephone, watch television, or go to any of her friend's houses. Movies, dances, and other non-school-related activities were strictly forbidden. The Rexall Pharmacy was along the way as Becca walked home each day from school. If she didn't tarry, she could duck in there for a quick snack with her friends, and her parents would be none the wiser.

Jimmy met Becca outside her school on his first day back in Boiling Springs. As he walked her home, they passed the Rexall Pharmacy. Mr. Boyter recognized him and, happy to see his former employee, invited the pair in for a snack "on the house." Soon thereafter, he offered Jimmy his old job back until he had to return to Vietnam. Perhaps due to his tactical military training, Jimmy immediately recognized the loophole in Becca's punishment regimen and was keen to exploit it. After one glance at Becca, he gladly accepted the temporary position, providing the couple with a covert rendezvous location almost every day.

Maybe it was just coincidence, or maybe Mr. Boyter recognized young love and wanted to nudge it along. Regardless the reason, every day, about the time Becca came in to the lunch counter after school, Mr. Boyter would appear at the counter, tap Jimmy on his shoulder, and tell him it was time for Jimmy to take his lunch break.

In the entire time Jimmy had worked at the pharmacy before being drafted, he'd never taken a lunch break. Most certainly, he had never taken breaks of *any* sort during the after-school rush, but he was more than happy to do so now. Soon, he and Becca were sharing the back booth for thirty-minute snippets of every school day. More often than not, she'd sneak out her window at night to meet him too.

A week before Christmas, Jimmy surprised Becca with a tiny, quarter-carat diamond ring and a proposal of marriage. Her parents notwithstanding, about the only person in Boiling Springs who seemed surprised by his proposal was Becca. But she recovered rapidly enough from her shock to enthusiastically accept. Then, she surprised *him* by expressing her wish for them to marry *before* he returned to Vietnam rather than after his second tour ended, as Jimmy initially had planned. Additionally, she informed him that she wanted to be married on Christmas Day.

It thrilled Jimmy that she was so excited. What better day could there possibly be for the two of them to begin their lives as man and wife. As an added bonus, because of the date, Jimmy knew he'd *never* forget his anniversary.

With Becca, for all practical purposes, still on house arrest, Jimmy was left to make all the arrangements. The short suspense had him scrambling. Immediately after leaving Becca, he called his uncle in Scottsdale to share his news.

Thrilled, Howard told Jimmy, "Son, I'm happy for you. You know, Doris and I got married on Christmas Day and that worked out pretty well for us. If your marriage to Becca is anywhere near as happy as ours was, then you'll have a truly blessed life!"

"Thank you, Uncle! I know it's short notice and all, but do you think there's any chance that you and Char—"

Uncle's interruption boomed through the telephone's receiver. "James, nothing short of trumpets blaring and the four horsemen of the apocalypse galloping down Main Street Scottsdale could keep us away! Besides, as I recall, you served as best man for *our* wedding. It seems only fitting that I should return the service."

Jimmy's heart leaped into his throat. The two chatted a bit longer and then with regret, Jimmy ended the call. He'd almost forgotten how much he loved and missed his uncle.

Both Jimmy and Becca wanted to be married by a clergyman. They figured that if their union was to be ordained by God, then the ceremony binding them should be officiated by a man of God. With so little notice, and with the wedding being planned for Christmas Day, finding a preacher both willing and able was a challenge. Most were busy because of the chosen date. Others refused to marry non-congregants. Still others, noting the rushed nature of the event, suspected an underlying pregnancy and refused to perform the ceremony without several months of premarital counseling.

Jimmy tried the First Baptist, First and Second Methodist, and Presbyterian churches in Boiling Springs without success. He was turned away from the local Church of Christ after receiving a pointed lecture about the evils of fornication. Exhausting venues in town, Jimmy cast his net toward churches in Spartanburg and was refused by the Anglicans,

Lutherans, and Adventists. The priest at St. Mary's Catholic refused even to talk with him.

Out of desperation, Jimmy even tried a Jewish Syna-gogue. The kindly old rabbi there declined to marry those outside his faith, but suggested Jimmy try the Spartanburg County Jail. The chaplain there, according to the rabbi, was a former Marine Corps chaplain who might be willing to help out a serviceman in need.

Having exhausted other options within a fifty-mile radius, Jimmy figured he had nothing to lose and went to the jail. There, he found Chaplain Edwin Lynch, who, to Jimmy's surprise and great relief, agreed to perform the ceremony. Chaplain Lynch informed Jimmy that he'd be giving a noontime Christmas service for the inmates, but if the couple could be in his office around two in the afternoon, he'd be happy to officiate the wedding service for them then.

With this task behind him, Jimmy's relief was almost palpable. The next day, he purchased wedding rings and procured a license. Thereafter, there was only one more hurdle left for him to cross.

Jimmy was a little old-fashioned, and although Becca was eighteen, he wanted to get her father's blessing for their marriage. With this in mind, he stopped by Hansen's Hard-ware in search of Burt Hansen, hoping to have a pleasant and earnest conversation, and left sorely disappointed...and at a run.

Hansen's Hardware had been in the same location since 1874. It was a long, deep, free-standing two-story red brick building. Out front, a weathered green awning sheltered old timers who sat, gossiped, and played checkers atop an upturned pickle barrel. Inside, the floors were bare wood, stained almost black by nearly a hundred years of foot traf-fic and tobacco juice. Just inside the front entrance, a giant four-bladed fan wobbled and turned slowly but moved no air. The walls were covered with peg-board and cubbyholes bearing knickknacks, nails, and sundry tools. Three long rows of shelves bore everything from barbed wire to an impressive collection of hammers and mauls. The counter holding the cash register was all the way in the back, before a wall lined with rifles, shotguns, and ammunition.

There, Jimmy found Emmitt Hansen, who, at least initially, seemed happy enough to see a new customer enter his store.

"You!" Hansen shouted after Jimmy introduced himself. "You're that warthless som-bitch who seduced my sweet little Becky and dragged her off t' the big city."

"No, sir, that's—"

"I always said you Hamiltons wuz nothin' but warthless trash!"

Hansen's accent gave each "short *A*" a "long *I*" sound, which, to Jimmy, was like nails on a chalkboard.

Hansen continued, "How dare you sully my l'il girl! Becky wus a good girl till you came along and started writin' her them letters."

Jimmy couldn't get a word in edgewise.

"You're jest like that warthless brother of yours, Mack Lee."

"Sir, I—" Jimmy began to protest.

"I'll show you what we do to molesters like you 'round hear!" Hansen spun to the wall behind him, selected a pump-action shotgun, and ripped into a box of buckshot.

Jimmy, having seen enough, bolted for the door.

"Yeah, you better run!" Hansen shouted after him. "If I catch you 'round here again..."

Jimmy heard the shotgun's slide being racked as he dashed through the front door, and he didn't stop running until he was two streets away.

Later, Becca teased him mercilessly, assuring Jimmy that her father was all bark and no bite, but Jimmy wasn't convinced.

CHAPTER 34

CHRISTMAS 1966

O N CHRISTMAS MORNING, THE HANSEN family arose early and opened their presents. Becca received a silver-plated mirror and comb set from her parents. Although they'd still not forgiven her for her Thanksgiving weekend escapades, her parents—after some discussion—allowed her to go off to church with her friend, Shelby, unchaperoned. They figured it was pretty safe. Emmitt had run off that Hamilton boy, and besides, how much trouble could a girl get into at church?

When asking for permission from her parents, Becca had been very careful with her phrasing. She never actually *said* she was going to *church*. Rather, she requested permission to attend a "Christmas service" with Shelby—that it was to be a Christmas *wedding* service was left unspoken. If her parents assumed, well, that was just on them and not her. She was a good girl, after all, and preferred never to lie.

With that, the girls sped off toward the Spartanburg County Jail and Becca's assignation with Jimmy and the chaplain.

In the chaplain's office, Jimmy paced nervously as he waited for Becca to arrive. His thoughts swirled. What if she couldn't get away? What if she'd changed her mind about marrying him? What if instead of Becca, her gun-toting father turned up at the jail?

Uncle Howard's amused efforts to calm Jimmy's frazzled nerves failed miserably. Charlotte fared no better. By the time Becca finally arrived, the nervous tension in the room could have snapped an aircraft carrier's anchor chain.

One look at Becca's smiling visage, and immediately everything was right again in Jimmy's world. She was beautiful! And she had shown up.

A moment later, Chaplain Lynch returned to his office with his five-year-old son in tow. The little boy had wanted to come to accompany his father to the jail that day hoping, in Tiny Tim fashion, that his presence there would give comfort to the incarcerated men who could not be with their own children on Christmas Day.

With Uncle Howard by his side, Shelby serving as Maid of Honor, and Charlotte as a witness, Jimmy and Becca stepped into place side by side in front of the chaplain, ready to be married.

Jimmy was overwhelmed by emotion. No sooner had Chaplain Lynch started the ceremony, tears began streaming down his face. Try as he may, he could not stop. Twice, Becca reached up and dabbed tears from his face. The tears only accelerated when the chaplain's little boy, seeing Jimmy in apparent distress, tugged on Jimmy's sleeve and interrupted the ceremony.

"Mister, are you okay?" the little boy asked with an air of earnestness.

Jimmy looked down, speechless.

"You can play with my racecar if it'll make you feel better," he said, holding out the toy 1966 Corvette Stingray with which he'd been quietly playing on the chaplain's desk up until that point in the ceremony. He'd received the car for Christmas that morning, and it was his most favorite-est thing in all the world.

Chaplain Lynch was mortified and moved to scold his son.

Jimmy, however, waved off his objections, knelt down to eye level with the five-year-old, and thanked the little boy for his kindness, at which the child gave him a mighty hug. After that, there wasn't a dry eye left in the room.

The remainder of the ceremony went off without a hitch, and Jimmy and Becca, to the delight of all present, were declared "man and wife."

Afterward, there were smiles and congratulations all around. Jimmy beamed, and Becca never looked more lovely. Sadly, no one had remembered to bring along a camera to record the event.

Grinning like a Cheshire Cat, Howard produced two beautifully wrapped gifts from the pocket of his overcoat—one for Becca, the other for Jimmy.

"Uncle, you shouldn't have. You've done enough already," Jimmy objected. "Just having you and Charlotte here today is more than I could've hoped for."

"Oh, hush and indulge an old man's fancy," Howard replied.

"There's no use arguing with him, James. You know your uncle. If Howard Hines ever gets something into his head, it's going to happen. There's no use fighting it. Resistance is futile. That's how *we* wound up getting married," Charlotte said with a laugh, nudging her husband in the ribs.

"That's not the way I remember it," Howard groused, although *clearly* he was not displeased. Then, he continued with a smile and deferential nod. "Now, for the newest Mrs. Hamilton, this is for you."

Becca blushed and tore into the proffered gift. Inside, she found a beautifully lacquered, tortoiseshell fountain pen, a vintage Pelikan 400N, with a rose-gold nib, cap-band, and clip. It was exquisite!

Becca gasped. "Oh, Uncle Howard, this is too much!" She was sure the pen must have cost a fortune.

"Not at all, my dear. And now you have something you can use to write our James while he's away keeping the world safe for democracy."

Becca leaned in and gave the old man a kiss on the cheek. Then she turned to Jimmy, wondering what magic *his* gift box held. And she was not disappointed.

Jimmy stared in amazement into the open box before him. The gift veritably screamed Uncle Howard. The old fellow had somehow found a gold Bulova wristwatch with three bas-relief circles in the shape of a silhouetted Mickey Mouse head and ears on the face. Jimmy gazed down at the watch, awestruck, then carefully removed the watch from the box and turned it over in his hands.

The case back bore the engraved inscription, "A song that never ends."

Jimmy gazed up at his uncle. "The inscription...isn't that from *Bambi*, Uncle?"

Howard punched the air in triumph. "See, Charlotte, I told you James would recognize that quote."

Observing Becca's puzzled expression, Charlotte explained, "It's the opening theme from *Bambi*, dear. 'Love Is a Song.' You know, Howard, he just loves all things Disney."

"Uncle, this is amazing." Jimmy gave the old man a hug.

Howard beamed. "Maybe you can keep it set to Eastern Time so you can better remember your beautiful bride until you two can be together again. Just a suggestion."

After the gifts had been opened, everyone followed Howard into the parking lot. From the trunk of his Cadillac, he produced a cooler, and from it, a bottle of 1959 Bollinger *La Grande Année* champagne and four flutes.

Charlotte passed around the glasses as Howard opened the bottle and poured. Then Howard lifted his glass to eye level and said, "A toast to the bride and groom."

The small wedding party turned to the old man and raised their glasses expectantly.

"To James and Rebecca, may your song never end!"

CHAPTER 35

A FTER THE WEDDING, SHELBY DROVE Becca back to her parents' house. In her excitement over the day's events, Becca almost told her parents where she'd really been, but lost her nerve each time the opportunity arose.

That night, after everyone was asleep, Becca packed a suitcase and slipped quietly out her bedroom window. She stole across her lawn to the street where her husband—Becca couldn't believe she was really married—was waiting in a borrowed car.

In the front seat, they briefly kissed. Then Jimmy eased away from the curb. He did not dare put on the headlights until they were well away from Becca's parents' house.

Becca slid across the bench seat and rested her head on Jimmy's shoulder. He tuned the radio to 950 on the car's AM dial. WORD was still playing all Christmas music, so the two sang carols all the way to the Howard Johnson's motel in Spartanburg, where they would share their first night as husband and wife.

Becca laughed to herself. *My husband couldn't carry a tune in a bucket*, she thought. His lack of musical talent didn't seem to faze Jimmy in the least as he continued to belt out his "joyful noise unto the Lord" with gusto.

The Spartanburg Howard Johnson's was one or maybe two steps above the Travelodge where Becca had stayed while visiting him at Walter Reed, but she didn't care. She was with Jimmy, and that's all that mattered.

Becca felt a tingle run up her spine as Jimmy swept her into his arms and carried her across the threshold. Most of the motel room was taken up by a double bed with a swaybacked mattress. Over the headboard hung a framed reproduction print of Thomas Gainsborough's "Blue Boy." Against the window stood a round table with two cracked plastic chairs. A floor lamp leaned in the corner, appearing ready to topple over at the slightest nudge. A Philco portable color television was bolted atop a faux-wooden desk/dresser combination near the foot of the bed. Through the window, a sign for Burger Chef Hamburgers and Shakes flashed on and off, intermittently illuminating dust motes eddying above the rattling heater vent.

Jimmy ducked into the bathroom to brush his teeth as Becca unpacked her suitcase. When he returned, she excused herself to do the same and slip into the scandalously short, pink satin baby-doll nighty Shelby had purchased for her from Mossberg's Department Store.

In spite of the glass of water she'd gulped down after brushing her teeth, Becca's mouth still felt full of cotton when she emerged from the bathroom. Jimmy had turned out the lamp and was waiting expectantly at the foot of the bed, wearing only his army boxer shorts. She stared at her husband's face as she glided toward the bed, trying to look like Audrey Hepburn, and promptly tripped over the shoes she'd kicked off while he was brushing his teeth. He caught her before she could fall.

So much for my elegant entrance, she thought, but then she soon forgot all about it as his lips met her own.

After that, nothing else mattered. Feeling the front of his boxers bulging toward her, she broke their embrace long enough to help Jimmy wriggle free of the constricting undergarment. The two kissed passionately, totally lost in one another. Becca pushed herself forward, arms wrapped tightly around his neck. With the back of his knees pressed against the mattress, he was unprepared for the sudden shift in their center of gravity and began to fall backward, drawing Becca with him. As the two struck the mattress, their bodies abruptly coupled with Jimmy on his back and Becca straddled atop. She gave a startled cry, and the two froze like a pair of frightened bunnies hiding from a hungry fox. After a moment, she shifted her position ever so slightly. An instant later, he gave a groan and she felt his body lurch inside her.

Afterward, they lay together in silence, their bodies still coupled and their breaths coming in shuddering gasps. It had been the first time for them both and lasted no more than a few seconds.

After a moment, Becca giggled. "I guess this means we're *really* married now!"

"I suppose it does, Mrs. Hamilton," he replied, laughing past his embarrassment.

Becca kissed him and asked, "Do you think we can do it again?"

Jimmy nodded enthusiastically. "Give me a minute, but I think so...and I'll do better next time!"

And he did. Oh, God, how he did! As the newlyweds explored their newfound sexuality, Becca felt things she had never felt before. Jimmy was a considerate, enthusiastic, and gentle lover, and he adored her...and she him.

CHAPTER 36

JANUARY–MARCH 1967

J IMMY AND BECCA ENJOYED FIVE glorious days together, the majority of which they spent in bed. However, after the fifth night, the real world intruded upon
the couple's bliss. He had to catch a flight that would return
him to the fighting in Vietnam, and she had to return to her
parents' home.

Given the choice, Becca would rather have been going to
Vietnam. She'd purposely elected *not* to contact her mom
or dad since the wedding and was certain, beyond all doubt,
her homecoming was *not* going to be a pleasant experience.
There was going to be Hell to pay!

And Becca wasn't wrong.

Her parents' initial response to their prodigal daughter's return was one of relief at finding that she was okay.
Relief rapidly gave way to anger when she told them she'd
been with Jimmy. Their anger transitioned into an atomic
rage when she informed them that she was now a married
woman.

For the first and only time, Becca actually was *glad* that
Jimmy was on a jet flying to Vietnam. Had he been any-

where else, she was certain her father would've hunted him down and killed him on the spot.

Over the first weeks in January, the Hansen household was an armed camp. On one side of the wire were her parents, who thought their daughter a harlot who was scandalizing the good name of Hansen. On the other was Becca's fourteen-year-old little sister who thought Becca's marriage was the most romantic thing she'd ever heard. Between them, enveloped within a minefield of hormones, hurt feelings, and teenage love was Becca.

Emmitt Hansen, over Becca's profound objections, actively pursued annulment proceedings for the marriage, but found the process significantly more time consuming and expensive than he'd anticipated. Eventually, he let the issue drop, allowing a certain détente to fall over the Hansen household.

Becca relaxed a bit. Maybe everything would be all right after all. Her parents would come to love Jimmy just as she did. All would be well.

She was unconcerned when in January her monthly menstrual period did not come. Her cycle had always been hit-or-miss, so she was unperturbed. Around Valentine's Day, she suffered a bout of stomach flu but thought little more of it, even when her February period was also missed. By March, when Becca was throwing up in the school bathroom every morning, her breasts had become tender and swollen, and her period still hadn't started, she began to panic.

Becca wrote Jimmy about her suspicions and was quite relieved when he seemed happy about the possibility of becoming a father. Actually, "happy" was not a strong enough descriptor. He had been thrilled at just the possibility.

A covert visit to Shelby's OB-GYN in Spartanburg confirmed what Becca—if she was being totally honest with herself—already knew. She was pregnant, and her baby would be due sometime around September 24.

Jimmy, upon receiving the news, was ecstatic.

Becca was terrified. She would've liked to have been able to confide in her mother about her pregnancy and share her fears and experiences but knew this was *not* an option. Her parents would be livid.

By April, she was beginning to show but managed to keep her pregnancy hidden by wearing loose clothing. The cat was let out of the bag in early May when her mother happened into the bathroom one morning while she was taking a shower. What followed was a scream and a string of epithets to include strumpet, harlot, floozy, and Jezebel, among a litany of others. And when Emmitt came home that evening, matters became even worse. It seemed that the Hansens' social standing and position within the church were not so secure that they could bear the shame of having a "fallen woman" for a daughter.

Becca's objections stating she was legally married when the child was conceived fell upon deaf ears. If the father was a Hamilton, then she must be a tramp.

The last words Becca heard as she was unceremoniously turned out into the night with nothing more than a suitcase of hastily packed clothes were her father yelling, "You git outta here, you shameless hussy, and never come back. No daughter o' mine's gonna be a common whore. You git an' stay gone. Don't you *never* come back! Ya hear?"

Expelled from the only home she'd ever known, Becca stumbled to the curb in tears. There, she was met by Shelby, who promised Becca she could stay with her for a few days until her parents calmed down again.

In her heart, Becca knew that was never going to happen. She was homeless, just like Jimmy had been, and he'd only been eight years old! If it felt that bad for her, she could only imagine how terrible it must have been for him.

The Suttons were kind enough to allow her to share Shelby's room but made it clear that the arrangement was only temporary. Becca was expected to actively seek more permanent accommodations. Having someone "like her" living under their roof could set a bad example for their younger children and would "look bad" in town.

Becca detailed her expulsion from the Hansen household to Jimmy in a letter. Afterward, there was little to be done but wait for his reply.

Jimmy was appalled to hear about Becca's ill handling at the hands of her parents. He'd not expected Becca to require housing so soon after their wedding. He'd thought her to be safely ensconced in her parents' home until his tour of duty and military service came to an end in late December. Thus, he'd not filled out the myriads of paperwork required for dependent housing when he'd redeployed after their wedding. Now, it was too late. The military bureaucracy moved slowly, and Becca needed somewhere she could stay *now*.

Immediately, he thought of Uncle Howard and Charlotte. He was certain they'd be more than happy to help in his and Becca's hour of need. Then he remembered that Howard and Charlotte were continuing to indulge their shared love of travel and would be unavailable until mid or late July, much too late to accommodate Becca's more urgent needs. After returning from Carnival in Rio de Janeiro in early March, they'd soon set out again on a three-month cruise of the South Pacific from Los Angeles to Auckland, New Zealand, with stops along the way in Hawaii, Tahiti, Pago Pago, and Bora Bora.

He smiled at the thought of his uncle out there, living his best life. He deserved it! Charlotte was a wonderful woman, and it was clear the two were happy together.

That still left him with a problem, though. Thinking a bad option was better than no option at all, in desperation, Jimmy sent a telegram to his mother. He knew his mother would never open one of his letters and, besides, Becca couldn't wait for the glacial pace of mail delivery from Vietnam, anyway. In his telegram, he used the only incentive he had available that held any possibility of moving his mother into action—money. He promised to send almost his entire military pay to support Becca, and later his child, until such time as he could return and assume those responsibilities himself. As a show of good faith, he wired five hundred dollars by Western Union to cover Becca's initial expenses with the understanding that any surplus funds could be used in whatever manner his mother saw fit.

Serendipitously, Jimmy's telegram arrived on the same day Margaret Hamilton received news of a new tax lien on the farm. Finding herself in desperate need of cash, she reluctantly scrawled out her reply.

The following evening, on a bunk in Vietnam, Jimmy breathed a sigh of relief as he read the first response he'd received to a communication from his mother since December of 1957, a one-line telegram.

MOVE IN APPROVED STOP ADDITIONAL FUNDS REQUIRED STOP

CHAPTER 37

APRIL 1967

A FTER SENDING THE TELEGRAMS TO his mother and Becca, two hundred thirty-four dollars and seventeen cents represented every cent Jimmy had left to his name. But without hesitation, he sent it back to South Carolina. Two hundred dollars he wired to his mother. The other thirty-four dollars, he sent by mail directly to Becca at the Hamilton farm's address. As for the seventeen cents, he'd need to scrounge up another eight before Sunday if that kid, Thanh, was going to shine his boots for him.

Jimmy didn't mind sending the money. There was nothing to spend it on in Vietnam anyway. Besides, if it would've guaranteed Becca a warm, safe place to stay until he could arrange more permanent accommodations, he would've happily sent along a kidney too. It made him feel a little proud knowing he was providing for his wife, even from half a world away.

Becca had been staying with Shelby since her parents kicked her out of their house, the only home she'd ever known. Becca fought back a sob at the thought. Shelby's parents had been kind enough to allow her to stay at their house for a few days, but had made it abundantly clear when she moved in, her welcome there had an expiration date. So, when Jimmy's telegram was delivered, Becca let out a sigh of relief.

With trepidation, Becca repacked her few belongings into her suitcase. She'd grown up less than a mile from the Hamilton farm, yet she really didn't know Jimmy's mother or brother. Of course, she recognized both from around town, but she'd never had any extended interactions with either. Jimmy, of course, never said anything bad about them. In fact, he rarely mentioned them at all.

It was sad, she thought, that Jimmy's family had sent him away. But with Jimmy being so sweet, how could his family be anything less than wonderful? Then, Becca remembered *her* own parents, and the reason she was needing to move into the Hamilton's home, and her anxiety returned with a vengeance.

"It's going to be okay...it's going to be okay...it's going to be okay," she whispered to herself like a mantra. Then she got into Shelby's car and rode to the Hamilton farm.

When they arrived, Becca thanked Shelby for her family's hospitality and for the ride. She watched Shelby leave, then took her suitcase and marched gamely to the house. She mounted the steps to the covered front porch and rapped smartly on the door. With a pleasant smile affixed to her face, she was determined to make a good first impression. Becca waited. No answer. She knocked again; still no response. Becca pounded on the door. Nothing.

Growing concerned, she left her suitcase on the porch and walked around the house, looking for the back door. As she rounded the corner, she heard sounds of a television playing in the front room at high volume. Becca listened for a moment at the window. It sounded to her like Ed Bauer was having a heated argument with his brother Mike on *As the World Turns.* Becca couldn't quite catch the gist of their spat but hoped they'd work out their differences soon.

At the back door, Becca peered through a gap in the window curtains by the door, but observed no movement or other signs of life. She tried the door—locked—and knocked as she had up front, with the same lack of response from inside.

"Nobody home? But they knew I was coming today. Jimmy's telegram said so," she said to herself and began walking back to the front porch.

It was then that the first fat raindrop slapped the ground, followed immediately by another. Before Becca reached the corner of the house, the rain was a torrent. By the time she reached the shelter of the front porch, she was soaked through to the skin. The temperature outside when Shelby dropped her off had been near seventy. Over the past few minutes, it felt as though it had dropped at least twenty degrees. Cold and wet, she plopped, shivering, into one of the rickety wicker porch chairs and bawled her eyes out. This wasn't how it was supposed to be.

The storm raged for another hour. As the wind and rain began to abate, an old Chevy pickup with mismatched doors and large patches of rust on its hood sloshed into the driveway. A moment later, Mack Lee Hamilton leaped from the cab. He skirted a large puddle and limped through the wet grass to where Becca was still waiting on the porch.

"And who might you be, Drowned Rat?" he asked, leering at Becca. In the cool air, her pretty white blouse—the one she'd selected specially to impress her new in-laws—had yet to dry and was almost transparent. It worked; Mack Lee was impressed, although not in a way she would've liked. In fact, it made her skin crawl.

Becca had earlier taken a second blouse from her suit-case and draped it over her shoulders for warmth. Now, under Mack Lee's gaze, she pulled it tighter around her shoulders.

"I'm Rebecca." She briefly held out her hand, but im-mediately brought it back to her neck as the second blouse began slipping from her shoulders.

"Oh, that's right, you're my new sister."

"Nice to meet you...I mean, officially. I've seen you at the gas station."

Mack Lee was immediately defensive. "Yeah, well...that's just a temporary job for me. You know...until somethin' better comes along. I hurt my leg playing ball, ya know."

Becca nodded noncommittally. Mack Lee had been at that station for at least three years, maybe longer. She'd seen him there.

"C-can we g-go ins-side? It's s-sort of c-cold out."

"Oh yeah, yeah, sure. Ma must be asleep. When she takes her pills, a freight train crashing into an accordion factory wouldn't wake her up."

Mack Lee unlocked the door. He sidestepped around Becca's suitcase and stepped inside, making no attempt to bring the heavy case in for her.

Becca shrugged her shoulders, picked up the suitcase, and lugged it into the foyer after her brother-in-law.

Once inside, Mack Lee said, "Yeah, Ma told me you were coming to live here for a while. You'll be stayin' upstairs in the room on the right side of the hall. That's my kid sister's room; or it was until your hubby, well, you know..." He made a gun with his thumb and forefinger, then dropped the "hammer" thumb. "My room's across the hall...you know...if you ever get lonely, or want to talk or somethin'."

CHAPTER 38

APRIL–OCTOBER 1967

J IMMY WAS PROUD THAT HE'D been able to provide for Becca. Still, he knew the situation was not optimal for her. The sooner he could get home and take care of his wife and soon-to-be child, the happier he was going to be.

The second tour in Vietnam was very different from his first. Although he returned to the same unit, his friends from his first tour were gone. Each had been killed, wounded, or completed their own tours and rotated home.

Only Rikki-Tikki-Tabby remained. Jimmy was glad his cat had somehow avoided stew-pots during the months he'd been away. Remarkably, no one reported having seen the animal around camp for the entire time Jimmy was gone. Yet, on Jimmy's first day back, the cat had appeared on his bunk as though by magic.

Not just the environment around him had changed. Jimmy, too, was different. During his first tour—at least in the beginning—he had been the classic newbie, skulking along behind the grizzled old vets, practically afraid of his own shadow. For the second, he was the confident, battle-hardened veteran who'd seen and done it all. *He'd* become the one to whom the newbies gravitated.

Jimmy simply did his job and did it well. Unlike many of his fellow vets, he never talked about his experiences unless it was to teach the newbies, which gave him a certain mystique to the men around him. They gawped at his many scars and whispered stories about his rumored prior exploits.

Still a prolific letter writer, he spent his evenings composing missives to Becca and Uncle Howard. He finally gave up on writing to his mother other than to send money. What was the point?

During his first tour in Vietnam, Jimmy had been excited to be there, to be doing something important for his country and the men around him. He cared little for his personal fate. After all, he had nothing back home that he'd cared to return to. Little would change if he never made it home again.

All that had changed now. Jimmy had a wonderful wife he adored and who was carrying his baby. Now he had someone at home he loved and who loved him, someone he couldn't wait to see and hold again. For the first time since he'd stepped off the boat at Cam Ranh Bay in 1966, Jimmy dared to dream. He waited impatiently for each of Becca's letters and was crestfallen on the rare occasions when he returned from mail call empty-handed. He followed her pregnancy by letters and could almost feel the baby's movements as he read.

More than anything, he wanted to be a dad, and not just any dad but a *good* dad. Luckily, he'd had the perfect role model. He figured if he was a tenth the dad Howard had been for him, this was going to be one lucky kid.

Around the post, Jimmy was known to be quiet, capable, and serious. On patrols, he was totally unflappable under fire, decisive, and more than compassionate. He was the medic everyone *wanted* along with them.

His competency soon brought him to the attention of his superiors. Noting that Jimmy had a few years of college under his belt, his commander offered him a recommendation for OCS—Officer Candidate School. In ninety days, the commander told him, he could be an officer. Although the idea of becoming an officer appealed to him, Jimmy knew that if he attended OCS, he would accrue additional years of commitment to the army.

Had he not met and married Becca, Jimmy likely would've taken his commander up on the offer. As it was, he just wanted to go home and take care of his little family. Perhaps someday he'd finish college and maybe even go on to medical school like Howard, but that was for later. Now, all he wanted was to be with Becca. Beyond that, he really didn't care.

Consequently, Jimmy thanked the lieutenant colonel for his offer but respectfully declined.

CHAPTER 39

APRIL–OCTOBER 1967

Becca officially "met" her mother-in-law on the morning after her arrival to the Hamilton farm. Margaret was in the kitchen preparing breakfast, cigarette in one hand and a spatula in the other, when Becca came downstairs from her room.

"Good morning, Mother," Becca chirped as she entered the kitchen.

Margaret turned from the stove and gazed appraisingly at Becca. "So you're the wife," she said in a flat tone before turning back to the stove.

"Yes, ma'am, I'm Jimmy's wife," Becca replied cheerfully. "You have a wonderful son!"

"*You* would think so," Margaret said over her shoulder, idly stirring her scrambled eggs.

"It is very kind of you to allow me to stay here, Mother, you know...until Jimmy comes home." Becca continued agreeably, "If there's anything I can help with around the house while I'm here, you've but to ask."

Margaret grunted, "Well, you can start by feeding the chickens." With that, she spooned a mound of eggs and bacon onto her plate, and plopped into a chair at the kitchen table. She looked at Becca expectantly, and picked up her fork. "Go on, now. The feed's out back in the shed by the henhouse."

Becca was taken aback, but complied with her mother-in-law's directive without complaint. After all, this *was* Jimmy's mother, and although she was clearly a hard woman, Becca wanted to stay on her good side, if at all possible.

After feeding the chickens, Becca collected three eggs from the henhouse. She returned to the kitchen and prepared her own breakfast. Afterward, she washed her dishes, along with Margaret's, and went in search of her mother-in-law.

As with the day before, Becca heard the television playing in the front room. She followed the sound to find Margaret engrossed in the TV. Becca tried to engage her in conversation, but Margaret was too absorbed in that day's episode of *Candid Camera* to be bothered with getting to know the newest member of the Hamilton family. Becca watched along with her for a while, but soon it became apparent that there was no conversation to be had. So Becca excused herself, returned to her room, and spent the rest of her day blissfully reading *Valley of the Dolls*, a novel by Jacqueline Susann she'd found at the public library.

After washing and putting away the dinner dishes that evening, Becca collected her toiletries and went downstairs to take a bath. The hot water in the old claw foot tub felt heavenly. She lounged lazily in the water, with her thoughts wandering where they may; first to Jimmy, then to their eventual lives together, and then on to possible baby names. She hoped the baby would be a boy. Every daddy needs a little boy to follow him around. But then, every daddy also needs a little girl who has him wrapped around her little finger, too.

Her reverie was interrupted by Mack Lee barging into the bathroom.

"Oh sorry, sish." He sounded drunk to Becca and he looked anything *but* sorry to have found his sister-in-law in the bath, her nudity concealed by nothing more than a thin layer of bubbles. "Didn't know you were in here."

Then he unzipped his fly, urinated into the toilet and stumbled from the bathroom.

Becca was mortified.

The next day, she walked to her father's hardware store in Boiling Springs. It was a Thursday, so she knew he wouldn't be there—he always took Thursdays off—and bought two lock kits: one for the bathroom door and the other for her bedroom. She had no desire for Mack Lee to return home after a night of carousing and "accidentally" slip into *her* bed! The thought was enough to make her want to vomit.

Becca resolved to make the best of her living situation. Over the next several months, she helped out around the house as much as her growing belly would allow. For the most part, Margaret and Mack Lee ignored her, and that was more than okay with Becca. They were neither outwardly hostile to her nor were they particularly kind or welcoming. Becca figured it was only temporary. If Jimmy could live in a tent with people shooting guns around him, then she could live in a house where nobody talked and where she was treated like a glorified scullery maid.

Sometimes late at night, she'd hear Mack Lee's footsteps clomping unsteadily up the stairs and pause by her door. She could practically *feel* his hand on her doorknob before the steps retreated back across the hall to his own room. The two dollars and ninety-eight cents she'd paid for that lock was the best investment she'd ever made!

As Becca's time drew near, with Jimmy's assistance, she made arrangements to see an obstetrician in Spartanburg.

Margaret had objected loudly, stating that doctors and hospitals were unnecessary expenses just to have a baby. She'd had all her children with a midwife right in the room Becca was staying. "If it was good enough for me, it should be good enough for you, Rebecca," she'd argued.

On this point, however, Becca held firm, and when her time came on September 30, a full week after her due date, her friend, Shelby, drove her to Spartanburg General Hospital. The next day, Becca welcomed a little boy, who she named James Wiley Hamilton Jr., into her heart and into the family.

CHAPTER 40

OCTOBER–NOVEMBER 19, 1967

I 'M LOSING MY MIND, JIMMY thought. *Not a great loss for humanity, but I'll miss it!*

He removed his helmet and poured the contents of his canteen over his head, hoping his thoughts would clear. The tepid water had little effect.

"It's the heat. Gotta be the heat," he mumbled.

Jimmy had always had a sharp mind, but recently things had begun to slip, probably the aftermath of the head wound suffered the preceding year. The headaches had become less frequent, though, which was good. But he was starting to see things, and that wasn't so good.

"Please, God, make it be just the heat," Jimmy prayed. He didn't even want to consider the possibility that his subdural hematoma was beginning to reaccumulate.

He rationalized that, technically, he wasn't seeing *things*. He was seeing people. And not really *people*—just one person, his little sister Anna.

Jimmy knew she wasn't actually there, that she was just a hallucination. Anna had been dead for over twelve years. He knew it, having been there when she'd died. After all, he'd killed her. Certainly, being aware that a hallucination wasn't real made it less of a hallucination and thereby less scary.

Anna's death had been an accident, and the guilt Jimmy felt was still almost palpable. His own mother didn't even forgive him, and he certainly wasn't about to forgive himself either, accident or no. Regardless, her death was his fault. Anna was gone forever, never to return.

Yet there she was or, at least, there was her visage.

Since his eighth birthday, Jimmy had often talked with his little sister. She'd been his constant companion in death as she'd been in life. Great or small, no life event was *real* until he'd told Anna about it. Of course, she only listened. She never responded, but he knew what she would've said if she'd been able to talk.

Last month, all that had changed.

Jimmy was officially a short-timer with thirty days and a wake-up before he completed his second and final tour as a combat medic assigned to the 173rd Airborne Brigade at Da'k To, Republic of Vietnam. Two weeks earlier, he'd received a letter from Becca informing him that he'd become father. A little boy! The news sent him over the moon with excitement, and now he kept the letter with him always.

Upon receiving the letter, Jimmy had run about the camp compound like a madman, showing any and all the photograph of his newborn son. Afterward, he'd returned to his tent, where he lay on his bunk reading and rereading the letter aloud. After the fourth—or perhaps fifth—reading, he heard clapping outside his tent.

Proud new papa that he was and not wishing to miss another opportunity to show off his new son, Jimmy grabbed the photograph and stepped out into the compound. Probably one of the local Vietnamese "camp kids" had overheard him reading. Maybe it was Thanh, the boy who shined his boots each week for a quarter and a bar of chocolate. The boy was totally incompetent at shining boots, but he was cute and Jimmy had built a rapport with him. Thanh would be very excited for him.

But Thanh wasn't there. In fact, no one was within earshot.

Puzzled, Jimmy returned to his bunk and stared at the photograph in wonder. Becca appeared radiant and so incredibly beautiful holding that perfect little bundle—*his* son. Smiling, he wondered how he'd gotten so lucky. Then, with a contented sigh, he set down the photo and returned to his letter.

Almost immediately, the clapping began again from just outside his tent flap. This time, it was accompanied by a peal of childish laughter, followed by a little girl's singsong.

"Jibby's a daddy, Jibby's a daddy! Yay!"

Jimmy knew that voice. He threw the letter onto his bunk and tore out of the tent. Again, the compound was empty. Shaken and with a pounding headache, he returned to his tent.

"It's the heat. It's gotta be the heat," he said as he stripped off his uniform and headed to the camp shower. The alternative explanation was too horrible to contemplate.

The water was cool and refreshing but did little to lessen his headache. He returned to his tent, crashed onto his bunk, and prepared to sleep. As was his habit, he whispered, "Good night, Anna," and began to doze.

"G'night, Jibby."

His eyes fluttered briefly. Then he was asleep.

The following morning, he awoke early. His unit was scheduled to deploy into the hills north of camp where a large North Vietnamese force had been reported. He penned a letter to Becca and assembled his kit. Slipping her last letter with his son's photograph into the pocket of his fatigue jacket, he posted his letter home and reported for deployment.

As a medic assigned to HQ Company, Jimmy was subject to be "drawn" by any company within the battalion in need of his services. For the duration of this foray into the hills above Da'k To, he would be seconded to Bravo Company. He'd deployed with Bravo before and felt comfortable with the assignment. They were a good bunch of guys. His job was the same regardless which men were around him. He whispered his usual premission mantra, "As long as I take care of them, they'll take care of me." Since he'd be marching through hostile territory with no weapon other than a .45-caliber pistol, this knowledge reassured him.

Several days out from base, Jimmy's squad lumbered in echelon formation through the jungle. He trudged along fifth in line behind the point, when suddenly the same voice he'd heard in the tent shouted, "Jibby! Stop!"

Nobody else seemed to hear. Nonetheless, he froze. Glancing around and then down, he noticed a length of fishing line stretched between two trees at ankle level, a mere six inches in front of his left boot. Attached to one end of the line was a grenade. *One more step and...boom!* Once again, his head began to throb. Still, he paused to flag the tripwire and then moved along with the rest of his squad.

On 19 November, elements of 2nd Battalion, to include Bravo Company, were ordered to take and hold Hill 875. There, a large North Vietnamese force ambushed them, and Bravo Company immediately began taking heavy casualties. From almost everywhere came calls for "Medic!" He and the other medics responded, doing whatever possible to stabilize the wounded before dust-off choppers evacuated them to field hospitals.

That afternoon, Jimmy responded to a call from a firing position located behind a deadfall which formed a natural barricade near the crest of the hill. He dashed through a hail of small arms and mortar fire and en route was painfully grazed by several shell fragments but managed to reach the wounded man's side without any serious injuries to himself. A detonating RPG round had severely wounded the man's face, leaving both eyes dangling from ruined sockets. The man was writhing in pain. Jimmy gave him a shot of morphine, then rinsed the eyeballs as best he could and tucked them back into the damaged sockets. Once there, he wound gauze around the man's head to hold the eyes in place. As he prepared to evacuate the man down the hill to the aid station for dust-off, another rifleman screamed that he'd also been hit. Jimmy assessed the man and found no wounds other than a minor cheek graze. He was stunned when the soldier threw down his M16, abandoned his position, and started downhill toward the casualty collection point under his own power. Jimmy briefly watched him go, then ducked his head as automatic weapons fire ripped through another soldier not far away. Jimmy immediately moved to help the man, but sadly, there was nothing to be done. Half the man's head was gone.

At one end of the deadfall, Jimmy noticed an officer there who'd turned his attention away from the enemy. Perhaps he was trying to get his minimally wounded rifleman to return to his post, or maybe he was concerned about his other wounded men. Either way, he wasn't paying attention to the battle in front of him, which was a great way to get himself killed.

"Jibby! Look out!"

Jimmy spun around.

Two NVA soldiers with bayonets gleaming were breeching the barricade and approaching the distracted officer. Without thinking, Jimmy drew his .45 and fired two rounds into the chest of the closest enemy and another into the head of the second.

"Fucking officer's gotta to learn to pay attention, dammit!" he muttered to himself.

Once again, Jimmy's head pounded, and he began seeing spots. He turned. Near the barricade, he glimpsed Anna's face framed by blonde ringlets. He shook his head and looked away. When he looked back, the face was gone, replaced by a thick cloud of yellow spewing from a smoke grenade canister.

Another soldier, apparently a radioman, was hit, and Jimmy crawled to his side. While caring for the man, Jimmy felt like he'd been struck in his left hip by a baseball bat. A second later, a red-hot poker drove through his right calf. He'd been shot, but in spite of his own wounds, he managed to reach the injured man and, once there, worked feverishly to get him stabilized.

Next, the officer was hit. One instant, he was crouched behind the barricade firing, and the next, there was a hole the size of a golf ball through the right side of his chest. Blood instantly blossomed over the front of the man's olive drab T-shirt, and he collapsed to the ground, pale as a ghost, his wound wheezing and bubbling with each labored breath.

Weak with blood loss from his own untended wounds, Jimmy's vision began to fade. He blinked. Before him, he no longer saw the wounded officer. Instead, it was Anna just as she had looked twelve years ago, with blood bubbling from a chest wound and a look of terror on her little face. In the back of his mind, Jimmy wondered why Anna should be holding a pistol.

"Anna!" he cried as he scuttled to his sister's side.

His strength was waning, but he managed to roll her onto her side and slap an occlusive plastic dressing over the exit wound beneath her right shoulder blade. Easing her onto her back again, he moved to dress the entrance wound, but he'd used his last occlusive dressing while earlier tending to the radioman. He cast about for something else with which to partially seal the wound. Finding nothing, he slipped the photograph from his pocket and taped it over the wheezing, gurgling wound in the little girl's chest. "I've got you, sis! Stay with me, Anna!" He had to save her.

Another NVA soldier clambered over the barricade and, with the last of his strength, Jimmy fired four times, emptying his pistol. One of the rounds must have found its target, for the man crumpled to the ground at his feet.

Jimmy dropped his empty pistol and grabbed Anna's. "You shouldn't have a pistol, Anna-panda. You might get hurt!" he chided.

Just then, something slammed Jimmy in the chest—hard. Suddenly, it was very difficult to breathe and he couldn't seem to keep himself upright. After a moment, he slumped sideways to the ground, bright red blood spurting from the wound.

From somewhere far away, he heard Anna say, "It's okay, Jibby. You'll like it here."

For Jimmy, time stopped and his mind became again perfectly clear. At once, he knew it hadn't been the heat causing his headaches or hallucinations. It was the missing splinter of bone in his brain. It hadn't been removed after all and was continuing to migrate and do damage. Then he looked down at his chest. He'd seen wounds like this before—arterial bleeding from a *very* big artery, or more likely, the heart itself. He smiled. The splinter wasn't going to matter much longer.

Images flashed into his mind. The first was of Anna. He smiled inwardly as she begged, "Read me the birdies, Jibby! Read me the birdies!" Then she faded.

Next was Uncle Howard. After losing Aunt Doris and Charles, Jimmy knew the old man was going to take his loss very hard. He was glad his uncle had Charlotte there to help him through it.

Then he thought of Rikki-Tikki-Tabby, hoping his cat would be okay without him. He deserved better than to become somebody's supper.

The next image was of Becca, smiling adoringly at him on their wedding day. *I'm sorry I have to leave you alone,* he thought. *But I know we'll be together again. Take good care of our boy!*

Finally, he thought of little James Jr. *I wish I'd gotten to know you, little one!*

All of these things occurred in a fraction of a second.

Then, out of the corner of his fading vision, Jimmy saw a grenade roll in among the wounded men around him. It was close enough for him to touch. At this, his psyche, protecting him to the end, gave in entirely to his hallucinations.

"Look, Jibby! It's a birdie. Catch the birdie, Jibby!" Anna cried with glee.

Through his mental haze, Jimmy saw it and thought, *Whaddya-know, Anna's favorite bird, finally...a long-tailed broadbill...and close enough to touch.* He groped for the bird with his free hand. He couldn't quite grasp it but managed to cup his hand around it well enough to drag it beneath him. Somewhere, his rational mind thought, *Funny, I thought a bird would feel softer.*

There was a brilliant white flash and then...nothing.

CHAPTER 41

NOVEMBER 19, 1967

T AKE GOOD CARE OF ME *when I'm wounded. Take* *even better care of me when I'm dead, and bring* *me home.* That is the hope of combat soldiers everywhere and the job of the Graves Registration Service, a unit within the Army's Quartermaster Corps. Their mission is retrieval, identification, transportation, and preparation for burial of American military personnel who have given their lives on foreign shores, and then to return them home to relatives and friends.

In more genteel times, as though there has ever been a time when war might've been described as "genteel," it was common practice for warring factions, during protracted engagements, to call a cease-fire in order to allow for the removal of the dead and care for the wounded. Since the dawn of the twentieth century, this custom has largely fallen by the wayside, making recovery of battlefield dead...tricky.

The wounded officer, radioman, and machine gunner were rapidly evacuated downhill to the casualty collection point and flown via medevac helicopter to army hospitals. Jimmy and the two dead riflemen lay where they fell as the battle raged around them. It was late in the day before their bodies could be recovered and moved to the collection point.

Members of the GRS unit cut away boots and uniforms from the fallen soldiers. Personal items were carefully cataloged and placed in plastic pouches stenciled with the name of the fallen soldier.

Into Jimmy's pouch, the GRS team placed his wallet containing four dollars, a gold Bulova Mickey Mouse watch with a cracked crystal, a simple gold wedding band, and the letter from Becca. They left his dog tags in place and applied a toe tag to his left foot. His body was carefully washed and then bundled into a canvas tarpaulin. Normally, a rubberized green body-bag would have been employed rather than the tarp, but with the high numbers of KIA for the day, the detail had run out of the specialized bags.

Jimmy's body had just been loaded onto the helicopter for evacuation when two medics ran up to the LZ, carrying a litter bearing a badly wounded soldier. The crew chief indicated that the aircraft was overloaded. Therefore, the crew off-loaded Jimmy's body and deposited it underneath a nearby tree to await the next chopper to make room for the wounded soldier. In the confusion, the GRS personnel forgot about Jimmy's pouch of personal items until the chopper had already lifted off with his possessions on board. By then it was too late.

The separation of personal possessions from remains was technically a violation of protocol, but the breach was minor and not uncommon. There was enough daylight for another run to base, and the chopper pilot had already promised to return. The possessions and remains would be reunited back at Da'k To airfield in less than an hour.

The chopper pilot was as good as his word and returned half an hour later. The GRS detail loaded Jimmy's tarpaulin, and thirty seconds later, the ground crew saluted as the chopper lifted off.

The chopper had risen no more than fifty feet when it came under fire from a Chinese-made heavy machine gun and immediately began taking hits. The windscreen exploded, and rounds killed the copilot and crew chief. Simultaneously, the pilot yanked the cyclic, wrenched the collective and kicked the foot pedals, desperately fighting to maintain control of the stricken craft. As the helicopter gyrated, its rotors narrowly missed the crest of a tamarind tree, and the body of the crew chief tumbled out the side door and into the jungle. The pilot regained control of the damaged Huey and escaped the LZ toward the northwest.

CHAPTER 42

NOVEMBER 21, 1967

I N THE CHAIR BY THE living room window, Becca rocked contentedly, gazing down at the tiny little bundle in her arms. James was perfect—a scrunched-up little button nose over a heart-shaped little mouth, a shock of wispy-thin blond hair, ten tiny little fingers, and ten even tinier little toes-eez. He grunted and cooed and had a reedy little warbling cry, but to Becca, his was an angelic vibrato. How could anyone possibly love *anything* this much?

The sound of crunching gravel drew Becca from her reverie. She glanced out the window and could make out the back of a dark sedan as it came to a stop in the driveway.

She rose and called softly so as not to wake her sleeping baby, "Mother, we have guests. I'm going to put James down for his nap."

As Becca climbed the stairs, a sharp knock sounded on the front door behind her. A moment later, Margaret answered the door. A short time later, her mother-in-law called out, "Rebecca, it's for you."

Wondering who could possibly want to see her at this time of the day, Becca kissed James on the forehead and placed him in his crib. She descended the stairs and, upon seeing two men standing in the entryway wearing army dress greens, took them to be friends of Jimmy and put on her most radiant smile.

The shorter of the two men wore captain's bars and the taller appeared to be some kind of sergeant. Becca thought Jimmy would be proud to know she was learning to recognize military ranks.

In a somber tone, the captain introduced himself and the sergeant, then asked, "Are you Mrs. Rebecca Hamilton?"

Becca extended her hand in greeting, excited to be meeting some of Jimmy's friends for the first time. "Yes, I'm Becca Hamilton," she responded, smiling warmly.

"Mrs. Hamilton, is there somewhere we might sit and talk?" asked the captain.

Becca's smile faltered slightly when neither man accepted her handshake. She shrugged it off, however, figuring it was probably just a military thing. She motioned the men to the living room and asked, "Would you like coffee or perhaps a glass of iced tea?"

The captain shook his head.

"No thank you, ma'am," the sergeant replied, speaking for the first time, a pained expression on his otherwise kind face.

"Ma'am, I think you should sit down," the captain began. "I'm afraid that we have some bad news."

Becca, thinking this a bad joke—maybe some kind of military-wife initiation ritual—sat as directed and waited for the gag to be sprang.

"Mrs. Hamilton, the Secretary of the Army has requested me to inform you that your husband, Corporal James Wiley Hamilton, was killed in action on the afternoon of 19 November in the Kon Tum Province, Central Highlands, Republic of Vietnam, near the village of Da'k To."

The captain rattled off the information in a clipped, professional tone while Becca sat in stunned disbelief. Her previous smile not yet completely faded, she was thinking that if this was a gag, it wasn't very funny. Then, *This might be real.*

"Corporal Hamilton's unit was attacked and surrounded by a numerically superior Vietnamese force, and in the ensuing firefight, he was wounded several times."

In desperation, Becca seized, uncomprehending, upon random words. "Oh, thank God he's only just wounded! Will he be okay? Will he be coming home soon?"

The captain continued, "Corporal Hamilton was wounded several times by small arms fire, and I regret to inform you that he died on the battlefield from his wounds."

Becca began to shake uncontrollably. Her eyes darted around the room and from the faces of the two soldiers before her. "This must be a mistake," she croaked. "Jimmy's a medic. He doesn't fight, doesn't even carry a rifle."

"No, ma'am, I'm afraid there's been no mistake." This time it was the kind faced sergeant who answered.

Becca buried her face in her hands and began sobbing. After a moment, her head snapped up again. She leaped from her chair and raced from the room. An instant later, she returned excitedly waving a letter. "See," she said triumphantly. "It really *is* a mistake! You say that Jimmy died two days ago, but I just got this letter from him this morning. He *can't* be dead!"

"Ma'am, I hate to tell you this, but this letter was written on November seventh and posted on the eighth. Your husband was killed on Novem..."

Nausea and a hot, flushed sensation swept over Becca as the room began to swim about her. The sergeant's awful words seemed to be coming through a tunnel a thousand miles long and then were gone.

Awareness came back to her in stages. She heard a buzzing sensation in her ears, which slowly transformed itself into discernible voices, although she could understand none of them. Before her eyes, everything was dark, save a pinpoint of light that seemed terribly far away but appeared to be slowly growing. As the light expanded, the voices became clearer.

When she awoke more fully, Becca found herself lying on her back on the sofa. There was a throw pillow beneath her head and two more under her feet. She felt cold and wondered if someone had left the front door open. Then she heard music—Westminster chimes—and the grandfather clock in the corner struck three o'clock.

Somewhere in the distance, she heard Margaret Hamilton's voice. Becca knew that if anyone on this planet could put an end to this cruel hoax, it would be Mother. She wouldn't stand for this nonsense. Becca listened, trying to focus on the words.

Mother was saying, "...family has very few resources. What becomes of his pay? May I presume that the army will pay for transportation and burial?"

Through the miasma of Becca's clearing mentation, it sounded to Becca as though Mother had already accepted Jimmy's death and was less concerned by his loss than the financial ramifications associated with it. In horror, Becca struggled past the thought and continued to listen.

Once again, it was the captain speaking. "That would typically be the case, ma'am. However, it seems that Corporal Hamilton's remains are missing."

Desperately grasping at imaginary straws, Becca sat up quickly from the couch. "Missing? Jimmy's only missing? He's not dead?!"

The three turned toward her, and the sergeant spoke in a pitying voice, "No, ma'am...Mrs. Hamilton. The helicopter carrying Corporal Hamilton's remains was hit by ground fire and it is believed to have crashed somewhere in the jungle. Efforts to contact the helicopter have been unsuccessful, and we fear the craft, and all aboard, have been lost. Search and recovery efforts are ongoing and we—"

From somewhere in the distance, Becca heard a muffled *THUMP-BUMP* as her head bounced off the coffee table, and an instant later, the hardwood floor. She felt nothing. Afterward, she heard nothing...nothing but merciful, blissful silence.

TO BE CONTINUED...

Thank you, dear Reader, for allowing me to share the Hamilton family's story with you. I hope you enjoyed reading *A Song that Never Ends* it as much as I did its creation. If so, please tell a friend, share a review, and revisit the family in *Roses in December*, the next installment of the Hamilton family's saga.

HISTORICAL FACTS
AND MISCELLANY

During the nineteenth century, Europe's John Gould was as well-known as North America's John James Audubon. He is credited with the creation of almost 3,000 beautifully hand-colored lithographic folios.

Gould was fascinated by the diversity and beauty of the bird species in Asia and spent thirty-four years in the creation of volumes I-VII. Volume I, Jimmy's first edition *The Birds of Asia*, includes 76 giclée prints. My description of the book and contents in this novel does not do it justice. It is a work of incredible accuracy and beauty.

Herb Parsons was a famous trick and fancy shooter who began working for Winchester in 1929. He toured the country in a red Pontiac station wagon and by the time of his death from a heart attack in 1959, he was performing up to 130 shooting expositions per year.

The Battle of Da'k To took place between November 3-27, 1967 in the hills around Da'k To in the Kontum Provence in the Central Highlands of South Vietnam. The battle was among the fiercest and bloodiest of the Vietnam War and involved ~16,000 American troops. 376 US troops were listed as killed or missing and presumed dead, and another 1,441 were wounded during the fighting. The centerpiece of the battle was the 110-hour fight for Hill 875, where in this work of fiction, I have placed Jimmy Hamilton.

The Battle of Da'k To generated three recipients, all posthumous, of the Congressional Medal of Honor.

Private First-Class Carlos J. Lozada of Puerto Rico:

On November 20, 1967, PFC Lozada, a machine gunner assigned to Company A, 2nd Battalion, 503 Infantry, 173rd Airborne Brigade, observed a North Vietnamese Army company rapidly approaching his outpost. He alerted his comrades and opened fire with his machine gun, killing at least twenty enemy soldiers and disrupting their initial attack. He realized that if he abandoned his position, there would be nothing to hold back the surging North Vietnamese soldiers and his entire company's withdrawal would be jeopardized. As a result, he told his comrades to fall back while he provided covering fire for them. He continued to deliver a heavy and accurate volume of suppressive fire against the enemy until he was mortally wounded and had to be evacuated from the field.

Lozada was posthumously awarded the Congressional Medal of Honor in December 1969.

Major Charles J. Watters of New Jersey:

While moving with one of the companies engaged in the battle on November 19, 1967, Major Watters, a chaplain assigned to the Army Chaplain Corps, 173rd Support Battalion, distinguished himself during the engagement with a heavily armed North Vietnamese battalion. As the battle raged and the casualties mounted, Chaplain Watters, with complete disregard for his safety, rushed forward to the line of contact. Unarmed and completely exposed, he moved among as well as in front of the advancing troops, giving aid to the wounded, assisting in their evacuation, giving words of encouragement, and administering last rites to the dying. Chaplain Watters repeatedly exposed himself to both friendly and enemy fire between the two forces in order to recover wounded soldiers. Later, when he was satisfied that all of the wounded were inside the perimeter, he began aiding the medics by applying field bandages to open wounds, obtaining and serving food and water, giving spiritual and mental strength and comfort. During his ministering, he moved out to the perimeter from position to position, redistributing food and water and tending to the needs of his men.

At 18:58, in one of the worst friendly fire incidents of the Vietnam War, a Marine Corps A-4 Skyhawk dropped two 250-pound Mark 81 Snakeye bombs on the 2/503's perimeter. The rounds landed short. The first was a dud. The second hit a tree and detonated in an airburst above the field HQ and casualty collection point where Watters was then ministering to the wounded. Watters and forty-one other men were killed outright and an additional forty-five were wounded.

For his gallantry in repeatedly exposing himself to enemy fire to retrieve the wounded on Hill 875, he was awarded a posthumous Medal of Honor.

Private First-Class John Andrew Barnes, III of Massachusetts:

On November 12, 1967, PFC Barnes, a grenadier assigned to Company C, 2nd Battalion, 503 Infantry, 173rd Airborne Brigade, manned a machine gun after its crew had been killed. He then eliminated nine enemy soldiers who were assaulting his position. While retrieving more ammo, Barnes saw a grenade tossed among a group of severely wounded soldiers. In an instant, he leaped on the device, shielding the blast with his body.

Remarkably, PFC Barnes's commanding officer refused to endorse the recommendation for Barnes's decoration, stating he didn't think medals were for "men who committed suicide." Saner minds prevailed and PFC Barnes was awarded his posthumous Medal of Honor in 1969.

SNEAK PEEK

ROSES IN DECEMBER
(HAMILTON PLACE BOOK II)

I T HAD SEEMED LIKE A good idea at the time. Chalmers wondered how many of life's misadventures began with just such misplaced assurances. Each decision was, he thought, well pondered with the permutations and computations compiled, collated, and analyzed so that the plan for his life was foolproof, or at least *fool-resistant*. As Dr. Horne, his mentor and a dedicated cynic, had once told him, "If you try to make something foolproof, they'll just build a better fool."

Oh, Doctor Horne, if you could only just see me now.

Even in retrospect, his thought processes *seemed* at least *mostly* sound. And yet, here he was, hiking through this steaming, *stinking* jungle, a walking buffet for millions of mosquitoes and biting flies, with forty pounds of equipment strapped to his back and blisters on his feet the size of soccer balls. Well, maybe they were not *quite* the size of soccer balls, but dammit, they still hurt!

"I'm in the air force, goddamn it! We don't do this kind of shit in the air force," Chalmers muttered to himself. "One joins the air force to live in air-conditioned comfort where a 'difficult hike' is traversing a hot parking lot to the O'Club. The only bag I should ever be carrying ought to have fourteen golf clubs sticking out of it and a flask of Jack Daniels in a zippered pocket."

"Did you say something, Major Chalmers?" The man actually seemed to be enjoying himself.

"No, Sergeant Ryals. Just singing to myself to pass the time." He secretly hated Technical Sergeant Ryals. "Half Navy SEAL and half mountain goat," he muttered under his breath. The thought of *that* unholy coupling actually made him chuckle, and he was still chuckling when the toe of his left boot became ensnared by a vine. His forward momentum being too great to overcome, he fell flat into the mud— or at least he *hoped* it was mud.

"Fuck!" Chalmers yelled as he started pushing up from the ooze.

"You okay, sir?" asked Ryals, trying to suppress a grin and failing.

"I'm fine, Sergeant! Thank you for your concern." And then he mumbled, "Just fucking peachy! How could I *possibly* be any better? I'm just sweating my ass off, having a nice stroll through a freaking jungle, using fucking cobras to play jump rope. I can't believe we actually fought for this steaming dung heap! We should have paid the fricking Viet Cong to just keep it. Geez, what the fuck am I doing here?!" he asked himself for the now thirteenth time that day.

Chalmers had been in Vietnam for ten days, which in his mind was nine and a half days too many. He'd felt professionally trapped by a bad assignment to an airbase in Japan and it really *had* seemed like a good idea to jump at this opportunity at the time, his ticket out of Japan. The initial excitement of escaping that unpleasant military posting had rapidly been replaced by the reality of "camping" in a tropical rainforest. The first few days had been spent tramping through the bug and reptile infested mountain wilderness of central Vietnam in search of a battle site that had been completely swallowed by the jungle. Upon finding it, the next week had been spent sifting, quite literally, through the contents of a twenty-five-year old bomb crater. Now he was off on another wild goose chase.

"Only three more weeks to go, then I'm out of this pit and out of Yokota...permanently," he muttered. "I wonder if there was another way?"

As his concentration drifted in search of an answer, Robert Frost's "The Road Not Taken" popped into his mind. How did the poem go?

> *Two roads diverged in a wood, and I,*
> *I took the one less traveled by,*
> *And that has made my life this living HELL!*

Not an exact quote, but just as well.

Maybe not exact, but close enough...and his version of the poem summed up his life perfectly. Had he taken the right fork, he'd be on a beach with an umbrella drink in one hand and a hot travel agent in the other. The left fork had him humping it through the jungles of Vietnam.

Instead of the right fork, I took the wrong fork! What the hell was I thinking!? How exactly, did I get myself here?

Chalmers supposed it was a lot like World War I. Nobody really *wanted* a war. No leader woke one day and said, "Hey, I know, let's start a war." Instead, they made a series of small moves and seemingly logical decisions that unknowingly and unwittingly edged the world closer and closer to catastrophe. Each step brought them nearer to the precipice until finally, a minor spark turned the planet into a conflagration and an entire generation had gone up in flames.

Chalmers continued muttering to himself. "Give it a rest, Chalmers. Don't be so melodramatic. You're slogging through a jungle, not sucking down mustard gas in some mud-filled trench on the Somme—"

He kicked at a vine and tangled his foot in another, stumbling again, almost falling. He'd just about regained his balance when his right foot came down on nothing but air. Technically, the ground was still there. It was just falling away at a sharp, downward angle. The effect, however, was the same. He pitched forward, tumbling, bouncing, and cursing all the way down the declivity until coming to rest, he thought, against the trunk of a tree.

He lay still for a moment, dazed after his tumble. He tentatively moved first one arm and then the other and stretched his left leg and then his right. Nothing seemed to be broken, and everything moved more or less normally. He tried to open his eyes but couldn't. They were caked with mud. Groping for his canteen, he poured water over his face and rinsed his eyes. As his vision cleared, two huge black eyes the size of Ping-Pong balls came into focus, staring back at him...and then six more. And then eight hairy legs. It was a tarantula the size of a dinner plate.

Startled, he jerked backward and banged his head against the tree trunk, causing a metallic *thunk*.

"Wait a minute!" Chalmers reflected when his slightly concussed and addled mind cleared enough for rational thought. "Trees don't sound like that." He slowly turned to look behind him.

It wasn't a tree but an olive-green painted tail boom.

"Hey! Hey, guys!" he shouted. "Guys! I think I've found something."

In Washington, DC, Senator Alexander Wentworth Prescott, III kicked back with his feet up on his burlwood desk. He liked burlwood. Its unique grain pattern was unmatched in its beauty and complexity. More importantly, it looked *nothing* like the desks in the other ninety-nine senatorial offices. No, this was no polished mahogany, ebony, teak, cherry, or glass behemoth. His desk, unlike those of his peers, featured a swirling honey, sienna, and cinnamon grain pattern painted by the hand of God and merely polished by man.

He held a vintage, unlit Cuban *Romeo y Julietta* cigar between his teeth. Beside him on the blotter, a crystal highball glass held a generous measure of thirty-year-old Macallan. Both the cigar and the Scotch had been gifts from some lobbyist or other. Prescott didn't really like either—the gifts, or the lobbyists—and he didn't smoke, but this was what his father had always done after a win. He'd probably never completely measure up to the old man's standards, but he might still *look* the part.

Prescott stared contentedly out his window, in the general direction of the US Capitol Building. His was a spacious, well-appointed office, perhaps not as nice as his father's had once been, but he wasn't complaining. The old man would've hated the burlwood. He would've said the desk didn't "adequately project the power of office," or some crap like that.

The elder Prescott had been a powerhouse in the Senate for almost four decades. The younger Prescott had been appointed to his Senate seat by the Governor of New York after his father's unexpected death in office. He had been only meant to serve as a place-holder until the November elections later that year. That had been almost eighteen years ago.

Apparently, the placeholder had found a place of his own—not bad for a man with precisely zero political ambition. He aspired—*who didn't?*—but his aspirations had never been in the political arena. His motivations were more personal. Unlike the majority of his peers on the Hill, for Prescott, politics was the means to an end; *not* an end in and of itself.

During his years in the House of Representatives and more recently, the Senate, Prescott had fought for veterans' rights and championed the Joint POW/MIA Accounting Command. JPAC's mission was to achieve the fullest possible accounting of all Americans missing as a result of the nation's past conflicts. JPAC's motto was, "Until they are home." He'd forced JPAC through committees and gotten it funded, then sent them out on their first mission into Vietnam. And today, the project had borne fruit. Three previously lost Americans were finally coming home from the war. Without politics, today's win would never have occurred.

Prescott held the tumbler of Scotch to his lips. "Here's to you, Dad...you son of a bitch!"

ACKNOWLEDGMENTS

Dear Reader,

Consider yourself lucky that I've been allocated but finite space and word count to render my thanks, for my list is long.

Thank you—up in heaven—Doctor Homer Pittman Hines. You were my friend and mentor as a child, and served as the perfect model for Jimmy's Uncle Howard.

Katherine Duello, you challenged me and encouraged through example. You gave the snowball its first nudge down the hill, and look what it's become!

Next, I'll single out Charles Campbell, my partner across the hall and friend. Chuck, but for you, this story would've moldered away in an unkempt corner of my mind for posterity. Without your constant antics and unfailing belief in my ability as a writer, I doubt I would've made it very far past the Prologue.

For all the members of my family and friends who've put up with me chattering away nonstop about scenes being written, I thank you for your forbearance and for at least giving the *impression* of listening.

I must also thank my colleagues who helped with technical details outside the scope of my personal military and medical knowledge. Any errors that persist are mine alone.

Next, I thank you, Dear Reader. I hope you will enjoy reading my little story as much as I enjoyed writing it.

Finally, I must thank Debra L. Hartmann of The Pro Book Editor (TPBE). I dropped a pile of electronic straw onto your desk, and like Rumpelstiltskin, you spun it into gold. You guided, you taught, you listened, you nudged, and you encouraged. Most importantly, you believed...even when I did not.

Doc

Finally

ABOUT THE AUTHOR

Dr. Mark A. Gibson is a physician who practices Cardiology in the mountains of rural North Georgia. He was raised on a small farm in upstate South Carolina—the last postage-stamp sized sliver of a much larger parcel granted to the family by land grant from Charles II in 1665—and may or may not have once gotten in trouble for digging up his mom's calla lily bed in search of the family's long-lost charter.

Dr. Gibson graduated from the Citadel in Charleston, SC with a BS in Biology. Afterwards, he received his medical degree from the University of South Carolina School of Medicine in Columbia, SC. He received his Internal Medicine training through the University of Tennessee Medical System and Cardiology training through the Wilford Hall USAF Medical Center. He served for eight years on active duty with the US Air Force, before leaving the military for private practice.

Although a cardiologist by profession, Dr. Gibson is a dreamer by nature. He is a self-styled oenophile who enjoys travel and fine food. In his spare time, he builds sandcastles and dreams of distant shores.

A Song that Never Ends (Hamilton Place Book I) represents Dr. Gibson's first foray into the world of literature. All previous publications have been of the professional, peer-reviewed medical variety, and make for lovely sleep aids.

Printed in the USA
CPSIA information can be obtained
at www.ICGtesting.com
JSHW021255311223
54545JS00003B/14